CONFESSIONS OF EDEN

A "Michelle Reagan" Novel

by

SCOTT SHINBERG

SPECIAL NOTICE

CONFESSIONS OF EDEN
Michelle Reagan - Book 1

FIRST EDITION SOFTCOVER
ISBN: 1622536657
ISBN-13: 978-1-62253-665-8

Editor: Whitney Smyth
Interior Designer: Lane Diamond

EVOLVED PUBLISHING™

www.EvolvedPub.com
Evolved Publishing LLC
Butler, Wisconsin, USA

Printed in Book Antiqua font.

BOOKS BY SCOTT SHINBERG

DEDICATION

To my wonderful wife, Janice, whose unconditional love and encouragement throughout this process have meant the world to me.

To all the family and friends whose support and insight continue to guide me along the rocky path of storytelling.

And to all those who do what needs to be done to protect our country, whether you serve in uniform or in the shadows. You know that everything in this book is fiction... except the parts that aren't.

CONFESSIONS OF EDEN

A Michelle Reagan Novel
Book 1

SCOTT SHINBERG

PART ONE

TOTEM POLE

Chapter 1

I held my pistol three inches from the back of her head and pulled the trigger for the second time that night. This time, my pull was quick and smooth.

She looked almost peaceful as she lay motionless, face down on the floor. A grotesque mixture of blood-matted brown hair strewn wildly about the floor and a dark burgundy stain spreading from the fatal head wound I had just caused jarringly interrupted the illusion of tranquility.

I fixated far too much that evening on my concern about ruining the resort villa's rather bland beige carpet. *Come on, Michelle,* I reminded myself, *focus on the plan, not on the body... or the blood.*

With the obstacle—her—now out of the way, the silence of the empty bedroom drew my thoughts back to my primary target. I hadn't heard Gutierrez for a while, so I peeked around the corner to see if he was already there. He was not.

The lifeless body lying at my feet held me spellbound. Standing over her, what I saw was a beautiful woman with thin, tanned legs in a short silver dress riding up on her more than she probably would have liked. I could see no hint of the belly wound caused by my first shot.

The tightening starting up again in my gut was interrupted by the sound of shoes tapping up the hardwood stairs outside the master bedroom. The noise yanked my attention away from my fascination with the dead woman. The bedroom door was pushed open with a tell-tale *clunk.*

I inhaled deeply and reminded myself that this was my reason for flying down to Aruba from Washington, DC, the previous morning. I kept my mental pep talk quick and to the point: *Okay, Michelle, now!*

Chapter 2

I remember quite clearly having decided early that sunny morning before boarding the United Airlines flight to Aruba that if she were there, I would kill her.

Those who know me now—at least the handful of people alive who know what I do for a living—might be surprised to hear me say that the thought of it sounded awful, even to me. In the moment—*at* that moment—standing on the departures level in front of Dulles International Airport outside of Washington, DC, I shuddered as uncertainty descended over me.

The specter of self-doubt pitted my brain against itself. One half desperately wanted to believe the internal debate had ended in my favor. The other half repeatedly chided me: *Don't kid yourself, Michelle, this goes far deeper than mere flesh and bones.*

My new boss, Michael, had made his expectations of me perfectly clear back when he extended his invitation to join his team. He didn't beat around the bush about the way outsiders might view us if they knew the details of our team's missions. He warned me from the get-go that I would have to get used to killing people who were simply in the way, even if they were not my primary target. It didn't have to be something I would like; it just had to be something I would do.

The concrete sidewalk led me to both the airport terminal and the first test of my less-than-concrete self-confidence. The strength required to carry out my mission lay buried somewhere deep within me. Part of my mind wanted to prove I was more than capable of succeeding and resolutely believed it would carry me through my mission to Aruba. But there was still that irritating other part asking the same recurring question: *Really, Michelle?*

I didn't delude myself into thinking the question could be answered while sitting safely in Michael's sterile office or at home in my apartment, seven miles east of the airport. This question—the one that had been ricocheting around my skull for days prior to my flight—could not be answered until the fateful moment arrived in which I found myself face to face with a human being standing in front of my pistol.

I breathed deeply to try and calm the quivering that wreaked havoc upon my stomach. I silently affirmed my decision to take the next step in the plan: board the plane. That gave me enough courage to walk towards the automatic door with renewed conviction and at least the illusion of having enough self-confidence to complete my mission.

Through the corner of my eye, I spied my reflection keeping pace with me in the lowest pane of the gleaming fifty-foot-high sectional plate glass window of Dulles' towering terminal. That's precisely where I now think of myself being at that point of my life, at the bottom of the totem pole—the beginning of my story.

We walked abreast each other, my reflection inside the terminal and the real me outside. The two mes could only regard each other from afar, forever occupying disconnected worlds. What an apt description that turned out to be.

Sweet, naïve, innocent Michelle only one year out of high school peered in from the outside, wondering what the future held in store for her career. Loving, experienced, hardened Michelle on the far side stared out, wondering whether the gains have been worth the costs.

I was only nineteen years old back then—so young. Innocent. Willing. Eager.

What would have happened if the two of us crossed the barrier, converged in that instant, and touched? What might have happened if our fingers had made contact through the impenetrable membrane of time or if our minds had connected on an emotional level? Maybe nothing at all. Maybe the world would have stopped spinning on its axis, or maybe only my world would have changed and no one else would have even noticed.

I checked my appearance in the window one last time while still on American soil. Hardly any nineteen-year-old girl can pass her reflection and not double-check her hair or clothes. In that glance, some sense of reassurance calmed me ever so slightly. I confirmed that my disguise looked just as it should: blonde wig, neutral makeup, non-descript black pants, and a dark blue blouse. Boring. Unremarkable. Perfect!

I took a personal, intimate mental snapshot of my reflection to remember how I looked at that particular moment—the moment at which I made *the* decision. That image would be my last mental *before* self-portrait. Before my first mission. Before boarding the plane. Before my life changed forever. Before I became a killer.

My apparition grinned a thin-lipped half-smile back at me.

I reflected on my new boss's advice about making decisions before starting a mission. "Once you make the decision and commit to it," Michael said with the smooth elegance of his fading West Texas drawl, "following through becomes automatic. Your training will take over. Trust your training."

As always, time has proven him right. I've learned to trust his wisdom and decades of experience implicitly. Michael is walking proof that you don't have as long a career running covert action operations as he has had without being right almost all the time. In the field, small mistakes can be fatal, and big mistakes can be even worse.

With *the* decision behind me, I inhaled deeply again and walked both literally through the now-open sliding glass door and figuratively into my new life as the youngest covert action operator in CIA's Special Activities Division—SAD.

Covert action can be a very messy business. Much of what we do in the Directorate of Operations, the DO, is messy. Many, maybe most, civilians would call me an assassin, but on our team, we prefer to use the military's term: operator. *Assassin*? No, that word just doesn't fit with my personal view of who I am as a woman or my feelings about why the profession in which I've specialized for over a decade is so important to my country.

Officially, the US government doesn't engage in assassinations. Officially. Even if the CIA doesn't acknowledge it, every Director has had a team like ours at his disposal. We're his option of last resort.

Only one person has ever used the word *assassin* to my face. I smiled at him warmly when he did and, yes, he's still very much alive. Someday I'll marry him. If I live that long.

My longevity was not something I thought about much in those early days, being caught up in the excitement and freshness of my new life.

I dove head-first into it all—the training, travel, learning to live undercover, working entirely in the shadows—and woke up one day having realized with a start that I had real, tangible control over people. Those feelings were powerfully intoxicating, stimulating, and liberating.

No one had handed me the power to control others. Rather, I incubated it somewhere deep inside me, somewhere so far down that I didn't even know such a place existed. This potent but fragile creation of mine both excited and, at the same time, terrified me. Could I keep it under control or would it destroy me?

Thoughts of my own mortality have been on my mind more and more recently. That's one reason Michael suggested I write this memoir. Whether anyone ever reads it or not doesn't matter to me at all. For all I care, it can sit unread in his office safe until it rots. Right now, I just need to sort out my twisted, conflicting emotions. My goals are to recognize and understand what these feelings are and then to figure out how to untangle their complicated web. For me, this is my attempt at preserving my sanity. It may be my last chance to control the power and not succumb to it.

As I write this, I'm working infuriatingly hard just to keep myself from becoming my own final victim. Some would no doubt say that it would be a fitting end. They might even be justified in that opinion, but I refuse to let that happen. Not on my watch. I will not lose!

I will *not* become a casualty of the inner hostilities and contradictory feelings that fight within the recesses of my mind for doing the things the CIA asked of me. My country asked and I answered the call, knowing what my missions required were necessary for the good of my country and my team. They were my choices to make, and I made them willingly. So, now, the question before my internal inquisitor is this: how do I feel about myself, considering the many lives I've taken?

I need to know what part of me will come out on top in my quest for self-approval—a quest begun on that beautifully clear and warm night in Palm Beach, Aruba.

Chapter 3

I struggled to walk at a casual pace and not run along the white sandy beach towards Rodrigo Beltran Gutierrez's rented oceanfront villa. The churning and tumbling in my stomach made me question whether I would even get to the villa's back gate before losing my dinner.

I approached the rear of the three-bedroom villa with the same self-doubts and consternation experienced by all first-timers—an abject fear of screwing up my all-important inaugural mission. Over the previous two weeks I had made dozens of dry-runs at the Farm, the Agency's clandestine service and covert operations training facility in Central Virginia. Even after extensive preparation, my hands still shook on my first foray into the real world. The corners of my mouth drooped upon the disappointing realization that I was only human after all and did not have mythical nerves of steel.

I felt scared. There, I said it.

The light from the half-moon hanging low over the Caribbean Sea lit my way along the paved path. I had to consciously refuse the appealing distraction of the water lapping upon the glistening sand a dozen or so feet to my left. The soft *whoosh-slap* of the small waves breaking on the sand was the only sound I could hear along the still beachfront.

The rear of the villa sat quietly, half concealed in shadows. I was happy to see that the moon only partially illuminated the wrought-iron gate set into the wall surrounding Gutierrez's vacation house. The minimal moonlight would make me harder to spot as I broke in.

The gorgeous rental probably cost ten grand for the week. The owners maintained it well and kept the backyard free of the fallen palm fronds littering so much of the rest of that tropical island paradise. No doubt, as the transportation coordinator for a Peruvian drug cartel, Gutierrez made good money. I'm sure he could have afforded an even more luxurious spread, but for a week-long getaway with his choice of *chiquitas*, it was perfect.

The rental cost him more than I could afford as a newly hired GS-7 civil service employee, even with the hazard pay that just about doubled my salary for being in this line of work. By my standards, Gutierrez was living large.

I traced my eyes across the tall privacy walls of his villa and those surrounding the neighboring houses for any of the usual threats: people, dogs, or security cameras. I scanned horizontally first, then vertically along the eaves, empty balconies, and curtained windows of each house, but saw nothing obvious. Dogs and cameras are rare around vacation properties, but people are what vacations are all about, and I did not want neighbors out for a late evening stroll to spot me.

Physical security at vacation properties is laughable, I reflected appreciatively, striding purposefully away from the water and towards the rear of the villa. The cheap locks were relatively easy to pick, even for a novice like me, only four weeks out of my second attempt at locksmith training.

With little likelihood of encountering surveillance cameras on this mission there was no need for any of my more complex disguises. Agency artists excel at crafting complex disguises such as silicone facial pieces. Regardless, I didn't want to end up featured on the next episode of *Aruba's Most Wanted*, so that night's disguise consisted of a basic blonde wig and a pair of large-framed glasses, just in case. Even routine actions like driving past an ATM machine can get you photographed nowadays, so my rule about disguises is to never leave home without one. Or three!

Every girl enjoys dressing up for the important events in her life. I'm no exception, although *What to Wear When Making Your First Kill* has not yet made it to any of *Cosmo*'s Top 10 lists. That night in Aruba, my medium-length dishwater blonde wig covered my short brunette bob. In addition, I wore only a touch of makeup. Who would want mascara smeared all over if she ended up sweating a lot and rubbing her face? I anticipated being awfully nervous that night.

Safe-ish missions like this one are the usual first jobs for new operators on our team. Frankly, it was a mission that didn't even need to happen. Normally, Gutierrez would not rate anywhere near the top of the list of people the CIA would deem worth the effort or risk to kill. Unfortunately for him, he chose to go on vacation at the same time I was finishing my advanced training. Timing is everything.

I would never meet the Case Officer in Lima who learned of Gutierrez's travel plans through a source working at LAN Perú Airlines.

Analysts in the Agency's Crime and Narcotics Center reviewed the cable describing Gutierrez's travel plans and decided they would not learn anything useful by spying on him during his vacation.

Michael, on the other hand, read the message in a completely different way. Knowing that no one else would be watching, he decided this would be the right opportunity for me to earn my bones, as it were, by ridding the world of yet another up-and-coming prince of the drug trade.

That sat well with me for my first mission. Safe-ish. Easy-ish. Worthwhile-ish.

At the rear wall of the villa, a quick push on the gate's handle confirmed it was locked from the inside. With the assistance of one of the half-dozen palm trees decorating the rear of the property, I took the next-most obvious way in by shimmying up the tree closest to the red-painted wall. I hopped over where the wall met a tan concrete pillar, dropped to the pea gravel that passed for a back yard, and reassessed the situation.

Inside the protective wall and seemingly alone, I looked carefully across the rear of the stucco house. I searched again for any sign of security cameras that might expose my participation in the coming events of the evening. There were none.

The clean, white stucco and bright-red trim spoke of the care with which the house was maintained. Yellow, red, and green flood lights gave the backyard a festive atmosphere and lit the Jacuzzi with a playful and tropical character that would have been a favorite of any vacationing couple.

I unlatched the gate to ensure an unimpeded escape later, then headed for the back door. Gravel crunched quietly under my shoes as I took my first, tentative steps towards the house. My realization that I was walking hunched over, essentially skulking, gave way to a wave of embarrassment at my own foolishness. My attempt to hide from occupants I already knew had left for the evening was probably not my first mistake of the night and would not be my last.

My surveillance of Gutierrez and his mystery lady earlier in the evening as they drove off to dinner made me confident that I was alone at the villa. Besides, if anyone was in the house and watching me, it would be the gun under my windbreaker that would solve that particular problem and not scooting to the back door in a half-crouch.

I stood upright and ran my hands down the front of my jacket in embarrassment. At least there was some relief in knowing I could suffer this one indignity in private and not have to watch it replayed on video in front of my entire class, as was the case with so many of the training scenarios I endured over the previous year.

A Kwikset lock secured the rear door. I smiled briefly at my good fortune that it wasn't a high-security brand, which would have been harder to defeat. For this job, a standard shallow-hook lock pick and a sturdy tension wrench would do nicely. I pulled the pair of thin-metal tools from the pocket inside my jacket and spent thirty seconds lifting and jiggling the five pins inside the lock's tumbler one by one until they all aligned at their sheer lines. The L-shaped tension wrench lurched clockwise in my hand as the lock jumped open.

I breathed a small sigh of relief and allowed myself a brief self-congratulatory grin, pleased that I wasn't having problems with the parts of the mission that were supposed to be easy.

As the villa's back door swung open, what Michael said to me two days earlier flooded back through my mind. I cherish the advice he has given to me over the years, and the last thing he told me before my flight to Aruba is something I will remember to my last breath. As we stood at the door to his office, he squeezed my shoulder gently and said, "When the time comes for it, Michelle, remember this: I'm giving you permission to pull the trigger." His words didn't mean that much to me at the time back in Virginia, but they echoed loudly through my mind as I stepped into Gutierrez's villa.

Starting at the rear door, I searched the living room, dining area, and kitchen to find hidden weapons or anything else of importance. I ran my gloved hands and novice's eyes across the cushions, cabinets, and closets, but found nothing.

The sterile rental villa was also devoid of anything to personalize it or give it character. No photographs sat on the countertops. No kids' awards, diplomas, or artwork graced the walls or refrigerator. A Cabernet Sauvignon from Bordeaux and an Argentinian Riesling on the countertop gave me the only hints the house was even occupied.

I looked up and eyeballed the stairway that climbed to the villa's second level. A single potted plant decorated the small loft at the top. French doors leading to the master bedroom commanded the view above me.

As I climbed the wooden staircase, the magnitude of my reason for making the trip began to weigh more heavily on my mind, on my heart, and on my legs. I labored to lift one foot over the other to reach the loft outside the master bedroom. With my gloved hands responding less and less reliably to my brain's commands to move, I pushed myself forcefully along the railing one hardwood step at a time.

Somewhere around the sixth step, a sobering realization burst through my mind. I would not come back down these stairs the same woman I had been upon entering the villa only minutes earlier. The emotional belt tightening around my chest cinched down another notch.

I doubted that a patriotic soliloquy about the substance of the career upon which I was embarking and its importance to national security would have motivated me to conquer the remaining stairs any quicker. Instead, I urged myself forward with the more plain-Jane method of simply agreeing with myself that getting my sorry ass upstairs would earn me the reward of plopping down in the chair closest to the door. If I had had any inkling that Gutierrez might have had a chocolate bar upstairs, that kind of bribe might have worked, too. Collapsing into the overstuffed leather chair in the corner of the master bedroom worked for me that evening.

I sunk into the well-padded white leather chair breathing heavily and franticly trying to find my inner resolve. The most active flock of butterflies that had ever inhabited my stomach whirled faster as I struggled to calm them with deep breaths. With little success, I tried to imagine how difficult a future mission—one with real danger—might be. My nearly debilitating case of stage fright had put even this easy first job at risk.

Oh man, what am I getting myself into? I focused on coaxing the acrobatic butterflies doing barrel rolls across my abdomen to take the rest of the night off. With my hands more than full simply trying to steady myself, I could not conceive of how to handle greater challenges on future missions. If walking up a flight of stairs posed such a problem for me, I wondered in dismay how would it ever be possible to succeed on a more complex mission? How do people handle their nerves on jobs that actually matter, such as one against an important target who has bodyguards, armored cars, or an alarm system to defeat first? Will I ever be able to do that, or should I just go back to Michael and admit defeat?

I refuse to be a failure, I answered myself with certainty. *Never have been and never will be. That's not me. I will not quit. I will not lose!*

From the reassuring embrace of a soft and welcoming chair, I surveyed the large master bedroom. Against the far wall, a king-sized bed sat draped with a colorful print bedspread replete with tropical yellow and orange flowers. A peach loveseat, wood-and-glass coffee table, and the mate to my plush white chair completed the vibrant theme of the room.

To my right, French doors led to the balcony where two wicker chairs and a matching table overlooked the evening surf. From that angle above the beach, I could appreciate the silvery moonlight reflecting across the small waves lapping up on the fine sand of the Aruban coast.

After regaining enough of my strength and nerve, I rifled through the dresser, nightstands, suitcases, and closet for weapons. As expected, I found none.

I sat back down on "my" chair and reflected on the woman who left the house earlier that evening with Gutierrez. Whoever she was, she'd regret having come to Aruba with him. I started to feel sorry for her, but only a little.

"When you take up with drug smugglers, you're choosing your own fate, right?" The empty room didn't answer.

I wondered whether she was his wife or if he had brought along a girlfriend instead. Either way, the outcome would be the same. One singular question bugged me incessantly for the two weeks since I first briefed for this trip: who would step through the doorway first and end up as my first kill? Him or her? Either way, that evening was not going to end with the loving embrace she anticipated as she got all dolled up to go out to dinner.

I drew the 9mm pistol and a cylindrical suppressor from the holster under my dark blue windbreaker. The threads inside the suppressor mated smoothly with those on the tip of the pistol's barrel. I bided my time twisting the two together while sitting silently in the dim light filtering through the balcony's sliding-glass doors.

The long wait for my targets to return from their last-ever night on the town gave me plenty of time to study the face of my watch as the hours passed. I honestly hoped they were having a wonderful evening.

With little else to do, I ran my gloved fingers over the length of the pistol, repeatedly caressing the rounded top of its frame and the smooth tube-shaped suppressor, studying a shape I already knew by heart.

On future "business trips," I would switch from that 9mm automatic to a harder-hitting .45 caliber with either a three- or five-inch suppressor. Sometimes, though, the firearm or suppressor I chose to use depended on what I wanted to or had to wear that evening.

Both are popular weapons for which good accessories are easy to find. I've accumulated a drawer full of holsters that work especially well with my assortment of skirts, pants, and jackets under which I conceal all sorts of weapons and equipment when in the field. After all, a girl has *got* to accessorize well!

Stealth, surprise, and an accurate first shot are my only real advantages. At five-foot-five-inches tall and one hundred thirty pounds soaking wet, I'm not a powerhouse and wouldn't likely survive a fair fight. So that's my goal: plan so that the fight is never a fair one. I either obtain and maintain the advantage or make an entirely new plan.

In this line of work, there are no silver medals for second place. If you're not the winner every time, all you get is an anonymous star engraved on the Memorial Wall of CIA's McLean headquarters. I've worked with a few of the people who have posthumous stars on that wall and, while I respect them greatly, I have no interest in joining them on that edifice of honor.

Chapter 4

My heart leapt into my throat as I heard the loud revving of a car engine that pulled around the villa's small circular driveway. They were home.

To this day, I still get nervous entering a target's house, hotel room, office, or whatever. On those missions, I'm inserting myself into their environment and stepping into the unknown. The unknown is unreliable. Nerve-racking. Deadly. That night in Aruba, I felt every emotion under the sun... or moon, as it were.

A rush of adrenaline set my thighs and arms quivering. My throat dried and tightened to the point that I needed to open my mouth wide to get enough air through my narrowed windpipe. I half-feared that the sounds of my wheezing breath and pounding heart would be enough to warn away Gutierrez and his lady-friend before they even made it upstairs.

I hefted the black Sig Sauer P228 semi-automatic pistol in my hands and needlessly double-checked the suppressor, feeling through my gloves that it was screwed onto the barrel securely. Weighing over two pounds, the Sig-and-suppressor combo is not terribly heavy, but nonetheless takes a good deal of concentration to control. The dense metal of the German-made pistol felt solid and reassuring. The hammer gave two metallic clicks as I drew it back with my thumb to its fully cocked position.

My chair was getting less and less comfortable. I crossed my legs and immediately re-crossed them, shifting awkwardly in the padded leather. With a frown, I settled on placing both feet flat on the floor and gently tapped my toe on the carpet.

The deadbolt in the front door made an unmistakable scraping sound as the key turned. The well-oiled wooden door's hinges were not noisy, but rubber weather stripping on its bottom screeched across the foyer's pink tile floor.

I heard the woman's voice first, speaking Spanish. Her vicious complaints about the ugly waitress who spilled a tray of drinks at the club that evening were not going to matter to her for much longer. She told Gutierrez to bring a bottle of wine and two glasses upstairs, referring to him as *querido*, "dear." That struck me as more wife-y than girlfriend-y, but still didn't settle the issue in my mind.

The clicking of her high-heels on the foyer's inlaid tile echoed upstairs as I moved with purpose across the master bedroom. The tenor of her heels changed to more of a clunk as she left the tile floor and started up the wooden stairs.

That she had told Gutierrez to bring wine with him meant she would come upstairs first, alone. I scooted around the corner to my left, made a U-turn down the short hallway leading to the bathroom, and stood out of sight, silently waiting for her.

If this were her own home, I would have expected her to head to her closet first to take off her shoes and dress. Since it wasn't, I gambled that she'd make a beeline for the bathroom to either change into "something more comfortable" or slip into a robe.

The carpet muffled her footsteps so well that when she rounded the corner of the short hallway between the bedroom and bathroom and we first saw each other, it surprised us both. I flinched, and my eyes quickly took in the entire scene.

The woman branded indelibly into my brain was standing four feet in front of me. She wore a short, silver, sleeveless dress with a sheer panel that wrapped from the top of one of her thin hips, around her back, to the other. Her gorgeous brown hair hung over well-tanned shoulders, down to the middle of her back. She had the kind of long, shiny hair that looks so easy and natural, yet women know from experience that hair like hers looks so beautiful specifically because in reality it's so damned hard to take care of.

Fashion magazines say beauty comes from the personalized and creative ways in which a woman mixes, matches, conceals, and reveals the elements of her individuality—hair, clothes, boobs, shoes, butt, makeup. There's an intangible element to beauty. Some women have it in spades while others never will, no matter how hard they try. This woman had it all, and she made it seem so natural and easy. Whatever *it* is, she most definitely had *it*, with plenty to spare.

I had flown to Aruba to kill Gutierrez, but now a brunette beauty stood between me and my target. Intellectually, I knew that completing my mission meant going through with the plan. I didn't create the plan, I just had to carry it out. To execute it. To execute *her*, a woman who made the fatal mistake of going on the wrong vacation with the wrong drug dealer at the wrong time.

She's so beautiful, I thought, *how could it be right for me to kill her?* All my life, people have repeatedly told me how pretty I am, but standing in that hallway, pistol cocked and aimed at her gut, I felt ugly inside.

Had I really signed up for this? In that spectacular moment back at the Farm when Michael asked me to work for him, a wave of joy had flooded my mind—elation, euphoria, or maybe it was relief knowing that my career would be in the confident hands of a man like him. A senior CIA executive wanted *me* and not any of the more educated or experienced new hires! Had I genuinely appreciated the magnitude of what he was asking me to do? Had I actually agreed in that glorious moment to do anything asked of me, regardless of the consequences? I realized, looking at the woman standing in front of my pistol, that yes, that's exactly what happened.

My inaugural mission—the final exam after a grueling year of intelligence operations training—left no time for hesitation. I came to understand in that specific moment that this is exactly what I wanted. No, what I *needed*: to pass the test, to be *in* and fully accepted on Michael's team. If that meant going through this chick to get to Gutierrez, then so be it.

"When the time comes for it, remember...." Michael had counseled.

I remembered.

My distracting thoughts seemed to take all night but likely only lasted a second. The calm of surety enfolded me, and I knew what path the rest of my career was going to take.

Decide. Act. Move. Live. Repeat.

After thousands of routine trigger pulls in training, *that* particular trigger on *that* particular night pushed back against my index finger as I drew it tightly against the arc of the smooth black metal. I doubt my squeeze was as smooth as my father had taught me to make them from that wonderful day—my tenth birthday—he first brought me to the firing range. From that exhilarating afternoon until he suddenly and without explanation or even a goodbye left my mother and me when I was sixteen, he made me an expert marksman.

I was a natural with a pistol, but pulling that particular trigger at that particular time felt anything but natural. I squeezed for what seemed like forever and flinched when the Sig jerked back in my hands. The empty brass case ricocheted with a surprisingly loud *ping* off the mirrored closet door to my right.

My memory of pausing to see what happened after that first shot is crystal-clear. It seemed perfectly natural to want to see the results of my first shot—never mind that Gutierrez was somewhere downstairs gathering glasses and a bottle of wine to bring up. I became overly fixated on the slowly spreading red spot in the middle of the knockout brunette's silver dress and wasn't focusing on the critical tasks still ahead.

In front of me stood, well, staggered really, a supremely surprised woman in terrible pain. She lurched backwards into the wall and the *thud* snapped me out of my self-induced haze.

If she collapsed against the wall, Gutierrez would be certain to see her and I wasn't strong enough to drag a hundred pounds of dead weight out of sight quickly.

I rudely grabbed ahold of her perfectly coiffed hair and pulled her a few feet down the hall toward the bathroom. There, bent forward, brown hair spread between the fingers of my gloved hand, she fought to say something. The anguished contortion of her face communicated more than the incomprehensible, guttural noise that emerged from her throat.

I don't recall having a strong reaction to shooting a woman I'd never met, but oddly, grabbing her by the hair felt too intimate and made it personal; it left me queasy.

I could only hope that from downstairs Gutierrez had not heard the muffled gunshot or the spent brass's ricochet off the mirror. Contrary to pop-culture TV shows and movies, suppressors don't make a weapon completely silent, even with the subsonic ammunition that is my typical. Sure, there's no loud bang, but there are still a few not-always-quiet sounds to contend with. As the gun fires, its slide scrapes across the weapon's metal frame, followed by the bouncing of an ejected shell casing against whatever it hits. In this case, I also had to deal with a surprised woman repeatedly mumbling, "*Guuk.*"

I dropped her to the floor in the middle of the hallway where she couldn't be seen from the bedroom. As ugly as it sounds, I wanted to get her on the ground so my soon-to-come second shot would not leave a large red stain on the wall to warn Gutierrez.

Yes, it's gross. You never quite get used to it, but you do learn to avoid the splatter.

I aimed straight down and leaned forward until the barrel of the suppressor hovered three inches from the back of her head. This time my trigger pull was quick and smooth. I had to look away and tell myself to focus on the plan, not on the body. Or the... mess.

It had not occurred to me at the time that I needed to pay attention to the path of the bullet. If it ended up going through both the woman and the floor, it might have alerted Gutierrez downstairs and ruined my element of surprise. Even if I had thought about it, I needn't have worried with a 9mm. Later, with more powerful .45 caliber rounds, it would matter quite a bit and I trained repeatedly to take great care with every shot.

With the "obstacle" now out of the way, I turned my attention to my primary target. I hadn't heard Gutierrez for a while and peeked around the corner to see if he might have come into the bedroom while I was dealing with the woman. He had not.

I removed both shoes from the now-dead woman and tossed them onto the bed.

Waiting quietly, I learned repeatedly that evening, is a whole lot harder than it sounds. I breathed deeply trying to slow my racing heart, with little success.

Unable to see the bedroom door from my position near the bathroom, I had nothing to look at except the body of the woman on the floor, which was not a calming sight.

The painful twinges in my gut were interrupted by the clacking of heels on wooden stairs outside the bedroom. The sound of his shoes on successive steps as he made his way up brought my focus back to the bedroom and away from my fixation on the dead woman sprawled at my feet.

"I hope that dress comes off as easily as those shoes did," he said loudly to ensure he could be heard all the way to the bathroom.

I heard him perfectly well.

Without hesitation I pushed the Sig forward, rotated around the corner, and confronted him in the bedroom.

Gaining the element of surprise is an art form, the success of which can be read on the faces of those on the wrong end of it. Surprise birthday parties are usually appreciated, and I'm sure being surprised by a beautiful woman in the bedroom would normally have ranked right up there on Gutierrez's list of things that would have made his vacation even more enjoyable. But not *this* woman. If the Sig alone wasn't menacing enough, the imposing presence of the suppressor made it perfectly clear that I was there for only one reason and I meant business.

He held the bottle of Riesling in his left hand slightly extended in my direction, obscuring my view from his upper chest to his chin. From my position, I could not make a clean headshot and absolutely did not want to miss him completely or have the bottle of wine deflect the bullet. I made the split-second decision and fired a hollow-point bullet into his belly.

I watched his white dress shirt redden as a circle of blood spread rapidly across the front. Gutierrez's face contorted as he crumpled to the floor at the foot of the bed and disappeared from view. I didn't hesitate to admire my handiwork or reflect in real-time on my career choices. I raced forward towards the bed, not knowing if he might be reaching underneath for a hidden gun.

Damn, I forgot to check there! Isn't that the most obvious place to hide something in a bedroom? Shit! Michelle, you idiot, how could you have made that kind of beginner's mistake?

I jumped onto the foot of the bed and fired four rounds in rapid succession. My tight shot grouping left four holes in the upper-back of his shirt. His head bobbed as he convulsed. Groans slipped weakly out of the dying man.

After a few seconds, his guttural complaints faded, becoming softer and more distant. With a final, rattling exhale, what little life that remained wheezed out of his lungs. Without any internal debate this time, I held the barrel of the suppressor a few inches from his left ear and pulled the trigger for the final time that night.

I caught my breath for a few seconds while I knelt on the bed and listened intently. I strained to hear anything that might indicate someone else was also in the house.

I heard nothing.

Make a plan and follow it, Michael always says. *What's next in the plan? Follow the plan, Michelle.*

I rifled through Gutierrez's pockets and pulled a wad of cash from his wallet. I checked his ID to confirm it was him and pocketed the money, just as Michael told me to do. I flipped the wallet onto the bed and emptied the contents of the dead woman's purse next to it, then let it drop to the floor in a rather feeble attempt to give the impression of a robbery gone bad.

An apparent motive like robbery would give the police an easy way to classify the case if they didn't want to work too hard. If they didn't buy the robbery theory and instead investigated it as a targeted killing, they would certainly look at rival Peruvian or Colombian cartels. There'd be no reason to suspect American involvement, unless I ended up getting caught red-handed. *To avoid that,* I reminded myself, *it was time to leave.*

Downstairs, I stopped just short of twisting the handle of the back door and making my escape to freedom. I glanced over my shoulder at the stairway and realized that one last task remained for me back in the bedroom.

The plan said to leave—to go out the back door, walk the few blocks down the beach to where I'd left the car, and drive away. First, I needed to do something else. While not part of the plan, I had to do it just for me. I ran back upstairs, made sure not to step in the pool of blood spreading around Gutierrez, and walked down the short hallway.

The woman's body lay outside the bathroom, right where I had unceremoniously pushed her to the ground and ended her life. The tightening in my gut returned as I caught sight of her open eye staring blankly at itself in the mirrored closet door. I wanted to close her eye, which seemed like the right thing to do, but there was blood all over her head. Selfishly, I didn't want to get it on my glove. The scene was by far the most disgusting thing I'd ever seen, much less created. I didn't want to touch her at all, especially not near the head wound. A wound that I caused, my gurgling stomach reminded me in no uncertain terms.

Carefully, so as to not get blood or worse on my gloves or pants, I pulled her left hand out from beneath her. I looked, but *it* wasn't there. No ring. Not his wife. Okay, now I knew.

Why it mattered to me so much, I couldn't be sure. I had never killed another human being before and simply needed to know. If not for my sake, then for hers.

With that settled, I walked downstairs to make my escape.

Chapter 5

The sky to the east glowed a light orange as I drove up the ramp into the three-story parking garage. I eased the car into an empty spot on the second deck at the Megaplex 8 Cinema in Palm Beach, just a few miles from Aruba's Queen Beatrix International Airport where I'd catch my morning flight home in less than three hours.

I popped the trunk to stow my gear and methodically ran through my memorized checklist. I had to make sure not to keep anything on me that shouldn't be carried through an airport security checkpoint.

I only travel using tourist passports and am not graced with diplomatic or military exemptions from any of the security restrictions that apply to civilian travelers. I have no easy way to get a weapon through an airport and certainly did not want airport security or the police to find me carrying lock picks or ammunition.

My professional life being what it is, I live under an alias and travel under Non-Official Cover—a NOC in Agency lingo. NOCs don't have any special privileges or get-out-of-jail-free cards like those afforded to Clandestine Service officers working undercover as diplomats at US embassies around the globe. Those officers enjoy diplomatic immunity; NOCs don't. If we're caught, we're screwed and we know it. We take extra precautions to evade and escape from local authorities, are extremely good at using disguises, and pay exceptionally close attention to the aliases and cover stories we use. Our careers and often our lives depend upon mastering the tradecraft required for covert operations.

I gently placed the pistol and suppressor into the briefcase-sized blue Pelican case in the trunk first. The lock picks and my gloves went in next, followed by my jacket containing the baggie of cash for our team's informal slush fund, and then two unused magazines of ammo. I ran my hands along my legs, pockets, and shirt, feeling for anything I might have missed. Better for me to find it in the garage than airport security catches me with it later that morning. Nothing. Good. Done.

I tossed the car keys in, then locked the case before grabbing my overnight bag and finally closing the trunk.

I would never meet the logistics specialist who parked the Agency-supplied vehicle in that garage a day or two before my arrival in Aruba. The Agency excels at covert logistics, moving everything from cars and cash to guns and explosives to any spot on the globe that a Clandestine Service Case Officer or covert action operator like me needs. All the Logistics Division needs is enough time and their teams make magic happen.

For one mission, they might fabricate a corporate cover and send equipment via a commercial ship or plane. Another time, they may take advantage of a government diplomatic courier to move weapons and electronic intelligence collection equipment to wherever it's needed. Michael fills out the right forms and whatever we need gets delivered to the right place at the right time, just like a great big covert Santa leaving presents for me year-round. Yes, even in the secret world of covert action, there are still government forms to fill out.

My brisk walk from the parking garage to the taxi stand at the Hyatt hotel lasted only ten minutes. I arrived at the airport with a little less than two hours until my flight to Miami, plenty of time since I wasn't checking any bags.

My hands started quivering as I entered the security queue. Even if no one at the airport knew what had happened a few hours earlier at the villa, *I* still knew. My restless hands moved with a mind of their own, much to my chagrin, since fidgety is exactly how you do *not* want to act at an airport. Even after double-checking myself at the car, confident that all of my gear remained securely locked in the trunk, I couldn't shake the jitters. My scalp itched from the feeling of invisible eyes watching me from all directions.

I squeezed my thumbs into my index fingers to keep my hands occupied while mentally digging back to my surveillance and counter-surveillance training. As one instructor taught, "Observe your surroundings by looking around with your eyes. Don't turn your head."

I ran my hand nervously through my hair and froze. My wig had shifted. I felt it move! Could anyone else see it? Did the slip give me away?

My exfiltration plan read like the textbook definition of an easy trip home. Step one, get on the plane. Step two, sit tight until the plane lands. The bodies of Gutierrez and his girlfriend still remained undiscovered in the villa's bedroom, and no one was the wiser. How could anyone possibly screw up such a simple exfil? Get on the plane—it's that easy. Did I lack the capacity to do even that much correctly?

I fought against the nervous energy welling up in my thighs, shoulders, and even my eyebrows. I had to control the shaking and channel it productively, but how?

It was winning. I was losing.

I appeased my inner tormentor by twisting slowly to my right and letting my bag slip gently off my shoulder and drop to the ground. That gave me a reasonable excuse to look to that side. Not counting the uniformed officers, I spotted at least six people who could have been plain-clothed security.

Stop worrying, I ordered myself. Intellectually, I knew no one was looking for me, but, emotionally, the fear of being hunted grew incessantly.

Are those people over there police? Are they plain-clothed security? I asked myself pensively, worried that my first mission would also be my last.

With a smirk, I chuckled at the answer to my self-interrogation. *Yes, Michelle, it's an airport. They probably are all security and, yes, they're all looking at you. But they're not looking* for *you, girl. Buck up. Face forward. Quiet the hell down and just go home.*

Everyone in an airport is under surveillance and we all know it, I reminded myself. Uniformed police, security officers, Customs and Immigration agents, and closed-circuit TV cameras are everywhere, even in a tropical paradise like Aruba. The sight of one after the other made my scalp itch and it required every bit of self-control I could muster not to reach up and pull at my wig. Finally, I shoved my hands into my pants pockets to keep them from betraying me as I inched through the security line.

Some secret agent you're turning out to be, kiddo, I chided myself.

Upon reaching the head of the line, I presented my CIA-issued real-but-fake passport to the woman in the dark blue security uniform at the podium. My mind flashed back to the dread of high school final exams. I knew going into the classroom that I was as prepared as could be, but still suffered the trepidation that comes with knowing you're not in control of what happens to you next. At the front of the security line, the only thing standing between me and the freedom of a return flight to the USA was a woman wearing a badge. With nothing else to do and nowhere else to go, I watched her examine my passport and boarding pass and simply hoped for the best.

No such angst bothered me when leaving the US a few days earlier. I knew the passport was a real one, issued by the same State

Department office that issues regular tourist passports. No one in the world could tell the difference between the one I was using and any of those issued to any other American citizen because there was no difference. The photo in this passport showed me, wearing the same wig I wore there in the security line, only the name printed on the passport was most certainly not the one my wonderful mother and asshole of a father gave me at birth.

Of course, I had nothing to worry about when leaving the States just days earlier as I hadn't done anything wrong up to that point. On my return home, however, memories of my violent actions at the villa engulfed my mind, and yet, somehow I had to convincingly pretend I knew nothing about the events of the previous evening.

Later, I would learn from experience that there are only two types of countries in the world—those in which American passports and citizens are welcome and those in which we're not. Aruba is most certainly the former. The security officer glanced at my passport only long enough to ensure the name printed inside matched what was on my boarding pass.

A gust of cool wind blew across my face when the inspector handed the blue booklet back to me and said, "Next." I walked forward to the X-ray machine and gently placed my bag on the conveyor belt. This was the easy part, since I knew that nothing on me would set off the metal detector or show up on an X-ray.

With the security line behind me, I made my way to the first bathroom along the terminal and gave in to an overwhelming need to check my wig. With a big sigh of relief, I found that the only things askew were my nerves.

Would I ever get used to the anxiety and second-guessing? Or, maybe having such feelings is what keeps us on our toes and always alert? I silently applauded myself for a successful mission and hoped my self-congratulations would calm me. Unfortunately, I'm stubbornly hard to convince and have always been my own harshest critic. It's just my nature.

I didn't start to relax until after takeoff when the landing gear retracted into the belly of the airplane. Through the thin cushion of my economy-class seat, I felt the bumping of the gear locking into place below me. That eased my fears of being caught and becoming known on the team as a miserable failure on my first mission. As the airliner accelerated skyward, I relished my release from the jitters inflicting my limbs and eked out a subtle grin on my way to safety, back to the States. Once there, I'd be untouchable.

As I stared out the jet's small window, a steady stream of questions paraded through my mind. How long would it be until the bodies were discovered? What will the police do then? Could any evidence left in the house be tied to me? I wore gloves in the house and didn't leave any fingerprints on the shell casings. The blue equipment case containing what little incriminating evidence that did exist would be spirited out of Aruba by a Logistics Officer in no time, likely in an un-inspectable diplomatic pouch. My equipment would arrive at the Farm within a week for me to clean and return to the armory.

Nagging questions I couldn't answer stayed with me long into the flight. Somewhere over the Caribbean Sea, self-consciousness about whether I should feel guilty about my actions intruded into my already unsettled mind, which was definitely not an improvement.

Part of me contended that I should be happy to rid the world of the likes of Gutierrez. Part of me worried incessantly about being caught. Part debated whether killing his girlfriend was okay or not, and part enjoyed the adrenaline rush of the newness and exhilaration of the whole damned thing.

Throughout the four-hour flight, too many parts of my brain pulled in too many different directions. I couldn't decide which would win the tug-of-war or even which one should. It dawned on me later that I was subtly grilling myself about whether or not I could ever do it again.

During the short taxi ride from the airport to my apartment in Reston, Virginia, I studied the face in my passport one last time and said a silent goodbye to my first disposable alias. Marcia Davis existed for less than a week, and now she would disappear forever. I never used that name again, had to forget all about that ephemeral persona, and went back to living my cover as a saleswoman for a catering supply company. Goodbye temporary alias Marcia Davis; hello permanent alias Michelle Reagan.

Warm, welcoming relief engulfed me as I stepped into my apartment. Even though I'd only been living there for a month, I relished that apartment. It was the first place I could truly call my own.

My bag landed with a dull thud on the hallway carpet as I made a beeline for the bathroom to rip off the wig and scratch my scalp to my heart's content. Oh, that felt *so* good! As the wig separated from my body, so did the alias. As Marcia's hair fell to the floor next to the sink, my worries about being caught fell away with it.

I stared into the bathroom mirror and saw myself. Myself at home. Myself successful. Myself relieved. But I was not the same *myself* who had looked back from that very mirror just a few days earlier. More than a little about that reflection had changed from the *myself* I remembered.

I showered, ate, and flopped down on my futon for a while to see if I'd found answers to any of the questions that jockeyed with each other through my head during the long flight home.

The painful mental image of the bloodstain spreading across that silver dress had stayed with me all day.

That night, I pulled back my new floral print bedspread and got under the covers. I hooked my arm around my favorite pillow and closed my eyes. Feeling conflicted and insecure I cried myself to sleep.

***

The next morning, anxious and still at odds with myself, I left for work earlier than usual. I hadn't slept well and wanted to get moving to keep my mind off the disturbing dream that had awakened me so early. For some inexplicable reason, I dreamt about Gutierrez's girlfriend's hair. Who knows why I fixated on what would seem like the least-significant aspect of everything that happened in Aruba, but obviously that's what was on my mind.

In my dream, I ran my gloved hand through her long brown hair. It started out as if it were something I was doing in a sweet and caring way. The sudden sight of blood and brain matter on the floor shocked me awake when the full realization of what I had done hit me. She didn't just die—*I* killed her. Me!

I bolted upright, shivering violently. The beads of sweat on my forehead and upper chest were all the evidence I needed that the battle inside me raged on.

With little likelihood of falling back to sleep, I got out of bed and started my day early. I headed into the office on edge and with an unsettled stomach, driving the ten miles slowly and in no rush to relive the events of the previous few days during my mission debriefing.

The elevator dropped me off outside our team's undercover office on the fourth floor of one of the many mid-rise office buildings in Tysons Corner, Virginia. That area, situated at the western edge of the DC beltway, is popular with a mix of commercial businesses, government agencies, and defense contractors, so we blend in well.

The small sign on the front door states that it's the sales office of Eastern Catering Connection, purveyors of commercial catering supplies. If it were a real business, it would be a pretty bland and uninteresting place to work, if you ask me. That's what makes it such a good cover. Providing catering supplies is not the kind of business anyone ever thinks of, much less wants to ask too many questions about. It's just not at all interesting, but it does provide a good excuse for frequently being out of town on "sales calls," so I don't have to make too many excuses to friends when I'm away for training or operational work.

A sales job also justifies the BMW 328i company car Michael gave me to use. There's nothing special about the car—it's not bullet-proof and doesn't have ejector seats—but it goes incredibly fast when I stomp on the gas pedal. With no badge or government ID to get me out of speeding tickets, I need to be careful. After all, as far as the rest of the world knows, I'm just a nobody sales girl.

Michael greeted me with a huge smile as I entered his office. "Welcome back. Close the door and take a seat. I want to hear everything. How'd it go?"

He didn't have to point to the seat he wanted me to take. Only one remained in his office that day—the old wooden chair with the cracked, burgundy leather seat that usually sat empty and ignored in the corner by the window.

"Where'd the sofa and good chairs go? Are you making some changes in here?"

"In a manner of speaking," he responded dryly, in a way that told me absolutely nothing about what he meant.

The chair creaked once and wobbled to the left as I lowered myself onto its faded leather upholstery. Stuffing flowed as the cracked leather pulled itself apart along the chair's front edge with little other than the weight of my thighs to keep it contained. I shifted in the seat trying to get comfortable, a prospect made more difficult by my outfit. My black and white striped skirt, which didn't quite reach down to my knees, simply refused to cover enough of the cracks and shield the bottom of my exposed thighs from the sharp edges of the battered leather. I found some solace by sitting far enough forward that the thin material of my skirt protected me as best it could from the unrelenting scratching of the seat's worn edge. If nothing else, it made my posture perfect.

"Fine," I answered. "Everything went fine. No problems." Michael knew that wasn't nearly all. I could see by the questions his eyes were asking that he knew there was more being said by the tone of my voice than by my words.

"My trip down to Aruba and picking up the car left for me by Logs went as expected," I told him. "I found the villa easily and had no trouble getting in."

"What kind of locks did it have?"

I expected that question from him since he had to send me through locksmith training twice in the previous six months. He knew of my troubles learning that particular skill. During my second time through the class, though, it finally clicked, pun intended.

"The back door had a five-pin Kwikset, so it was straightforward. No one was around, and it only took me thirty seconds to get in." Thirty seconds is actually a long time to spend picking such an easy lock, and I didn't want to admit he hadn't hired the world's greatest burglar.

I also didn't want to start out my first professional relationship by lying to Michael. That's no way to build trust. I had to accept that if he felt a half-minute was too long, he'd send me back through training again and I'd suck it up and train even harder, if such a thing were possible. He didn't make an issue of it, which made me happy considering picking the lock ranked pretty far down the list of the most important things that happened to me in Aruba. I desperately needed to get something off my chest and hoped he'd lead into the conversation about Gutierrez's girlfriend so I could share my feelings about her.

Michael, a tall, slender, grandfatherly man, ran his fingers up his scalp through his thick white hair and pushed the one wayward lock that always seems be drooping into his eyes up over the top of his head. "Then what happened?"

Crap. He wasn't going to directly ask about her. I didn't know how to bring up my feelings about killing the girlfriend while not making it sound like he made a mistake choosing me for his team. I definitely wanted to work for him and do a great job, but was certainly not yet comfortable with it. Sure, I was the new kid on the team, but the last thing I wanted my teammates to view me as was actually *being* the new kid on the team.

I dove into my explanation at a breakneck pace. "Gutierrez and his girlfriend arrived home from the club, and she walked upstairs first. He stayed downstairs to get a bottle of wine from the kitchen. I was hiding near the bathroom in the master suite when she rounded the corner.

"Do you want the gory details? I mean it was really gross, you know...." I said as my voice trailed off. "Really, it was utterly disgusting."

"It's okay, Michelle. I understand. I've been an operator since before you were born and have been there myself many times," he said, reminding me that he has seen everything I just experienced, and more, throughout his career. "Just tell me about the shots you took. Who was first? How many total? That kind of thing. Go slowly if you need to."

Michael understood perfectly well that I had difficulty talking about it. He had the air and patience that comes with experience. He's a true professional. Would I ever be able to match his level of self-confidence? I always found important lessons living inside the tales he told—his war stories, literally, from his days as an Army Green Beret during the failed hostage rescue in Iran at Desert One or his later missions after joining the CIA in the early 1980s. He had seen it all and I have been incredibly fortunate to have him teach me the tradecraft he'd learned during his career.

I know he took a risk bringing me, a completely inexperienced and fresh-off-the-street Agency recruit, onto his team and training me from scratch. Michael's belief in my potential to rise to the challenge became my personal motivation to train hard and live up to his expectations. His became the voice in my head constantly urging me forward, encouraging me when even I questioned my own resolve. Sometimes, it was a kind and encouraging word and other times a motivational kick in the ass.

Before Michael selected me, there hadn't been a woman on the team for twenty years. I consciously dedicated myself to becoming the best I could. I didn't want to make him think I couldn't handle it and regret picking me.

It didn't take me too many years to start feeling the right level of self-confidence and pride in my skills, but at that moment in his office, I could not fathom how such a thing would ever be possible. How had he done it a million years ago, before his slicked-back hair was stark white? *Maybe it's just a male thing,* I thought, sitting there squirming on the red leather chair.

"Okay.... Yeah.... Right...." I rambled on a bit trying to figure out how to admit out loud what I'd done. Everyone's taught from a young age how to behave, and for little girls it's always the same. Be *nice* to people. Don't hurt people. Make people smile and they'll like you. You want other people to like you. Smile more. You'll make yourself happy by making other people feel good about themselves. Treat people the way you want to be treated. Do unto others as you'd have done unto you.

In my head, my mother's voice recited all of these things over and over, but no matter how many times she said it, what I did in

Aruba was anything but *nice*. I couldn't reconcile her sweet voice with my repulsive memory of Gutierrez's girlfriend as she lay face down outside the bathroom. I was certainly never going to tell my mother about my mission to Aruba, and that morning I struggled to even tell Michael.

"I knew she was coming upstairs first because I could hear her high-heels on the wooden stairs. In the bedroom, she walked around the corner, and I was a bit surprised, you know? She looked so beautiful. I expected that the woman a guy like Gutierrez would have with him would be pretty, but she was stunning. That caught me off-guard. I heard her coming up the stairs but seeing her suddenly appear so close in front of me still kinda surprised me."

"I know what you mean," Michael said, leaning back in his chair. "You wait hours and hours until it happens and you're so shocked when it finally does that sometimes you hesitate for a split-second."

He truly did know what I was feeling! My eyes brightened, partly in surprise and partly in relief at not being as much the oddball as I'd feared. Had he hesitated on his first mission, too? Maybe my reaction in that hallway wasn't any different than anyone else's on their first mission?

I wasn't completely sure what Michael thought of me at that point so early in my career. I found it exceedingly difficult to open up to my new boss even though he was the only person around for me to talk to about my work and my jumbled feelings. I didn't feel comfortable opening up to him completely. Not by a long shot, but still so desperately needed someone to talk to. I felt compelled to hold back about my blatant imperfections, so I skipped over the part about my hesitating in the hallway.

"I made my first shot to her gut, disabling her, just like you said to do. She stumbled backwards into the wall, so I pulled her down to the ground for the *coup de grâce*." I've always felt that using the French term for a quick and merciful kill-shot gave this work the necessary veneer of impersonal professionalism I needed it to have. Although, when you have to look your target in the face before killing them, it's intimately personal in spite of my abundant wishing otherwise.

I described the rest of what happened in the bedroom and waited for Michael to say something. Any rookie would want to hear their team lead say "good job" or "way to go" or something similar. I did, however, deserve exactly what he finally said.

"You didn't look under the bed first?"

Man, oh man. I kicked myself about that in the villa when it happened and suddenly felt deathly afraid that *that* would be how I'd be known on the team from then on: the girl who forgot to search under the bed. Reality proved kinder than I feared, and Michael let it drop. He knew he made his point and didn't need to rub my nose in it. I promised myself right then and there to never make the same mistake again.

Michael told me what I was expecting, that Gutierrez had not yet been reported missing. It was too soon. He offered some good advice about not searching for news about him or what happened in Aruba. I had no believable reason to look into it, either inside or outside the CIA. Internally, officially, the Agency had nothing to do with what happened. My trip to Aruba never happened—a completely deniable Op. Outside the agency, I had to live my cover story at all times, and there's no way that newly hired catering supply sales girl Michelle Reagan would know anything about Rodrigo Beltran Gutierrez.

As far as anyone should ever know, nothing that happened had anything to do with me. If anyone asked, and no one ever did, I spent those few days in Miami at business meetings, a cover story Michael could make real, if needed. But he never had to. No one in America ever missed Rodrigo Beltran Gutierrez, nor ever mentioned his name to me again.

As I got ready to leave, Michael raised a finger. "By the way, how do you know she was his girlfriend and not his wife?"

While I had wanted to know, it never occurred to me that he would even care. I told him about my sprint back upstairs to check her hand for a ring.

"Michelle, don't you *ever* do that again!" His intensity caught me completely off guard and deflated my growing sense of accomplishment over my first mission's success. His face tightened in a way I'd never seen before and I immediately felt very, very small.

I'd never seen Michael get angry before and never want to suffer that shame again. The instant I realized that my actions had disappointed him so immensely, a suffocating darkness descended over me.

"Michelle," he said more calmly, "you never, *ever* go back to admire your handiwork. Do the job and get the hell out. You may think you're safe, but you never know who else may be coming through the door. Do the job you're there to do and get out right away. I want you back here in one piece every time."

He was right, of course. I *had* felt entirely safe after finishing Gutierrez off. In the heat of the moment, I hadn't thought about the risks of staying in the villa longer than absolutely necessary.

"I've told you this before: you're only safe once you're back on US soil. I can get you out of any jail in America, but that's as far as it goes. I don't want to see you end up in a melancholy situation in some third-world country."

Michael had a few pet phrases. "Melancholy situation" is his euphemism for getting shot or arrested overseas. Operating under non-official cover is a serious risk for CIA officers, and we NOCs know it. To my detriment and Michael's disappointment, I didn't think about that at all back there in the villa.

I nodded my understanding and acceptance of his rebuke. He went on a little while longer, rebuilding my self-confidence about my successful mission. I appreciated it, but the sting of disappointing him so badly remained, and it motivated me to do better the next time.

As I stood to leave, the bottom of my thighs thanked me for their release from the red leather's biting grip. Michael watched as I rubbed the backs of my legs, searching with my fingertips to discover what kind of damage the chair had inflicted.

"There's one last thing," he said as I started towards the door.

"That's the same chair I sat in when I had this same conversation with my team lead back when I was in your shoes. It's the same chair everyone who has joined this team for the past four decades has sat in during their first mission debrief."

I looked at the uncomfortable chair and it hit me why Michael had the rest of the furniture in his office removed while I was traveling.

"Whether you consider it a worthwhile connection to the past," he continued, "or just a silly tradition, I keep it here as a reminder to us all that we each had our first mission, and we each felt then the same way you're feeling now. There's a mixture of confusion over whether what the team does is right or not, some measure of happiness that you were successful, and more than a little relief at not getting caught. I understand all of that. I sat in that chair after my first mission to Honduras—something I'll never forget. No one ever forgets their first, and no one ever forgets sitting in that chair when they get back.

"I see great promise in you, Michelle. I saw it while you were in training at the Farm. That's why I wanted you—and still want you—on this team. I saw your determination clearly while you were working through field scenarios in the basic Operations course. You clearly had the firearms skills, but more importantly, you had fire in your eyes. You still do. Even if you were a bit rattled by your first mission, I can see it's still there. It's vital to your future success. Not everyone has it. In fact, most don't. In training, you showed me that you had the willingness to do whatever it took to get the job done. That's key. Equally important, your mind is wide open to learning. That's critical for any position in the Directorate of Operations. No matter how much you ever think you know, don't ever lose that willingness to learn and use what you know to make the world a better place, one mission at a time.

"You might even find that, in a way, your missions resemble that chair. You may never be completely comfortable in them, and they're not always pretty, but they serve an important purpose. They are neither trivial nor are they ever the first option considered. This team gets the call to go in when no one else can achieve the necessary outcome.

"Things may seem to you like they've been going at a hectic pace, but you'll get used to that. Operationally, you'll start out slowly and before long, get to deploy with your teammates. You'll learn the ropes and be a mission lead before you know it. Now that you've successfully completed your first mission, the other members of the team will be more open to having you involved in the missions they lead. This first success shows them that you can handle the work.

"As I told you before you left for Aruba, it's important for everyone to succeed on their first mission flying solo. On those missions, you know full-well that there's no one to fall back on. You must rely on your own skills and training, and you can't expect others to do for you what needs to be done when the critical moment arrives. Now you've shown the whole team that you have the skills and can handle the pressure where it matters most—in the field. I have every confidence in you and am extraordinarily happy to have you on my team."

Michael walked around his desk, shook my hand, smiled, and gave my shoulder a squeeze.

"So, welcome to the team, Michelle. Now get out of here and I'll see you next week."

As I look back at my career so far, I now realize that *that* particular conversation with Michael crystallized my resolve to become the best covert action specialist the CIA has ever seen. I joined the Agency with almost nothing in the way of knowledge of the world or marketable skills. Michael took me under his wing and over the years trained me to do some unbelievable things. For my own reasons back then, I wanted to be the best. I still do.

I desperately wanted what little recognition anyone in this line of work could ever get for being the best in the Agency, the country, or maybe the world, in a profession that by design gets no recognition or appreciation for the dangers we face.

But Michael would know and be proud of me. My teammates would know. I would know. That would be enough.

I don't know how to determine who's the best at this job. Maybe it's just the person who lives the longest; I'm not sure. No one publishes batting averages for people like us.

As I sit here today in a hospital bed typing this and thinking back to that specific conversation, it's obvious just how much I appreciate the gamble he took, betting he could teach me everything required for me to do this job well. He taught me the ropes and most of all, believed in me unequivocally at a time in my life that called for—no, demanded—exactly that. Michael's mentoring and support has enabled me to survive this long and succeed at a job few can ever know we do. For that, as well as his friendship, I owe him a tremendous debt for his faith, acceptance, encouragement, and support over the years. Have I lived up to his expectations? That's a question I will never have the courage to ask him directly.

Early on, Michael told me of his policy of giving his operators a week off after each mission to decompress from the stresses of fieldwork. At first, I thought of it as a nice bonus. Since then, I've come to relish those weeks and recognize the wisdom of his ways. Sometimes it takes more than a week for me to calm down after the long international flights, cover stories, endless lies, and of course the killing. That, too, takes quite a bit of getting used to.

During my first week off, I didn't have much to do other than buy a few things to decorate my new apartment. That still left plenty of free time.

I began two fitness routines that became important to me, both personally and professionally. I ran a few miles each day and signed up for my first yoga class.

The running is obvious. Being in excellent shape has saved my life more times than I can count.

What I didn't expect was how important yoga and the friends I made through it would become to saving my sanity. That was something I would only discover years later.

PART TWO

MESSAGE RECEIVED

Chapter 6

Allison DeMott practically gulped her smoothie after our yoga class one April morning. "Well? Are you going to tell me, or do I have to start guessing?"

"Tell you what?" I asked in return before taking a sip of my blended banana-strawberry lunch.

"What has you so excited? You could barely hold still during class. Does it have something to do with Tony?" she asked, hoping I'd dish some dirt on the current man in my life.

"No, nothing like that. It's work," I answered truthfully. "I should find out this week whether I'll close a new account that I've been trying to land for a while."

That part was a complete fabrication. In reality, I was amped up because Michael had scheduled a mission briefing for that afternoon. This would be my fourth mission, and the first on which I traveled with a teammate. I could hardly hold still, anxious to move past training with the other members of the team and start working with them where it mattered—in the field.

Throughout our liquid lunch, I strained to hide the electric feeling in my gut knowing that I stood poised to take a significant step forward towards finally being accepted by my teammates as a first-rate operator and an equal on the team. At least that was my hope. I knew in my heart that a lot of hard work remained ahead of me before they'd see me in that light and not just as "the new kid."

"That's great! I hope you get it, Michelle. Sorry to eat and run," she said looking at her watch, "but if I don't get to the hospital in time to shower, I'll be late for my shift. You'd think I could make the twenty miles to Georgetown University Hospital in much less than an hour, but with this damned DC traffic, it's impossible. I hate that. Why don't I just move back to North Carolina?"

I smiled. "Because you don't have friends like me there, that's why. Go. Don't be late."

"Okay, but on Thursday, I want to hear everything you did with Tony. And if there's nothing good to tell, just make something up. My love life is at a standstill now, so I need to live vicariously through you for a while. See ya!"

I struggled to keep my lies consistent with Anthony. Even remembering them all became a part-time job in its own right. I had to keep my true professional life completely hidden from him, which made building a trusting and supportive relationship between us unexpectedly hard. The unpredictability of my travel schedule made it that much worse. All that and having to invent new and believable excuses for not returning his calls promptly exacted a terrible toll on our two-month-old relationship.

He seemed like a good guy. I wanted to get to know him better and tried every trick in the book to make it work. I was frustrated with myself, being caught between the competing demands of wanting to have a healthy personal life, needing to maintain my cover, and working hard to grow and succeed on the team.

That afternoon, I arrived at the office for the mission briefing and settled into one of the black padded leather chairs. All Michael had told me about this one was that my teammate and I would be traveling as a married couple—a common cover.

About half of our missions were pinpoint strikes on which we worked solo. On the others, we would travel together. Sometimes, that's because the final phase of the mission required more than one person to carry it out. Other times, it's simply easier to live a convincing cover story if you're not alone. It also never hurts to have someone you trust watch your back and help with surveillance.

My first three assignments had all been solo missions against minor targets and had gone well. Not all of them had succeeded, technically. On my third, it turned out that my intended target got run over by a drunk driver the day before I was supposed to intercept him on his way to work. Throughout the flight home from Rome, I was never able to decide whether I should have been pleased that the target ended up dead anyway or upset that I had not accomplished what I'd been sent across the pond to do.

With three missions under my belt, I felt increasingly comfortable with our team's routine: training, briefings, work-ups, missions, debriefings, and a week off to decompress. Nothing on our team is ever truly routine, but I found myself easing into the pattern of what my professional and personal lives were becoming.

I enjoyed the expanding sense of self-respect I got from doing well, by my yardstick anyway, and becoming a reliable contributor to an important organization. Back home in California, I never felt the enticing sense of unlimited freedom that came with this job.

Michael was starting to understand and trust me, but the other two operators, Claude and Arnaud Payeur—fraternal twin brothers in their late thirties—were not there yet. Not by a longshot. They still viewed me as the new kid and were nowhere near ready to trust me with their lives. I could well understand their feelings since they had not yet seen me in action in the field where things were unpredictable. I planned to use this mission to change that.

This mission captivated me because it would be my first with a foreign political angle to it. I practically fantasized about the myriad roles I would soon play running sneaky covert action missions in another country's sandbox, which is exactly why the Special Activities Division, SAD, existed in the first place.

I would be working with Claude on this mission. Ensuring things went perfectly would be my best chance at becoming more accepted by the twins. Get in good with one and you'll get in good with both, I figured. This would be my one and only chance to make a good first impression.

Chapter 7

Wilson Henry began the pre-mission intelligence briefing after Michael joined us in the conference room. Michael took his usual spot at the head of the table and Claude, Arnaud, and I sat on one side of the large oak table across from Wilson. Arnaud sipped from a can of Diet Coke. I had my ever-present bottle of water at hand and waited anxiously for the briefing to start.

Wilson, a career intelligence analyst on permanent assignment to our team, passed out the mission briefing packets. An employee of the Directorate of Intelligence, he did the detailed research necessary to ensure the operators on our team have the best possible information at hand before we're sent into harm's way. He's been on the team since long before I joined it.

Once someone gets assigned to our team, there's precious little cause for them to leave. The nature of our work being what it is, Michael has the ear of the Director and the political power to get the right people transferred onto our team and keep them there. On the upside, with his influence, Michael gets everyone promoted fast enough to make it worth their while to stay for most of their careers.

In his strong Bostonian accent that I've become quite adept at deciphering, Wilson gave us the background for the mission.

"For as long as banks have existed, they've been getting robbed. As one man famously said, it's because that's where the money is," he began. "For most of history, bank robbery has been a high-risk, low-reward crime. Until, that is, banks decided to connect their computers to the Internet and essentially put their money out in the open for anyone to take."

Wilson often spoke somewhat dramatically. He went on to describe how banks choose to make things more convenient for their customers, even if it means taking significantly greater losses from theft and fraud.

"Once Internet banking became the norm, bank robbery became far more sophisticated. Nowadays, the best bank robbers are hacking into banks quite literally from the other side of the world. Over the Internet, they wire the money out of the country where it's picked up by intermediaries. Those people then walk the cash down the street to another bank or a Western Union office and wire it to the boss's account. Each intermediary keeps a small percentage for his efforts. The organizers could not care less if any of those money mules get caught—the bosses themselves remain safely overseas and out of the reach of law enforcement. In this case, the boss is in Samarkand, Uzbekistan."

Michael looked at Claude and with a wry smile said, "I hear Uzbekistan is lovely this time of year." Claude just shook his head and smirked, trying hard to not break out in a full smile. I never found out why he thought Michael's comment was funny, and soon realized that they were not going to let me in on the joke. I remained an outsider.

Before being promoted to a Senior Intelligence Service executive, Michael was an operator. He, Claude, Arnaud, and a guy named Aiden were the four members of the team. They'd worked together for years until Aiden was killed on a mission. They had worked together for almost as long as I'd been out of diapers and knew and trusted each other unconditionally. I'm sure there were a thousand such inside jokes I would never be privy to.

Michael did not intend to alienate me with his joke, and anyone could see the close rapport between the two of them. Something else shone as clear as day: while I may be *on* the team, I was still not *one* of the team. I focused all of my energies on this mission to change that. Actions speak louder than words, and I was becoming a woman all about action.

"For lack of a better term," Wilson continued, "the boss of the group is who we're after: twenty-three-year-old Faruk Altyaryk. As far as we know, he doesn't have any partners-in-crime who live physically close to him. He recruits his associates on underground hacker websites and gives them a slice of the profits from whichever bank they're going to fleece that month. Faruk is clearly the brains of the operation and writes the software used to exploit vulnerabilities in the banks' computers. His custom software is what has enabled him to become so successful. The tech guys tell me it's something called polymorphic code. Basically, the software changes its own executable code every time it's run so that anti-virus and other security scanning systems don't know what to look for the next time. This has made it almost impossible for the banks to keep him and his cohorts out.

"Faruk and his co-conspirators have been very busy and unusually successful. Over the past four years, Faruk, who goes by the online nickname of *Annex*, has stolen an estimated fifty million dollars, mostly from American banks, plus a few in the UK. That's some serious money already lost, and banks across the US are still bleeding cash to Annex and his group."

Stealing over twelve million dollars a year is quite a crime spree. Not that I knew anything about robbing banks, but even if he netted half of it for himself after giving his partners and the money mules their cuts, what in the world, I wondered, did someone do with that kind of money in Uzbekistan?

Wilson continued his briefing, describing what other CIA analysts thought about Annex and his exploits. "The analyst who has been following Faruk's exploits for the past year or so told me he thinks that the nickname *Annex* comes from a rather rough abbreviation of the transliteration of the Russian word for Dillinger. As in John Dillinger, the infamous bank robber from the 1930s. If so, he's living up to his namesake's reputation for effectiveness. The FBI got Dillinger in Chicago in 1934, but they've been unable to get Annex."

"Wilson," I asked, "why is the Agency interested in Annex for robbing banks? Granted, it's a lot of money, but even so, isn't that more of a law enforcement problem and not one for an intelligence agency to address?"

"Good question, Michelle. Annex was tracked down a year and a half ago by the Justice Department, which has been trying to extradite him from Uzbekistan ever since. Obviously, they've not been able to do that. We found out why, and it has nothing to do with robbing banks."

That peaked my interest. Still new to the world of intelligence, I marveled at the extraordinary level of detailed information we could gather on people half a world away. I didn't think the CIA would be all that interested in a bank robber, even someone operating on Annex's scale. Finally, Wilson was leading into the meat of the briefing.

"Sometime last year, the Russians found out about Annex. Maybe he was robbing their banks, too. I don't know. What we do know is that they recruited him to expand his repertoire. They've been using him to infiltrate malicious code—computer viruses to you and me—into the networks of major American defense contractors, including, or perhaps especially, the big ones like Lockheed Martin and General Dynamics. From what our Information Operations Center analysts report, Annex is targeting the defense giants' networks to implant his malicious code and steal the software used by our stealth aircraft, which is exfiltrated out to servers under Russian control. In return, Russian intelligence, the

SVR, is providing political cover for him from Moscow to and through the Uzbeks.

"Whether they're blackmailing Annex into helping them or not, we don't know, nor does it matter. As long as Annex is useful to Moscow, there's no way Uzbekistan is going to permit the kid's extradition to the US," Wilson concluded. "For all we know, the Russians are helping Annex launder his stolen money too, but that's just speculation and not all that relevant to the mission.

"What is relevant, and why Annex is now in your crosshairs, is that he began targeting our most sophisticated weapon systems. No doubt at the SVR's direction, Annex is going after the two most sensitive parts of Northrop Grumman's B-2 stealth bomber. Specifically, he's trying to obtain the chemical formulas used in manufacturing the radar-absorbing material the bomber's skin is made of and the algorithms running inside their onboard computers which fool the Russian military's search and acquisition radars. If he's successful at stealing those technologies, the B-2 itself becomes useless against Russia and any country that buys their radar systems. Plus, there's a real likelihood the Russians could duplicate the technologies and use them against us. Or if not us directly, our NATO allies whose militaries don't have their own stealth and counter-stealth capabilities."

Wilson simplified the military analysis of the situation for us and made the seriousness of the threat against our technological advantage clear. He excelled at that, and it certainly helped since I don't have a background in military weapon systems. Essentially, if we wanted to keep a step ahead of the Russians, our team had to stop Annex.

The briefing got more interesting by the minute. I found myself sitting up straighter and hanging on each word. Next, I knew and anxiously awaited, Wilson would explain the part I would be playing in the latest post-Cold-War chess match between the USA and the former USSR.

"As long as they want their goose to keep laying its golden eggs, Moscow will continue to protect Annex and he'll have a free hand to continue robbing us blind. We don't care about the money. It's the protection of the few game-changing technologies we still have that really matters," Wilson said.

"As for Faruk personally, he appears to be an orphan. An old newspaper obituary reported that his mother died in childbirth. There's no sign of his father. Either he's dead or out of the picture. Faruk lives in a single-family house with his aunt and uncle, Nila and Ruslan

Dotorov. Your principal target is Faruk, but the tasking came down from the Director. He wants to send a clear message to the SVR and the Uzbeks that no one has a free hand to fleece America or protect those who do."

Michael chimed in to add his own emphasis on why he had agreed to send us into harm's way. "As always, there won't be any direct statement of responsibility for any this, but the Agency will be putting out the word through Annex's favorite hacker websites that it doesn't pay for anyone to ever work for the Russians or to target American industries. Most importantly, though, Annex will have been stopped. Frankly, he's really good at what he does. We just can't tolerate him doing it against us anymore."

Wilson continued his briefing more hesitantly. "In addition to Faruk, you should expect that Ruslan and Nila Dotorov will be at home. The disposition of those two is not part of the mission parameters."

I imagine Wilson felt that phrasing it that way—the way he always did—softened the message for us. At the same time, he emotionally distanced himself from what he already knew would become of Faruk's aunt and uncle. Even before he said it, Wilson knew exactly what Claude and I were going to do to all three people living in that house. Our team's unofficial motto of "Leave no one alive" is emblematic of the fact that we are the Director's choice of last resort.

When I first joined the team—only eighteen months earlier at that point—it seemed cruel and unnecessary. I learned through experience that in most cases it *is* necessary, like it or not. Over time, I learned to rationalize it—after all, it's either them or me. I didn't want to end up hating the woman looking back at me in the mirror each morning. Sometimes in this line of work you just need to set certain feelings aside to keep moving forward.

"What is a mission parameter, however, is Annex's custom-written software." Wilson continued, describing the uniqueness of the software to an unnecessary level of detail. I know enough about computers to get by and am perfectly happy living digitally ignorant. My eyes glaze over when the tech guys start talking about bits and bytes.

Wilson boiled it down to the salient point. We had no way to bring Annex's computers out of Uzbekistan, so we needed another way to get the information stored on their hard drives out of the country. CIA's wizards in the Directorate of Science and Technology—DS&T—send us into the field with a simple, yet effective, device for just that purpose. I call it a magic wand.

It's a small USB thumb drive that an operator can plug into just about any computer. We don't have to run any programs ourselves; it works automatically, or auto-*magically,* as I like to say. I just plug DS&T's little wonder into a PC and wait until the light on its tip blinks three times. When it does, the spell has been cast and the magic is done. I just pull it out and insert it into the next computer. Simplicity itself.

The tech guys tell me that the CIA's virus on the stick infects all the computers it can reach on the local network and sends everything back to Langley. I don't specifically care how it works, as long as it does. To me, when the tech geeks talk to each other, they all sound like wizards casting technobabble spells. Technology is not my cup of tea. Give me a pistol instead of a computer any day of the week, and I'm all smiles.

"Travel on this trip will be a bit more complicated than usual," Wilson said with a cautious tone to his voice. "In the time available, Logistics was only able to get your vehicle and equipment into Ashgabat, the capital of Turkmenistan. From there, you'll be driving across Turkmenistan to neighboring Uzbekistan. Judging purely by the distance from point to point, you might estimate it to be a ten-hour drive. In reality, the road conditions are fairly poor. Plus, you'll have to cross a border and who knows how long that can take. Expect the drive from Ashgabat to Samarkand to take two days."

Ugh, I lamented silently. Two days in a car, mostly just sitting quietly in the passenger seat. Two days each way! I didn't expect Claude would let me drive, especially since he spoke Russian, and I don't. Not a word of it beyond *da* and *nyet,* both with what I'm sure is an absolutely horrible accent.

With a little luck, I would get to know Claude better and started hoping mightily that he'd suddenly turn into a talker on this trip. Wishful thinking, I know, but I committed to giving it my best effort anyway.

"You'll fly military airlift to Turkey," Wilson continued, referring to the US Air Force transport jets we'd take from Andrews Air Force Base outside of DC to one of the US air bases in Turkey. From there, we'd fly commercial from Istanbul, through Baku, Azerbaijan, across the Caspian Sea to Ashgabat, Turkmenistan.

"The visa stamps in your passports are good for ten days in each country, so even though you'll have a lot of connections to make, you won't have any problems in that regard.

"You'll stay overnight in Ashgabat and pick up the car at the hotel. The car, a Mercedes SUV, contains all your equipment. The vehicle has a bench-style backseat and releasing the concealed latches will open it up. Inside, you'll find your weapons, radios, electronics, and spending money in Uzbeki Som. At checkpoints or if stopped along the way by local police, expect to pay fees—what in America would be considered bribes—to make things go more smoothly. Paying forty or fifty dollars a pop is usual and customary in that part of the world, so don't sweat it if it happens."

Claude nodded knowingly, so I just trusted his experience. I'd not been stopped by security or law enforcement on any of my first three missions, so it'd be a new experience for me if it happened. Claude's experience on the team and traveling the world made feel far more reassured than if I'd had to make this trip alone.

I still had a lot to learn and couldn't decide whether on that trip Claude would more likely play the role of teacher and partner, or all-around jerk. I could only wait and hope.

Chapter 8

Claude and I stowed our gear aboard the USAF Gulfstream jet for our flight to Turkey and settled into a pair of back-row seats. An Air Force Brigadier General and two of her staff officers took up residence in the front row. They looked at us a few times quizzically, trying to decide why two civilian interlopers were on *their* airplane.

From the sounds of their conversation, they were Medical Corps staff on their way to inspect hospitals on two Air Force bases in Turkey. We didn't exchange more than pleasantries during the overnight flight. Besides, I couldn't have added anything interesting to their conversation. The little I knew about medicine I learned during the first-aid class everyone goes through at the Farm or the more advanced "bullet-and-blade" wound-treatment class Michael sent me to at the Navy's medical training facility in Bethesda, Maryland.

The seats reclined all the way back and we all got a good night sleep on the red-eye flight over the Atlantic. At Ramstein Air Base in Germany, we deplaned to stretch our legs and eat breakfast while the Air Force refueled the jet. Claude's silence on the aircraft didn't surprise me since we were within earshot of outsiders, but it began to worry me that he seemed to take great pains to ignore my very existence during the next leg of our trip, a four-hour flight to Turkey.

I mulled over my options to ensure the forced isolation would not cause problems for us once we landed in Turkey. Once there, we'd spend the next week masquerading as husband and wife. That would be a brand-new role for me. I didn't relish the thought of playing it all the way to Turkmenistan with a fake husband who was unwilling to even make fake conversation.

***

We walked through the parking lot of the Sofitel Hotel in Ashgabat, Turkmenistan, and located our SUV right where Wilson said it would be. I smiled from ear to ear and might just have been falling a little bit in love with the Agency's Logs officers. They never failed to impress me. Certainly, at that point, they ranked a few steps higher than Claude in my book.

I expected Claude would be tight-lipped that night in the hotel and he did not disappoint. Intelligence officers assume all hotel rooms are bugged and never say anything of interest anyway. Traveling as we were, with no obvious connection to any government, military, or private-sector company worth spying on, we didn't think we'd warrant being under surveillance, but it's always safest to assume the worst. We made the casual chit-chat expected of a married couple and stuck to the script, just in case.

That night, Claude stayed on his side of the bed and I stayed on mine.

At breakfast the next morning, I started to feel out of place. No matter what country you're in, English is the most commonly spoken language for international travelers, but Claude stuck to Russian and some Arabic on this trip. I'd not experienced any language barriers on my missions in Europe or the Caribbean over the previous year. In Ashgabat, however, I felt completely out of my element and at a real disadvantage.

I've studied Arabic since then, but throughout the week, I had found myself wholly reliant on Claude even for such simple things as ordering breakfast. My utter dependence on him rubbed me the wrong way. I loathed being unable to read the signs around me or even the breakfast menu in my hands.

That trip served as good practice for my later travels in male-dominated parts of the world that are not especially accommodating to women. It also gave me my first insight into the realities of being a woman operating in parts of the Muslim world. Many times since then, I've found that being ignored by the majority of the people around me can be a distinct advantage while traveling. Women are often completely overlooked such that, if I dressed the part, it was as good as being invisible.

The drive north to the border crossing between Köneürgench, Turkmenistan, and Nukus, Uzbekistan, became an all-day ordeal on poorly maintained highways cleaved through drab brown fields devoid of crops or livestock. The occasional cluster of yellow or faded-red houses in various states of disrepair spoke to the lack of industry in that part of the world.

I got sick of the silence after four or five hours and our first pit stop. We were still only halfway to the border and the day was dragging on. I decided to play the conversation into Claude's position as the mission lead and the much more experienced operator.

"How do you want to handle things when we get to the border? What's the best way to do this, since I won't understand anything the guards might say."

"Just let me do all the talking. That's pretty obvious. I don't mean to make that sound belittling, though," he said quickly glancing at me. "Police or border guards in this part of the world won't take offense if they ask a woman a question and she just politely refers them to her husband instead of answering directly. If you can help it, I'd suggest you don't speak at all. If they hear you speaking English, they may look at us more closely or hold us longer while they try to find a guard who speaks English.

"Of course, we're traveling on American passports, so if anything is going to make them look at us closely, it'll probably be that. English is expected of Americans, naturally, but I'll respond to them in whatever language they start talking."

"Okay, sounds good," I replied, pleased to have gotten at least that much out of him and seeing that he wasn't completely ignoring me anymore.

"I'm expecting the border guards at this small checkpoint will be a bunch of lazy, underpaid misfits. The main benefit of going out of our way to the Köneürgench border crossing is that it's a much smaller site than the main international artery on the M37 at Turkmenabat. That'd be a much more direct route to our objective, but they'll have lots of dogs there to inspect cargo trucks. With the weapons and ammo in the car, we don't want to take that risk."

"Mm-hmm," I agreed.

I hoped to build up some momentum in the conversation and decided to press my luck.

"So, you and Arnaud were, what, sixteen years old when your brother was killed in Beirut?"

Claude looked at me sideways and nodded slowly. A hint of sadness crept into his voice. "Charles," he said, pronouncing the name in the French he grew up speaking. It sounded like *SHAR-el*. "He was my identical twin.

"He tagged along that day in the Marine barracks compound with our mother who was translating for the French paratroopers stationed there when the first truck bomb detonated. He was killed, and she was really banged up bad, but nothing permanent. We were all evacuated to the States after the Marines were recalled by President Reagan."

"I'm really sorry," I said. "I never had even one sibling, much less two. I can't imagine what it was like for you. So, you didn't grow up in the States, then?"

"Thanks, and no. We were born and grew up in Lebanon. Our father was a professor of European Literature at the American University of Beirut and mom was a linguist for DoD. Dad's French, but since our mother is a US citizen we have dual US and French citizenship."

Claude looked at me and asked the obvious question. "What about you? Born in Los Angeles?"

I shook my head. "Not quite. I was born in New Jersey where my parents were stationed when they were in the Army, but I was raised in California. I grew up in Gardena, which is part of LA county. If you've never been to Gardena, you haven't missed anything. It's stuck right between very poor Compton to the east and very rich Manhattan Beach to the west. It might not have been as international as Beirut, but was about as multicultural as you can get. I grew up speaking English at home and in school, and Spanish with a lot of my girlfriends."

"We most often spoke French at home," Claude went on, "and had friends from all over the region. Just about everyone grew up speaking French, English, and Arabic. Our next-door neighbors were Russian professors with kids our age, so we learned Russian from them.

"Beirut was called the Paris of the Middle East back then. It was a beautiful, modern city before it was largely destroyed during the Lebanese civil war. Growing up there was great. I didn't really appreciate that until we moved to Virginia and my mother hired on with CIA's Foreign Broadcast Information Service. FBIS was my and Arnie's first introduction to the Agency. DC's fine, I guess, but it's nothing like Beirut was back then."

"Your language skills must have been a real draw for the Agency. Even here, I can see you're really good at blending into the local culture. That's experience. Not something that training back in Virginia can duplicate."

I knew the reasons that got the Payeurs onto Michael's team ran far deeper than just their excellent language skills. At least as important was the bothers' deep resentment for the Iranian-backed terrorists who funded and carried out the attack that had killed their brother. They were natural choices for recruitment in the Special Activities Division.

I chose to not press my luck further by dragging the conversation out and leaned back to get more comfortable in the seat. I enjoyed my small but significant win having gotten Claude to talk at least that much.

***

The border crossing at Köneürgench popped with color. The new and well-maintained white building with green trim and yellow lettering made it clear that the Turkmen people took pride in their country and cared what visitors thought about it. The facility looked a lot smaller, but much prettier than the border crossing between San Diego and Tijuana. I'd crossed there with friends a few times in high school on day trips to do some *el cheapo* shopping south of the border.

The Turkmen border guards barely glanced at the photos in the pair of passports Claude handed over. The officers energetically waved us across and in no time at all we were in Uzbekistan.

Compared to the colorful Turkmen buildings, the Uzbek side appeared flat and dim—more subdued, with its faded yellows and grays. The boring, functional view left me uninspired.

The Uzbek border guards looked with far greater interest at our passports than had the Turkmen inspectors. I grew nervous that the visa stamps were not valid. None of my previous trips required visas and, although Wilson told us they were good for over a week, I was on pins and needles watching Claude discuss something I couldn't understand with the duo of armed officers at the window of our SUV. The conversation grew more animated as the minutes ticked by.

Like my mother used to say when I was young, the ants in my pants were starting to dance.

I kept my eye on a German Shepherd off to our left. A guard had tied its leash to a hand railing against the administration building. It looked as though the dog's handler parked him there while he'd gone off to the bathroom and might return at any moment. I didn't want to think about what might happen if the dog sniffed around our SUV with two handguns, one hundred rounds of ammunition, two suppressors, and some cash concealed in the backrest of the vehicle's rear seat.

The conversation between Claude and a chubby border guard got noticeably louder. Claude repeatedly gestured to the passports and slapped his finger against one of them a few times. I imagined he was repeating for the umpteenth time that the visas were good, and we should be allowed to enter Uzbekistan. Clearly, the border guard had quite a different opinion.

My heart raced when Claude moved his right arm down to his side as if to draw a weapon from a holster. I didn't think he was carrying, but maybe he had hidden one under his shirt while I dressed in the bathroom this morning. I wouldn't have put it past him.

My mouth ran dry. Not being armed, I didn't see how I could help him. Images raced through my mind of Claude drawing his weapon and shooting two border guards in broad daylight. Insanity! What the hell was he thinking?

Claude raised himself up and shifted to his left in the driver's seat, reaching his right hand all the way behind his back. I glanced through the passenger-side window and debated whether it'd be better, tactically, to run behind the Jersey barrier to my right or around the front of the car to wrestle a weapon away from one of the guards.

Things were happening so fast and unexpectedly that I didn't have time to guess what our next move would be, assuming we survived the shootout at the border. Drive forward into Uzbekistan? Try to return to Turkmenistan? This was not the plan by any stretch of the imagination. What was Claude doing? My right hand moved instinctively to the door handle, ready to open it either on my way to freedom or an early grave. I dared not even guess which way things were going to go that morning.

Claude's hand emerged from his pants holding a small wad of cash. He peeled off a dozen bills of Uzbeki Som for each of the guards. I tried to act sly by letting my breath out slowly upon seeing Claude pull money out of his pocket for a payoff instead of drawing a weapon, which would certainly have meant the end of our mission. A bead of sweat rolled along my right armpit. A shiver ran down my side as the Mercedes' air conditioning blew up my sleeve, evaporating the remnant of my nervousness as it ran towards my elbow.

With the press of a button, Claude rolled his window up and shifted the SUV into gear, starting us back on our way. As the miles passed and the border crossing shrank away behind us, I focused my attention on getting my racing heart to return to a more manageable post-embarrassment rate.

Crisis averted. At least, the crisis I had hallucinated was upon us—one which, fortunately, only existed in my head. Claude had everything under control the whole time while my inexperience led me to think the worst.

Boy, I still had a lot to learn.

Chapter 9

"I'll check us in. Stay close to me with your suitcase," Claude advised. Well... ordered really, as we entered the hotel lobby in Bukhara.

The sparsely furnished and dimly lit lobby spoke to me of the thrift with which the hotel was run. Not nearly as upscale as the Sofitel in Ashgabat, it was a good candidate for our purposes. While certainly a few steps above a No-Tell Motel, the place looked clean but not extravagant. It would work just fine for the three days we planned to spend in town taking photographs of the local architecture—or, at least that's the cover story we would tell anyone who asked. From the hotel, we would stage our four-hour drive the next night to Samarkand and our unannounced drop-in on Annex.

We slept late the next morning, anticipating we'd be up working the entire following night.

I awoke with a start, feeling a hand where it shouldn't have been, especially considering that it was not my hand. Claude's incursion onto my side of the bed was unexpected and startled me. I spun over to push him away, still shaking the cobwebs out of my head.

I thought better than that of Claude, and it immediately soured my impression of him.

I half-slid, half-jumped out of bed and landed on my feet. I turned toward Claude and opened my mouth to give him a piece of my mind. His slow, rhythmic breathing punctuated with short, throaty snorts stopped me in my tracks.

I didn't need Claude to be awake to have the obvious conversation with him. It all played out in my head.

"How dare you do that, Claude!"

"Sorry for touching you there, Michelle, I realize that I'm neither your doctor nor your boyfriend, but in my own defense, I was fast asleep at the time."

"Yeah, well, don't do that again."

"What, sleep?"

"Exactly."

Never mind, I told myself, scrunching up my nose and shaking my head. Clearly, I had to learn how to sleep *next to* a guy I wasn't sleeping *with*. That would take some getting used to.

The hands on the hotel-room clock showed it was just after 11 a.m., and after my rude awakening I was up for the day. I sat down on the floor, stretched my legs out in front of me, grabbed my toes, exhaled deeply, and sweated through my morning workout routine to get ready for an important day at the office.

***

The luminescent hands on the dashboard clock reached 2 a.m. I continued to stare silently out the SUV's side window and imagined I could see the barren Uzbeki countryside through the impenetrable blackness.

Mile after mile of highway passed quietly, each one looking the same as the last... and the next. The low rumble of the Mercedes' tires on the worn pavement had been my reliable companion for two long days, speaking to me continuously as a poor substitute for Claude's lack of participation in the conversation.

Despite not speaking a word of Russian, after a couple of days I had figured out how to read the road-side signs as we approached each city. When I saw one showing we were twenty kilometers outside of Samarkand, I felt it was past time we discussed the plan for the evening.

I'm not sure whether or not I succeeded at keeping my pent-up frustration from coming through in my voice. "When do you want to gear up?"

"We're getting close to the city," he answered without even a hint of enthusiasm. "The briefing package showed a truck stop just inside Samarkand. I'll top off the gas tank, and we can take turns using the restrooms. At this time of night, the car's tinted windows will be enough concealment for us when we pull the gear out of the seat-back and get set. Ten or fifteen minutes, tops, and we'll be on our way. Very straightforward."

"Okay." I knew it would indeed be straightforward for Claude, especially since he wasn't going to make entry into Annex's house. I would be doing the hard work on this mission while he'd stay across the field behind the house and watch me through a thermal scope.

Claude would be my guardian angel on this mission, using the scope to see heat signatures of occupants through the walls. He'd watch my back, warn of any possible ambushes, and guide me through the house from target to target. Just as we'd done a hundred times in training, he'd radio the locations of anyone he saw, giving me the advantage of knowing exactly where they were, even—or especially—when I couldn't see them myself.

"I'm ready."

"Don't worry, Michelle. You'll do fine," he said, glancing at me briefly. Apparently, that represented the closest thing to a motivational speech I had any hope of getting from him that evening.

I stared out the side window again and envisioned how the mission might have gone if Claude were teamed with Arnaud instead of me. Maybe the two of them could do this kind of job in their sleep by now. They probably didn't have to talk about it at all. Both still saw me as an interloper into their world and not the experienced pro they were accustomed to working with. Without ever saying so, their cold tones told me that I had essentially been forced upon them by Michael. Whether they wanted a new team member or not, the boss brought me in anyway, and they were expected to just get used to it. To just get used to *me*.

I had never said a word against either of them during our year of training together, and as far as they knew, I had not made any mistakes on a mission, either. I simply had not yet had the opportunity to make a positive impression on them. The mission to kill Annex would be how I proved myself to Claude. Then, hopefully, he'd put in a good word for me with his brother when we got back.

For now, at least in Claude's eyes, that night's mission represented my coming-out party. Good thing I was dressed to kill.

Chapter 10

"I'm in position now," Claude called out over the encrypted radio. The earpiece wrapped around my left ear carried his voice with a clarity that made our expensive digital comms system a pleasure to use. "Head up the side of the road, and I'll start scanning the house. Ruslan and Nila Dotorov's house is the second one in on this block."

Seriously? Did he think I hadn't studied Wilson's briefing package before we left Virginia? I'm not an idiot! *Ugh.* Do all men think women aren't capable of doing a good job or was it just him? Or, did Claude think he was actually being helpful while the adrenaline working its way through my bloodstream made me overly sensitive?

"Okay," I replied tersely into the throat-mounted microphone, deciding to keep my acidic thoughts to myself. "Where are they?"

"Upstairs. There's a large heat blob in the center of the house. Must be the aunt and uncle in the master bedroom. One less intense but longer heat blob is farther off to the left, as seen from my vantage point. That must be Annex's bedroom. No heat on the first floor—you're safe. I count three heat signatures, so they're all home. You're good to go in."

Good, now we knew they were all in the house. Without a larger team available for a full pre-entry surveillance, it's never guaranteed that the target is actually at home. If we couldn't place Annex there that night, we'd have scrubbed the mission and tried again in a day or two. With the thermal scope letting us see right through the walls, we didn't have to guess.

I looked along the row of houses at my end of the block and confirmed Wilson's intel that none of the first three had a fenced-in backyard. Good. Hopefully, that meant no dogs. Dogs are unpredictable and can complicate the situation terribly.

Two wooden steps led up to the back door of the Dotorovs' house. From the bottom step, I could easily reach the deadbolt's keyhole above the door handle without stretching or being off balance. With the lock-pick gun in my right hand and tension wrench in my left, I squeezed the trigger mechanism several times in rapid succession to bump the lock's pins upwards, enabling me to twist the deadbolt open in seconds.

"One lock done," I radioed quietly to Claude. "Any change?"

"Negative. I see you clearly. Nothing resembling an animal in sight. No dogs."

"Copy. Both locks open. Making entry now."

Stepping inside, I slid the pick gun back into my jacket pocket and removed a pair of night vision goggles from the belt pouch in the small of my back. While NVGs give a green tint to everything you see, they certainly beat having to turn on the lights when you're trying to sneak up on someone in their own house.

"Claude, I'm in the kitchen. The house is a dump, but they've got every new appliance in the world in here."

"I guess crime actually does pay."

"I've never seen a coffee maker that big before. I'm going upstairs."

A double click from the radio served as the only reply Claude needed to send—an unofficial but readily understood, "Okay."

I drew the Sig Sauer 9mm pistol from my shoulder holster, screwed the suppressor on firmly, and thumbed the Sig's hammer into the cocked position. With my head on a swivel, I walked towards the front of the house and the stairwell leading upstairs. On my left, the door to the powder room stood open. A glance into the small bathroom proved it was unoccupied. Claude had already told me there were no heat signatures on the main level, but safe habits are good habits.

On my right, a door under the stairway hid what looked like a closet. I didn't open it since I had no need to risk making unnecessary noise.

From the bottom of the stairway, I looked up to the second level and saw no one. I tested the first step gingerly with the weight of my left foot, not knowing how much noise it might make. If it squeaked too much, it might wake the home's occupants, and I'd lose the element of surprise. I slowly ascended the first three steps, stepping only on the front edge of each and was pleasantly surprised that the wood barely made a sound. *No need for me to go on a diet,* I smiled to myself.

On the third step, I paused to peer up to the second level. The empty hallway had a wood floor with a carpet runner down the middle. I couldn't tell what color it was. Everything looked green.

To my left, the open door of a full bath revealed an empty room.

The closed door in front of me led to the master bedroom. The two doors to my right—one open and one closed—were the other two bedrooms.

I ascended the stairs two at a time, passed by the master bedroom, and walked directly to the open bedroom door. I pulled the Sig close to my chest while keeping it pointed forward and at the ready. With a quick thrust, I rounded the corner and rotated to my right, ready to shoot anything that moved.

Nothing did.

Boxes and clothing littered the floor and lay scattered across three tables. Some of the clothes still had tags attached. Clearly used for storage, the room didn't hold so much as a guest bed. As is common with European housing designs, the room had no closet in which anyone could hide.

I made my way back to the master bedroom, walking along the carpet runner to muffle my footsteps. That room, I already knew, was not empty.

I drew a deep breath and steeled myself for what was to come.

I twisted the knob, pulled the door open quietly, and slipped into the master bedroom. I kept my weapon trained on the pair of figures sleeping in the queen-sized bed.

I approached the left side of the bed and regarded the Dotorovs as they slept. On the side closest to me, Nila rested on her left side facing her husband. Ruslan slept on his stomach, head tilted away from me.

Good, at least I don't have to look him in the face when I do this.

I aimed across the bed at Ruslan's head while my trigger finger tapped the gun's frame. I jumped as he let out a sharp, nasally snort.

Calm down, Michelle, I coached myself. *Smooth is fast. Just remember, smooth is fast.*

My right index finger moved naturally to the trigger just as it had done in training a million times before. My pulls were swift.

From his perch outside, Claude radioed in. "I saw two muzzle flashes. Are you done in the master bedroom?"

Click-click, I replied silently.

"The other heat signature has not moved. You're still black," Claude said, using the counter-surveillance term for having not been discovered. "Move to the other bedroom. You're doing great."

Click-click.

Annex had decorated the door to his bedroom with what I thought at first was a movie poster, prominently featuring a large biohazard symbol. I squinted to read the smaller words printed in English on the poster and realized that it referred to a video game, instead. I didn't think a bank robber and uber-hacker like this kid would also be trafficking biological weapons, but I made a mental note to mention it to Wilson during the mission debriefing, if only for thoroughness.

"I see you're near the other heat signature. No change. You're good to go," Claude radioed.

Click-click.

I felt tremendously reassured by Claude's report that Annex slept just a few feet from me, and there were no other threats in the area. In what has since become my standard routine for mentally preparing to face my target, I inhaled deeply and pushed the door open wide. I burst through the doorway to fire a pair of hollow-point bullets into the sleeping man before he had time to react.

I pushed the Sig out in front of me, ran my eyes across the room, and came face to face with an empty bed. *Shit! Where the hell's Annex?*

I dropped to my knee and looked under the bed eager to not repeat the big mistake from my Aruba mission. The gaping void under the bed stared back at me, hosting nothing more than a medium-sized suitcase much too small for anyone to hide in.

I stood and spun. LEDs blinked on a half-dozen computers that whirred quietly on a table under the half-open window. Without closets in the room, the last refuge for someone to hide was the wooden wardrobe against the far wall, but no one could lie down in a six-foot-tall but only three-foot-wide armoire. Claude hadn't reported a vertical heat signature in the room, but I had to check anyway.

Thinking about playing it safe, I considered firing a few rounds into the wardrobe first. Would that be helpful or just an act of obvious desperation?

I decided against random acts of violence and jerked the doors open in rapid succession. I was hit in the face by nothing more hostile than the smell of musty clothing and a hint of mothballs.

Crap.

"Not here. He's not here," I reported to Claude with an unintended urgency in my voice. "The room's empty."

"I see you upright, and the heat signature is horizontal. What do you mean he's not there?" Claude retorted anxiously.

I answered with a good deal of frustration and much louder than I should have. "Computers. Six PCs and a laptop are all on, lights blinking like crazy. That must be the heat you saw. I'm telling you, he's not here!" The realization wrapped itself around my brain that I had just killed the primary target's aunt and uncle, likely now for no good reason. Meanwhile, Annex was nowhere to be found.

Not only did I have to live with that, but the mission ended in complete failure.

After everything that happened in the house that evening, of course Annex would move out. Who would want to continue living there? The Agency will lose track of him, Russian intelligence might very well resettle him into a more protected environment—maybe in Moscow—and we'd never get another shot at him. Meanwhile, he'd continue his attacks on us.

Maybe he found a girlfriend and is spending the night with her? Now *that's* what I call getting lucky.

I pulled the magic wand from my pocket and plugged it into the first PC. The green light illuminated and when it blinked the third time, I withdrew it from the USB socket and moved to the next machine.

"Working on the computers now," I reported to Claude. "Any changes?"

"Negative."

With an obvious tone of desperation in my voice, I asked, "No other heat signatures? Nothing? There's no garage, and I can see what Wilson said is his car out the window in front of the house. Anything, Claude? Anything at all? Something small, maybe that you thought was a dog? A cat? Hell, a goldfish?"

"Nothing. I've got a good view of the whole area. The next house to the right is empty, and the one on the end of the block has four heat signatures in it. The scope's working perfectly."

Crap, I failed. Crap. Crap. Crap!

After training my ass off for what seemed like forever, working solo for a year on successful missions—if you don't count Rome anyway—I finally had the chance to prove myself to Claude and Arnaud and the mission fails miserably. Damn!

I knew it wasn't my fault, but I'm the one who made entry into the house and failed to kill Annex. It didn't matter that he wasn't home on the one night we happened to come for him or that Claude was the one who had screwed up by saying there were three people in the house when only two innocent people and a bunch of lousy computers were home.

None of that mattered. People would only remember that Michelle had traveled halfway around the world to kill Annex and failed to accomplish the mission. Inch by inch, a band constricted around my chest. No one would say Claude had failed, no, only that Michelle failed.

"Done with the computers. I'm coming back."

Click-click.

My need to act stealthily gone, I walked downstairs and headed for the back door.

"I see you on the main level."

Click-click.

I glanced down the hallway towards the kitchen and stopped in my tracks. I raised the Sig and pointed it down the hallway while taking stock of the situation. Earlier, I had ignored the main level because Claude told me there were no heat signatures present. Maybe, or maybe not. He had been proven wrong once that night. Why not a second time? Even though he said he saw no one on the main level, I decided to check for myself.

The stairs from the second floor led down to the first level and let out in the foyer by the front door. To my left, I looked into what was an obviously empty dining room with a large china cabinet filled with plates and cups, all neatly arranged. Along one wall stood a small sideboard. Nobody could be hiding inside that, I concluded.

The living room extended to my right and continued around the corner, out of my line of sight. I pointed the Sig in that direction and eased my way in a half-step at a time. Slowly, I inched my way into the room sideways, placing each foot down deliberately and never crossing my legs. I made each step its own individual, distinct, controlled, tactical movement. I peered over the barrel of my pistol into the fuzzy green image of the Dotorovs' living room. I eased my way in a foot at a time, exposing myself to any danger it contained in a slow and controlled manner. A sofa, coffee table, and large leather recliner faced a flat-panel television. It struck me that the recliner wouldn't be a La-Z-Boy, exactly. Maybe a La-Z-RussianBoy? *What's the Russian word for boy?* I asked myself silently, trying to cheer myself up. Not even a bad joke could pierce the dour attitude consuming me.

Nothing. No one was in the living room either.

Crap and more crap. Crap. Crap. Crap.

That's all this mission had turned out to be, crap.

"Are you sightseeing or coming bac—" Claude whispered into my left ear as I walked towards the kitchen and past the powder room. The static cutting off the end of his question caught me by surprise.

Besides the clarity of the voice transmissions, the beauty of our new digital radios over the old analog ones is that they don't screech in your ear, and you're never supposed to hear any static. If there's radio interference, the digital signal just doesn't go through and there's silence, not static. While no techno-geek, I'd used both the old and new radios enough in training to appreciate the differences.

That static interrupted Claude's transmission immediately struck me as odd.

"*Shhhh,*" I ordered over the radio.

Click-click.

The static in my left ear came and went, but the fact that I heard Claude's clicking meant his mic button was working just fine and not stuck open.

I pulled the earpiece out of my left ear and turned my head from side to side to listen without the distraction of the radio.

I heard it again.

Soft sounds spilled from the bottom of the door across from the powder room. I'd not checked the closet under the stairs earlier and, in fact, hadn't even given it more than a passing thought. That changed in a heartbeat.

With my Sig at the ready, I twisted the doorknob and the door opened easily. The hinges squealed, slicing into the silence of the night with a high-pitched complaint of neglect.

I cringed from the sudden noise and practically jumped for joy at seeing steps leading down to a basement. The flickering light from a television played off the wall at the bottom of the staircase. The TV sat somewhere off to the right and out of sight.

Holy shit, there's a basement! No wonder Claude didn't see another heat signature—Annex was downstairs, underground, and too well-insulated by the surrounding earth to show up on the thermal scope.

The noise from the TV must be what I'd heard and thought was radio static.

I cautiously started down the staircase. A shrill *creak* from the second stair sliced into the quiet night. The racket froze me in my tracks. *Damn it! I might as well have worn a cowbell.* My nose wriggled at my bad luck.

No, not at bad luck.... The scent of the basement differed tremendously from the other two levels of the house. The aroma wafting up the stairs transported me back to the beach party my then-boyfriend Jimmy Hernandez had thrown the night after we graduated high school.

I wiggled my nose and smiled into the darkness, pleased as punch with myself for having not only found Annex, but also recognizing what he was doing. Annex was in the basement getting wasted. Apparently, marijuana is not just a Southern California pastime.

"*Babushka*?" Annex yelled over the noise of the TV.

At least that's what I thought he asked.

"*Babushka*?"

For the life of me, I could not figure out why he would call out *head scarf*. It made no sense to me. None at all.

It also told me that he knew someone was on the steps. Of course, the straining of the old wooden stairs and the cry of door hinges made that painfully obvious. So much for stealth. I'd lost the element of surprise entirely.

Of course, he didn't know *who* was on the stairs. Nor *why* I was there.

Every now and then in life you have to make a snap decision and just go for it. Right or wrong, you just need to make the call on the spot and act decisively.

I dispensed with any more sneaking and walked straight down the stairs. In the quiet of the night, the complaints from the creaky stairs were as loud as a herd of elephants. Generally, I prefer the more subtle, graceful, and stealthy movements of a gazelle, but that night I walked directly down the stairs confidently, noise be damned, and rounded the corner.

I found Annex on a plush leather sofa, sitting alone in his underwear watching two almost comically buxom, naked blonde women enjoying the company of an equally naked and exceptionally well-endowed man in the porn video playing on his TV. Annex pulled hard at the remaining half of the joint he had been enjoying and held his breath. He turned towards me and his eyes sprung wide at the sight of a live woman and fourteen inches of Sig Sauer and suppressor extended menacingly in his direction.

My heart leapt. "Hello, Annex," I said almost gleefully. The words flew out of me. To this day, I have no idea why I said that or if he even spoke enough English to understand. My surprise and the elation I felt from having turned the mission around completely got the better of me.

Hmmm, I thought looking at Annex. *You really know what you're doing with that blunt, don't you? Not your first one, I see, but it is your last.*

Annex sat less than fifteen feet away. I smoothly adjusted my pistol the last few inches up to my sight-line, aligned the sights of the Sig with the left side of his head just above his ear, and squeezed the trigger with no hesitation.

Annex's head jerked back from the impact of the bullet. His body slumped and angled slowly to his right over the arm of the sofa. A green cloud, as seen through my night vision goggles, escaped his mouth slowly while his body relaxed and marijuana smoke took its leave from his lungs. My head tilted slightly in appreciation of the visual of his life force escaping his body. Out through his mouth. Out and up, it rose to the basement's ceiling, disappearing, dispersed among the wooden beams, exposed wiring, and bare insulation where it faded from view. Annex's last hazy breath would forever remain a part of the house in which he had lived and died. It all seemed perfectly fitting.

I shifted my aim from Annex's head to his chest, moved a few steps to my left, and stood between him and the TV. Annex didn't move, not that I expected he would. Out of an abundance of caution, I fired two hollow-point rounds into his upper chest and moved smartly past him to clear the rest of the small basement.

I walked briskly past a portable bar hosting an assortment of top-shelf whiskies, vodkas, and a few bottles of champagne. Annex has pretty good taste. *Had*, I corrected myself.

Farther in, an imposing mass of metal in the center of the far wall caught my attention. At the back of the small basement rested a large metal safe—and I mean large with a capital *L*. Not Fort Knox large, but I had no idea how anyone could get an object with that much steel down into the basement. They must have brought it down in pieces and assembled it there.

As I approached the safe, my jaw hit the floor.

"Holy shit," I said aloud in utter shock, peering—or perhaps *leering* is the better word—wide-eyed into the safe. Below the shelf containing more marijuana than I'd ever seen before sat stacks and stacks of one-hundred-dollar bills. Perhaps I'd seen piles like that on TV or in a movie, but having that much cash arrayed right out in front of you in person is a sight to behold. It took my breath away. There was so much money that you'd have to measure it in feet or pounds.

It could have been five million dollars. Who knows? I had no way to get that much currency out of there, even if I wanted to.

Grunts and pants from the TV awoke me from my marijuana-induced gawking at Annex's safe. The din of bad acting had become annoying. I returned to the sofa, picked up the remote control, and struggled in the green glow of the NVGs to figure out which was the *off* button on a remote I'd never seen before. I had no idea what the Russian word for *off* was, so I picked the largest button on the top row and aimed it at the TV.

With a click, they were gone. Sorry folks, no happy ending for anyone in this house tonight.

At the thought of the word *click*, I cursed under my breath and grabbed the dangling earpiece. I gently pushed the piece of soft plastic back into my ear.

Claude shouted into the left side of my head. "—elle, come in! Can you hear me? Where are you, dammit?"

"I'm fine. Mission accomplished. I found him!"

"What? Really?" he asked more calmly. "Where are you?"

"In the basement. Annex was in the basement, not upstairs. Can you see me? I'm guessing not. You're never going to believe what I found."

"If the mission's complete, get out of there. Did you place the sign? We've got to go."

Click-click, I replied.

Michael sent us to Uzbekistan to kill Annex not only to stop him from pilfering our military technologies, but also to send a message to others who might in the future consider cooperating with or working for Russian intelligence. If the magic wand I used upstairs worked, the CIA's software had already begun transmitting Annex's programs to HQ. And if the message we were going to send worked, fewer smart hackers would line up to take his place.

I eased my way up to Annex's body ensuring not to get blood—or worse—on my shoes or clothes. From beneath my jacket, I pulled the homemade sign Wilson had created specifically for this occasion. With a safety pin, I attached the message to the dead man's undershirt just below the two distinctive red stains from the pair of bullet holes in his chest.

The Russian text read, "I was Moscow's bitch." Or something to that effect. I stepped back and snapped a few photos.

Michael had a simple plan for the pictures. One of CIA's Information Operations teams would post it anonymously on the right underground hacker websites to discourage others from working for the SVR. The visual message spoke loudly: "If you work for them, you'll not only end up like this, but so will your entire family. Don't do it. The price is too steep. It's not worth the Russians' money. You won't live to spend it."

I zipped the small digital camera into my jacket's inside pocket and glanced again at the safe. It was time to leave, but first, I needed to do one more thing.

***

"What the hell is that?" Claude asked as I arrived at the SUV.

"Walking around money, apparently." I let the heavy suitcase drop and shook my wrist until feeling returned to the palm of my hand. I was in good shape, but dragging a medium-sized suitcase full of cash just the hundred yards or so from the house to the car winded me more than I wanted to admit.

"You'll have to lift it into the car," I said huffing as if I'd sprinted from the house across the dirt field instead of walked, half-carrying and half-wheeling two million dollars or so in cash.

"I thought about bringing you either a bottle of Macallan whisky or a bag of pot from his safe, but I couldn't take even a fraction of everything he had down there."

"Pot?" Claude asked incredulously as he hefted the suitcase into the rear of the SUV.

"Oh, right, I didn't explain that part over the radio. So, Annex was in the basement smoking a joint and watching porn. He had a huge safe—and I mean *huge*—with more money and Mary Jane than I've seen in my life. Stacks and stacks of bundles of hundred-dollar bills. The safe was the size of one of those bank safes you see in old photos from the 1800s or something like that. I brought as much cash as I could fit into the suitcase I found under his bed, but I didn't think that bringing the weed along would help us get through customs at the border more easily," I said smiling.

I made a big show of reaching my right hand under my jacket. "But I did bring you the porno DVD."

Claude started the Mercedes' engine and looked over at me. Maybe I just imagined that his eyes got a bit wider.

"Just kidding," I said, withdrawing my empty hand. "You'll have to buy your own smut."

That drew a smirk from Claude.

With a more serious tone, he asked, "So, you tagged the six PCs and got Annex, right?"

I nodded. "Yes. Well, seven computers. One was a laptop. Does that count as a PC? Anyway, I got Annex in the basement. That's why you couldn't see him on the thermal scope. He was below ground level. One to the head and two to the chest, as usual. Got the photos right here," I said and gave the camera under my jacket a pat.

Claude smacked me on my thigh and beamed. "Good job, Michelle. I was afraid this was going to turn into a complete bust. Well done. Let's go home."

That made my day. Hell, that made my year. Since the day I first joined the team, I'd yearned for little else but for Claude and his brother to take me seriously. Now, having seen me in action, I hoped Claude would have a much more positive attitude towards me and, of course, put in a good word with Arnaud. After almost two years of training and a couple of successful missions under my belt, I didn't expect they'd treat me as an equal just yet, considering how much more experience they had. However, finally being treated as though I did indeed belong on the team would be a tremendously welcome change.

"But you left the pot, porn, and most importantly, the Macallan behind, eh?"

"Afraid so."

Claude smiled and did his best school principal imitation. "Complete mission failure, then. Sorry, lady, that's going on your permanent record."

We both laughed far, far more than the joke warranted. The release from the stresses of the evening did wonders to free my mind from the anxiety that had built up over the previous few weeks.

I settled in for the long drive ahead of us and enjoyed my contact buzz.

Chapter 11

"The door hinges squealed, and the stairs made a real racket, too," I said looking from Michael to Wilson as the debriefing was coming to a close. "It seemed especially loud in the middle of the night. There was no way I could get downstairs without Faruk noticing unless he happened to already be dead.

"He called out *babushka* a couple of times while I was on my way down. I still can't figure out why he called me a scarf, though," I mused aloud to the four men sitting at the conference table in our Tysons Corner office.

That generated some serious laughter from both Claude and Arnaud. Wilson and I looked at the brothers, puzzled.

"He wasn't calling you a *scarf*, Michelle," Arnaud said trying to catch his breath between fits of laughter.

Laughter he was enjoying at my expense, I noted.

"*Babushka* is the Russian word for *grandmother*. They're so stereotyped for wearing those big scarves on their heads that the word has become synonymous for both. *Babushka* literally means *grandmother* or *elderly woman*, but has a slang meaning of *scarf*. In particular, the kind of large scarves they wear to cover their hair from the rain or snow. Faruk was sitting on the couch getting high and heard someone coming downstairs. It seems natural he'd think you were Nila coming to hassle him for it. Maybe that's why he had to get high in the middle of the night, I don't know."

"Oh," I said sheepishly as my face flushed a light shade of rouge. Maybe I should have known that. "That makes sense now, but at the time, I couldn't figure out why he said that."

I could appreciate why Claude and Arnaud, who both spoke fluent Russian, would find it so funny, but didn't enjoy them laughing at my expense.

"And you also liberated a suitcase with a million dollars in cash, is that right?" Wilson asked.

"At least," Claude chimed in. "It may be closer to two mil. Unbelievable. That'll do wonders for the Trust Fund."

Michael's eyes narrowed. With little enthusiasm, he said, "It will be another couple of weeks until Logistics gets the SUV back to Germany. Logs will send whatever's in the seatback compartment to us then, and we'll take a look." Clearly, he remained unconvinced about that element of our report.

I wanted to get the real scoop on why Michael always told us to bring back whatever valuables we can reasonably get away with. "So, I know you've said that the Trust Fund pays for some of our expenses, but what is it, really?"

"The Agency pays the vast majority of our expenses through appropriated funds. That means that taxpayers cover our salaries, facilities, equipment, training, and most travel. The downside to that, however, is that there's a paper trail for all of it. Even if it's classified, it's all auditable, which is not a good thing for our missions, to put it mildly. Sometimes, we need to go places and not leave a trail that can be traced back to the CIA in general, or to any of us, in particular. In those cases, I arrange payments from what we colloquially call the Trust Fund. Those costs are not paid from Agency funds. That way, there's no possible way for the Inspector General, Congress, or law enforcement to trace any of it back to us. That protects us all. It protects the Director, too, so it's good for everyone. Unfortunately, we can't replenish those funds from the usual sources. So, we need to be at least somewhat self-financed.

"The nature of our work being what it is," Michael continued, "it's best that we keep this just between the five of us. That's one reason the people in this room are all on the Agency's Do Not Polygraph list. Only a few dozen other officers across the Agency are on the list. No director wants the Security Division to stumble upon what we're doing."

"Yeah, no, I get it. I have no problem with that," I said with certainty. "I'm just glad it all worked out in the end."

"You both did a terrific job," Michael said. He stood up, indicating that the debriefing was over. "You've been on the road for almost two weeks. Rest up, and over the next week I'll find some grueling training course or other for you to take next."

I appreciated his compliments and shook my head at his mention of another exhausting training class, pretty sure he was only half-kidding. I walked out of the conference room holding my head higher than at any time in the two years I'd been a CIA officer.

Before the mission to kill Annex, I couldn't even spell Uzbekistan. At least for the duration of the debriefing, I enjoyed the status of "hero for a day." If Claude—with a bazillion times more experience than I had—had been the one who entered Annex's house instead, maybe he would have missed the guy in the basement completely. Who knows?

The compliments from Michael and my teammates made me smile so hard I could feel the corner of my eyes crinkle. After almost two years on the team and a painfully silent drive with Claude across most of two third-world countries, I finally got to hear them say "good job," "terrific work," and "well done." I'd have to settle for those compliments for the moment and work up to a good ol' American "shit hot" later. Everyone needs a goal.

That afternoon, I made my short-term goal to look up when the next yoga class was. And also, to figure out what lie to tell my boyfriend, Anthony. Maybe I'd gone to Denver this time. I've always wanted to see the Rocky Mountains.

As it happened, I didn't have to worry. Anthony broke up with me a couple of weeks later to reunite with his ex.

PART THREE

FIRST IMPRESSIONS

Chapter 12

Michael stood up from my workbench in the Farm's advanced electronics classroom and pushed his white hair straight back and out of his eyes. He looked down at the circuit board in front of me again and said, "Looks like you've gotten the hang of defeating alarm systems that have integrated cellular uplinks. That's good progress."

"Thanks." I smiled, pleased as punch not having had the siren scream in my ear during the last dozen run-throughs on a series of advanced models we learned to defeat in class that week. "I can't really say I understand exactly *why* the circuit bypass works when you do it the way they teach," I said, pointing to the three jumper cables I'd installed on the circuit board in front of me, "but as long as it does, I'm fine with that. It's quieter this way than when I just gave up and shot the damned siren in Indonesia last time."

"No, you don't want to do that again," he said with a chuckle, more laughing at me than with me. "You also don't have to understand all of the inner workings of the electronics, either. Just follow what the instructors teach so you can defeat the boxes you're most likely to encounter in the field on our missions—essentially just the medium-strength systems. When a mission calls for defeating an exceptionally hard system, we have entire teams of engineers in DS&T who specialize in that sort of work. For those jobs, rely on the technical services officers to get you inside and then you do your thing.

"When you go in alone, you just need to be good at getting around the types of alarms you'll find in residences and small offices. You won't be the one breaking into banks or embassies," he said, resting his hand on my shoulder for reassurance, "so don't sweat it. We have some amazing high-tech equipment for those jobs. Those are incredibly fun missions when they do come up, but they're rare, unfortunately. Now, clean up, and I'll buy you a birthday beer in the Cantina."

***

"Happy belated twenty-second birthday, Michelle," Michael said with a broad smile. He reached across the table and clinked his bottle of Michelob against mine. "Sorry I couldn't be here yesterday. Claude and Arnie had to brief for a trip to Nigeria. Cheers."

"Cheers," I echoed. I took a sip and smiled, thrilled to have someone to share my birthday with, even if the party was a day late.

"So, three years in the Agency so far. What do you think?" Michael asked against a backdrop of laughter from a couple of tables at the other end of the Cantina.

The occupants of the two loud tables up front were dressed too formally for DO operations officers. They stood out at the Farm against the jeans- and khaki-clad instructors and students who usually spend their Thursday nights enjoying happy hour. *Clearly not DO, and probably not S&T officers, either,* I thought. They just didn't look like geeks. *Maybe Logistics?*

I've always enjoyed looking around the walls of the Cantina. Officers post some of the craziest photos from their travels to the ends of the Earth. Many are of the "hey, look where I've been" type, while others are hero shots with para-military officers in full combat gear surrounded by whatever tribe or resistance group they were training at the time. Some would call it the world's greatest travelogue and others, a Rogue's Gallery. It all depends upon your particular political bent.

One photo I particularly adore is of a past Chief of Station in Moscow standing in front of Vladimir Lenin's body in the famous Red Square mausoleum. With a big smile on his face, the COS is holding a sign that reads, "Lenin's Tomb is a Communist Plot." Political humor and tweaking the nose of the Russians are favorite pastimes of many CIA officers, especially those who served during the height of the Cold War.

"I'm feeling good," I said, answering Michael's question in my own way. "I'm getting the hang of the technical training, and the military courses are good. The close-quarters combat class last spring at Fort Bragg was a real challenge. I still need more practice shooting in the Smith house, but I learned a lot, especially about tactical movements in small teams. That's not something I've done much of, particularly communicating with teammates as you shoot and scoot. Even when traveling with Claude, I've gone in and done most of the work alone, so that hasn't been an issue in the field, but I can see when it would be important. Of course, they focused a lot on target identification and not shooting non-combatants. It means a lot to them." Continuing quietly, I added, "Although that's not much of a concern for us...." The words I still found difficult to say aloud hung in the air for a moment but generated no reaction from Michael.

"Also, I'm enjoying the advanced Spanish classes much more than Arabic. After working with Claude and Arnaud in the field, I feel so lost when I can't speak the local language. I'll never be as good as they are in that department."

"Don't try to compare yourself to them in that respect. They grew up in an environment that forced them to speak multiple languages just to survive. You grew up in California speaking some Spanish with friends, which was a great start for you. Back when Claude and Arnie lived overseas, Lebanon was a different place. I worked there a few times, and I miss parts of it. Beirut was a great city before the whole country imploded."

One particularly high-pitched laugh rose from the loud group at the front of the Cantina. A tall, prematurely graying man at the head of the table waved his arms wildly a few times as he spoke to his companions. *Loud Laugher,* as I nicknamed the scrawny, forty-something man, captivated the occupants of his table with whatever story he was telling them.

Most of the men at the table—and there were only men seated with him—seemed to hang on his every word. Two professionally dressed women sat at the adjoining table with three well-dressed men whom they clearly preferred over Loud Laugher. The ladies regarded their animated neighbor with clear distain. Their faces showed both happiness at not being seated at the same table with him and a clear measure of disapproval with whatever past exploit he regaled his friends.

The volume of Loud Laugher's voice and the velocity of his arms showed he was getting way too drunk way too early in the evening, even for a Thursday happy hour in a place as laid-back as the Cantina.

"I'm working the schedule to get you into the Army's Green Beret hand-to-hand combat class at Bragg later this year," Michael continued. "I'll warn you in advance, though, it's a tough one. You'll almost certainly be the only woman in the class, unless the Agency has another female officer to send, but that's unlikely. I'm certain you'll do well, but if you want my unsolicited advice, I recommend you hit the gym and work on upper body strength to get ready. Claude and Arnie have both been through it before, but it's been years. If I can get the slots, I'm going to send all three of you down at the same time. If not, it'll be just you."

"Okay. Sounds good," I said, even though it most certainly did not. I couldn't think of any training less desirable than spending two weeks getting stabbed with rubber knives and choked by a bunch of sweaty Army commandos. The Green Berets I'd trained with in CQB earlier in the year were all extremely skilled troops—in great shape and many were quite handsome. Most were perfect gentlemen around me, the only woman in the class. They understood that being five- to nine-inches shorter than most of them and about half their weight, I couldn't carry as much gear as they did, especially the heavy door-breaching equipment. The instructors pressed all of us mercilessly, but they understood that as the only civilian in the group I didn't need a passing grade and they couldn't flunk me out. I learned the combat tactics I need for my missions and chalked it up as a successful, albeit draining, month.

I downed the remainder of my beer, mostly to create a pause in the conversation and pointed my empty bottle at Michael. "I'll get the next round. Same again?"

"Okay. Sounds good," he said, echoing my words with a wry smile.

Maddie was working the bar, lined up two bottles for me and popped the caps. I pulled a ten-dollar bill from the pocket of my jeans for her and walked the beers back to our table. I could feel my cheeks getting flush and enjoyed the slight floating feeling. The beginnings of a good buzz held great promise for me, especially since I was staying in the dorms and didn't have to drive anywhere that night.

As I leaned forward over the table to hand Michael his beer, his eyes angled up over my right shoulder.

"That's a good lookin' girl you got there. Are you keeping her all to yourself or are you going to share?"

I handed Michael his beer and turned to see Loud Laugher towering a foot above me. Even from that distance and over the aroma of the bottle in my hand, I could smell the beer on his entirely unpleasant breath. While not the first unwelcome advance I'd ever experienced, it astonished me that an Agency employee would be so crude.

The buzz I'd been enjoying dissipated as the tall lout reached his left hand around my waist and pulled me against him. I pushed him firmly with my elbow, but the combination of his larger size and my lacking anything against which to brace myself made for a singularly unsuccessful attempt to escape his grasp. I felt trapped, but not threatened by his pull against my hip.

"You need to let go of me," I said loudly, my voice amplified by a combination of surprise at his drunken overstepping of common decency and my absolute disinterest in having anything to do with him. "And I mean right now."

Not content to just be disagreeable, he dropped his hand from my left hip to my butt. His large hand cupped almost my entire left cheek. He leaned down slightly, smiled, and looked at me with unfocused eyes.

"C'mon," he said, his breath almost as offensive as his grasp, "we're all down here to get out of the office and have some fun. So, let's have some fun, honey."

My jaw dropped at the audacity of his affront. Sure, there are assholes in every bar in the world, but I really thought better of CIA officers. In my experience, they—we—are some of the most professional people in the world. Clearly, there are exceptions to that rule.

"What I know," I hissed, "is that if you don't remove your *hand* from my *ass* immediately, I'm going to remove it from your body permanently."

"Aww, now, there's no need to be like that," he went on digging the hole deeper for himself and, in the process, managing to add utter disgust on top of my complete contempt for him.

It might have all ended there if he had just chosen to walk away to go sober up, but he didn't. Instead, he squeezed.

When a woman is with a man she wants to cozy up to and he gives her a playful pat on the tush, it can get her blood pumping and be the enjoyable start of an evening's foreplay. But only if it's the *right* guy in the *right* situation.

Loud Laugher was *so* not that guy.

I shifted my right foot behind me and to the side, twisted my hips, dropped my weight over my right leg, and landed a roundhouse kick squarely across his face with my left foot. I snapped my leg back and drew it in front of me as he bent forward in pain and covered his face with his hands. I used my still-raised leg to push him sideways hard enough to drop him to the floor, but not so hard as to hurt him again.

I recovered upright with my back to Michael and faced Loud Laugher's compatriots across the room. I reflected that while my unarmed-combat instructors might be impressed with my kicking technique, they probably would not be all that sanguine about my landing it on the face of another Agency employee.

I didn't care. The moron more than deserved it.

I got a chuckle from the thought that what this bozo wanted from me that night was to make him moan. Well, he was moaning all right. He was also bleeding on the floor.

Across the bar, the slack-jawed faces of his tablemates exhibited their utter surprise at what had just happened. I saluted them with my bottle of beer, drew a sip, and plotted my next step.

I'm not the type of woman to give up an advantage once obtained. With a confident stride, I advanced to the now-empty chair at the head of the table and sat down. I crossed my left leg over my right with an intentionally overemphasized refinement calculated to contrast the nose-bashing I had just given their friend.

"So, which one of you went and let your dog off his leash tonight?" I asked the group in general and no one in particular. I motioned to the red stain on the laces of my white sneaker. "He made a real mess of my Keds."

"I'll go see if Sheldon needs help," the prematurely balding man on my right said. He grabbed a fistful of napkins and rushed to where Sheldon-the-Shithead was kneeling and dripping blood onto the Cantina's floor next to Michael's table.

I turned after him, pointed towards the Cantina's back door, and announced helpfully, "The Infirmary is about fifty yards that way."

I'd spent enough time there getting my own scrapes and bruises looked at that I knew the way by heart. Later in my career, it became my home away from home on too many occasions.

"So, what's your excuse?" I asked the guy to my left, not actually meaning anything by the question. I just wanted to see what he'd say.

"From the imprint of your shoelaces on Sheldon's face, I can see that you really know how to make a lasting first impression." He managed to say it with a straight face, which made it that much funnier. I tried pretty hard to keep my reaction in check, but the corners of my lips rose ever so slightly.

I took another sip of that evening's second beer, not wanting to let this guy see I thought his comment was funny. I hoped to recover my buzz before the guards showed up, figuring they'd drown me in paperwork or some such mess for the rest of the evening.

While good looking, he wore his brown hair, parted on the left and curling on the ends, a bit longer than I thought fashionable for most men. I found his hazel eyes engaging when they caught mine. He regarded me with honest interest and didn't betray any fear.

That intrigued me. Any guy that saw me deck a man that much taller than I am and not instinctively pull himself away was definitely worth a second look. His friend had escaped the table as soon as I walked over, but this guy sat up straight and joked with me right away. That made him someone I wanted to keep talking to and, with no wedding ring in sight, maybe get to know better.

I failed to hide my grin as it broadened into a full smile. "That's funny," I said and chuckled. "That's actually pretty funny." I had lost my internal battle for control and looked away, slightly embarrassed. I sipped my Michelob again and gestured in a circular motion to include the others at the table who were watching our conversation. "What are you all doing down here. Clearly, you're pretty far out of your element. There are no pencils to push at the Farm."

His companions sat with rapt attention, either too scared to get up and leave or too fascinated with the evening's entertainment. Perhaps they hoped I'd brain someone else, if only for their amusement.

"Our DI division's having an off-site at the conference center," he said, referring to CIA's analytical element, the Directorate of Intelligence. "We're branch chiefs in Sheldon's division. He wanted to come here for a drink. Or five, it may have been. I'm not sure. He's been here before, but we don't come down from Langley all that often. You do, though, huh?"

I nodded and looked around. With the evening's title fight behind me, I debated what to do next. I was getting a good vibe from this guy, whose name I did not yet know. How could I capitalize on that?

"So, you're DI weenies, then," I said.

He ignored my verbal jab. "What do you do?"

Any guy who didn't make some lame excuse and run away after seeing me clock his boss was okay in my book and worth talking to for a while longer. I had no idea how much time I had left, though. Surely, someone must have already called the Security Protective Officers about the "incident in the Cantina." I figured the SPOs would be arriving shortly to end the party and my conversation with the branch chief who made me laugh.

To answer his question, I recited my inside-the-CIA cover story. "I'm on a Technical Penetration team in the Special Activities Division. And before you make any jokes about the word *penetration*," I said gesturing to him with my bottle of beer and a half-smile, "you might want to first consider what happened to your friend over there when he had similar ideas."

As intended, that got a laugh from all the men at the table. The women at the adjacent table smiled silently at my defense of womankind. Girl power!

"I said he's our boss, not a friend. Actually, we all think he's kind of a jerk. Although Jon," he said, pointing to the vacated chair across from him, "is a bit of a brown-noser. But Jon's a good guy, just the same."

"What division are you in? I mean, what subject matter or geographic region do you work?"

"Western Europe. Mostly political and economic topics. They're almost all NATO countries, so there's no real reason to spend much time on their military forces. If we want to know about that, we usually just ask them."

Jon returned, running his hand over his expanding bald spot. He looked down at the branch chief I'd been flirting with. "Steven, Sheldon will be in the Infirmary for another half-hour, at least. She, umm," he stammered. "You, uh, broke his nose and they had to set it. He'll have to see a doctor when he gets home."

I shrugged, deciding to play it cool and not be seen by these guys as having any regrets about my actions.

The screen door at the back of the Cantina opened and all eyes turned to watch a pair of armed SPOs in black uniforms enter. For an instant, I tried to think how I might impress Steven with another joke: 'Two SPOs and a spy walk into a bar....' The serious demeanor of the two officers in body armor, however, sucked any remaining lightheartedness from the room.

Michael gestured them over to him. It didn't take an FBI agent to spot the glinting of fluorescent lights off the small pool of blood on the floor next to our table.

Jon excused himself to go back to the Infirmary, either to keep Sheldon company or possibly just to get away from me. Maybe both. I inhaled deeply, drew a long belt from my rapidly emptying bottle, and steeled myself for whatever tongue lashing or disciplinary action was about to come my way.

"Do you have a pen, Steven?" I asked.

Silently, he removed a Cross rollerball pen from his jacket pocket and held it up for me by its cap.

I laid my empty left hand on the table in front of him, palm up, and commanded him in an enticing way to hand over all advantage in whatever relationship might develop between us by saying, "Write your secure phone and office numbers."

I hooked my thumb back in the direction of the SPOs. "From the looks of it, I'm going to need to call you to bail me out."

"Anytime." He spread his left hand across my fingers, pinning them to the tabletop with a firm but gentle touch. His thumb swept an arc across my palm, coming to rest at the base of my hand, drawing the skin a little more tightly, so much the better for writing on. At first, I thought of it as the motion of a windshield wiper clearing the view ahead, but that was not a romantic-enough analogy. Later, I imagined his thumb wiped away the remnants of all past relationships to ensure a clean start for the two of us.

When he finished writing, he held my hand in place for a few heartbeats longer than the simple task required. The warmth of his hand on mine—flesh on flesh—warmed my heart, and I enjoyed the floating sensation returning to my head. Or, maybe that was the beer at work, I thought, interrupting my own ruminating and ruining my growing buzz.

"Try to stay out of trouble," I said and reluctantly withdrew my hand from his. I tipped my now-empty bottle at him in a salute.

"You, too." He tipped his pen in my direction, a parting gesture of his own.

"Not likely," I answered truthfully. Girding my strength, I walked back to my table to surrender myself to CIA's boys in blue. Or black, in this case.

Still seated at our table, Michael was addressing the higher-ranking SPO sergeant as I approached. I only caught the tail end of their conversation. "—being drunk does not, however, excuse his actions."

Michael looked at me as I neared the group. He spoke in a calm and seemingly over-restrained tone, something quite uncharacteristic of him. "Michelle, if you would like, you can go with these gentlemen and file a complaint against Mr. Donaldson for anything from simple assault to sexual battery. It's your choice."

I struggled to keep my surprise at the change in direction of the conversation from flashing across my face. So, the SPOs were not going to lead me off in handcuffs, eh? Michael had turned the conversation with them in a way I hadn't expected. *Damn, he's good!*

Faced with the opposite of the situation I feared, combined with the effects of my second beer, nervous contractions rippled across my belly and assuredly unattractive sweat progressed down my bare arms. A fear of sweating so much that it might wash Steven's office number from my palm percolated up from the back of my brain. If what he wrote got smeared, I'd be in a bit of a pickle. I didn't even know his last name and would have to do some real detective work to find him at headquarters. Who wants to have to work *that* hard at it? Picking up guys is supposed to be so easy for women, right?

The hint from Michael's tone and the slight emphasis he placed on it being my choice made his suggestion clear to me. The SPOs, who hadn't spent the past few years working closely with him, wouldn't notice that. I, however, caught it straight away. Michael had somehow convinced the officers that, while Sheldon Donaldson's actions were clearly wrong, my response did not constitute an unforgivable overreaction. CIA's HR department might not agree, but I felt certain that Donaldson had no intention of filing a complaint against me when the sun rose. That would surely be digging a grave for his own career. Even a chucklehead like him would be able to figure that much out for himself.

"No, I guess he's learned his lesson," I replied nodding slowly, approving of the outcome, and both feeling and sounding more than a little contrite.

"Sure," the SPO sergeant said, "but if you change your mind, just come over to the Security Operations Center and we'll take your statement."

I nodded and thanked the officers as they left.

Michael stood up. His smile reinforced my conviction that I had done the right thing. As he headed towards the Cantina's door, he left me with a soft, "Happy Birthday, Michelle."

I smiled appreciatively at him and walked off to get a late dinner.

Chapter 13

I planned to ambush Steven that Wednesday, but ambush in the *nicest* possible way. At the Cantina, I made him write his office room number on my hand and intentionally did not give him my cell phone number in return. That way, I held all the cards. Hell, I hadn't even told him my name.

I wanted my visit to surprise him and debated how long to wait after our brief encounter. Both the logic and emotion of it fit together nicely. Friday wouldn't work since my alarm-defeat class didn't end until early afternoon and he'd certainly be on the road home after his conference wrapped up. The weekend was out, for the obvious reason. Going right in to see him on Monday would make me seem desperate, a definite no-no even if it might be partially true. Tuesday was an option but is the next possible day after she-must-be-desperate Monday, so I ruled that out, as well.

Maybe I *did* feel slightly desperate, not having had a successful relationship in... well, essentially my entire life. But I wanted Steven to be the one feeling wanting and anxious for my call. Basically, I wanted to take all my primal feelings of uncertainty, insecurity, and lack of self-confidence and make him feel those things.

I had a terrible time deciding what to wear on my ambush lunch-date. I planned to surprise Steven in his office, so I had to wear something that would be respectable at headquarters, especially in the Directorate of Intelligence. They're much more formal on a day-to-day basis than we are in the Special Activities Division. How hard could picking out one outfit be? I had five days to figure it out and select that one ideal outfit conservative enough not to be frowned upon in the Ivory Tower of the New Headquarters Building, yet sexy enough to ensure Steven would ask me out.

Actually, that last one was a given. He's cute, but I'm way hotter than he is.

For starters, I had a darling white button-down blouse that when unbuttoned far enough, stays closed most of the time, but flops open a bit when I lean forward just so. I wanted him sneaking a few peeks, but not staring. In that top, his co-workers would be looking at me with respectful envy. *Is respectful envy even a real thing?* I wondered about that while closely surveying my reflection in the bathroom mirror. Either way, I liked what I saw.

The skirt, however, was most definitely a problem. I rummaged from one end of my closet to the other at least a dozen times, certain that if I repeatedly flipped through everything I owned, the perfect one would just fall across my arm, screaming "Wear me!" Instead, I discovered that my closet contained skirts of three distinct lengths: mid-calf, at the knee, and third-date. None would do for Wednesday.

The answer, of course, was a trip to Nordstrom. I absolutely loved the way I looked after my decadent splurge on a blue pencil skirt. It hung to about three inches above my knees and hugged my butt just perfectly, yet covered the myriad flaws I hallucinate my bottom to have before each of my stretch-and-sweat yoga classes with Allison.

I wore my freshly washed, shoulder-length hair down that Wednesday morning, shining, brushed out, and smelling slightly of lavender.

I saw no sign of Sheldon Donaldson in his division's office suite. *Good,* I thought, *maybe he's out at a meeting or at the doctor's planning a short-notice nose job.* Either way, I breathed far more easily without him around.

Just as they were when I sat down at their table in the Cantina, Jon Brady was sitting across from Steven, who was behind his desk.

Steven's eyes lit up when he saw me appear in the doorway. "Hi," he said.

I crossed my arms and leaned against the door frame.

Jon took a long, slow look at my legs and was not subtle about it. "Well, look who it is. Broken any noses yet today, Special Activities lady?"

Let him look, I thought. If all goes well, I'm going to want the others in Steven's office being jealous. Besides, that's why I overpaid for my new skirt in the first place.

"Yes, two so far," I replied. "However, I'm still behind my quota, so I'm glad you're here. Hold still, would you?"

Jon smiled. "On that note, Stevie, my boy," he said pushing down hard on the arms of the visitor's chair and standing up, "I'll leave you two to write on each other's hands. Or wherever else either of you might want to start scribbling."

"By the way," Jon asked as he passed me, "do you have a name?"

"Yes," I replied, grinning slyly as I gently closed the door in his face.

"So," Steven said with a smile, "you managed to avoid being led off by the SPOs in handcuffs. Glad to see that."

"Yeah, well, maybe what I did was wrong, but Sheldon was more wrong. I'm glad I haven't run into him here, so far."

"Don't worry. He hasn't been in the office all week," Steven said, assuaging my apprehension over the possibility of running into his boss on his home turf.

I hadn't decided what, if anything, to say to Sheldon if we passed in the hallway. After all, I had just come into *his* division's office space. After what happened the previous week at the Farm, any incident that occurred at headquarters would make me look like the aggressor. I certainly didn't want to give him any ammunition to use against me.

"Good," I said, feeling as though a weight had been lifted from around my neck. "Even though he's not in, what do you say we get out of here? Meet me for lunch in the cafeteria in twenty minutes?"

"Tell me your name, and I'll consider it," Steven said, grinning.

"Well, if you don't show up, then clearly you don't need to know. Meet me there and maybe I'll tell you. But only maybe."

***

He took me on our first date the following Saturday afternoon. With all of the possible things to do in DC, I had no idea what to expect. It turned out perfectly and truly characteristic of Steven. We walked around the National Mall people-watching, sat on the steps of the Lincoln monument, strolled aimlessly along the Reflecting Pool, meandered through two Smithsonian museums, and had a great time getting to know each other.

Dr. Steven Krauss, I learned, earned his Ph.D. in History from Columbia University in New York City. At first, I marveled at how much he knew about the men immortalized by the monuments on the Mall, the exhibits in the Museum of American History, and the world in general. No wonder he ended up as a CIA analyst.

Beyond just being so damned cute, he showed me his strong suit right off the bat. Without a doubt, Steven is the kind of genius that makes *Intelligence* the CIA's middle name.

As the afternoon stretched into evening, I was smitten and found myself getting lost every time I gazed up into his hazel eyes. The more we talked, the more I enjoyed exploring their beautiful depths. My thoughts turned from reminiscing about history to wondering what the future might be like on our next date or two. Somewhere along our walk on the National Mall, my hand slipped inside his; it fit perfectly.

The weeks that followed sped by. He treated me royally, but I found myself holding back, waiting for the inevitable betrayal that never came. No man could be this good, could he? He was sure to leave me just when I needed him most, right? Like my father had. Isn't that just the way men are?

The soft caresses of his hands contrasted harshly with the coarseness of my lies about what I do in the Agency. I busied myself fabricating elaborate stories about my travels and work.

For the next month, keeping up pretenses about my real work consumed me until I realized something I had trouble believing at first. Something intimately disturbing. It wasn't until he picked me up to go out one Friday night that it struck me. Only then did I finally realize what was going on and what I was doing. Steven wasn't asking about my work, but I still found myself throwing falsehoods around faster than a cardsharp dealing off the bottom of the deck. He wasn't asking about my trips. He wasn't asking about any of that.

No, he only asked about *me*. He didn't ask what I did during our time apart, he asked me how I felt. He didn't care where I traveled for work, he was just glad to see me when I returned. No, that's not quite right... he was ecstatic to see me on each of our dates. I didn't need to keep Steven in the dark, I realized with a start, but rather that *I* needed to see the light.

This revelation scared the hell out of me, and I almost made some weak excuse to cut that date short. I'm so very, very glad I didn't. On that date and the next and our next and the one after that, I never talked about my trips for work and he never asked. He asked me about my long-distance relationship with my cousins back home in Gardena, not about my work. I spoke generically about my job—never telling him it involved killing people—and he just asked about whether I missed my mother and was making new friends in Virginia.

Almost too late, it hit me that I had made Steven work double-duty to forge the emotional connection between us while I hampered his efforts, keeping the relationship shallow and superficial. How had I let it come to that?

The months sped by and our dates grew from weekends at his condo to mini-vacations at a quaint B&B on the waterfront in Annapolis. My explorations of him grew from finding that his hand was just the right size for mine to discovering that one perfect spot on his shoulder on which to rest my head.

Our hand-holding turned into kissing, and kissing into hugging, and hugging into falling....

PART FOUR

ALL IN

Chapter 14

Arnaud looked back at me from the front passenger seat of the BMW 740iL. "Michelle, you've been awfully quiet back there since we crossed the border from Germany. What's the matter, don't you like Switzerland?"

"I've never been to Switzerland before and was admiring the scenery. The Alps are unbelievably big, and they're so beautiful. I've never seen anything that even comes close. It makes me feel so small. And anyway, it's really comfortable back here. I love my 3-Series back home and have never been in a 7-Series before. I'm perfectly happy to let Claude drive again. He did a great job in Turkmenistan and Uzbekistan a couple of months ago. Now Germany and Switzerland. I'm going to start keeping a list of all the countries he chauffeurs me across. He's a good driver."

"Nah, he drives like an old lady," Arnaud chided his brother at the wheel of one of the CIA's most luxurious undercover vehicles. "This thing has power, but Claude doesn't know how to use it. On the Autobahn, he drove like he was on the DC beltway, stuck in traffic. The pedal on the right make the car go faster, *mon frère*. Learn to use it." Arnaud slapped the back of his hand across his brother's shoulder playfully.

"How was Barcelona, Michelle?" Claude asked.

"Oh, changing the subject on me, are you?" Arnaud sniped. "That's entirely too passive-aggressive of you."

"Fine," I replied. "I had fun, actually. It's one of the few places I've been operationally that I'm comfortable with the language. Although they have a weird accent."

"I'm going to go out on a limb here, Michelle," Arnaud added, uninvited, "and say it was probably *your* accent that was out of place. By about five thousand miles, I'm guessing."

"It's not just the difference between a Spanish accent and a Mexican accent. Like the way they pronounce Barcelona. It comes out as bar-*THEH*-lona," I explained. "But anyway, the surveillances went well.

And counter-surveillance. And counter-counter-surveillance. It all gets confusing pretty quickly. We were watching to see if there are people who are watching the people who are watching our people. Madrid Station said they found the guy they were looking for, and the SAD team was amazing. Even though I knew from the team briefings who all eight of the surveillance specialists were, I could barely pick them out of the crowd along Las Ramblas or in the stores of the Gothic Quarter. Technical Services Officers make some absolutely amazing disguises."

"Then you're all ready for your new look," Arnaud said, pointing to the silicone ears and nose piece he helped me apply a few hours earlier at the safe house on Ramstein Air Base.

"They feel weird. Not so much uncomfortable as entirely out of place—as though they make me more obvious, not less. My ears feel like they're sticking out like antennas. Do they look really big to you?"

"No, I told you, with that wig covering most of your ears anyway, you can barely see them. Depending on your hair or wig that day, maybe next time you don't even need the ears. You can try the silicone eye-sockets instead. The nose piece does change the shape of your face. Not in a bad way, though. You're still pretty, don't worry. It's just a *different* look, that's all. It doesn't look as much like you. That is what a disguise is for, right? It's enough to fool computerized facial recognition programs, or so the DS&T guys tell us."

"So, the pirates have surveillance cameras, huh?" I asked Arnaud, circling the conversation back to the reason for our trip to Switzerland. "You saw them on your recon trips here?"

"Yes. Well, of course the guys in Zurich aren't the pirates themselves. These shitheads just launder the ransom payments the pirates collect in Somalia. These are the bankers. The pirates' intelligence cell is in London, and the money-men are here in Switzerland. You missed the mission briefing, having fun in the sun in Bar-*theh*-lona all week," Arnaud said, mimicking my mimicking of the Catalonian accent. "Getting the pirates themselves in Somalia is too big a job for even the US military to handle. They tried doing that a few years ago, and it was a miserable failure. We're just cutting off the flow of money. Take away the profit motive and maybe they stop hijacking Western yachts and freighters for ransom. It's worth a shot, anyway."

"London would be fun," I mused aloud. "Any chance we're headed there next?"

Claude answered for his brother. "No, the Brits don't want anyone messing up their intelligence collection against the pirates' team there.

Wilson said the bad guys don't appear to know that the good guys know all about them. He said it's a treasure trove for the limeys."

"So, let me get this straight. We're going to watch the Brits who are watching the Somalis' cell in England, who are watching out for the pirates in Somalia, who are watching the American shipping companies to identify the next ship they want to highjack. Is that right?"

Arnaud jumped back in. While the twins didn't finish each other's sentences, they did seem to enjoy taking each other's place in the conversations almost at random. I had trouble imagining how confusing it must have been for others when all three triplets tried to talk with and for each other. "Something like that, I think. Except we don't actually watch the Brits. We generally just give each other whatever's asked for. It's a good relationship. We don't screw with them and they don't screw with us. Same with the Aussies."

"And the Canadians," Claude added.

Arnaud chuckled. "Yeah, true, but they're barely even considered foreigners anyway."

"So," Claude said glancing back at me and wagging his right thumb at his brother in the passenger seat, "*mon frère* over there and I have been surveilling these six guys in Zurich on and off for the past four months. They play poker together the last Friday night of the month like clockwork. It is Switzerland, after all. They like clocks."

"Nice stereotype, Claude," Arnaud said, teasing his brother. "Does that make you racist?"

"Swiss is not a race, Arnie. Shut up," Claude retorted.

"Weak comeback. Even after all these years, you still need to work on that."

I interrupted the brothers' sniping, heading off any more of the annoying sibling rivalry for the moment anyway. "Back at the Ramstein safe house, you said there'll be nine of them there tonight, but you just said *six*."

If they were going to continue being so childish in the future, I decided, my first mission working with both Claude and Arnaud might also be my last. Although only half their age, apparently it fell to me be the adult of the group.

"Yeah," Claude answered. "Eight or nine guys show up to play each month. The core six are there every time, and a few of the others are regulars. Every now and then, one or two new guys show up at a game. For the others who might show up at tonight's game, well, it's just bad luck for them.

"Wilson said the analysts back at Langley are reading enough of these guys' emails to confirm that this month's game is on so Mike gave us the green light. Since you were already in Europe, you get to join us. Lucky you. And lucky us, actually. With that many targets to control, we can certainly use the third set of eyes and hands."

"And we volunteered you to zap the *reinemachefrau,*" Arnaud said.

I responded abruptly. "The what? Can't you just speak English, Arnaud? This is serious. You wouldn't tell me the whole plan back in Germany. Now's the time. Stop screwing around."

"Cleaning woman. Sheesh, Michelle, chill out. Or housekeeper, in this case. Maid, if you prefer."

"Thank you," I sneered. "Was that so hard?"

"We've already done all of the advance work, and the plan is just what we told you. You go to the mansion's service entrance. Knock to get her to open the door. Zap her with the stun gun, and then Claude and I come in. There are a few external security cameras at the doors, so that's why you're wearing the big ears and clown nose."

"They are not big. Stop that, Arnie," Claude said, defusing his brother's unflattering comment. "We zip tie her and go downstairs to where the guys will be playing cards."

"Zip tie *her*?" Arnaud asked Claude, grinning impishly and hooking his thumb in my direction.

Finally, I'd had enough of his attitude. I reached forward and slapped Arnaud across the right side of his head. Not too hard, but I made my displeasure known.

"Ouch."

Arnaud had moved well past simply getting on my nerves. "You *do* realize that in an hour I'll have a gun in my hand, don't you?"

Claude tried to play referee. "Stop it, both of you!"

Arnaud rubbed the back of his head. "Hey, she's the one who hit *me.* Control your girlfriend. You're the one sleeping with her across every former Soviet republic."

I smacked Arnaud across the back of his head again, this time not holding anything back.

"We were *not* sleeping together," Claude interjected defensively. "You know that. Just sleeping next to each other. That's all."

I scowled, crossed my arms, and quietly stewed in my seat. I knew Claude was not taking my side against his brother, but mostly just defending himself from an unjust insinuation.

Arnaud continued to needle his brother. "I should tell your wife. What would Monica think?" He *tsk*ed, and smiled from ear to ear, enjoying himself thoroughly as he dug the hole deeper.

"I'm stopping for petrol," Claude said, not chasing his brother down the rabbit hole. He pulled into a gas station just off the A3 highway.

Arnaud shook his head. "There you go being passive-aggressive again. When will you ever learn?"

"Michelle," Claude said, ignoring his brother's quip, "you're wearing the disguise, so you get to fill 'er up. Arnie, give her fifty euros. They'll give you change in Swiss francs, but everyone takes euros here, even if they do kind of screw you on the exchange rate."

I snatched the colorful bill from Arnaud's hand and hoped it gave him a paper cut. I exited the car glad to get away from him for the few minutes needed to fill the gas tank. That breather gave me an opportunity to calm down before we headed for the serious business ahead and the real reason for our trip to Switzerland.

Chapter 15

Claude guided the BMW between the decorative stone pillars that sat as silent, impotent guardians on either side of the driveway's entrance. We approached the service entrance, bypassing the circular driveway, which sat clogged with Maseratis, BMWs, Mercedes, and a Ferrari. I looked along the line of cars in amazement and stared wide-eyed at what was likely as much money on that driveway as I would make in my entire career.

"Is that a Maybach?" Arnaud asked no one in particular, sounding impressed. "I wonder if the Air Force crew will notice if I sneak it aboard the C-141 for the flight home?"

I had never heard of a Maybach before. Arnaud was our resident car buff and drove a company-leased Porsche 911 back home. Michael treated the three of us well, and deservedly so.

I broke away from ogling the cars and double checked the equipment in my pockets and under my jacket: stun gun, Sig Sauer, suppressor, four magazines, black balaclava mask, and plastic zip cuffs. Check.

"Got the packet?" Arnaud asked.

"Yes," I replied and patted my jacket pocket.

I touched my nose gently, self-conscious about the silicone disguise glued to my face. Along with the jacket, wig, and fake ears, that small piece of rubber was supposed to keep anyone from identifying me from any surveillance videos. The flimsy contrivance did not build my confidence or make me comfortable with the prospect of betting my future on it, but it was too late for second thoughts.

I donned my tactical gloves and rested my right hand reassuringly on the handle of the electronic stun gun in my jacket pocket.

Claude stopped the car a few yards past the "servant's entrance," as he called it. I approached the house from an angle to avoid being seen from inside until I stood at the side door.

A red light glowed on the rectangular box above the door. Claude and Arnaud were right about the cameras. Even if nobody was watching the video feed at that moment, the cameras still recorded images of everyone who approached the house onto their hard drives.

I knocked lightly on the glass pane in the center of the door and waited for the housekeeper to investigate.

A disembodied mop of gray hair appeared around the corner at the end of a hallway that looked as though it might lead to a dining room. The *reinemachefrau* peered towards the door and asked me something in German, which I did not understand in the least.

I smiled and simply repeated the one German phrase Arnaud had taught me on our drive to Zurich. "*Guten abend, frau.*" I waved my left hand and, in my right, held the stun gun out of sight, past the door frame.

"*Guten abend, fraulein,*" she replied as she walked down the hallway towards me. "*Kann ich dir helfen?*" She opened the door so we could speak face to face.

"*Ja,*" I replied and jammed the stun gun into her ample belly.

The pudgy housekeeper convulsed violently from the twenty-thousand volts the small black device discharged into her soft paunch. She fell to the floor and hit the tile so hard I feared she might have hurt herself.

I knelt next to her, yanked her left hand behind her back, and cinched down the plastic flex cuff around her meaty wrist. I climbed over the large woman to reach her right arm and pulled hard to cuff it next to its mate.

Arnaud and Claude appeared at the door, pistols in hand and faces covered by black balaclavas. Even without disguises, the fraternal twins didn't look that much alike to me. Arnaud had the trim, almost scrawny figure of a triathlete. He wore his hair close-cropped with tight curls, much shorter than his brother's longer brown waves, the outlines of which were visible along the top of his balaclava. While athletic, Claude didn't have the taut physique of his insanely fit brother.

"Nice of you to join us," I said. "Watch where you step. I think she peed her pants... well... dress, in this case."

I reached into my left jacket pocket and removed the silver zip-lock foil packet. I thumbed the packet open and re-read for the umpteenth time that day the entirely uninformative label: Product Strength 4.

I inhaled deeply, extracted the moist pad from the packet, and cupped it firmly in my left hand. With my right hand, I grabbed a handful of the housekeeper's short gray hair, hefted her head up, and covered her mouth and nose with the pad.

The ten seconds it took for her groans slowly subsided seemed more like minutes. As her guttural complaints transformed into raspy rhythmic breathing, I returned the pad to its pouch and resealed it.

"You really don't have to hold your breath when doing that, you know," Arnaud said through the balaclava covering his face. "Just keep it at arm's length, and you won't end up asleep next to her for the next four hours."

"Okay, well...." I said, returning the packet to my pocket and zipping it in securely. "It's my first time, you know? Just playing it safe."

I retrieved my balaclava from my back pocket and pulled it over my wig, careful to not dislodge my silicone ears.

"Okay," I said, while screwing the suppressor onto the barrel of my 9mm Sig. "I'm ready."

Arnaud gave a silent follow-me wave to us as he took point, leading the way further into the house. We made our way along the hall and descended the wide, polished mahogany staircase into the basement. Claude followed directly behind his brother and I brought up the rear as we walked silently down the carpet runner.

The bottom of the stairs opened straight away into a large basement with more of a London pub motif than anything particularly Swiss. Instead of the ski-chalet vibe I expected, we were greeted by a twenty-foot-long cherry-wood bar to our right, with two shelves of dark German beers and top-shelf liquors.

Arnaud darted for the green poker table in the center of the room and started barking orders to the eight men seated around its padded oval rim. Claude swung to the right and went behind the bar where the ninth banker was pouring himself a dark beer from one of three built-in taps. With my pistol raised, I followed Arnaud and covered the table of money launderers.

The unwelcome appearance of three uninvited, masked intruders interrupting their monthly male-bonding ritual caused an eruption of yelling and arm waving, focused largely on Arnaud. The bankers, comfortably dressed in a mix of dress slacks and khakis for a night of drinking and gambling, were well into their Friday evening of beer and poker. The array of half-empty glass steins on the table told me the men were doing at least as much drinking as betting.

A blond banker perched at the left end of the table dropped his cards on the green felt and raised his hands. The tall, thirty-ish man gestured energetically at Arnaud and yelled with equal measures of anger and surprise. Clearly the host of the group, he raved angrily in German. If I spoke his native tongue, I'm sure I would have learned a few choice curse words that evening.

Claude pushed and prodded the sandy-haired banker from behind the bar to the middle of the floor in front of the three of us.

"I'll cover. You cuff," Claude said to me. He turned a bit, so I could more easily reach the stack of flex cuffs hanging from the rear of his belt.

"English? You speak English?" the player whom I assumed was the host asked Arnaud in slightly broken, but certainly passable, English. "What do you want here? You here to steal from us?"

"Shut up," Arnaud replied pointedly, aiming his pistol at the man's face for emphasis.

The host remained standing while his compatriots sat perfectly still. The initial shock had worn off, and I could see the gravity of the situation begin to dawn on him. His eyes lingered anxiously on the intimidating length of the suppressor on Claude's pistol. A sight more common in movies than in real life, the otherworldliness of seeing a suppressor on a firearm aimed at him made the fair-skinned man blanch.

Around the table, eight faces drooped. Smart men, the bankers rightly reasoned that three intruders wearing three identical masks, armed with three identical pistols topped with three identical suppressors, and carrying a stack of plastic flex cuffs had planned this intrusion well in advance. Around the table, sixteen eyes darted from the taller Payeur brothers, both giving orders, to the silent, shorter third intruder doing their bidding. Most of the players followed my movements more than they watched either of my partners'.

Did they pay more attention to me because I was the one doing most of the work, cuffing Claude's banker and kneeling him down on the floor? Was it because I was the only one moving and that's simply where the action was? Or did they single me out because I was the only woman in the room and even when faced with guns pointed at them, that's simply what gets men's attention?

"You want money? It's in the safe behind the bar," our host volunteered. "Take it and leave, please." No doubt he wanted to make our visit as short as possible and get us out of his house before anyone got hurt. Unfortunately for him, their wealth was not what brought us all together. Rather, the human cost behind it caused the inevitable convergence of our two groups.

"You, big mouth, come here. You're next," Arnaud ordered. "Kneel down next to your friend."

In quick succession, the men lined up and were all cuffed in short order.

Arnaud lifted the group's host to a standing position by his hair and pushed him towards the stairs.

"Let's go find your other safe. Where is it? In the office? Maybe your bedroom?" Arnaud prodded the banker forward not caring at all what the answer to his question was. The two ascended the stairs and disappeared from sight.

A few minutes later, Arnaud returned alone and nodded to his brother. Claude selected the banker he had collected from behind the bar and marched him upstairs. Two minutes later, Claude, too, returned alone. Finally, it was my turn.

I picked the man directly in front of me because he was the smallest of the group and if he gave me trouble would be the easiest for me to control.

We ignored the protests of the remaining men, leaving their questions about where we were taking their friends unanswered. I certainly had no good answers to give.

I navigated the banker to the top floor of the house and directed him to the bathroom in the master suite. As planned, Claude had left the door ajar, and I instructed the banker to push it open.

Blood stained two of the walls and red liquid oozed along the white tile floor. The banker gasped and clutched his chest at the sight of his two dead friends. His outburst was short-lived, interrupted by agony as the 9mm hollow-point bullet I fired into his upper back mushroomed, shredding muscles, bone, and his right lung. As he collapsed to the floor, his surprise turned into a guttural growl of agonizing pain. Pain that I ended for him swiftly—mercifully—with a second bullet, this one to his head.

I closed the door and returned to the basement where I nodded to my teammates that the job was done.

Another round of trips by Claude and Arnaud to other rooms upstairs left us with four bankers kneeling in front of us. The man on the left end of the line complained vociferously in German, making me glad I didn't speak his language. The banker second from the right cried softly, looking away to keep anyone from seeing the tears rolling down his cheeks.

Claude looked at Arnaud and me and made a shooting motion with his left thumb and index finger.

There would be no more forced marches up the stairs. Since none of their friends had returned from such a trip, the odds increased dramatically that the remaining men would start taking chances and fighting back. Even though we had not been violent with them in the basement, we had to figure that at least one would try to get away. Cuffed or not, a desperate banker might attempt to grab a gun or push one of us down the stairs hoping to gain the upper hand.

We shot the remaining four in quick succession as they knelt on the basement floor. Claude and Arnaud shot one each, leaving the two on the right for me.

I looked closely at the four lifeless bodies as I loaded a full magazine into my Sig. Once reloaded, I returned my pistol to the holster under my jacket. As I watched the unmoving corpses, the thought occurred to me just how anticlimactic the whole thing seemed. We had paraded five men up the stairs slowly and rhythmically, followed by what can only be described as an execution of the remaining four in the basement.

There was no jumping around on beds like in Aruba. No crazy driving around the streets of Rome. No unaccounted-for targets hiding in basements in Uzbekistan. No confusing counter-surveillance concerns as we had in Barcelona.

No adrenaline.

Then it hit me. *That's* what felt different. I stood still, mesmerized and unable to look away from the four bodies splayed about the floor in front of me. The simplicity of the mission made it methodical, not adventurous. Shouldn't such a serious affair as this have more ceremony to it? This time, we never faced any real danger.

Was there more to it than just completing the mission? *Should* there have been more to it than that?

Was that all it was to *me*? Just a task from headquarters to kill six money-launderers?

What about the three men who were not our real targets? What about the housekeeper? Did they have to die too?

Sometimes, being in the wrong place at the wrong time is just part of life. Arnaud calls them WPWTs, which sounds like "whipperts" when he says it. Bad luck all around when it happens. It's all just part of life. Right?

Is that right?

Is that *right*?

Expanding pools of bright arterial blood made the light-brown floor shiny and slick. Reflections of the overhead lights flickered like sparks in the crimson liquid.

Transfixed and lost in thought, I peered down at four motionless bodies lying on the polished hardwood floor. I did not expect the men to reanimate or mystically answer my questions but expected I would be able to answer them myself at that point of my career. That I *should* be able to answer them. I disappointed myself that I couldn't.

The two men whose lives I had just ended laid on the floor facing each other, lifeless eyes open.

Were these two the pirates' bankers or were they just WPWTs?

Either way, would it matter in the end? I suddenly found myself wanting to know the answer to a question that was not part of—could not be part of—the mission briefing: would killing these nine men take any of the profit motive out of the business of piracy? Would taking out these nine really do anything to stem the flow of money? Or, as with the drug trade so prevalent back home in California, is there simply so much money for greedy men to make that when nine fall chasing it, ninety more anxiously step forward to take their places regardless of the risks or how many before them have died trying to get rich?

Was it worth doing this at all?

Was it worth *my* doing this?

"—elle. Earth to Michelle," a voice behind me said.

Arnaud stood at the bar with Claude and motioned for me to join them.

"Here are the two hard drives from the surveillance system the owner of the house kindly showed me upstairs. I'll put some bullet holes in them here and take them with us on the flight home tomorrow night to make sure they're destroyed properly.

"And these," he said, dropping a dozen envelopes and a half-dozen loose stacks of currency on the bar, "are the contents of the safes from behind the bar and the owner's bedroom. He got quite helpful and talkative up there.

"The envelopes are marked with the players' names. He told me they leave their money here from month to month. It must be safer for them to leave their dough here between games instead of carrying this much cash around the streets of Zurich."

Arnaud looked over the bar at the bodies of the four dead men and shrugged. "Or, then again, maybe not."

I was impressed with the piles of cash. "The envelopes have, what, about ten thousand euros, give or take? That's about thirteen grand."

Claude nodded. "Each."

"And there are, what, fifteen envelopes? That's one hell of a poker game these guys play."

Arnaud made one large stack of bills and started piling up looser collections into three smaller stacks. "There's about a hundred thousand euros in this pile." Arnaud dropped the largest stack into a plastic bag he found under the bar. "That'll go to Mike for the Trust Fund. Here's for you," he said sliding one of the three remaining smaller piles towards Claude and another towards me. "And you."

I had no clue why he divided the money between the three of us. "What's this for? Shouldn't it all go to the Trust Fund?"

Arnaud looked at his brother and asked, "With all that money in Samarkand, did you—?"

Claude shook his head. "No, we didn't control the logistics on the way back."

Arnaud scrunched his eyes slightly and asked me, "Have you started setting up your Out?"

"My *what*?"

"Your Out. A way for you to get away quickly if everything goes to shit all of a sudden."

"No. I don't know what you mean," I confessed.

"Alright, pay attention. Your Out is how you'd get yourself to safety if something really bad happens back home. If suddenly the Agency weren't backing you anymore, for whatever reason, or the wrong people get wind of what we're doing, and you have to get away and start over somewhere. Somewhere you can be safe for a few weeks or, if need be, for a few years. Maybe a log cabin in the woods, if you're like me and enjoy that kind of thing. Or maybe a beach house in a country that doesn't have an extradition treaty with the US. It has never happened in the history of the team, but you want to be prepared for worst cases, you know, just in case."

Claude joined the conversation. "What you do is slowly collect the things you'll need. Start with this cash. Over time, keep a couple of the aliased passports you use. Keep a few of the firearms, suppressors, magazines, ammo, lock picks, and so on that you use in training or in the field. Every now and then, just say that something got lost.

"But you only do it on missions for which you control the logistics, like this one," Claude continued. "We flew over with the gear in the car, and we're taking it home with us tomorrow on the C-141. When we get it all back to the Farm, you turn it in... except for the cash and maybe one magazine. Next time, maybe one of your weapons doesn't come back because you had to ditch it in a river to avoid getting caught with it by the local cops. Next year, it's a suppressor. Every now and then, one lock pick doesn't make it back. Get it?"

"After a little while," Arnaud said, "you'll have enough gear to use in an emergency if you have to beat feet and get out of town *tout de suite*. It's for your own safety, Michelle. Here."

Claude picked up one of the small piles of euros and Arnaud handed another to me. I looked at it for a while and, following the Payeur brothers' lead, stuffed it into my jacket pocket.

"One more thing to do," Arnaud said, putting the two hard drives from the surveillance system on the floor. He stepped back a few feet and shot each four times before putting them into his jacket pocket.

Claude headed for the stairs. "Let's get out of here."

In the kitchen, Arnaud looked at me and gestured towards the housekeeper.

"Claude will start the car. You get her."

Innocently, I asked, "What do you mean 'get her?'"

"Get her. Shoot her. Come on, hurry."

"Shoot her? But she's unconscious. She didn't see anything. I mean, other than me. She never saw you or Claude. She's no threat to anyone. By the time she wakes up in three-and-a-half hours, we'll be back at the safe house. She can't identify me. All she saw was some blonde woman with a big nose. Why do we have to shoot her?"

"You know why. We always clean house. Just do it," Arnaud commanded.

"No," I said defiantly. "There's nothing she can tell the police, and she's not one of the bankers. She's not involved. She's a nobody. She's just the maid."

I bent down, unzipped the back of the *reinemachefrau*'s large dress, and stuffed about half of the Out money from my pocket into the bra strap of the obese woman as she snored peacefully on the kitchen floor.

I zipped up the back of her dress. "Besides being the one who'll find nine dead bodies later tonight, she's also out of a job because of us. She's fine. There's the car. Let's go."

Arnaud glanced out the open doorway and saw that Claude had pulled the BMW up for us. He looked back at me and shook his head in resignation.

"You're a piece of work, you know that? Fine, go," he said, gesturing to the car.

I stood my ground. "You first."

Arnaud smile and nodded. "Yup. A real piece of work."

In the car, Claude drove us slowly down the long driveway. I turned and watched the line of luxury cars parked in front of the house recede from sight and disappear behind one of the stone pillars sitting where the driveway ended and the street began.

I sank into the firm embrace of the BMW's soft leather and eagerly pulled off the balaclava, wig, fake ears, and gloves. I stretched out my legs, massaged my scalp, ran my fingers through my hair down to the base of my neck, and gave myself a mental high-five at the thought of having won at least a small victory that evening.

PART FIVE

SECOND THOUGHTS

Chapter 16

The large red digits on Steven Krauss's alarm clock blinked in the early morning darkness as 3:29 became 3:30, and I gave in. Simultaneously, I both won and lost my internal battle. I couldn't hold it in anymore and desperately needed to share my feelings with him. The *what* and the *why* were both important, and I couldn't leave our conversation from earlier that evening unfinished. Not the way I'd left it. Steven deserved better, even if it hurt me to talk about everything. Especially the *why*.

I pushed my back up against the headboard, crossed my legs, and pulled down the Columbia University t-shirt I usually wore when spending the night at his condo as far as it would go. I wiped a few tears away with my right hand and gently stroked his shoulder with my left.

"Steven.... Steven...."

His guttural response rose in timbre slowly. "Mmmmmm?"

I was waking him up in the middle of the night and understandably all he wanted to do was sleep. I was probably about to come across as an over-stereotyped emotional train-wreck of a girl that smart guys like Dr. Steven Krauss did everything they could to avoid. But I had to get my feelings out in the open. Not just off my chest, but shared fully and laid bare, no matter how much it hurt.

"Steven, are you awake?"

"Um humm... whu...?" Slowly, Steven ran a hand across his face. "What's wrong?"

"Nothing's wrong," I muttered, choking back a quiet sob. "It's what you said."

He pushed himself up on one elbow and squinted as his eyes adjusted to the few rays of moonlight streaming between the slats of his bedroom's Venetian blinds. Steven rolled towards me and saw the remnants of my tears in the dim light. He reached up and gently wiped my cheek with his thumb.

"I'm sorry for whatever I said. I'm sure I didn't mean it. I take it back."

He laid back down, bunched his pillow under his head, and settled in for a longer conversation than he undoubtedly would have liked to have had at that early hour.

Tears again cascaded along the curves of my cheekbones. "No, you're not sorry and no, you can't take it back." My next statement sounded more venomous than intended. "I know you meant it."

I fought to get the words out of my mouth, words punctuated by loud, body-shaking sobs this time. "I—love—you—too."

"Oh, that. No, I don't take *that* back. Not even a little bit. I didn't know we were talking about that. I love you too, Michelle."

"I can move in with you, if you still want me to." I wiped both hands across my face, clearing the slow streams that ran from my eyes. "That's not what I was so upset about last night. It's not what you asked me, but what you didn't ask."

"Now I'm back to not understanding—"

"This is hard for me to talk about. Really hard. You have no idea." I inhaled deeply for strength and looked into those hazel eyes I find so irresistible.

"Take your time," he said, rolling his cupped hand across my knee sweetly. Comfortingly. Reassuringly.

My mouth contorted into a twisted grimace. "I'm just going to say this. I have to get it out. I can't hold it in anymore. You've been so wonderful. You *are* so wonderful. I've been up most of the night thinking a lot and crying a little and I know it's not fair to you and even after dating for a year you don't really know that much about me and you just came out and said you loved me and I didn't say it back to you and we got into bed and I didn't tell you why or tell you anything, but if you love me and I love you and we move in together then someone will be thinking of whether we have a real future together and getting married and I want to have a future with you but I don't want to get married. I can't get married. I don't know how to be married, but I really do love you and...."

My voice hissed to a halt as my lungs ran out of air. The breath I hurriedly inhaled streamed back out as a long string of sobs. I buried my face in my hands so I didn't have to see Steven looking at me in my condition.

"Slow down, honey," he said softly. "Slow down. I'm here for you. Catch your breath and talk to me."

"You're so great, and I'm such a mess tonight.... It's not you, it's me." I smiled and laughed between sobs. "Like no one has ever said *that* before, huh?"

Steven answered slowly. "It's okay. If things are going too fast for you, we'll just—"

"No, that's not it. That's not it at all. My parents were married for nineteen years and then my dad just left us. You have no idea what that's like. Without a word, he just didn't come home one day. I never saw him again after that. Ever. It hurt so, so deeply. I can't even begin to explain the pain. I mean, it physically hurt and turned my stomach inside out. I barely came out of my room for a week. Didn't eat. Didn't go to school. Didn't shower. I didn't even notice that my mom didn't notice because she didn't come out of her room for, like, a month. Her cries were so loud the neighbors stopped by a few times.

"I ended up having to care for her and she never completely recovered. Maybe the main reason I applied to the CIA was just to get out of California. I didn't want to join the Army like they both did out of high school, but I needed to have a reason to leave and be able to say I had no choice—they were making me go. I just had to get away from that place."

"I'm sure it was hard for you."

"Yeah, it was," I said, putting my hand on his shoulder, appreciating his support and understanding. "I thought my parents were happy. What the hell did I know? I was just sixteen. I mean at that age you think you know what's going on, but I never saw the problems or whatever drove my dad away. Later, my aunt said she thought my mother was being too hard to get along with, and my dad just couldn't take it anymore. I don't know, but I hate him for leaving us. Abandoning us. Abandoning *me*. Even if it's true that he couldn't stand my mother anymore, I can't forgive him for not saying goodbye or even leaving me a note. He never sent a letter or birthday card or anything. He just didn't come home from work one night. There's simply no excuse for that.

"So, I don't want to get married. I mean not just not to you. Not to anyone. In my job, I can't see myself ever having kids and, besides, if people can just up and leave even if they *are* married, then what's the use?"

"Michelle, lots of undercover officers get married and have families. Having kids or not is probably worthy of its own conversation. If you want, we can have that conversation sometime. It doesn't have to be today. Tonight, I mean."

I shook my head. "One thing I'm absolutely positive about is not having kids. There's no way I would ever want my child to experience what I felt when my dad left. I can't bring a child into the world knowing I have to travel on short notice for work and, given some of the things I do, that I might never come back and there wouldn't be any explanations or goodbyes. I've *been* there when a parent doesn't come home one day, and no one can tell you why not or where he went. I absolutely cannot, not, not, *not* ever do that to a child I gave birth to.

"Steven, if you want kids, it's okay, just tell me and we can part on good terms. The best of terms. I mean, you're twelve years older than I am, which is fine. It's great, really, and I'm not just saying that, but if you've always wanted kids or you have a biological clock that's ticking or something, just tell me. Do men even have biological clocks? I don't know. Kids are fine and all, but not for me. You need to know that... to understand that much about me. That's just how I feel, and I had to tell you. I owe you at least that much. I'm sorry it happened like this, though."

"I don't know what you get into when you're in the field, and maybe I don't want to know everything—"

"No, you don't," I said with more urgency than I'd intended or would have liked to infuse into those words.

"—but, you know that plenty of officers, both men and women, change positions within the Agency throughout their careers. I'm sure you could find a great job at headquarters, if you wanted."

"No, I know. I mean, yes, I do know that they do, but no," I said, managing to confuse myself in the process of figuring out what I was trying to say. "That's not going to happen for me. I do what I do and it's my career now. I didn't have a clue what I would be getting myself into when I first got to the Farm. Maybe nobody ever does, but I'm in too deep now and it's pretty much for life."

I hated having to talk around what I actually do on Michael's team, especially at that moment, half-naked in Steven's bed. I felt rotten having to deceive the one man in the world with whom I so badly wanted to share everything.

I looked at Steven and ran my hands through his hair. "You can think about it and we can talk more tomorrow, or next week, or next year, if you'd like. If you want me to move in with you, I'd love to, and I will. But the deal is that you can never ask me to marry you, okay? I know that last night you didn't ask me anything about marriage and maybe you're not thinking about that, yet, but my mind is racing forward a few steps. That's just the way I am. You say, 'move in,' and I just naturally started thinking about what comes next, even if you're not close to thinking about that. I don't want to move in with you now if it means moving out in a few months if or when you do start thinking about such things. We can get married when we both retire from the Agency. If this relationship lasts that long, then I'll agree it will be until 'death do us part,' but before then, you have to agree that you won't pop *The Question*, okay?"

Steven thought for a moment. "I didn't realize your dad's leaving had that kind of impact on you. I had no idea it was so intensely painful."

He sat up, pressed his lips firmly against mine, and silently wrapped me in his arms. I always lose myself in his firm embraces. Between his hypnotic eyes and the arms I always want around me, he knows just when I need the reassurance of being held tightly.

I ran my hand down the side of his face and said, "I love being your girlfriend, and I love you. I would love it if we shared the rest of our lives together, but I'm just not the marrying type. I would never, ever want to take that away from you, though. If what you honestly want more than anything else is a wife and kids and a minivan and little league games, then I'm just not the right woman for you. I would prefer that we figured it out sooner rather than later, and I'd be perfectly willing to help you find Miss Right. It'd hurt me to lose you, but I would never take away from anyone the opportunity to have a family, especially not someone I love and respect so much. And by that, I mean you." I poked him gently with my index finger to emphasize the point.

"With you," I went on softly, "I feel... I feel... when I'm with you, I just feel safe. With you, and really only you, I can let down my defenses. You have absolutely no idea how good that feels. How liberating. With you, I can be the real me, and that's so important. I don't have to pretend around you. We know enough about each other's work to know we need to leave work at the office and not ask the wrong questions. That's important to me. I love being here with you. We can look at each other and say to ourselves, 'Yeah, I know the basics about what the other does. I don't need to know the details.' That's exactly what I need. Here, in your condo, I feel safe. I feel welcome. When I'm in your arms, I feel... at home. If you still want me here, that is."

Steven stumbled through his thoughts. "I appreciate your telling me this. I can tell—I mean it's the middle of the night—that it wasn't easy for you to get up the strength to have this conversation. I imagine you've been up most of the night trying to find the right way to say it. I don't know if you thought that if you did bring this up... or maybe *when* you did bring it up that it might be... it might mean... it might be the end of what we've had. What we *have*, I mean," he said, caught somewhere between confusion and defensiveness.

Steven chuckled, deflecting his discomfort. "See, Michelle. It's difficult for me to find the right words, too. But here's what's not difficult for me to say: I choose you."

Steven looked into my eyes and wrapped me into his warm smile.

"In whatever way we build our lives together, the only thing that's important to me is that we do it together. Whether we're singles dating, a married couple, or cohabitating life-partners—if that's even a real thing," he said with a grin. "I only care that we're doing it together. I choose you, Michelle Reagan, and I want to spend the rest of my life with you."

This time, it was my turn. Gently, I guided Steven's face up and kissed him firmly with the pent-up passion that built during the hours I laid in his bed, physically next to him but emotionally separated by the gulf created by my fears. While lying there building up the courage I needed to wake him, I had hallucinated every possible way the conversation could go wrong. I overthought everything I could think of and had no space left in my head or heart to hold another drop of love or self-doubt. I had bottled up my fears, hopes, dreams, and dreads until they boiled over, leaving me no choice but to wake him. His love for me was overwhelming and the pure joy I felt flowed from my lips to his, from my hands to his face, from soul to soul.

I pulled back from our kiss just far enough that I could focus on his face to see his reaction to what I was about to tell him. I smiled, tilted his head up towards mine, and softly said, "Kopechne."

"Huh?" Steven's head tilted slightly in my hands, an unconscious reflex betraying his confusion.

"If we're going to live together, then you need to know the real me. That's my real name, Michelle Kopechne. I live under cover as Michelle Reagan. Most UCs don't live under aliases, it's too confusing for the families, but Michael decided it would be best if I started out that way right from the beginning, so he gave me that name."

"Not that your knowing will make any practical difference. There are probably only five people in the Agency who know that fact. You, me, Michael, Security, and someone in HR. But since we're going to live together now, I wanted to share that one last bit of trivia with you."

I looked at him and smiled again. "I wanted to tell you about that. It's not really a big thing, but it's the one last thing I've been keeping from you," I lied.

Right through my teeth.

Right to his face.

PART SIX

SOUTH AFRICA

Chapter 17

Michael routinely sends me encrypted text messages, but getting one at 10 p.m. on a Sunday struck me as anything but routine. The succinct message was clear enough, but at the same time, gave me no insight into what was going on: "Meet at Starbucks tomorrow. 5 a.m. Business attire. Tell no one."

I raised an eyebrow and wondered about the real meaning behind it. "Tell no one" clearly meant Steven—no doubt about it. Whatever was going on, I couldn't tell him about my visit to headquarters bright and early the following morning. That made me sit up and take notice of the highly unusual nature of the summons.

Michael was celebrating my birthday with me at the Farm three years earlier when I first met Steven and knew I'd been living with him for the past two years. Michael probably even ran an additional background investigation on Steven once I moved into his condo in Arlington. For all I knew, Michael might very well know more about my beloved Dr. Steven Krauss than I did. The opposite was not true, however. Steven still believed I worked on a Technical Penetration team. I knew Michael wouldn't trust Steven—whom he viewed as just an analyst—with the truth.

I found the part of Michael's message about dressing up highly unusual. He wears a suit when at headquarters, as do most CIA executives. A man in a suit never looks out of place there. I usually wear khaki slacks or some boring skirt and a nice blouse the few times a year I go to Langley. This time, whatever we were going to do, Michael wanted me to look the part.

I was intrigued and should have paid more attention to my feeling of foreboding instead of pushing it back down into the recesses of my mind. Always trust your gut.

***

I could see clearly down the long, empty corridor outside Starbucks from my seat on the padded bench. The black-and-gray speckled tile hallway stretched from one end of the Original Headquarters Building, OHB, on my left, off to the atrium of the New Headquarters Building, NHB, on my right. Behind the wall against which I sat, employees in the cafeteria and food court were preparing breakfast and brewing that much-desired caffeinated black gold for the rush of employees who would stream through later in the day. Starbucks, I discovered much to my disappointment, would not open for another hour.

I always marveled at the contradiction that this particular portion of CIA headquarters represented to me. On one hand, these buildings contained some of the most advanced supercomputer systems in the world, while at the same time, the bathrooms still sported the same porcelain toilets installed when the OHB was built in the 1950s. With all the money that flowed *into* this building each year, why couldn't they spend at least some of it to help ease what flowed *out*?

Michael came into view far off to my left as he rounded the corner at the OHB end of the corridor. He wore his white hair slicked straight back and it contrasted elegantly against his dark blue suit. A red tie with a yellow diamond pattern repeating up and down its length and matching pocket square completed his look exquisitely. Michael's a handsome man, and I find it completely unacceptable that men can look so good with hair a color that we women fight so hard and spend so much money to avoid. It's just not fair.

"The boss called, eh?" I asked, already knowing the answer.

"Yes, we're going to the seventh floor," Michael confirmed. "Have you met the new Director?"

"No, of course not. He's only been here for two months, and I must have let my membership at the yacht club lapse last year."

Michael frowned at my snarky reply as we entered the elevator for our quick ride to Seventh Heaven, as the executive floor was sometimes sarcastically called by us mere mortals.

"Don't worry, I'll be nice." I smiled sweetly to reassure him as the doors closed. The elevator accelerated and the white circular floor indicators counted their way up to seven. "You do all the talking, and I'll do all the nodding in agreement. Is that the plan?"

"Basically," he said, stepping forward as the elevator doors opened. Truth be told, I had never been to the seventh floor before and was happy to let Michael lead the way.

Michael walked into the Director's office suite first while I trailed closely behind. Out of habit more than anything else, I scanned the assortment of well-appointed offices and briefly admired the attractive, polished oak and cherry furniture. Later that morning, the suite would also host the Deputy Director, the Director's Chief of Staff, and a dozen staffers, secretaries, and schedulers. In one corner of the outer office sat two unobtrusive plain-clothed Security Protective Officers who served as the Director's bodyguards.

More in response to training than any real interest, I tried to assess what kind of weapons the two men in their late twenties might be carrying under their sport coats. Or maybe that's just the woman in me—always checking out the cute guys and wondering what they might be "packing." The bulges in their jackets told me they had more than just six-shooters under there. Much more.

Not far from the seated SPOs, the beginnings of the Director's Christmas tree lay in pieces. Pushed against the wall at the end of a senior secretary's desk, the metal base and red quilted tree skirt sat on the floor, awaiting the facilities team to finish setting it up later in the day.

That reminded me, I had to start thinking about what to buy for Steven this year.

As we walked further into the suite, I must have looked to the SPOs like a tourist in wide-eyed appreciation of the extensive decorations and pageantry on display to impress visitors. Pictures of intelligence-collecting satellites, submarines, amazing Agency-designed aircraft such as the U-2, and the obligatory photos of the President and Vice President hung on the wall.

Agency psychologists had carefully selected each element in the suite to serve multiple purposes. The message they subtly infused into the design and decor was one of well-earned superiority—we're the CIA and you *will* do as we say.

As we approached him, Director Richard Duncan was standing behind his desk watching silently as two female electronics technicians packed up the remainder of their equipment and rolled their cart out of his office.

The green polo shirts the women wore sported the famed fly-swatter logo of the Directorate of Science and Technology's Technical Security Counter-Measures team. They're the electronic security experts who sweep Agency offices and vehicles for surreptitious microphones, cameras, or other unauthorized surveillance devices—bug hunting, in the vernacular.

Their obvious familiarity with the room made it clear that these women scanned it frequently and served as the regular crew Richard

Duncan had become used to entrusting with such a vital task. I'm sure the Director had his suite swept for bugs on both a regular schedule and at random times. I did not have to guess that this occasion was neither of those. Clearly, the Director wanted to take no chances anyone could possibly overhear the discussion we were about to have.

Several photos hung from the wall opposite the Director's desk. In one, Duncan wore a Key West baseball cap while standing in front of a boat in a marina. Next to him stood a round-faced woman—his wife, I presumed—in a pink Miami Beach tank top. In another photo, the Director stood in the Oval Office next to the President as they shook hands and smiled big, politician-sized grins.

That morning, there was no smile on the Director's face. Instead, his lips were drawn thin and the ends of his mouth turned up. As the saying goes, things were about to get real.

The Director motioned for us to sit around his circular conference table. Michael pulled out a chair for me before taking the adjacent seat. What a gentleman!

A new voice spoke from the doorway. "Thank you, ladies." I watched as Dagmar Bhoti entered and closed the door behind her, shutting out the TSCM sweep team. The first female chief of counterintelligence in the Agency's history, her sandy hair not much longer than a military crew cut, wore one of her characteristic gray pant suits. Her reputation for being a pit bull resounded throughout the agency. Her reputation for having no fashion sense whatsoever was also right on target, I saw, certain to keep that opinion entirely to myself.

The CI Center that Dagmar had run for the previous two years is CIA's version of Internal Affairs. They hunt down spies within our ranks. Relentless in their pursuit, CIC is charged with finding both technical leaks of information as well as human traitors. Technical vulnerabilities can usually be countered with our own application of technology, whether it's an electronic signal jammer or additional sound insulation applied to the walls of offices. Traitors are turned over to the FBI for prosecution.

Echoes of the Aldrich Ames investigation that Dagmar led in the early- and mid-1990s as the then-deputy chief of the CIC still echoed through some corridors of the Agency. Even a casual mention of Ames' name is enough to send shivers down the spines of many career Agency officers. The damage he did to CIA's technical collection capabilities and—perhaps especially—the agents-in-place who were executed by Russia because of his treachery set CIA's intelligence collection efforts there back a decade. Dagmar Bhoti earned her well-deserved reputation from her handling of that monster of a case.

As much grief as most employees give CI officers, we know deep down that Dagmar Bhoti and her staff don't just keep foreign spies at bay—they keep our agents and officers alive.

I've never met him, but Dagmar's husband, Dr. Samuel Bhoti, had the reputation for being one of the best cardiac surgeons in the DC area. The joke around the Agency was that you never wanted to find yourself in the unenviable position of having either one of them looking into you too deeply.

Michael maintained a perfectly neutral expression as Dagmar sat down. He was an experienced intelligence officer with a practiced poker face. Even having worked with him closely for years, I still had difficulty reading him sometimes. What he was not controlling well that morning were his eye movements. The rapid shifting of his gaze from Duncan to Bhoti betrayed his discomfort with her presence. Clearly, the Director had not told Michael in advance that Dagmar Bhoti would be joining us. Duncan was about to let someone new in on the secret of Michael's team and what we do. Michael did not fancy that, I sensed.

For the first time, I would get to see the reaction of another officer when she learned that we sometimes go well past just bending the rules and straight away to shattering them completely. This seemed like a big risk for the Director to take, but I suppose that's why he gets paid the big bucks. If things go badly, though, I wasn't quite sure where that would leave me or Michael. As instructed, I planned to mostly watch, listen, and nod.

Director Duncan rolled his chair next to Dagmar, who sat directly across the table from me. "Mike, after we spoke, I briefed Dagmar on my decision. I want her to give you two the same threat assessment she gave me last week and come to a consensus on what happens next. Do you want to introduce your team, first?"

Michael lifted his hand, palm up, gesturing to me to speak for myself.

"I'm Eden." I hadn't planned to say that—not at all. Those two short words have become so central to my life since the moment they jumped from my mouth of their own volition.

Michael's head tilted a bit in surprise. It was slight enough that the others wouldn't notice, but I caught his uncharacteristic display of emotion out of the corner of my eye.

I'd never used that name before and, in fact, didn't even consider it a name. A nickname, at best. Or a codename invented on the spot, maybe? Even I didn't know.

My ad lib was a knee-jerk done entirely in self-defense, not something planned in advance. The moment the word passed through my lips, a wretched fear cascaded over me that if things went sideways, I could suddenly have the Agency's CI chief looking to stick my head on a pike as the scapegoat for whatever Michael was about to send me to do. If that happened, I'd need every second I could buy using such an alias to have a better chance of getting away. It was a completely ridiculous thought; there would be little chance of getting away if it came to that, but, regardless, it's a thoroughly beautiful name.

"Eden," Michael said smiling, "is an experienced operator and is up to the task at hand."

After we all said our polite and obligatory "Good Mornings," Dagmar opened the clasp of the large brown envelope she held. On the polished conference table, she placed two color photographs of men seated in front of American flags. Each photo had the words SECRET NOFORN stamped across its top and bottom. I recognized them immediately as the kind of official employee portraits retained in government agencies' personnel files. The red, white, blue, and green logo of the Defense Intelligence Agency, DIA, sat in the upper-left-hand corner of each photo.

The classification stamp and markings stating that the photos were not releasable to foreign nationals told me these were DIA's official portraits of a pair of undercover officers. The men were members of what at the time was called the Defense HUMINT Service.

Dagmar rotated the photos and gently pushed them into the center of the conference table so Michael and I could see the two faces clearly.

"DIA officers Boggs and Srivinian were killed last year in South Africa, and the perpetrators have not yet been identified. They were both assigned as Non-Official Cover Case Officers working HUMINT collection on a Five-Eyes counter-proliferation Joint Task Force in Johannesburg. The JTF focuses on detecting and interdicting the transfer of nuclear weapons design and engineering information and materiel from those who previously worked on the now-shuttered South African nuclear program to other countries. In short, they're trying to prevent knowledge useful for building nuclear weapons from making its way to Pakistan, North Korea, or Iran.

"Even though neither were CIA officers, we provide integral support to other agencies' undercover programs. When something goes wrong, we get involved. Whether it's a cover getting blown or operations compromised, my office looks into it from a counterintelligence angle to assess the damage or uncover a penetration. In this case, two officers whose cover we supported were killed by an unknown party in what appears to have been a professional manner. Until very recently, however, we didn't know what connection, if any, there was to the US Intelligence Community."

"As you can imagine," Director Duncan interrupted, "I've been drinking from the proverbial firehose in the nine weeks I've been here." He ran his hand nervously over the few thin strands of hair remaining on top of his head. The sides of his head, in contrast, were downright bushy, a clear compensation for what he lacked above. "This was one of the first major issues I was presented with in my first week, and we've been working it non-stop. Dagmar and her team, of course, have been working on this since last year. She has done a terrific job piecing the puzzle together. Go ahead and give them the background on North Korea."

"Yes, sir," Dagmar said, settling back into her cadence. "The head of the JTF is the Canadians' Chief of Station in Johannesburg, Stuart Fenner. About three months ago, through analysis of information we received from the JTF and additional information our own Clandestine Service collected independently, we grew suspicious of Mr. Fenner. I won't go into the details, but essentially what we were hearing from the JTF about the deaths of the officers did not align with what we were able to develop ourselves. That was enough for the Director to authorize a highly sensitive operation against Fenner, even though he's a citizen of one of our Five-Eyes partners."

That intrigued me. Intelligence operations run against a close ally were so rare and sensitive that you never hear about them. The other four of the so-called "Five Eyes" nations—Britain, Canada, New Zealand, and Australia—are our closest allies. The US Intelligence Community simply doesn't spy on them. Duncan must have had a damned good reason for doing so, I thought.

The Director squirmed in his chair, clearly uneasy about the way events unfolded. Situations that developed years before he took the helm of the CIA were now his problem, but I didn't feel sorry for him at all. He wanted to sit in the big chair, so now he gets to deal with the big problems. For the life of me, I could not imagine why anyone would ever want to be a manager. Whenever something goes right, good bosses give the credit to the people who did the work and, when something goes wrong, the good ones take the blame themselves. To me, it always seemed like a lose-lose proposition. Budgets and blame, that's all management positions bring.

Michael remained expressionless as Dagmar continued to unfold her story for us. The Director must have briefed him the previous week, and he was hearing much of it for the second time.

"The closely held operation Director Duncan authorized against Fenner," Dagmar continued, "involved a deniable team of contractors from the Special Activities Division entering his residence surreptitiously. First, they swept it for listening devices and cameras and found none. Then, they placed our own devices in his apartment and inside the heels of several pairs of his dress shoes. We monitored him for almost two months and discovered that what we feared was indeed the case."

"As you can imagine," Richard Duncan interjected, "the very idea that we would collect against another Five-Eyes nation is abhorrent. The fact that we did must never be revealed beyond those who already know. The information we collected was compelling and made the risk worth it. Please, continue."

"We never learned anything while monitoring his apartment," Dagmar went on. "However, the team recorded two meetings Fenner had with a North Korean intelligence officer assigned to their embassy in Johannesburg. The conversations were blunt and incriminated both Fenner and the North Korean, who turned out to be his handler. Pyongyang had turned Fenner. We don't know how long he has been feeding them information from the JTF or anything else we share with the Canadians—which is quite a lot, as you can imagine—but specific reference to the two DIA officers was made. Pyongyang has turned at least one retired South African nuclear scientist into a source for them on nuclear warhead design. Fenner's information is helping to protect their source, which in turn is supporting the advance of the North's weapons research and development program."

Duncan smacked his hand on the arm of his chair. "It was Fenner who fingered our people to the Koreans—the North Koreans, I mean. Fenner got our people killed. He's still the head of the JTF and in a position to divulge the identities of many of our officers and agents across much of Africa, putting them all at unacceptable risk. And not just ours, of course, but DIA's and those from the other Five-Eyes nations, as well. I cannot allow that to continue."

I could see where this was headed. The most obvious options were to turn Fenner against the North Koreans, have him arrested by the

Canadians, or, since Michael and I were sitting at the conference table, kill him. Either of the first two options sounded good to me, but sure as the sun was rising outside the Director's seventh floor window, I already knew that they'd settled on what was 'behind door number three.' My right foot nervously tapped the floor under the table. I uncrossed and recrossed my legs to keep it under control, hoping the others would not notice my growing discomfort.

Duncan continued. "That put me in a bind. We can't use the information in open court to prosecute him for complicity in the murders of two Americans because we'd have to expose how we got it. I can't admit to Ottawa that I authorized collection against their Chief of Station. As bad as creating an international incident with *them* would be, I fear that it would hurt our relationship with the British even more. Since Fenner doesn't work for us, it's not as though I can transfer him somewhere harmless, either."

Duncan fixed his eyes on Michael and continued more slowly. "Mike, you told me when you first briefed me about your team that your operations have never been compromised. As bad as it would be to admit we collected against a Canadian—even if he is a traitor—having anyone discover that I authorized something like this would be the end of everything. I'm trying to *save* lives here, not create even bigger problems for us."

Michael responded calmly. "Correct. We have never had any of our operations compromised. I have a very small and highly specialized team of dedicated officers, such as Eden. I can't claim that we get our targets one hundred percent of the time. We don't. But we've never been exposed."

I thought hard to figure out what was bothering me most about the conversation so far. Was it that my target was a fellow intelligence officer from one of our closest allies, or that the Director of the Central Intelligence Agency couldn't bring himself to say the word *kill*?

If you can't say it, you can't do it. Of course, it wasn't his task to do. The whole mess would soon be dumped in my lap, and I didn't appreciate the way he tiptoed around the edges. Maybe my distaste for the mission I knew in my gut was soon to come was coloring my view of the new Director. Or maybe I was doing him a disservice. But at that point in the morning, I simply didn't care. The clock hanging on the wall between pictures of a boat and a president showed it wasn't even six o'clock yet, and I already wanted the day to end.

Richard Duncan nodded slightly in Michael's direction. "So, I decided that the talents of your team would be best to retire him involuntarily. Your way."

There, he said it. Or at least got as close as he ever would, using a terrible euphemism. Whatever makes him feel better about having made that decision, I thought. It made my skin crawl that he didn't have the guts to just come right out and say it, but if that's what he needed to tell himself so he could sleep better, then I guess that's all we'd get out of the man.

"It should be something quick," Duncan continued. "I mean, I don't want him to suffer, you know?"

Duncan wiped a drop of sweat from his brow and Dagmar shifted in her seat, disturbed by the severity of the event she was conspiring to commit.

Good, I thought, *he should be uncomfortable about this whole thing. Damned right, they both should be.* Part of me enjoyed watching the pair of senior executives squirm.

"Quick is messy," I said, speaking for the first time in more than a half-hour. With all eyes on me, I completed the thought, "and usually suspicious. Clean is slow. You need to decide what you want it to look like. Or at least what you're willing to live with it looking like. Natural causes? Accident? Mugging gone bad?"

I used the phrase "willing to live with" intentionally. I wanted them to think again about the gravity of what they were talking about doing. What they were talking about *my* doing, anyway.

Director Duncan choose his words carefully and asked slowly, "What are some of the options?"

I answered calmly, but with an edge to my voice. "Poisons, pistols, or pushes. With the right poison, it can look like a heart attack or a drug overdose. On the surface, that may sound clean, but that's not necessarily the case. All poisons are detectable, if you know what you're looking for. In any country, the death of a foreign diplomat is going to get the highest level of scrutiny. In this case, from both the host country and then a Canadian coroner when his body is returned home. That means a thorough toxicology analysis by RCMP's crime lab and, if they ask us for help, then by the FBI's lab at Quantico, as well. Poisons are risky, even if we use one of our own from DS&T. I don't think the FBI knows about all of those, but why risk it? If they were to find it, it could come back on us. Not good."

Duncan agreed. "No, not good at all. 'Pistols' I understand, but what exactly do you mean by 'pushes?'"

"Under the proverbial bus, down the stairs, off the roof, in front of a moving train, or, in the movies anyway, down an open elevator shaft. That kind of thing. In general, shaping events to appear accidental." I tried hard to not make it sound like a joke. "It's actually harder to arrange accidents than you'd think. There are also plenty of opportunities for witnesses or bystanders to get hurt. Rifle shots and car bombs look too obviously like targeted killings—"

Dagmar cut in. "Eden, earlier, you said 'mugging gone bad.' If not a mugging, exactly, what about a home-invasion robbery? We know exactly where he lives, what alarm is installed in his apartment, what kind of pistol he was issued—a 9mm Beretta, by the way. You can bypass an alarm system, right?"

I didn't answer her verbally. I could only manage to tilt my head in disbelief that she would even ask such a question. I have a real problem with people not believing that I train hard and have developed my skills through blood, sweat, and yes, tears.

"Yes, she can," Michael said, drawing attention away from my rather critical attitude. "Knowing the make and model would help, thank you."

"I can get you the access code from the previous SAD team that installed and removed our listening devices, if you want."

"No need," I said. "While that would be appropriate for another clandestine entry, in this case it could end up being a red flag leading people to ask questions that we don't even want verbalized. I can take care of any household alarm."

"Yes, alright," Dagmar said, realizing that I was certainly right. I'm sure she was just trying to help by surfacing ideas for the group. Clearly, she'd never planned a murder before.

"People get robbed all the time," Duncan said more as a conclusion than a suggestion. "Dagmar, do you know how many US Embassy staffers get robbed in any given year? Any staffer, I mean. State Department, military attachés, our folks—"

"Yes, it's about ten or twelve a year worldwide. Only one or two are CIA and some of those incidents are simply broken windows or thefts from an unattended vehicle. Whenever an incident happens to Agency officers or their families, my team investigates to see if there could be a state sponsor or terrorist group behind it and not just a random crime. Our security division investigates, too, and of course, so does State's Bureau of Diplomatic Security. The Canadians do the same thing for their people and we share information frequently in such matters, especially for violent crimes. No host government ever wants to see something happen to a foreign diplomat on their soil or suffer an international backlash because of a bungled inquiry, so it's always a very thorough investigation. The South Africans will put their A-Team on it."

Dagmar looked at the Director and caught on to what he was actually asking. "I can't shut down another agency's investigation, but what I can do is have my team come to a quick conclusion that it was nothing more than a robbery gone bad. If we're the first to come to that particular conclusion when it was an officer with whom we have such a close relationship—after a reasonable length of time, of course—then it could give the other investigating teams some political cover to come to the same conclusion themselves. We can't direct, but we can influence. Yes, that could work."

We all sat quietly for a short time and looked around asking with eyes instead of words for any competing suggestions. The shifting gazes made clear the lack of interest in dragging the discussion out any further. The discussion had reached its inevitable conclusion. *This sucks,* I thought and gave a mental sigh.

Early in the conversation, I had guessed the likely outcome, and even so, couldn't offer an alternative to the despicable task at hand. At *my* hand. I'll never know if with more time to think I could have done better.

For the first time that morning, Director Duncan turned his shoulders squarely towards me and asked without actually asking if I would kill Stuart Fenner. "Will you go?"

At least he had the guts to look me in the eye. That said something about him. Can't say the guy doesn't have a backbone.

I enunciated each word of my response clearly. "If Michael says to go, then I will go." I turned to look at my boss, confident that the other two Agency executives got the not-so-subtle message that he's the man from whom I take direction. I specifically did not say *when* Michael said to go—but rather *if.* That they both turned to look at Michael made it clear the difference had not been lost on either Duncan or Bhoti.

"There are some logistics to attend to, and Eden will have to practice on the specific alarm model, first. She will be on a plane inside of a week, sir."

"Good," Richard Duncan said, nodding. He placed his palms flat on the conference table to signal that he had made his decision and was satisfied with the plan. He stood and announced quietly, "I hope I don't have to remind you all that this conversation never took place."

How trite, I thought.

Michael waited until we left the Director's suite and got a half-dozen yards down the hall before looking at me. "Eden, eh?"

"Yeah." That morning's conversation and the mission in front of me left me in no mood to even fake a smile. "Something about this whole thing made me really uncomfortable right from the beginning. The thought of giving them my real name didn't sit well with me. I don't know why. It was a hunch, I guess, which turned out to be right. I just said the first thing that popped into my mind. I grew up in Gardena, California. Gardena... Garden of Eden.... It's that simple and probably seems silly to you."

"No," Michael said, nodding and smiling his approval as we arrived at the elevators. "I like it. It suits you. *Eden* it is."

The moment the elevator doors closed, I spun on my heel and looked up to give Michael a piece of my mind. The tone of my voice made my distaste for the assignment plain. "So, is *this* what we've become now? We go after our own allies?"

I would never confront him in public or undermine him in front of outsiders, especially other Agency executives. In private, though, I could be more transparent with him.

CIA Directors come and go every few years and change with the political winds, but Michael was a fixture within the SAD. Directors can think all they want that they're the ones who give the orders, but those few people in the Agency who know Michael need to know that only *he* can truly green-light a killing. Claude, Arnaud, and I are all happy to help him cultivate the image of powerbroker and king-maker.

And now the Director had added Dagmar Bhoti to the short list of those who knew the truth about our team. Michael had clearly not planned on that happening. I wondered what that might mean for us.

Still looking straight ahead, Michael added, "You heard the same damage assessment upstairs that I did. This guy has been wreaking havoc in Africa, is helping spread nuclear weapons to a highly unstable nation and gave up information that led to the murders of two undercover officers. You're going to put a stop to the damage he's causing, and in the process, hopefully prevent any other innocent people from getting killed. Right?"

He turned to look me in the eye.

Even when I'm wearing high heels, Michael is still four inches taller than I am. That he had to physically look down *to* me to lock eyes did not translate to him figuratively looking down *at* me. He respected me and knew full well that I saw the necessity of the situation. I just needed him to hear me out first. He understood he had to give me the emotional outlet I required. I couldn't talk about these things to Steven, so Michael did well to accommodate my occasional need to vent. He's my mentor and I'm his protégée. He knows me well enough to know what buttons to push when he needs to, and what stroking is occasionally necessary to soothe the emotional reactions he gets from me that he doesn't get from either of the men on the team.

"*Right*?" he asked again, more insistently.

"Right," I responded more calmly, "but I don't have to like it."

"I would worry if you did," he reflected.

That, I knew, was experience talking, and I appreciated his validation of my disdain for this mission.

"And if I'm flying all the way to South frickin' Africa, you're paying for a first-class ticket."

"And that's what the Trust Fund is for," he said, smirking at my petulance.

When the elevator doors opened on the first floor, Michael exited first. He strolled off to do whatever it is that managers do, probably shifting the Agency's covert logistics machine into high gear for this short-notice mission. He'd make sure that the right car would be left for me at the airport with my weapons, lock picks, alarm bypass kit, and so on. He knew what he had to do to kick the Logs team into motion. He wasn't being cold or unfeeling about the mission, just practical. He knew he had to give me some time and space to come to terms with my latest assignment.

I, however, felt as though I'd been emotionally ambushed upstairs. Michael must have already known for a few days what the Director had in mind. I needed some time to become comfortable enough with my assignment to be able to go do what he was sending me halfway around the world to accomplish.

No one had asked me to enjoy this mission, and I sure as shit was not going to. Somewhere deep down, the strength existed for me to carry through with it—I just had to find it. Or, if it didn't already exist, then somehow I had to create it from sheer willpower alone.

I stepped out of the elevator and looked down what seemed like a mile-long hallway from the Original Headquarters Building, past the cafeteria and Starbucks, and into the New Headquarters Building. People were arriving for the start of their workweek, while for me it felt as though I'd already had a bruiser of a day. I could easily imagine that

Stuart Fenner had walked these same hallways a dozen times while visiting CIA headquarters to confer with our Case Officers over the fourteen years of his career with the Canadian Security Intelligence Service. A career that I would soon be ending.

I checked my watch and cursed aloud at the realization that Starbucks wouldn't open for another ten minutes. Not that I needed the caffeine at that point, but I decided that a big cup of coffee would be my guilty pleasure for the day. With caramel *and* whipped cream, damn it! It had not been a good morning. Perhaps a guilty pleasure would assuage some of the actual guilt I felt about the task ahead of me.

With a few more minutes still to waste, I meandered along the hallway and surveyed the length of wall where paintings of all previous CIA Directors hang. I scanned the line of portraits of the men—all of them men, so far. Their looks varied greatly over the years. Some wore military uniforms while others dressed in now-dated suits which were the styles of their day. Generals, Admirals, and even a former President. For the most part, not a bad-looking group.

I pondered the orders that some of them might have had to give during their tenures on the seventh floor. Alone with my thoughts, I wondered how many had chosen to give an order such as the one I had just received from the man whose portrait would one day hang on the far end of that same wall.

To the left of the portrait of the CIA's first director, Major General William "Wild Bill" Donovan, a large mural of the Statue of Liberty caught my eye. The phrase painted in large letters adjacent to her jade crown struck me as if Lady Liberty were coldly mocking me, both personally and professionally: *We are the nation's first line of defense. We accomplish what others cannot accomplish and go where others cannot go.*

We do what others cannot do, I mentally paraphrased the well-worn saying so often repeated across the Agency.

Or, in this case, I added to myself with a heavy heart, *what others would not dream of doing.*

Chapter 18

The silver Audi sat parked in the garage outside Terminal A of Johannesburg's Tambo International Airport—right where the field note from Logs said it would be.

I frowned while dropping my carry-on suitcase into the empty trunk. I hate not being able to see my equipment. Life is so much easier when I can see that my gear made it. That way, I know that I'm good to go. When Logs conceals it inside a door or the back seat of the vehicle, I have to wait hours until after shaking any surveillance that might be watching me before checking to see it's all there. If it's not, no sweat off my back, I'd hop on the next flight home, and my mission is over. But it's always there. I've never had to abort a mission for lack of equipment. Never.

I just have a personal inner-need to see it with my own eyes. To wrap my fingers around it. To feel comfortable with it. To trust that I'll be able to bet my life on it, because that's what it truly is. But it's always there. Always. It helps immensely to know I've never been let down by the invisible men and women of the Logistics teams. But still, seeing is believing.

I closed the trunk and sighed with the realization that I had to go through with it after all.

I climbed into the driver's seat, adjusted the mirrors, and settled in for a four-hour jaunt around Jo'burg running a full surveillance detection route to identify and lose anyone who might try to follow me.

Counterintelligence is a fact of life that we deal with everywhere in the world. Host-country surveillance teams will occasionally pick arriving passengers almost at random to follow. Sometimes it's just for practice, sometimes it's because of something suspicious in the traveler's airline record, and sometimes it's based on nothing more than a hunch. Today of all days was not the time I wanted some well-meaning surveillance instructor to randomly pick me to sic his class on for practice.

I eased the car out of the garage for a few hours of "dry cleaning" myself on highways and side streets, angling in and about among the four-million residents of the Greater Johannesburg Metropolitan Area.

***

The mild summer afternoon seemed to bring out the entire neighborhood around Fenner's apartment complex. I wanted to make my entry no later than 3 p.m. and was a bit ahead of my self-imposed schedule. I assumed he would still be at work and figured that left me four to six hours to prepare before he arrived home. Plenty of time.

As I walked along the sidewalk, I hefted my large handbag over my left shoulder. The sizable purse looked much like any other, but this Agency-issued one concealed the many tools of my particular trade. How do men carry all this stuff when they'd look out of place with a bag in hand? A briefcase works sometimes, sure, but maybe they just get good at hiding everything under a suit jacket. Seems awkward to me when a purse is so much more practical. After all, it's specifically made for carrying stuff. *My* stuff. For me, it works perfectly well and never looks out of place.

I watched as children scurried about, playing on the small lawns in front of the apartment buildings. This must be their school vacation, I thought. I knew before leaving the States that it was summer in South Africa, but hadn't realized so many kids would be around. I was going to have to watch out for them.

Inside Fenner's building, I walked down the hallway towards his apartment while getting a good grip on the lock-pick gun in my pocket. I picked the lock on his door in five squeezes of the trigger mechanism—not bad, I reflected, grading my own performance. The pick gun clicked a bit louder than I would have preferred, but Fenner's door had a high-quality six-pin Schlage lock I had to defeat as rapidly as possible. A little noise was worth the small risk. His lock and door handle were a different model than any of the others I could see along the hallway. Clearly the Canadian Embassy's security team had replaced the apartment's consumer-grade unit with their own higher security model.

I dropped the pick gun into my purse, reached inside and got the alarm kit ready before pushing the door open. The alarm would only give me thirty seconds to disable it before things went to hell in a South African handbasket. With my purse on my left shoulder and gloved hand inside it griping a small crowbar, I depressed the door handle with my right thumb and pushed the apartment door forward.

Three soft beeps announced that the alarm system was active and armed. Just as expected.

Here we go, I told myself encouragingly as I pushed the door firmly closed. *Thirty seconds starts now, Michelle.*

My fastest practice run—twenty-two seconds—didn't give me much time to spare. I knew I had to work even faster this time since the stress of a real-life break-in makes everything more difficult than during practice in the safety of a sterile classroom. *Move, girl, move!*

The alarm's keypad glowed on the exterior wall to my left. Two steps further down the short entry hallway, the coat closet sat closed with a paper shopping bag dangling from the doorknob.

Ignore the keypad, I ordered myself, *and go for the control panel in the closet.*

I dropped my purse to the floor beside the closet door, gripped the crowbar in my left hand tightly, and flung the closet open with my right.

Crap!

The coat closet contained everything in the world except the hanging coats I expected to see. Stacked cardboard boxes stood taller than I am. Damn it! Fenner hadn't finished unpacking after, what, a year? He clearly used the closet as his "out of sight, out of mind" storage space for the "I'll get to it eventually" boxes. Men! Why can't they finish a job when they start it? When you start unpacking, you keep going until everything is in its proper place. You don't just shove everything into the closet to wait for "someday."

Beep. Beep. Beep. Twenty-five seconds.

I tossed box after cardboard box down the hall, further into the apartment. I no longer even tried to maintain any kind of sound discipline. Better for the neighbors to hear me tossing boxes than for them to hear the screeching of the alarm system that was going to happen in....

Beep. Beep. Beep. Twenty seconds.

The control panel hung on the back wall of the closet, right where it should be. I pulled the cover slightly just to check, and as expected, it didn't budge. The embassy's installation team had left it locked. Okay, no problem. They did their jobs well.

The thin sheet metal of the case proved no match for my crowbar. The left side of the cover popped off its hinges easily, leaving the lock attached on the other side of the cover and, critically, keeping the anti-tamper wire connected. The designers of the Honeywell ATX-7 alarm system accounted for the occasional clever thief when they created the ATX line—a considerably more advanced model than most residential users would ever consider buying.

The Canadians install first-rate equipment to protect their employees' homes overseas, I thought while propping the bottom of the cover up with the middle of my right thigh. *But nothing's perfect. Anything that can be built by a man can be undone by a woman,* I silently reminded myself, smiling at the thought.

Just as I'd practiced at the Farm, I pulled a yard-long blue wire from my purse and slid my hand inside the alarm case to feel for the anti-tamper wire's connector on the now free-hanging case door. I found it right where it should be, next to the lock mechanism. I pinched the alligator clip on my bypass wire and applied it to the connector on the lock. I affixed the alligator clip on the other end of my blue wire to the circuit board. It snapped cleanly onto the third post from the left on the circuit board's maintenance port, completing the bypass of the anti-tamper subsystem.

I lifted the now-disarmed cover safely off the case and peered inside. I let out a breath of relief when I saw the familiar integrated circuit board. Dagmar Bhoti's information on the model and configuration of the alarm system was spot on. As a double-check, I scanned the circuit board occupying the top half of the box, the gray metal loudspeaker in the lower right, and the folded clamshell-style cell phone in the lower left. Perfect—the exact model I practiced on.

Beep. Beep. Beep. Fifteen seconds.

Shit. Halfway there.

Move! I urged silently, coaxing myself forward.

I yanked the pair of insulated wire cutters out of my purse, knelt, and pulled myself the rest of the way into the bottom of the closet in my ongoing race against the clock. At that point, I knew the clock was winning.

Around the loudspeaker, I saw the familiar rainbow of wires running from the controlling circuit board to the speaker underneath. While practicing over the previous week, this is where things got tricky. To get to the green wire, I slipped the small wire cutters beneath the top of the speaker with my right hand and reached underneath the assembly with my left. With that little cheat completed, I squeezed the handles together, snipping the power wire in half. Done.

The black ground wire protruded more. I easily reached that one with my left hand alone. Another snip. Done.

Beep. Beep. Beep. Ten seconds.

If the alarm sounded at that point, I realized, doing a quick worst-case analysis, my having cut the siren out of the system would keep it silent in the apartment, but with the cellphone still attached, the Canadian Diplomatic Technical Security Service watch desk at the embassy downtown would be getting a data burst about an alarm activation in nine seconds.

Faster, Michelle, faster! While not all that original, it was the most motivational speech I could muster under the circumstances.

Two cables led into the small cellphone which sat affixed to the case. Fortunately, plenty of space surrounded that little monster. I skipped over the power cable and lifted the flat ribbon data cable attached to the bottom of the phone, pulling it the last inch it would stretch. That's where the data burst would go, from my left hand to the embassy watch in....

Beep. Beep. Beep. Five seconds.

I cut the eight wires in the wide ribbon cable as if my life depended on it. Maybe it did. I didn't want to find out what would happen if the alarm's report got through successfully.

Snip. Cut. Snip.

Faster!

The ribbon cable fell away, and I yanked the power cable out of the phone for good measure.

The sudden buzz from the alarm system's keypad startled me. The audible signal of my failure reverberated down the short hallway. I thrust my way out of the closet and jumped to my feet faster than I'd ever leapt before. I ripped the keypad off the wall and jammed it speaker-first against my body. As best I could, I muffled the plastic speaker grill with my left breast.

With absolutely no regard for which was which—power, signal, or ground—I cut the three wires that dangled between the keypad and the wall one by one. The buzzing stopped as the third wire dropped away, and I could finally breathe again.

Mentally exhausted, I slumped against the front door to catch my breath. I turned my head slowly from side to side, listening for any sounds in the hallway behind me. I had difficulty hearing anything over the near-deafening drumbeat of my pounding heart.

I reached inside my purse for my gun in case someone got curious enough to investigate.

Thirty-three seconds earlier, I had entered the apartment from a vacant hallway. Was the hallway still empty? Had anyone heard the keypad buzz? I strained my ears for any noise that might filter through the door behind me.

Would anyone even recognize the sound as an alarm since it wasn't the siren wail that the larger speaker I'd already disabled would have made? For all I knew, Fenner might be the only person in the building to have an alarm. They were not exactly luxury apartments. His ex-wife back in Canada likely got a significant portion of his salary each month. Perhaps all Fenner could afford was a small apartment in a middle-income building.

I focused on talking myself into thinking everything was going to be okay. Besides, the buzzing sounded more like an alarm clock or loud kitchen timer than a burglar alarm, didn't it? Even if someone had heard it, would they bother to investigate? I might not find out until it was already too late. A neighbor knocking at the door would be bad enough. I could ignore that, and they'd eventually go away. But if it ended up being the local police responding to the call of an alarm sounding, well, that would definitely suck. For both of us.

I detested the fact that I had to kill an allied intelligence officer that night. I certainly did not want anyone else getting involved. Even if everything went exactly as planned, my mission to South Africa would be hard enough for me to live with. Another death on top of Fenner's would make the whole affair a failure in my eyes, especially if my being two or three seconds too slow in disabling the alarm caused it.

Wow, I needed more practice with alarms. Electronics are not my strong suit. Although I don't have to defeat alarms in the field all that often, for someone whose cover is a Technical Penetration Specialist, I didn't feel this lived up to what I was sure Michael expected of me.

I looked at the cardboard boxes strewn about the hallway and decided to blame Fenner. *Clean your damned apartment, dude. Don't just shove everything that doesn't fit elsewhere into the front closet.*

The *thump-thump*ing of my heart that had pulsated in my ears slowed. The lack of a knock at the door during the couple of minutes I'd been sitting on the floor gave me the reassurance needed to feel no one would come around asking questions. I felt confident enough to continue my mission.

I stood up and inhaled deeply a few times while setting about to inspect Fenner's apartment. My walk through the modestly furnished open floor plan of the combined kitchen-dining-living room and the sole bedroom lasted all of ten seconds.

I weaved my way past cardboard boxes back to the front door and looked at the keypad lying on the floor. Options for how to doctor up the damaged alarm system floated through my mind. It had to look good for Fenner. *And the cops*, I reminded myself. They had to believe the story too.

I tucked the three brightly colored wires into the small hole in the wall from which their severed halves awkwardly protruded and angled the keypad back onto its bracket. It mated with a pleasing *click*. I tugged at the keypad a bit, but not too hard. The bracket held well enough. I didn't intend to give Fenner enough time to examine it in great detail before I....

Skipping the thought that would complete that sentence and my mission, I looked over my makeshift reconstruction. It would pass Fenner's cursory examination.

I could not say the same for the control panel in the closet. Fenner had a relatively sophisticated Honeywell alarm system for an apartment, but not something out of the league of a decent burglary team.

I looked over my handiwork and nodded in self-admiration to no one in particular. *I did a nice, clean bypass job, if I do say so myself. I'll need to work faster next time,* I admitted, critiquing myself modestly, but considered the end result a success.

The blinking LEDs remained the only visual clue to the silent scream going on inside the control panel's circuit board. It reached out repeatedly, demanding the attention of anyone who understood what it was so urgently trying in vain to report. Reds and greens blinked fast, then slow, then fast again. Green and red... repeating endlessly.

The rhythmic blinking of the lights, hypnotic in their forlorn cry for attention, cast me back to my lab classes at the Farm. Jack, our class's electronics instructor, somehow successfully taught those of us who could do little more with electronics than flip a light switch how to set and disable the entry-level alarm systems that every student learned to bypass. I think it was his dry sense of humor that, amazingly in my case, made the class enjoyable, if still puzzling.

I studied my craftwork hanging on the closet wall in front of me and finally understood what he was teaching us. "You only gain understand from doing," he'd say repeatedly, and now I could see that plain as day. The control circuit knew full well that someone had opened the front door but not tapped a valid disarm code into the keypad. The circuit furiously and futilely tried to send 110 decibels of ear-piercing sound through the severed loudspeaker and, at the same time, transmit its emergency data burst over the cell phone through the data cable which now sat cutaway and unreachable. The alarm's control system worked exactly as designed. It was broadcasting alerts via every available channel—channels I had cut right out of its electronic heart.

I ran my hand lightly over the severed ribbon cable and flicked it with my index finger while keeping its rended ends an inch apart—just in case.

One inch, I thought. That's all that stands between me and an apartment full of Diplomatic Security agents and Johannesburg's finest.

I thought it a shame to have to mess up such a nice alarm bypass. However, since the police had to conclude this was a home-invasion robbery gone wrong, I had to stage the crime scene appropriately. Or at least passably.

I levered the loudspeaker off the case with my crowbar and pressed the edge of the metal tool against the cuts in the wire to dirty up my earlier handiwork. I made a similar mess of the ribbon cable and retrieved my blue cable, returning it to my purse.

Done with the alarm. Good.

I withdrew from the closet and returned Fenner's boxes into their stacked configuration. With that completed, I closed the door and rehung the paper bag on the knob.

I placed the alarm kit back in my purse and followed it with my disguise—a wig of shoulder-length dishwater-blonde hair, silicone nose piece, and oversized glasses.

From the bottom of my purse, I retrieved my pistol and holster. The paddle holster for my .38 caliber revolver fit snugly into my waistband along my right hip. The speed-loader pouch with six extra rounds of ammunition I hoped I wouldn't need snapped easily onto my left. For my six-shooter, I brought along a smaller suppressor than is my norm since a .38 caliber weapon is quite a bit less powerful than a 9mm or .45. This mission, though, called for a revolver in particular.

I screwed the suppressor onto the barrel and spun the cylinder in which a half-dozen rounds of .38 Special jacketed hollow-point ammunition rested. The rapid clicking of the cylinder reminded me of baseball cards stuck into the spokes of a bicycle. I spun the cylinder again, enjoying the sound once more, just because I could.

A revolver doesn't leave shell casings behind and looks less professional than my usual 9mm would. Appearances mattered in this case, I reminded myself, glancing again at the closet door. Also, a .38 with a suppressor and the right subsonic ammo is virtually silent—a critical factor when planning to shoot someone in an apartment building where other tenants are just a wall or two away.

I holstered the revolver and set about to search the apartment before hunkering down behind the kitchen island to await Fenner's fateful return.

Chapter 19

The metallic scratching of a key being inserted into the door's lock brought my attention back to the kitchen. I'd been waiting for... how long? The black digits on my watch showed 9:34 p.m. I did some quick math and shook my head upon realizing how many hours I'd been pacing around Fenner's small apartment and sitting on the floor behind the island.

The moment I'd dreaded had finally arrived. Each hour I'd waited seemed to pass slower than the previous, and I just wanted to get the mission over with. I lifted the .38 and drew the hammer back in a single fluid, practiced motion as the weapon cleared my holster.

The slight slurring of Fenner's words foretold the beer I would soon be smelling on his breath. "Come on in. Close the door and lemme get the alarm."

And damn it, he wasn't alone!

If Director Duncan had made this an officially sanctioned mission, we would have had a full surveillance team on Fenner all day—hell, all week. But *noooo*, that's not my lot in life. I get all the one-woman jobs with far too many of what Arnaud calls WPWTs—Wrong Place, Wrong Time.

Crap!

A second man spoke over the sound of the front door latching closed. "Shouldn't it have beeped? Mine does. Hmm. The keypad's not lit up. Is it broken?"

"No," I said, standing up from behind the island. I pointed the .38 down the length of the apartment hallway and watched the faces of the two men who stood wide-eyed and frozen in front of me. I read the full measure of shock rippling across their faces. Awareness and fear spread through their minds and were displayed for all to see on faces which are usually, by necessity for men in their profession, expressionless. The horror of their situation became clear as they took stock of the intruder holding a rather ungainly revolver capped with a suppressor.

"The alarm was working just fine when I got here," I said, certain the humor would forever be lost in the moment. "Both of you, move into the living room and sit on the couch."

Fenner led the way while I trained my revolver on the second man. If he bolted for the door, he would get my first bullet of the night squarely in the center of his back. I recognized Fenner's companion from his photo in Dagmar Bhoti's file on the Joint Task Force in particular, and the Johannesburg Station, more generally. Douglas Benkert, CIA's Chief of Station in Johannesburg, trailed Fenner by three feet as they moved slowly from the entry hallway to the living room.

Benkert's eyes never left the gun in my hand. Clearly, this was the first time he'd ever been held at gunpoint in real life—not counting his initial Clandestine Service training at the Farm. Benkert was too fixated on the instrument of the threat and obviously didn't have the training or experience to focus not on the weapon, but on the person wielding it. The weapon was not a threat to him. *It* was not going to decide to shoot him. You can't talk a gun out of shooting you. The person wielding it is the threat, and that's who you have to deal with. *I* was the threat—couldn't he see that? He should have been paying more attention to me! Guess I'm just selfish that way sometimes.

Bhoti's file on Benkert said he'd spent his entire career as an intelligence collector. Not quite a desk jockey, but close enough to it by my way of thinking. Instead of focusing on the gun, he should have been looking at my eyes—my beautiful brown peepers—to try to anticipate what I was going to do and prepare himself to make his move against me when I inevitably turned my attention elsewhere. His eyes never left the revolver. I could tell right away that he posed no problem for me.

"Sit," I ordered my charges. "Opposite ends of the couch. Hands up all the way. Elbows straight."

Unable to use his hands to ease the drop from feet to seat, Fenner plopped awkwardly onto the couch. "What do you want? I don't have much money."

His question provided as good an opening for me as any. The open floor plan of the small apartment worked to my advantage. I rounded the kitchen island without hurrying while keeping my distance from the seated men who looked ridiculous sitting upright with their arms fully extended over their heads.

I aimed squarely at Benkert's chest, keeping my hands in the cup-and-saucer grip I'd learned as a girl on the firing ranges of Los Angeles with my father. I tightened my index finger against the trigger, taking the slack out of my grip.

I pivoted on the balls of my feet. The leather soles of my black ankle boots slid along the tile floor smoothly. Effortlessly, I transitioned my aim from Benkert's chest to Fenner's and squeezed. The trigger's single-action broke with little effort. The almost inaudible *pop* of the bullet sounded far quieter than Fenner's grunt and exhalation when the hollow-point bullet ripped into his chest.

A small red stain expanded across Fenner's button-down shirt, proving that my bullet found its mark just above his heart. The bullet most likely caused a non-survivable wound, I knew, considering the damage done to the major blood vessels around his heart by the mushrooming of the lead projectile now lodged somewhere inside him. Non-survivable, though, is not the same as immediately fatal in the way a headshot would have been.

Without waiting to cock the hammer, I squeezed the trigger again, more forcefully this time for the required double-action pull. My second round struck Fenner not far from the first.

I shifted my focus and aim to Benkert and said, "Don't move, Douglas. Do *not* move a muscle."

His panicked voice squeaked. "I'm not. I'm not. What the hell did you do that for? What do you want?" The sheer surprise of my shooting his host had overwhelmed his senses. No doubt his mind was screaming that this is not what happens to credentialed diplomats. His expectation of diplomatic duty being perfectly safe was crumbling before his eyes and paralyzing his ability to think under fire.

"You're still alive for a reason. Do not make me change my mind. Do you understand?"

"Yes," he said hoarsely, looking me in the eye for the first time. "What—"

"Shut up," I interrupted. "Sit still and be quiet. You're not out of the woods, yet," I calmly advised the local Chief of Station. More used to giving orders than taking them, his face betrayed his yearning to speak. To direct. To ask. But mostly to understand. His eyes revealed the alarm rising up his spine at the realization that his fate quite literally rested in my hands. He decided he was best off letting me speak first. It was not chivalry, just pragmatism.

Benkert nodded, taking to heart my advice for silence. He squirmed as if trying to merge his body with the arm of the couch and get as far away from the convulsing Fenner as possible. Fenner gurgled quietly at the other end of the sofa, languishing somewhere between being unable to breathe and not yet drowning in his own blood as it filled his lungs.

Not yet dead and probably in terrible pain, I thought, which did not sit well with me at all. Unfortunately for everyone involved, I couldn't finish him off with a clean headshot this time. I had to make the whole affair look more amateurish than that.

I maintained my aim at the American COS to disabuse him of any bad ideas as I moved. I approached Fenner's side of the sofa, aimed, and fired another shot into Benkert's fading colleague. Bullet number three penetrated Fenner's chest two inches or so below the first pair.

Bullet number four would be different. It had to be.

I watched Benkert closely to ensure his ongoing cooperation and lowered the end of the suppressor to within two inches of Fenner's abdomen. With one more pull of the trigger, I fired my fourth round into the Canadian spy. A shot from such a close range would ensure the forensics teams couldn't miss the powder burn on his shirt. A botched home invasion robbery would most likely have gone bad from close range at first. This little extra bit of evidence would make the story that much more believable.

I backed away and returned my attention and aim to Benkert. "Move to that chair in the corner. I don't want you to get blood on your clothes."

"Okay," the veteran CIA officer replied agreeably. Douglas Benkert's ashen face relaxed ever so slightly at what he felt was a good sign that I wanted him alive—for the time being anyway.

He knew he was not yet out of the woods. Beads of sweat stood out on his brow, and a sharp odor of abject fear drifted in my direction. The horror of the events of the previous minute held him fast. I wondered how much he would end up drinking at home later that night.

Although Benkert didn't realize it, he was seeing me without my disguise, and I had to decide what to do with him. "Now, what am I going to do with the Chief of Station who just saw me kill his friend, an allied nation's COS?" I asked rhetorically.

"Look, I—"

"Again, Douglas, shut up." I resumed my position against the kitchen island to stand between the cornered chief of CIA's South Africa office and his only avenue of escape. "Your covers at each embassy have nothing to do with each other. You're in the Cultural section of the US Embassy and he's in the Economic section of the Canadian Embassy. Why were you two even out together drinking tonight? You should be more careful about living your covers, no?"

I looked at Benkert's pale face as he watched Fenner's final exhale and became concerned that the man whose life I was trying to spare might end up passing out in the plush chair occupying the corner of the apartment. That'd make things more difficult for me than they needed to be.

"Look at me, Douglas, look at *me*. Eyes up here, big guy," I said earnestly, wanting to keep his gaze off of Fenner's body and his mind thinking about something other than the death of his friend. "Okay, Douglas, go ahead and ask me."

He tilted his head slightly to the side. "Ask you what?" At that instant, I firmly believed he was honestly and truly unsure. He really didn't know what I was talking about. I was shocked, but I could see that he was *in* shock.

"Why did I just kill your friend? Why haven't I killed you? Why did Madonna ever marry Sean Penn in the first place? Take your pick. Ask away."

Benkert's brown eyes squinted slightly. "Why did you kill him? He was a good man."

"I killed him because he was most definitely *not* a good man, Douglas. You just didn't know him well enough. Stuart Fenner made Aldrich Ames look like a boy scout," I exaggerated, possibly for my own benefit as much as his. "You remember Boggs and Srivinian from DIA last year? Fenner has been working for Pyongyang. He exposed DIA's NOCs to the North Koreans and got them killed. It fell to me to stop the bleeding and this way, it gets chalked up to a random act of crime that went from bad to worse—a botched home invasion robbery turned fatal. And now that you know the truth, you're going to help make the cover story about the death of your friend stick."

"Wait, how do you even know who we are?"

Holy cow! He hadn't figured it out? Sure, I hadn't been explicit, but come on. Wasn't it obvious? Or did he just want me to say it outright?

"We're on the same side, Douglas, and I know everything. I know it all. I know what your job is, and I know what Stuart's job is. I know where Fenner's ex-wife lives and where their kids go to school in Winnipeg. I know Fenner was providing intelligence from the JTF to the North Koreans. More importantly and on a more personal note, Douglas, I know where *you* live."

He looked at me more intensely for a moment, and I let that sink in for a few seconds before going on.

"Here's what's going to happen now. When I say so, you're going to go straight home tonight, pop an Ambien, and get a good night's sleep. You're going to need it. In the morning, you'll go to work as usual. Just another day behind your desk approving your Case Officers' cables and expense reports. When you hear about Fenner's death, you'll act shocked. Got it? *Shocked*. That will be the first you've heard of any of this. You're a professional liar, Douglas, that's what makes you good at recruiting agents. You'll pull it off, I have every confidence in you."

Benkert nodded.

"When you eventually talk to the Canadian Embassy's security agents or CSIS officers, do whatever you would normally do to help them. Other than telling them the truth, of course. Your life depends upon that. The story that's going to stick here is that this was a home invasion robbery gone bad. I did a job on the alarm up front and the two safes in the bedroom to make it look just like that. Understand?"

Benkert nodded again.

"Any questions?"

The Chief of Station shook his head and peered over at Fenner's body, still and quiet. A sullen expression looked etched into Benkert's face. Ironically, it was at that moment that he so desperately needed however many drinks he enjoyed earlier in the evening.

"One last thing before you go," I said, motioning for him to stand. "Just in case you get any stupid ideas about going to the cops, just remember that I have teammates you know nothing about but who know everything about you. Be smart and you'll be safe."

I was hoping for at least a nod from him, but he only pointed to the door.

"Go," I said, and lowered the revolver to my side.

Time would tell whether Douglas Benkert would be a problem for me or not.

Chapter 20

Thankfully, the British Airlines flight from Tambo to Heathrow lifted off right on time. Cradled in the soft gray leather of my first-class seat, I reclined half-way back as soon as the landing gear retreated into the fuselage.

The reassuring thump of the landing-gear doors locking closed in the fuselage beneath me is my personal finish line. I never truly relax until firmly back on US soil, but on board the plane, I was traveling alone, unarmed, and had nowhere to go but forward.

With no one chasing me and no way to escape even if they were, there was little worth worrying about at thirty-five thousand feet above the lush African plains. I removed my boots and soothed my feet in the tan comfort slippers to which first-class passengers are treated by their British hosts—the people who, while they didn't invent royal privilege, frequently brag about having perfected it, and for good reason. International first class is definitely the only civilized way to travel.

I enjoyed several servings of wine, cheese, and crackers by the time we leveled out at our cruising altitude for the twelve-hour flight to England.

I craned my neck to survey the first-class cabin and my fellow globetrotters. To the extent that one can even see other passengers in their privacy-enforcing mini-cocoons, my companions were pretty much what you'd expect: an assortment of business executives, rich retirees, and one family of four—perhaps flying on a frequent-flyer award vacation. Lucky them.

I wondered what they might make of me. Who was I?

Not dressed like an executive—I'm just a worker bee.

Not retired—I was still in my twenties.

Not traveling with a family—I have very little family. My mother had passed away over the summer, and who the hell knows where my father was. More to the point, who cares? There's Steven, though, and he's important to me. So very important. I count him as family. My *de facto* husband, even if I won't use that word around him. But it's as fake a family as everything else in my life, some part of my mind repeatedly told me. The love was real, but....

But what?

But I was still keeping so much from him. So much of the real me. So much of what I've done. So much of what I think about and brood over.

Alone on the airplane with only my thoughts to keep me company, the faces of the men I've killed played across the window to my right, the names dissolving away into the clouds outside.

The men. More than a dozen of them.

And the woman. Just one of those.

I didn't even know the names of all the men. I will never forget Rodrigo Beltran Gutierrez's name, of course. I might sooner forget my own true name and start believing I actually am Michelle Reagan before forgetting *his* name. They say that you never forget your first. How true.

Well, in my case, I never even knew my first. She will forever be just "the girlfriend." I never knew her name, and that still bothers me. She was the only woman I had killed up to that point, and she should have a name.

I mean, of course, she has a name... had a name... but I never knew it. In Aruba, I didn't think her name was important enough for me to stop and find out. Now I regret my lack of caring. I not only stopped to look at Gutierrez's ID, but even ran back upstairs to see if she wore a ring. I cared more about her title and social status—wife or girlfriend—than about her identity. I stole what little money she had in her purse but didn't bother to look at her passport for her name. What kind of woman does that make me?

That persistent, nagging regret rears up from the recesses of my brain every so often. It bothers me that I don't know her name and never will. She didn't deserve to die—she *had to,* but she didn't deserve to. What she did deserve was to have a name. I should have given her that respect.

I stared into the abyss through the plane's small oval window. The faces of the Zurich bankers reflected back from the plexiglass in turn, floating away one after another into the wild blue yonder. I never knew their names, either. They certainly had names, but, for some reason, I don't care about them. Probably because of the cars in the driveway. If you're making that kind of tall coin by kidnapping and ransoming people, well, then you *do* deserve it. No one needs to know your name, and you don't deserve to have anyone bother to remember it.

Stuart Fenner had a name. His face bobbed slowly up and down in the window, bounced around by the light turbulence of the thin air through which I was making my escape at nearly five-hundred miles an hour. His expression of shock was frozen upon his countenance for all time, exactly the way he looked when he first saw me standing in his kitchen with my revolver pointed at him.

I reclined in my comfortable seat watching his face bob up and down as the jet carried me away at nearly the speed of sound from the one name I never want to ever hear uttered again. From the one mission I will never own up to. From the one story I will never, ever tell. From the one kill I shall never claim as my own.

Fenner's face bobbed in the window, refusing to leave.

I slammed the window shade shut, drawing looks from my neighbors, and signaled the flight attendant for another glass of badly needed wine.

***

I dropped my carry-on bag on the floor just inside our condo's front door.

"How was Mississippi?" Steven asked.

My mind wilted trying to keep all my lies from all my missions straight. "Cold. Unbelievably cold. It's bitter down there in Mississippi this time of year, even that far south. The worst part of it is that the Navy SEALs don't ever seem to even feel the cold. To be honest, it's hard to tell whether they feel much of anything. The only difference to them between summer and winter is whether they wear shorts or jeans to work. Every day, I wore almost every bit of clothing I brought," I said, making up detail after detail about my fictional week of training with a team of Naval Special Warfare operators, "and still froze my butt off.

"But it was definitely cool when they breached the doors and cinderblock walls with explosives. My team won't be doing that kind of penetration work. It would kind of defeat the purpose for our needs, don't you think? But overall, it was really fun to try. I got to squeeze the detonators twice. Even with earplugs, it was loud." I increased the volume of my voice and smiled at Steven for effect. "Did I mention how *loud* it was?"

"I think I get it." He grinned and poured a glass of white wine for each of us. "Did you hear about South Africa?"

"No, what about South Africa? Are they back to building nukes?" I knew full well that was not what Steven meant, but didn't let on one bit. This is the secret I swore to keep from him until the day I died. This is the one he'd never, ever know. I had derided Douglas Benkert for being a professional liar but found myself living the part more often than I cared to admit.

"The Canadian Chief of Station was killed in a robbery. Right in his home. They cleaned out two safes and killed the poor guy. The diplomatic community in Johannesburg is going nuts, at least those from the western European governments my division covers. You're in the DO, did you hear anything from your folks?"

I shook my head and answered truthfully. "No, I was out of town all week, and we don't have an office in Mississippi. I mean, maybe the National Resources Division has an office down there. I don't know. I don't ever deal with NR. So, I've been out of the loop all week. That really sucks. Was he married?"

"Divorced. I don't think I said it was a *he*, but, yeah, it was a guy. I guess most station chiefs are male. Not all, of course... I mean.... Anyway, the rumor going around was that they cut his throat wide open. Sheldon said they gave him a Columbian Neck Tie, pulling his tongue out through the slit in his throat."

I was shocked at the way the rumor mill was twisting what actually happened into a grotesque fiction, and it showed on my face. "Oh, that's horrible. What a terrible thought. Leave it to Sheldon to say something like that. He's a complete asshole. And, by the way, you said that they, quote, killed him, end-quote. *Him*. I'm no analyst, honey," I said grinning, "but to me, that makes him a male."

"Oh, right. Well, drink up. I'm two glasses ahead of you, and the wine must be having the desired effect." Steven snuggled up to me and tipped the glass to my lips.

I desperately needed both that glass of wine as well as the one that would come next. I drank deeply and placed the empty glass on the kitchen counter next to the bottle of Sauvignon Blanc.

I slid myself between Steven and the half-full glass he held, wrapped my arms around him, and anchored my hands firmly in the center of his back. I pressed my head into his chest, hugged him tightly, and drew us together as if trying to merge our two hearts into one. The warmth of his body contrasted the inner coldness I felt about the mission I had just completed.

Steven is my refuge and how I re-center myself in this crazy universe. He is the one to whom I return each time I need someone to remind me who I am, or at least who I want to be. Our condo is Michelle's world; one in which Eden does not exist.

Steven returned my hug firmly with the arm-and-a-half he had available, careful not to drop his glass of wine.

After a minute, he eased out of our shared embrace and reached for the bottle to pour me seconds. As if he ever needed to get me drunk to get my clothes off!

***

"There's been a complication," I said to Michael the next morning while standing in the doorway to his office. I bit my bottom lip pensively, feeling more than a little apprehensive to have to tell him what happened and about the decision I made—a decision that could have serious repercussions for the entire team.

I closed his office door, sat down on the leather sofa, and briefed him on my run-in with Douglas Benkert.

"Do you think he'll cooperate?" Michael asked, still thinking through my report.

"I certainly thought so at the time or I wouldn't have let him go. Without a doubt, I scared the shit out of him. I think it'll be okay. What have you been hearing?"

"I've been speaking with Dagmar once a day since the news broke. So far, so good. The investigations will take weeks to run their course and, at this point, there's no reason to worry. I'm meeting with the Director the day after tomorrow on something else entirely, as it happens. I'll let him know. He may be upset, but I'll make sure he doesn't start having thoughts about Benkert that he shouldn't be having."

"Yeah. Good. Certainly want to nip that in the bud," I agreed.

I rose and glanced over at the empty red leather chair in the corner of Michael's office. The phantom scratching on the back of my thighs returns whenever I look at it. Relegated to its corner by the window, its presence remains a permanent fixture in the psyche of those who have sat in it.

"What are you going to do this week?" Michael asked as I opened the door to leave.

"Christmas shopping."

Michael grinned. "What are you going to get Steve? A pipe and sport coat with elbow patches?"

"Be nice, Michael," I said seriously. "Why don't you like him?"

"I never said I didn't like him. You two make a cute couple. I approve, and I'm glad he makes you happy."

"Thank you." I smiled at hearing that he approved of my relationship with Steven. "He may be a DI weenie, but he's *my* DI weenie."

"Go relax and, hey, Eden, good job. I know this one was not easy for you."

There was nothing else to be said. I had nothing to be proud of and certainly nothing to brag about. I nodded to Michael, politely acknowledging his compliment, and walked off into a week of nothing.

Chapter 21

Late that spring, Allison suggested we spend a weekend at the Lansdowne resort near Leesburg, Virginia. After a half year without a mission and having endured months of training, I was ready for a weekend at a spa for some TLC—a massage, facial, mani-pedi, and some all-around pampering. Not to mention some salacious girl-talk, too.

Allison is a talkative woman. I love that about her. Her penchant for just about anything suggestive makes it so much easier for me to not have to talk about myself quite so much. It also makes for some wildly entertaining and embarrassingly educational conversations. She's unusually open about her never-quite-going-well relationships and all the things she and her boyfriend—whichever one it is at the time—were doing or had done. She describes it all in such graphic detail that it occasionally puts me on the border between engrossed and grossed out. My face has gone flush more than once as she recounted what they did the night before. More often than I care to admit, I've learned a few things just by listening to her.

I called her on my drive out after passing Dulles airport to let her know I was halfway there.

"I've been here all morning, Michelle. My nephew's in a Little League playoff game, so I stopped by to cheer him on and keep my sister company. It's running long, so why don't you come by the field and when he's done, we'll head up to the spa? You can see my sister again. You met her once at my birthday party, maybe two years ago, I think?"

I found Allison and her sister, Deborah, on the bleachers watching Deborah's son pitch the bottom of the still-tied seventh inning in what should have been a six-inning game.

"I'm starving," I announced to the sisters. "I'm going to get something fattening from the snack bar. Want anything? My treat."

I stood up to a chorus of "I'm good," and "No, thanks."

"Okay, your loss," I replied, heading off to the concessions stand run by a local high school band.

As I walked past one of the other baseball fields, two teams were packing up their equipment bags. The Dodgers were celebrating, and the Pirates looked decidedly unhappy at the outcome. *No one likes to lose, but that's the nature of sports,* I mused. *And life, too. Someone always ends up on the losing end.*

While standing in the short line to make my purchase, I admired the painted sign above the snack shack proclaiming it as *Krauss's Korner.* No doubt named after *my* Steven, I thought smiling, knowing it was just a coincidence.

Behind me, a man spoke to one of the young players. "Terrific job catching that line drive, Tim, and awesome throw to second base for the double play. I'm really proud of you. You guys are going to do great in the championship game next week. Sorry I can't be here to see it. I have to head back out of town before then."

The voice of the man in line behind me sent a shiver down my spine. I knew that voice from somewhere, and hearing it felt as if someone dropped an ice cube down the back of my pink tank top.

Who *is* that? I asked myself with rare urgency. For the life of me, I could not place the voice in the right context. The kid's voice didn't sound familiar at all. Not even a little bit.

But who is this guy? I beat myself up mentally, taxing my gray matter to figure it out. *Who the hell is he? Am I supposed to know him outside of the office? Was it personal or professional? What part of my cover was I supposed to play around this guy?*

A dull ache in my jaw told me just how hard I was clenching my teeth. I forced myself to relax and think more clearly.

But it was just not coming to me. I'd heard his voice somewhere before, although out of context and unable to see the man's face, I simply could not place it. It was important—I knew that much beyond a doubt. Damned if I could figure it out just from his voice, though. I didn't know him well, of that I was certain, but I'd heard that voice before. In person. Telephones distort voices and give them a different tenor. I knew for sure I'd been in the same room with this guy, but who is he?

I didn't dare turn around yet. Eventually, I would have to face him after buying my Raisinets, but needed the next minute or two to figure out whether I'm even supposed to know him outside the office or not.

"Thanks, Uncle Doug. I hope I get to play shortstop again next game. That was fun," Tim said enthusiastically. The excitement of his recent win and game-ending double play lit up his tiny voice with delight.

Doug? Oh, crap!

The sudden realization brought a bead of sweat out on my forehead while my mouth ran dry. It was Douglas Benkert.

Home on vacation? Enjoying the warm weather in DC while it turned cold back in South Africa? Maybe he was just in town for one of the quarterly regional conferences the Agency runs? Or a training class? *Shit! What the hell do I do now?*

Whatever the reason for his return to the States, this time I was the one trapped. To my front, a high-school-band member handed me my candy while behind me stood Douglas Benkert. This time, *he* was blocking *my* easy escape.

To say the least, I did not enjoy the feeling of slow strangulation descending over me. Now whether he knew it or not, Benkert had me cornered like a rabbit with no way out of the trap. No, I did not enjoy it at all.

Holding my box of Raisinets and three cold bottles of water—to which I was going to treat Allison and Deborah whether they asked for them or not—I was ready to leave and had to face Benkert. I thanked Brittany the flute player—or so her nametag said—drew a big smile onto my face and turned around to make the inevitable confrontation.

I rotated in place and paused so Benkert could focus his attention on my face. I waited the two or three seconds it took for the look of recognition to wash across his face. The hair I'd worn tied back that night six or seven months earlier hung down now, swinging freely below my shoulders and framing my face quite differently than he'd seen it on that fateful night. Still, it didn't take him too long to remember me. I'm sure my face featured prominently on his short list of those he hoped to never see again as long as he lived.

Or did he see me in his sleep? Did he have nightmares about me and the five minutes we spent together in Fenner's apartment half a year earlier? He knows how close he came to dying that night, doesn't he? Does he awaken screaming at night as his subconscious replays the scenario over and over, each time with alternate endings, none of which ended well for him?

I looked him square in the eyes and spoke slowly. "I'm glad to see you're playing ball, Douglas. I told you I know where you live."

Benkert's face blanched. The thought crossed my mind that he might very well pass out right there.

I didn't wait to see whether he did or not. I wanted nothing more than to get the hell out of there. I walked right past him, striding purposefully away from Douglas, Tim, and Brittany, and headed back towards the bleachers and the top of the eighth inning.

PART SEVEN

HEAD TURNER

Chapter 22

"Come on, Steven," I implored, trying hard not to sound as though I was begging. "It'll be fun, I promise."

"Camping?" he retorted. "I don't really think spending an entire weekend tromping around the woods of West Virginia is my idea of fun. And I've never heard you talk about camping before, so even if your co-workers do want to go, why are you so interested in us going along?"

"It was Arnaud's idea for all six of us to spend the weekend together. He and Claude are getting used to the idea that I haven't been scared away from the team by now, and they need to get used to my being around for the long haul. They want to get to know both of us better, and I want to get to know Claude's wife, Monica, as well.

"It could be a good male-bonding weekend for you," I said hoping it might actually work out that way. Steven would clearly be out of his element, but maybe getting him away from his desk and computer would be good for him. And for us.

Our relationship had hit a few bumps in the road over the previous couple of months or so. I wanted to use the trip to get us back on track by getting away from DC and our usual routine.

"Besides," I continued, "I've gone camping plenty of times and not just in training. My dad used to take my mom and me camping in the Angeles National Forest every summer for, like, my entire life. She cooked s'mores, and he told the best ghost stories around the campfire. There's no way I'll be able to do his stories justice, but it'll be fun to try to tell one or two. And it's just for one night. We'll drive out there and hike in Saturday, camp at a site Arnaud heard about, and hike out on Sunday after lunch. We don't even have to buy any gear. We'll rent it all."

"You said 'six.' Who else would be going?"

I could tell the tide was turning in my favor. "Three couples. Claude and his wife, Monica, and Arnaud and his girlfriend-of-the-moment. I think her name is Paige. They don't seem to last too long and

I've never met this one." I tried to not sound judgmental, knowing full-well I was being exactly that.

"They don't 'last too long?'" Steven asked, raising an eyebrow.

I answered somewhat hesitantly. "Arnaud's not the settling-down kind of guy. He's more of a serial monogamist, near as I can tell. Not that it's any of my business, but I hear some of the details from Claude every now and then. Paige will be the only one there who doesn't know everyone else is CIA. Monica knows, as most wives of undercover officers do... and husbands, I mean, of course, husbands, too." I stumbled trying to cover my tracks. I didn't mean it in a bad way, but most of the time it's the wives who are the civilians and the husbands who are the undercover intelligence officers. Not always, but most often that's the way it is.

"You probably shouldn't say that you're CIA, either...." I said, letting the thought hang in the air for a second to try to gauge Steven's reaction to the idea. "Even though you're an overt employee, it'd just be better not bringing up that you're a division chief in the Directorate of Intelligence. It might start Paige asking too many questions. You can pretend for the weekend you're undercover, too."

I tried to get him even just a bit excited about a weekend in the woods, which anyone could immediately tell is definitely not his forte. "You can pretend you're a history professor at Georgetown University or something," I suggested, trying hard to make the thought enticing.

"If Paige asks too many questions, just start explaining all that stuff in your doctoral thesis about how Vercingetorix was such a great leader and all that. And, hey," I said while playfully thumping his chest with the back of my hand, "aren't you impressed that I remembered how to pronounce *Vercingetorix*?"

"Dissertation," Steven mumbled softly.

"Huh?" was the most articulate response I could come up with at that instant, clearly not following his train of thought.

"Dissertations are for Ph.D. candidates. Thesis papers are for Master's degree students," Steven explained as if I cared.

Steven could easily bore anyone to tears with a lengthy explanation of his doctoral dissertation on the political intricacies of pre-France Gaul and how the largest of the independent cities of the day banded together to blah, blah, blah, and resist the repeated Roman military invasions, many of which were led by Julius Caesar who, blah, blah, blah.... I know he has bored me to sleep a few times talking to his friends about it all. I love Steven, but, seriously. Yawn.

"Okay, I guess so," Steven said relenting. I think he just wanted to make me happy, and the thought of him agreeing to the trip for my sake did, at the time, exactly that.

Nobody would ever accuse Steven of being the outdoorsy kind of guy. He grew up in the suburbs of Atlantic City, New Jersey, and attended college in New York City. My wonderful Steven was an academic through and through. In hindsight, maybe I should have thought twice about taking him camping, but even after having spent several years on Michael's team, I still found myself working incredibly hard to become fully accepted by Claude and Arnaud.

Weeks later, I thought back to Arnaud's suggestion that the six of us go camping and began to suspect his real plan was more to embarrass Steven, and by extension, me. The possibility of that being his real motive upset me tremendously. I never figured out if that's what he intended or if I became a sore sport because of what happened.

Selfishly, my thoughts centered around what I might get out of the trip and not what it might feel like for Steven being pushed so far out of his comfort zone. But it was just one night in the woods, so how bad could things go, right? I readily agreed to the trip and convinced Steven that if he joined us, he would have fun, too.

My bad.

***

Bright and early that Saturday morning, Steven and I loaded our rented tent and backpacks into Claude's Jeep Grand Cherokee and climbed into the back seats behind him and Monica.

Arnaud and Paige led the two-car caravan in his black Porsche 911 convertible. I've always felt fortunate that Michael leases a BMW 3-Series for me as part of my cover, but how Arnaud convinced Michael to give him a Porsche as his company car, I'll never know. I am, however, absolutely certain that car is one of the primary reasons Arnaud never stayed single for long.

As we loaded everyone's gear into the Jeep, I made a comment to Paige about how good the Porsche looked.

"Don't you just want to smear your entire body all over it?" she asked, grinning wickedly.

"I've never felt like that about a car, exactly," I responded, somewhat taken aback by her feelings about that particular automobile. "But if you end up doing that, let me know how it goes for you, okay?"

I guess there really are all kinds of people out there.

On the long drive out to southern West Virginia, Monica and I got to chat a bit. With the guys in the car, though, the conversation remained mostly superficial. She delighted in asking Steven about being an analyst and an overt CIA employee. Since Paige wasn't in the car with us, it was safe for them to talk shop. As Claude and our entire team are all undercover, she didn't get to speak to many people who could freely say they worked for the Agency. She wanted to hear how people reacted when he'd tell someone he worked for the CIA. Monica itched to understand how Steven felt about being so open about it since she and Claude couldn't be.

Monica found it somewhat perplexing to socialize with an overt employee while Steven remarked how exotic living undercover seemed. What might have been a clash of cultures between them became a prized opportunity for the pair to share their entirely different experiences on life in and around the Agency. I enjoyed listening in.

I also looked forward to getting to know Monica better over the course of the weekend. I hoped that if we could connect in a social setting, my working relationship with her husband would improve. Although I'd spent a lot of time training and working with the Payeur brothers over the previous four years, I still felt too much like the unwanted girl that the cool boys refused to let into their clubhouse. They weren't holding me back professionally, but they were definitely excluding me emotionally.

Chapter 23

The ratty pre-fab trailer serving as the campground office in Lake Berwind, West Virginia, had seen better days, as had much of that part of the Mountain State. The torn window screens and thirty-year-old furniture spoke to the plight of the local economy and the lack of visitors to the park. While the natural beauty of the Red Oak and Aspen trees remained, the "Good Old Days" when coal mining and heavy industries thrived were long gone.

Arnaud, Paige, Monica, and I entered into the office to inquire about renting a campsite. Arnaud met with the manager, Dean, to get directions to the start of the hiking trail and pay the rental fee. Since this would be the last civilized stop we'd be making, Paige and I hightailed it to the ladies' room.

As we returned to the office, we watched Arnaud pay Dean the ten-dollar fee for the campsite from a wallet stuffed with cash. Why he would carry so much money around with him, I could not understand. Maybe he was trying to impress Paige. Some women go for fast cars and fat wallets.

"There's no utilities at that site," Dean said smiling. "No electric, water, or privies, but the fire pit's great for cooking and sitting around drinking at night." He obviously spoke from personal experience. "You can fill your canteens right from the river, too. Water's good there, and so's the tire swing. Swing out and drop off into the deep part of the river at the bend. Lots of folks get a kick out of that.

"Like I said, there's no bathrooms," he emphasized to Paige and me, having already seen that we made a beeline around the corner for the last toilet in civilization. "You'll want to head uphill a bit on the mountain trail for that and not down towards the river. Much more privacy if you go around the big boulder and up the trail a-ways. You'll see what I mean. Can't miss it."

"Thanks," Arnaud said. He gave Dean a half-wave of his hand in dismissal as we walked out of the office towards the parking lot.

***

It didn't take as long as I hoped it might for Steven to start asking questions. I honestly thought he'd last longer.

"How far do you think we've hiked so far?" he asked after only thirty minutes.

"About a half-mile," I replied quietly, absolutely not wanting the others hearing him start to ask the "are we there yet" questions.

I tried to sound enthusiastic and encouraging. "Over terrain like this, we'll only be covering about one mile an hour. Maybe a bit more, since it's not too hilly right here. It's not like walking on a sidewalk at home, honey. But it's fun being out in the real world." I stopped talking before it began to sound like a lecture.

"It'll be another two hours or so to the campsite. Let's enjoy the beautiful views," I said smiling and speeding up to catch Monica a dozen yards ahead of us. I hoped that by walking in front of Steven he'd have the motivation to keep up with me. If he weren't talking, then perhaps he'd not get too out of breath from the physical exertion he was simply not used to.

My four years on the team had whipped me into great shape through running and an almost slavish devotion to yoga workouts. Steven, on the other hand, sat at a desk all day and wouldn't know what the inside of a gym looked like if you showed him a photo. Being as smart as he is doesn't necessarily help when you're dropped in the middle of the woods with a tent on your back, but I loved him anyway.

Steven and I just had to figure out how to get back in sync with each other. My excessive traveling strained our relationship. I could feel him pulling away. I had hoped spending a weekend together somewhere other than in our Arlington condo would help us start to reconnect.

I caught up to Monica and Claude and asked, "Do you guys go camping much? My family used to go camping most summers in California, but I haven't gone since high school." I ignored for the sake of the conversation all the time Claude, Arnaud, and I had spent in the woods in various training courses, usually with one Army Special Forces unit or another. That wasn't camping. That was work—hard work.

"Not too often," Monica replied. "I camped a few times when I was in the Girl Scouts, but that was a few more years ago than I'd care to admit. We've gone, maybe, three or four times in the past ten years. It's almost always Arnie's idea. Almost always...." she said, pausing to think about it.

"No... it *is* always his idea," she said coming to the realization suddenly. "Now that I think about it, I wonder why he always wants to bring whatever woman he's dating at the time camping? I'm sure the girls would rather spend the weekend at a B&B, or spa, or something else. *Anything* else, actually. He'd probably get more appreciation from them with a gesture like that, if you know what I mean."

I giggled in agreement.

Claude nodded as well. That made me feel as if it might be possible for me to connect with him over the weekend on a level more personal than professional. Claude spoke more to me in the next hour of hiking than he had in all of the time we'd spent in the car traveling through Turkmenistan and Uzbekistan. Maybe he was just keeping up appearances for Monica's sake. Either way, I was thrilled with how things were going.

The conversation stayed light throughout the rest of the three-mile hike from the trailhead to our riverside campsite. The easy banter left me feeling happy with myself, as if confirming that I made the right decision to drag Steven away from the monotony of Arlington's concrete arteries and into the woods where, I had assured him, we'd all have a good time.

Chapter 24

After setting up the tents, we decided to go swimming before building a campfire and making dinner. In our tent, I changed into a yellow bikini with white shorts and my rented water shoes.

Visions of Steven jumping into the river from the tire swing Dean mentioned flittered through my head. I love Steven dearly, but he's not the most athletic guy in the world. So, I was charged up to see him do his best Tarzan impression and drop into the river from a tire on a rope. The bikini I brought along for the weekend would not work for me to join the gang in that particular event, though. I'd soaked my shirt with sweat during our hike in, so I was definitely looking forward to cooling off in the water.

Obviously, someone had spent a lot of time clearing the campsite. They had leveled the tops off four felled trees and placed the logs as seats in a loose square surrounding the stone fire pit. The site could easily accommodate groups much larger than just the six of us and our trio of two-man tents—twenty-five or thirty people could easily sit around a raging fire. That night, we would have the site to ourselves and all the privacy we could want.

I imagined with a shiver that the ghost stories told at the site over the years would have been chilling to hear by the light of a crackling campfire.

I told the other five that I'd catch up with them at the bend in the river just down the hill from the camp site. First, however, I needed to answer the call of nature. I grabbed the roll of toilet paper from my backpack and looked over at the group as they laughed at something Monica had said. I ambled away towards the boulder, which was easily the biggest rock I'd ever stood next to.

Just past the boulder, the path up the mountain was right where Dean said it would be, not that I doubted him. He certainly knew the area well. I couldn't decide how far to go along the path and went a hundred yards or so to ensure my privacy. My being out of sight for twenty minutes or so in the middle of the afternoon wouldn't be the end of the world. Everyone knew where I was headed anyway.

My return trip down the steep hill stressed my thighs more than my ascent had. My quads started to burn as I worked to control the rate of my descent to avoid tripping or breaking an ankle.

As I rounded the boulder and caught a view of the campsite, any complaints about the strain in my leg muscles evaporated instantly.

There is a particular type of mental disconnect that occurs when a person is suddenly confronted with a scene so completely different than what they expected that they're unable to process the visual rapidly enough. More than just doing a double-take, the brain needs to reboot. The onset of confusion is immediate and overwhelming, followed by a short bout of paralysis.

I see it all the time from the other side. I saw it on Stuart Fenner's face when he entered his apartment in Johannesburg and saw me standing in his kitchen with my revolver pointed at him. Now I know what my targets experience when they first see me, and I did not enjoy it one bit.

I rounded the boulder, toilet paper in hand, and froze. The scene in the campsite caught me so off guard that my brain skipped a beat and cost me the few precious seconds that would have enabled me to safely backtrack up the path. I probably made the same what-the-hell-is-this face Fenner did that fateful evening. The prospect for this situation turning out as badly for me as that one did for him was suddenly a distinct possibility.

In the campsite, four of the five friends I'd left smiling and laughing now knelt behind one of the four flat-top logs surrounding the fire pit. The fifth, Steven, knelt next to the empty ring of campfire stones. Three armed men whom I had never seen before stood guard. The shock of my having walked into a completely unexpected and obviously dangerous situation—one that was the polar opposite of the happy scene I'd left not long before—stopped me in my tracks.

"What the f—?" I blurted out entirely instinctively. I knew immediately that I got caught flat-footed—completely off-guard and armed only with a roll of toilet paper. My heart sank as the magnitude of my mistake became clear: I'd just surrendered the element of surprise.

"Well, lookee there. One more," the man nearest the fire pit said with delight. In one hand, he held a fistful of Steven's hair, and in the other, a pistol. "That makes more sense, Bobby. Now there's three guys and three bitches. More fun, more fun, more fun."

I had no idea which of the other two men was Bobby, nor at the moment did I give a damn. That ugly, gap-toothed asshole was holding a gun to Steven's head and just called me a *bitch*.

Strike One.

It was hard to even call him a man. All three of the bastards looked as though they were just teenagers and may well have still been in high school. If not, they were out by only a year or two.

The verbal slap in the face snapped me out of my state of shock. I took stock of the situation playing out in front of me while regaining my wits somewhat. To my left, Claude, Monica, Arnaud, and, closest to me, Paige knelt behind the log. Closest, yes, but still thirty feet away.

Mr. "More Fun" stood inside the square formed by the four logs around the empty fire pit. I nicknamed him *Pistol,* since that's what he was holding to Steven's head.

Pistol turned to face me, shifting the aim of his weapon in my direction. Pointing a gun at me.

Strike Two.

The other four of my friends were guarded by two men who, for self-evident reasons, I nicknamed *Rifle* and *Knife*. Rifle stood directly across the clearing from me, a few feet beyond the farthest campfire seating log. He held his weapon in the low-ready position. To my left, Knife stood a few steps behind Paige holding a fourteen- or sixteen-inch Bowie Knife.

If Knife were standing behind either Claude or Arnaud, either of the brothers would have had an excellent chance to wrestle the weapon away from him. Not that it would have done any good with Steven held at gunpoint twenty feet away and Rifle across the campsite. It does not take a genius to figure out who would win most confrontations between one man with a knife and two others with firearms.

Even if one of my teammates did relieve Knife of his blade, I asked myself, what would he be able to do with it against the other two? Steven would be dead before Pistol could be disarmed.

My mind stayed blank. For the life of me—literally, it might very well turn out—I just could not come up with a viable answer. If a man with a large knife and the Payeur brothers' hand-to-hand combat training couldn't come out on top in such a situation, how could a woman with a decade-and-a-half less experience and training succeed? Especially when she's armed only with toilet paper. My mind raced, but I could not devise a viable plan.

I had just interrupted whatever was going on and needed to stall for time to think, but didn't want to give up more of the initiative than I already had. In the moment, it made sense to find out which of them was in charge and making decisions.

I balanced a combination of a stern-but-hesitant and close-to-quivering voice and asked no one in particular, "What do you think you're doing?" I wanted to see which of them would speak first, but at the same time, did not want to come across too forcefully.

Pistol answered for his group. Neither of the others even made an attempt to speak, which for my purposes made him the boss of this gang of hick misfits.

"We was just gunna take your city folks' money," he said to me. With a glance at his buddies, he added, "Boys, now that a pretty bitch is here, I'm thinking we're also gunna have us some fun this afternoon." Pistol waved his gun in a circular motion around Steven's head and nodded to me. "You must be with the fat one, here."

Steven may sit at a desk all day and not be in great shape, but he was not fat.

"You're a real pretty one," Pistol said to me, "and I'm thinking that you don't want to see the fat one get hurt. So, you're gunna behave real nice now. We don't even need to go nowhere. You can just get on the ground right there, and we'll let 'em all watch. You're gunna enjoy it. I know *I* am."

My exact words are lost to the cosmos, but were probably something he didn't appreciate, such as "Like hell I will, you little shit." Of course, knowing me, they were likely *slightly* less polite than that.

Pistol pushed Steven over behind the log where the others were kneeling under guard, maintaining his distance from the group. He shuffled his feet in the dirt while watching Steven settle into his new position next to Paige.

Knife brought his blade lower and closer to Steven, reinforcing his pal's spur-of-the-moment plan, and to overcome my obvious lack of enthusiasm for it—which is putting it mildly. The emphasis he added to Pistol's idea underscored the message: if I didn't "give it up," Steven would pay the price.

Steven's face, while never all that tan to begin with, drained completely. He swallowed hard, and I felt horrible he had to endure this. I could see he felt responsible for what was about to happen to me—for being unable to prevent his girlfriend from being raped.

Steven's eyes narrowed, and his nostrils flared. A knot twisted in my gut seeing him in such a frustrated and helpless state. I watched what had started out as a fun camping trip unfold into a trauma poised to create a deep wound in his self-esteem. As brilliant as he is, I knew he was not able to think his way out this situation and, to Steven, that's not the way the world was supposed to work. To his way of thinking, the smartest always wins. In reality, that's not always the way things work in the field. Or the woods.

I turned my attention back to Pistol. If he and his band of merry morons thought that by holding Steven hostage they could take turns raping me as their afternoon's entertainment, they had seriously misjudged this particular group of "city folk."

Strike Three.

But now I had to figure out what the hell to do about it. They had me at a complete disadvantage in every way.

The saying is "rock, paper, scissors," not "knife, pistol, toilet paper." I could not even begin to comprehend in what world toilet paper could possibly beat guns and knives. Claude, Arnaud, and I had all taken the Special Forces hand-to-hand combat course at Fort Bragg, North Carolina, and trained on occasion with Delta Force operators in armed and unarmed silent attack scenarios. But not one of those scenarios involved the lethal use of double-ply toilet tissue.

For the five years since I arrived at the Farm, I've made my entire professional life one of learning how to craft situations that give me the insurmountable advantage over my targets. Now, caught completely off-guard while on what started out as a relaxing vacation in the woods of West Virginia, I found myself entirely unprepared and unequipped for what I faced. I ended up on the receiving end of all the disadvantages I usually create for my targets.

I stood there absolutely ready and willing to trade the Devil that entire toilet paper roll plus everything else I owned for my .45 Sig Sauer. Someone else must have made him a better offer that Saturday afternoon, because my gun stayed locked safely away in the weapons vault back at the Farm.

Mentally, I'd already run through and rejected the scenario of Claude or Arnaud getting the blade away from Knife and killing him. Even if one of the brothers managed to do that, he was still going to lose out to Rifle or Pistol. Both of the Payeurs knew that, which is why they hadn't made a move. All three of us were obviously wrestling with the same question: how can a man armed with only a knife win a gunfight? Neither of them could answer that question any better than I was able to. The answer is simply that he can't.

And that turned out to be the solution I had been ransacking my brain to find. *He* can't, but *she* can.

"Okay, okay!" I agreed emphatically, raising my hands in front of me to emphasize the point. "Don't hurt him!"

I'm sure I looked entirely foolish—a twenty-four-year-old woman in shorts and a bikini top holding a roll of toilet paper in her outstretched hand. The futility of my gesture underscored the point that I had no other way to prevent Knife from stabbing Steven. The toilet paper served as my own version of waving a white flag in surrender.

I lowered my hands and dropped the toilet paper, which rolled off to my left. It had served its purpose and, however the situation turned out, I wasn't going to need it anymore.

Pistol smiled at my willingness to yield to him. He didn't want a fight. He just wanted to get his rocks off and by the looks of it, I was going to let him.

To this day, I'm not sure who acted the most surprised when I reached up and removed my bikini top. Arnaud and Claude both gasped at my move, but Steven's face lit up in complete shock. Why would the man who had seen my boobs up close and personal so often for the past few years be the one who reacted so strongly? Maybe he was afraid I'd concluded that the only way for me to save his life was to submit myself to Pistol and his prurient friends. I didn't stop to ask.

I eased forward a few yards towards the fire pit, closing the distance to Pistol. I stopped three feet short of the nearest seating log. To further distract them all, I gave my audience the pleasure of a slow shoulder shake, sending my girls jiggling a little bit in their unconstrained freedom.

Pistol's grin widened to show off where both missing teeth used to be, and he started towards me. What an unattractive bastard. I fully expected he'd smell terrible, too.

My plan was an absolutely horrible plan, and I knew it. Unfortunately, I didn't have time to come up with a better one, so I had to make it work. As with most bad plans, each individual part had to come together perfectly, or it would not work at all. Bad or not, I had fully committed.

We were not playing a chess game in which both people started with pieces of equal power and the winner would be determined by who maneuvered theirs with the most strategically sound late-game plan in mind. No, Pistol had forced me at gunpoint into a fast-moving poker game and dealt me crappy cards. My measly little plan required me to push my chips all-in to prevent Pistol from getting in at all.

I stood my ground three feet shy of the campfire log and maintained my focus on Pistol while continuing to entice him forward with a slow but deliberate twisting of my upper body. My swaying breasts kept Pistol moving towards me. His eyes were glued to my chest while mine never left his legs.

I had only one chance to get this exactly right, and it all hinged on my judging the timing of how he transferred his weight from one leg to the other as he walked. While unscientific, inexact did not have to mean ineffective.

I didn't know if Pistol had a detailed plan in mind for what he'd do once he reached me. I, however, had one and was luring him right into it.

At the log, he lifted his left foot over the top as he moved in for some afternoon delight. The smile that never left his face showed me how intent he was to violate me in the most intimate way possible, right in front of my lover and two co-workers whom I'd been working so damned hard for the past couple of years to impress.

It required all my willpower to not react to his advance. I stood my ground and waited with as blank an expression on my face as I could maintain under the circumstances.

I had to hold out for exactly the right instant. Not just the right second, but that *one* precise instant in time. I channeled all my energy and focus into standing still, seemingly doing nothing while waiting for that singular moment to arrive. A blood vessel pulsated behind my right eye. The growing anticipation I worked feverishly hard to hide behind my best poker face was readily visible across Pistol's youthful stubble.

Stepping over an object is something we all do every day and don't think much about. You lift one leg over it, push off your rear foot, and land on your front. It's a routine part of life that we perform automatically and without much conscious thought. But for me at that moment, I was thinking about it intensely because it made all the difference in how the situation would play out. Done right, I might just be able to walk away from the campsite under my own power. If not...well, no woman wants to think about *that* possibility.

With his left foot raised over the two-foot-high log, Pistol pushed his weight off his rear foot. That launched me into action. With the weight of his body off his rear foot but not yet on his front, for that quarter- or half-second he had no control over his motion. The instant I'd so anxiously awaited had arrived.

Without hesitation, I sprang forward, released from my self-imposed limbo to strike my target with all the ferocity that dirt bag deserved.

I took the quickest half-step of my life and planted the instep of my right foot squarely into Pistol's groin. The bastard got a well-deserved combination of free-flowing adrenaline and more primal hatred than had ever come out of me. I could not have kicked harder if my life had depended on it—and maybe that afternoon, it did.

Pistol had walked over to me intent on finding out what my body felt like. Now he knew.

His weight never made it to his front foot. He collapsed directly to his hands and knees at my feet, paralyzed from the excruciating pain of my having tried to launch his family jewels out through his ears. It's not at all ladylike to admit that if I'd had time to take in the scenery and watch him suffer such agony, I would probably have enjoyed it.

After connecting with my kick and scrambling his *huevos*, I didn't wait for my own weight to transfer back to my feet. I had no time to waste gloating over my initial success. I still had two armed men to keep from hurting my teammates and Steven. Especially Steven... and my teammates, too, of course, but especially Steven. From my position in the air, I bypassed my feet, dropped straight down to my knees, and relieved Pistol of his pistol.

Now, I was in my element.

Now, I was back in control.

Now, I had the power.

Just minutes ago, I had walked back into the campsite as Michelle on vacation. Now, Eden was at work.

Rifle stood forty to fifty feet straight in front of me. I raised my newly acquired 9mm and aimed directly at his head. At the same time, he was raising his long gun towards me. That one shot—right then, right there—was the singular pull of a trigger for which I had painstakingly trained over the previous fourteen years of my life. No earlier trigger pulls mattered and, if I missed that shot, I would never get another.

From the firing range with my father all those years ago to the Smith house at the Farm just a few weeks earlier, I've trained tirelessly to make perfect headshots. I'd routinely dropped eight-inch head-plate targets in for a dozen years and didn't have to think about the mechanics. For me, it's all muscle memory. I can lift a weapon, line up the sights, drop one target and transition my aim to the next faster than anyone I've ever met. Those are *my* shots. That's what I've become known for on my team and what has enabled me to succeed as an operator.

Early on, Michelle trained hard to perfect her skills. But now, that particular superpower belongs to Eden.

I closed my left eye and focused my right on the gun's front sight. I raised the weapon so the notch of the rear sight bracketed the front. The three pieces of the puzzle aligned perfectly. With the front sight in focus, the target remains blurry, unfortunately. That's too bad since I wanted to see the look on Rifle's face as I aimed at his nose.

I drew my finger against the trigger firmly for the half-second it took for the double-action firing mechanism to break. The hammer dropped, slamming the firing pin forward against the primer seated in the rear of the cartridge. The impact ignited the patiently waiting gunpowder, giving rise to a maelstrom of expanding gasses which forced the bullet through the barrel of the weapon, hurling it downrange at my target.

I shifted my focus from the pistol's front sight to Rifle's forehead where a dark red-and-black spot that had not been there moments earlier appeared. He fell straight back, dead. Rifle died of lead poisoning—a single 9mm bullet to his brain.

Effortlessly, I transitioned my aim from Rifle to Knife, off to my left. My five companions remained kneeling between me and my target. I fervently hoped they would stay that way, letting me do what I needed to do. I looked over the sights of the pistol and realized I couldn't risk a shot from a kneeling position without putting Steven in unnecessary danger. I refused to do that.

I bounded from my knees to my feet and leapt onto the flattened campfire log, which would give me the extra height I needed for an unobstructed view of Knife's ugly mug, well above Steven's head.

As I moved into position, Arnaud sprang up. My teammate sprinted the few steps to Knife, grabbed the armed man's blade-wielding hand and pulled. In a tried-and-true disarming maneuver, Arnaud spun Knife by his outstretched arm, gripped the weapon-hand with both of his, and twisted it into a wristlock. Arnaud pushed the trapped arm left when it only wanted to go right. Knife's ulna and radius cracked in protest. His scream echoed across the campsite as Arnaud flipped him to the ground by his mangled arm.

Arnaud controlled the blade expertly, pulled Knife's arm to roll him over onto his stomach, and snatched the weapon away. He shoved his knee into the now-prostrated man's back and jabbed the blade into the base of Knife's skull—a perfect pith kill.

Claude raced across the campsite to retrieve the rifle, making Arnaud the first to reach me. He stood just beyond the seating log holding the red-stained Bowie knife and simply watched.

With Rifle and Knife safely out of the picture, I turned my attention back to pistol-less Pistol. Still on all fours, he fought unsuccessfully to breathe.

I knelt down next to my would-be rapist and placed the outside of my right thigh next to his head. I leaned slightly to my right, reached my arm around his head, and unceremoniously grabbed a handful of his chin. I pressed my left hand down on the back of his head and pulled up hard with my right, lifting and twisting until I heard the telltale crack from his neck—just as I'd been taught at Ft. Bragg. Pistol's lifeless body dropped to the dirt with a soft thud.

Across the campsite, Paige knelt with eyes as big as full moons. In unison, her baby blues rolled back in her head and, seemingly in slow motion, she crumpled to the ground unconscious. Arnaud rushed to tend to his overwhelmed girlfriend.

I recall feeling only a flood of relief that the danger had passed. Arnaud later told me that as I broke Pistol's neck, I beamed with the biggest shit-eating grin he'd ever seen. I won't contradict him although, in my defense, I feel that having avoided the fate Pistol had in mind for me that afternoon entitled me to feel tremendous relief at not having to endure one of the worst things that could happen to a woman.

Maybe I also got some personal or professional satisfaction from turning what might have ended up being an extremely melancholy situation into a victory.

As the rest of the group gathered around me, I stood up. Surprisingly, no one looked happy or even relieved.

I glanced around at the three bodies littering our campsite and gestured down at Pistol. I lacked anything intelligent to say at that moment, so with as upbeat a tone as I could generate under the circumstances, I jokingly said, "Well, he's definitely not a happy camper."

I knew it wasn't funny, and appropriately so, nobody laughed. They just looked at me, seemingly waiting for me to say something else or tell them what to do next. My mind raced but didn't get anywhere. I had no idea what they were waiting for and must have had quite the puzzled look on my face.

My wonderful, dear Steven pointed out to me that I was still topless.

Chapter 25

Claude and Arnaud did the heavy lifting and moved the bodies. They worked with fluid motions that spoke to their years of experience with the task. My partners buried the trio a hundred yards off the mountain trail. No doubt, the three sets of remains would eventually be dug up by animals and subsequently discovered by some hiker or other and reported to the local sheriff. We had no intention of reporting what happened ourselves.

No one wanted to sleep at the campsite that night. We didn't even discuss it—we were all of the same mind. None of us wanted to spend any time at all that close to the bodies. We needed to get the hell out of there.

Nor did we want anyone who heard my gunshot come around to investigate and find us in the area. Things could go badly for us if we were seen nearby or had to answer questions about what happened. Our fun vacation had turned into an unplanned exfiltration for which we were woefully unprepared. We were cutting our vacation short and hiking at least part of the way back while we still had daylight.

We finished breaking camp a half-hour later, intent on putting at least a mile between us and the campsite before dark. Sunset comes without warning in the woods, and we didn't have time to hike all the way back to the cars before the sun disappeared behind the trees. Arnaud, Claude, and I readily agreed we shouldn't take the risk of trudging through unfamiliar and uneven terrain in the dark. That was a sure way for one of us to end up with a broken ankle, which would turn an already bad situation into a real nightmare.

I gathered up and wiped down anything I could think of that any of us had touched and we weren't going to carry home with us. No good could come from us leaving our fingerprints behind on the knife or either of the firearms. Maybe some future rainstorm would wash all the prints away, but why take the chance? On missions, I always wore gloves, which made wiping fingerprints off everything in sight a task I never had to worry about. In West Virginia, though, that was a different animal altogether. Eventually, the police will have three bodies to examine. We didn't need to give them any additional leads to follow. With the help of the FBI, CIA's Security Division blocks all law enforcement access to our fingerprints, but why take any chances? If our prints were run by the local sheriff, he'd be told there were no hits. However, the Agency's security office would be alerted silently. That would bring around security officers asking questions none of us wanted asked, much less answered.

I disassembled the two firearms and wiped each piece down thoroughly. I threw the heavy metal frames and magazines into the deep part of the river and walked into the woods about fifty yards where I buried the rest. There was no guarantee the pieces wouldn't be found once the bodies were discovered and people started scouring the area, but at least none of it would lead back to me or my friends. That's what I cared about most.

As we helped each other don our backpacks, I looked back in the direction where my latest victims laid and reflected briefly on how drastically one's world can change in just an hour's time.

Those three shitheads forced me to play a high-stakes game of poker, and I won with a small pair and a big bluff.

***

I wasn't asking for my friends to throw me a ticker-tape parade, but I also wasn't expecting to get the silent treatment on the drive home, either.

For the first hour of our drive home, Monica stared out the front-passenger window lost in thought. I tried unsuccessfully to read her mind or at least her body language to figure out what she was thinking or feeling. I assumed Claude had only told her our team's cover story—that we broke into foreign homes and businesses to copy or steal documents, plant audio and video surveillance equipment, and the like. I'd never gotten the impression she knew the truth about our work but wasn't completely sure. I felt confident Steven didn't have a clue, but couldn't be sure what Monica may have figured out or overheard during the fifteen years or so that she'd been married to Claude.

I felt terribly conflicted throughout the ride home. On the one hand, shouldn't they think of me as the heroine of the day? I certainly did nothing to cause the incident or bring those three idiots down upon us, yet I managed to do what neither Claude nor Arnaud could:

successfully resolve the situation without anyone getting hurt. Well... any of *us*. That's what matters to me.

Maybe the others didn't feel that way, but what was the alternative? Letting ourselves get robbed or raped? I didn't see either as acceptable outcomes. I worried that the others may have thought my reaction was too aggressive.

I desperately wanted to speak with Claude and Arnaud in private, but that didn't happen until we'd rendezvoused back at Claude's house to unpack the gear.

Arnaud and Paige were sitting on Claude and Monica's front porch sipping Starbucks coffees when we arrived. I wondered just how fast Arnaud had driven his Porsche to beat us back by that much, and still have time for a caffeine pit-stop along the way.

"Michelle," Claude said as we stepped out of his Jeep, "would you help me get the packs into the garage? We can leave the tents in the car."

"Sure," I replied tersely, feeling dejected after sitting in silence for four hours.

With a subtle finger gesture the others likely missed, Claude motioned to his brother that Arnaud should join us in the garage. I braced for a tongue lashing and hoped that they'd at least go off on me in French, so I wouldn't have to bear the words. I'd surely get the gist of the barrage from their tone.

"What?" I asked Claude pointedly once the three of us were alone in the back of the garage.

Arnaud was the first to respond. "That was unbelievable, Michelle. Absolutely amazing."

"Arnie's right," Claude chimed in. "I hate to admit it, but they caught us flat-footed and not at all equipped for a confrontation. Steve was standing near the tents at the edge of the campsite, and they grabbed him first. I'm not blaming him, but once they had a gun to his head, we didn't have much room to maneuver."

"You took quite a risk," Arnaud continued with a huge smile on his face. I'd long ago gotten used to them alternating a conversation between the two. Even when the three of us were talking, it was as if there were only one of them and one of me. Before working with the Payeurs I'd not spent much time among twins much less triplets, but when you live your whole life with someone you're that close to, I guess it's just natural for them. "You could have been seriously hurt."

"Well, I had to think on my feet or I was afraid I was going to end up on my back. I didn't see another way around it," I said, starting to feel warm relief in my heart that I wasn't completely on my own on this one. My teammates have always reliably backed me up in the field. I felt so isolated throughout the drive home thinking that this time, though, I was hanging all the way out on my own.

I breathed more easily as the conversation continued, knowing my teammates were both on my side. As quietly as possible so the conversation wouldn't carry outside the garage, I said, "Since last night, laying in my sleeping bag and then all the way home, I've been trying to think of any way things could have gone differently. What were my options? If they were just going to rob us, I could have lived with that. Besides, it was Arnaud who flashed all that cash in his wallet. But once Pistol decided he wanted more from me than the little money I had in my purse—"

Arnaud's eyes narrowed. "Who?"

"The guy I kicked, obviously," I responded gruffly. "He was holding the pistol."

"Oh, him," Claude said. "One of the other guys—the one Arnie killed—called him Jack."

It never occurred to me to even pretend to care what his name was. "Jack. Jackass. Whatever," I muttered. "I guess maybe I didn't need to break his neck after the other two were out of the picture. But then what would we have done? Tied him up and called the police with two bodies there?"

The unattractive scenario of being subjected to a probing homicide investigation by the local police played through my mind. That would almost certainly end up revealing too much about our team for Michael's likes. It reaffirmed in my mind that I'd done the right thing not just to save myself, but also to preserve our team's identity, cover, and association with the Agency. The sun seemed to shine just a little bit brighter that afternoon once I could see my teammates were firmly on my side.

"I'll talk to Michael tomorrow and tell him what happened. You guys don't have to be there. It was my doing and if he wants to get mad at anyone, it should be me."

Claude responded abruptly. "Like hell you will. Arnie and I will be there to tell Mike what an amazing reversal you pulled off. It was quite a sight to behold."

I felt confident that Claude was referring to my tactics and not my breasts. If Arnaud had said it, I would not have automatically given him the benefit of the doubt.

Arnaud jumped in. "Yeah, and we certainly don't want *you* telling Mike the part about how Claude and I got caught flat-footed when Jack grabbed Steve." He winked at his brother. "We're going to have to make up a story about how there were twenty of them, and we got all but your two."

"You guys were unarmed, and they grabbed Steven before you even knew they were there. You two also had Monica and Paige to worry about," I said, giving the brothers a way to save face in their coming conversation with Michael.

"But you were unarmed, too," Arnaud said.

I smiled. "Not true. I had an almost-full roll of TP."

After years trying everything I could think of and working my butt off to earn my rightful place on the team, a new layer was finally growing in our relationship, strengthening the bond of trust between the three of us. At last, they seemed ready to accept me as a permanent fixture in their lives and someone they could rely upon to do anything and everything that's necessary to finish the job.

Even more importantly, they were opening up to me about how they felt about my being on the team. They were lowering the drawbridge to their clubhouse.

Arnaud summed up something else that disturbed me as it floated around my mind during the drive home. "Is it just me, or did either of you notice a bit of a family resemblance between Jack and Doug, the park manager? I've been wondering if maybe that's how those three morons knew we'd be out there alone last night."

***

"You've been very quiet. Is everything alright?" Steven asked me on the short drive back to our condo.

"Yes. I'm fine, thanks," I said, still delighting in the recognition I'd gotten from the Payeur brothers as the savior of the day. I relished finally being viewed by them as a professional qualified to work on Michael's team.

"Where'd you learn to do that?"

I should have expected him to ask but thought he would have waited until we got home and cleaned up. I deflected his question weakly with one of my own. "Do what?"

"You know... the neck thing. I mean, I've seen you shoot plenty of times. Every time you come to the range with us you put Jon Brady to shame. Every single time. He doesn't let it show, but it eats him up inside. He's been shooting for twice as long as you, but your groupings are so tight I've actually seen his jaw drop. But the other thing—"

"Oh, that... it's just something that we learn in training. Like first aid, everyone learns it," I lied, still wanting to protect Steven from the burden of knowing what I do for a living. "But you never expect you'll have to actually *use* it. It all happened so fast, I didn't know what to do. I'd never been in a situation like that," which was less of a lie, but still not the truth.

"And I hope I never will be again," I said. That part was completely true.

"I never should have agreed to go camping," Steven said, seemingly to himself. He glanced at me sideways. "I thought it'd be okay for one weekend. I really did want to have a good time with you... but I'm sure I should've said 'no' and just not gone. I don't know.... Once we were out there, it all happened so fast."

"Yeah, when thing go bad, it kinda happens all at once."

So, what was Steven saying? That it was all my fault? I stared out the car's side window and crossed my arms as we approached our building. It distressed me that not once did he so much as ask how I was feeling.

That night was one of those in which I badly needed Steven to hold me close and be supportive. Instead, the distance between us left me feeling isolated, even when lying in bed next to each other. We both had a stressful weekend, and whatever was going on between us had only been made worse by the trying events of the previous afternoon. My plan to spend some quality time with him away from the city to draw us closer together had clearly backfired.

Chapter 26

That Tuesday afternoon in his office, Steven found it a monumental task getting the right words out of his mouth. A mixture of apprehension and concern permeated his voice. "Are you... y-your fieldwork...." He stumbled repeatedly, tripping on the words, unable to verbalize the thought that both excited and, at the same time, terrified him.

The purely masculine part of him wanted it to be true so he could feel proud of me. That way, his ego would be buoyed in front of other men. Then he could think of himself as the Big Man on Campus when he's seen with me on his arm or holding hands as we walked through the halls of CIA headquarters. Even if few others would ever know the truth because so much of what I do is somewhere between highly classified and completely denied, *he* would know. It would be enough to supersize his ego, and I so badly wanted that for him.

At the same time, the intellectual in him already knew what he suspected was indeed true. I could see from the way he squinted his eyes as he repeatedly tried and failed to ask that the question was wrenching his gut. If I answered in the affirmative, the risks implied for me would be hard for him to stomach. Sometimes, ignorance really is bliss.

Throughout the time we'd been together, I consistently stuck to my cover story, telling Steven that I worked in the Special Activities Division as a Technical Penetration Specialist. On Michael's team, our missions largely involved breaking into homes and offices overseas to crack safes, steal documents, or wire the places with surreptitious audio and video equipment.

Steven knew that such missions are real espionage work with real dangers of being caught by security guards, employees, or police. I felt bad having to use a cover story and lying to him so blatantly while living with him, but it was safer for everyone that way. Armed with the knowledge of the serious risks my fieldwork entailed, he supported me wonderfully by helping me maintain my commercial "sales girl" cover publicly. That way, I could talk to him about my travel plans and still be confident that he'd keep up the charade to our non-Agency friends about my frequent and often short-notice business trips.

"Do you...." The fits and starts continued as he tried to verbalize his thoughts and form a coherent sentence. He couldn't bring himself to say the words. I needed to help my love do what he needed to bring himself to do, so I stood up from the not-all-that-comfortable government-issue visitor's chair opposite his desk. I stepped slowly toward the exit of his fifth-floor office in the Directorate of Intelligence, edging towards the closed door clearly intent on leaving him alone with his question unanswered if he didn't act swiftly.

With a slightly seductive twist of my hips, I made my way to the door, one brown strappy high-heeled sandal after the other. I made it obvious that I wanted him to ask but would leave whether he did or not. Although not completely confident it would work, I felt the pressure of my imminent departure should be enough to pry open his overly tense lips. Either way, I had to try.

I placed my hand on the doorknob and paused. I turned my head to look at him, flinging my shoulder-length hair around my neck and out of the way. I gave him a final verbal push. "Just ask me, honey, and we'll consider today the day that you finally popped *The Question*."

I said it softly with a combination of playful urging and mild sarcasm. Speaking softly is a behavior that just about everyone at CIA seems to adopt by nature, usually without giving it much thought. Even though his office was secure from foreign eavesdropping attempts, the doors are not soundproof, and I didn't want his secretary to hear that part of our conversation.

Steven didn't have to try to speak softly. He could barely get those four words out of his mouth and pushed them out hoarsely, barely above a whisper. "Are you an assassin?"

Whichever way I might answer, he was at that moment both anxious and apprehensive to hear it. If indeed I was what he wanted me to either confirm or deny, I knew he feared that by having figured it out, his act of just posing the question could be what ended our relationship. Although we'd had our problems recently, we've both invested our full energies in our relationship, had fallen in love, and still wanted to make work. Maybe he thought that if he did successfully figure it out, he might become my next target.

If, on the other hand, I was *not* what he suspected, he surely risked insulting me and hurting me deeply by showing he could possibly think such a thing of his sweet, innocent Michelle. For him, the embarrassment of being wrong and the inevitable ridicule I would assuredly visit upon him for years to come was an uncomfortable, albeit remote, possibility.

I also knew my man perfectly well and saw that the same insatiable drive for certainty that was propelling him to great heights within CIA's analytical ranks also made it impossible for him to not bring closure to *The Question* that plagued him.

Finally, he asked it.

And suddenly, I had to decide how to answer him.

A few years earlier when he asked me to move in with him, I told him that I did not see myself ever having kids and would not marry him until we both retired. I made it clear that he was free to ask me to leave at any time if he decided he wanted something else in a relationship—something I couldn't or wouldn't give him. But he was not to ever ask me *The Question*.

My wisecrack about him popping *The Question* that afternoon was going to remain an inside joke. From my point of view anyway, *at* that place and *at* that time, I thought it was funny. The answer I was about to give him, however, would be anything but humorous. I looked at him across the faux-pine-wood veneer of his government-issued desk and hesitated for dramatic effect.

"Yes," I answered simply and truthfully with a lover's satisfaction at having helped him verbalize what he so acutely needed to ask. A weight dropped from my shoulders—I no longer had to bear the burden of hiding my biggest secret from him. A tingle ran along my scalp as I relished the thought that we now had one more intimate detail of our lives to share between us, even if we could never admit it to anyone else.

I pulled his office door open and spoke loudly enough that his secretary could hear me clearly. "I love you, too. See you at home tonight, hon. I'll be waiting for you." I left his office wearing one of the biggest smiles of my life.

As I walked down the hallway towards the elevators, I tried hard to imagine whether the look on his face at that moment expressed relief or sheer terror. Was he wondering if I'd be waiting for him at home that evening with lingerie or a ligature?

Maybe I have a bit of a dark streak in my sense of humor. Perhaps that's uncharacteristic of a woman, but what in my life isn't?

Chapter 27

"I'm in the kitchen," I said loudly towards the hallway as our condo's front door swung open. "You're home early. Dinner's not ready yet. I'm still making the salads."

Steven's briefcase thudded onto the carpet next to the front door almost a half-hour earlier than I expected. Not that I always made it home first, much less cooked dinner most nights, but after our conversation in his office I wanted to do something special. No doubt, he'd have a million questions, and I'd need a glass of wine. Or two. Or three.

I slid a dozen red pepper slices off the butcher's block into the salad bowl and sauntered off to the hallway for a hello kiss.

"I'm making your favorite salmon dish with the Cajun spice rub," I said rounding the corner and coming face to face with my love. I expected a kiss and could not have been more surprised when Steven back-pedaled faster than I've seen him move in a long time.

His eyes flew open as wide as his face allowed, his hazel eyes trying to escape from their sockets. He stumbled back a step, which stopped me in my tracks as I paused to figure out what was happening. I reached my arms forward to calm him, and an electric current from the realization of my gargantuan mistake shot up my spine.

"No. No. No! I'm sorry, I'm *sorry*!" I yelled as I sprinted back to the kitchen. I threw the eight-inch Henckels chef's knife I'd been using to chop the peppers into the stainless-steel sink. It landed with a loud *clank*, making as audible a signal of disarming myself as I possibly could.

"I'm *soooo* sorry, Steven. I wasn't thinking, honey. Honest. I'm just so stupid. It's good, I promise. We're good," I yammered, not able to think of anything more articulate or reassuring to say in the heat of the moment.

With my empty hands up and fingers spread wide, I slowly approached him and offered my full surrender. "I didn't mean to come at you with a knife, especially after this weekend. Really. I was making the salad, and you walked in, and I wanted a kiss, and I wasn't thinking, and I... I'm sorry, sweetie. Truly."

Steven's eyes retreated back into the safety of his skull and he stepped slowly towards me in the hallway at the edge of the kitchen. Even in the dim light, I could see how fast his heart was racing by the rapid pulsing of his carotid artery along the right side of his neck.

He grasped my outstretched and obviously empty hands with his own, pushed them up over my head, and pressed me against the wall more aggressively than he had done since early in our relationship. His lips touched mine gently at first, giving me a welcome sign that my mistake was in the process of being forgiven.

After his rather meek manner earlier in the day, the smile of my surprise at the sudden, complete, and oh-so-welcome change in his demeanor must have showed clearly across my face. The shock of my sudden appearance in the hallway with a rather menacing blade certainly got his adrenaline flowing. His pulse pounded through his lips as they touched mine.

Steven pulled back an inch and whispered, "If this is going to be our last kiss, I want to make it the kind of kiss you deserve." He pressed his lips against mine more forcefully this time, increasing the pressure as he nestled his body against mine. Caught between Steven and the wall, I wanted to throw my arms around him and squeeze. With my hands still solidly restrained above my head, all I could do was return the passion of his kiss with my own.

I've never thought of myself as the kind of woman prone to swooning, but I came close!

"If you keep kissing me like that," I whispered, "I'm going to have to keep you around for a while. And if I didn't have two fish filets in the oven, I'd prove it to you right here in the hallway. I've got two bottles of wine on the table, and I'm already a glass into the first. Why don't you catch up and I'll get the rest of dinner ready?"

"Okay," he said as he took a half-step back. The start of a more relaxed countenance replaced the wrinkles of worry that I caused him to wear earlier. "But I think I'll need more than just a glass or two tonight."

***

Our dinner conversation was polite but bland. The wine must not have kicked in for him as rapidly as it had spread its wonderful warmth up through my belly and across both shoulders.

During a lull in the conversation, I bluntly asked, "What made you first suspect me?"

He must have expected I'd ask something of the sort but hesitated before answering as if he hadn't come up with a prepared answer before arriving home.

"The way you and Arnie handled yourselves in West Virginia this weekend made it obvious. Though, all the way home I believed, or at least wanted to believe, what you said: that it was just training you all get at the Farm, but never expect to have to use in real life.

"I knew you were a terrific shot from all the times we've gone to the firing range with Jon and the guys, so that wasn't a surprise. Of course, I'd never seen anyone actually die... in person... right in front of me. It probably should have surprised me more that it came so...."

He paused to collect his thoughts. "So, easily to you. Maybe *easily* isn't the right word, but I don't know what is. You didn't act as though it was easy and, anyway, I think we were all in shock afterwards. Especially Paige. By the way, is she doing alright?"

"It's never easy, and yes, Arnaud said she's fine, although she broke up with him by phone yesterday, not too surprisingly."

"You and Arnie acted as though you knew exactly what to do. I know it wasn't rehearsed, but it looked so... practiced. So effortless. Was it scary?"

"Honestly, Steven, I can't say that I've *never* been so scared in my life.... I *have* been... once or twice before. It's never easy, but, yeah. Even though what happened was all basically self-defense, it certainly sucked for all of us."

After another pause, he asked "When was your first?"

"Nice try, Dr. Krauss," I responded, heading off his inquiry. "You haven't answered my question, yet, so I don't have to answer yours until you do." I forked a slice of tomato into my mouth and smiled, clearly putting the conversation back in his court.

"Okay," he agreed with a chuckle. "Seeing it actually happen in West Virginia was what made it all click, but it's also the timing. It's always the timing. You've always said that your operational trips were sometimes dangerous, and those of us in the DI respect the Directorate of Operations teams that go into harm's way. You know we do, even if we don't always admit it aloud or feed your egos and tell you as often as you might like," he said with a grin.

"You've been pretty good about telling me when you're just away on training, so I don't have to worry as much those times. The other times... well, it's just the little things... things that have added up over the past couple of years. There were just too many coincidences between your trips and things that happen around the world when you were operational. Such as a banker moving money for terrorists gets killed, which prevents the attack they'd been planning. Or some courier is run over by a car and his briefcase—which we so desperately wanted oh-by-the-way—mysteriously appears and is suspiciously attributed to a new clandestine source nobody's ever heard of before and who never reports in again. Those kinds of things."

"And don't forget the North Korean double agent who very conveniently had a heart attack in Las Vegas," I added and foisted a slice of cucumber into my mouth. I pointed to him with my fork and continued relating my story. "Remember the time I showed up out of the blue one day with my hair bleached blonde? It was for that trip. It wasn't all fun and games, but as the saying goes, whatever spy goes to Vegas, stays in Vegas."

"*Ugh,*" Steven groaned. He motioned to the fork in my hand and asked, "And do you have to aim every sharp object in the house at me all in one night?"

I savored seeing his composure return and that he could laugh about my earlier misstep.

"But seriously," he said turning the conversation over to me. "It's your turn now, Miss Kopechne."

I nodded and reflected on Steven's use of my real last name—a name I hadn't heard since visiting my cousins in California two years earlier. It sounded odd to my ears—somehow hollow. I found myself identifying much more with my new life than I ever would have expected. In the beginning, I thought that a cover story would be something I had to work hard to live by, always hiding my true self. But it turned out that just the opposite became true. I *became* my cover story, and it started to define who I was. Who I *am.*

Michelle Kopechne may have become a CIA employee when she was eighteen, but she had no future after that. She didn't die that day, but she slowly faded away, gradually evaporating from the Earth. Everything I've done since then is entirely attributable to the new me—Michelle Reagan—who Michael created out of whole cloth with the mixture of a little need and a boat load of training.

Steven sat back and soaked up my recounting the details of my life from before we met on that crazy evening at the Farm. "Really, it's just like you've heard me say before. I joined right out of high school with no skills or experience. I still don't understand exactly why the Agency wanted me, other than they needed a blank slate with no public exposure from college or publications or anything. I had very little family back home and hadn't traveled to foreign countries under any identities at all—except Canada, of course, but that doesn't count. It's just Canada. My shooting, well, you already know about that. While in the Basic Intelligence Operations class that fall—and I still don't know exactly how—Michael found me. Probably the shooting, right? Makes sense, but he wouldn't tell me when I asked. He probably had certain instructors on the lookout, and they tipped him off. It's not as if he could publish a position description for this line of work, right?"

Without mentioning Aruba by name, I made my first mission sound sexier and less awkward than it truly was. I did that mostly for Steven's benefit, but maybe also a little bit for me, too, so I didn't have to dredge up too much of the internal conflict and pain I experienced after that trip. "I was so green and inexperienced. I made a lot of mistakes that night, Lord knows, but somehow I survived in spite of myself... and, here I am."

"I never realized what you go through...." he said as his voice trailed off in thought. He looked up suddenly as though he had just remembered something and asked, "So, why did you pick the name *Reagan* as your undercover name?"

"I didn't choose it, Michael did. Back then, I didn't give it much thought. I've come to think of it as his way of honoring his favorite president. When Michael was in the Army, he was one of the Special Forces officers that flew into Iran for the failed hostage rescue mission. You know, Desert One? Michael had friends who died on that mission. Anyway, he hated Carter for how that all went down but respected Reagan for getting the hostages back safely without a shot being fired. I think that's why he gave this particular name to me. I use the name *Reagan* for most things, although I travel under a lot of other names."

"At least your cover works well to give you an excuse for traveling all the time," Steven mused.

He never travels under cover but knows how much time we spend apart. Too much, if you ask me, and that contributed to the strain on our relationship. Now that he knew the truth about my work, I wasn't sure which way the relationship would go. He'd either accept what he learned and live with it, or his discovery was going to mean the end of everything we worked so hard to build. I could only hope for the best.

"Yeah, lots of travel," I said. "Sometimes the travel's fun, and sometimes it's not. Remember that trip to Vegas I mentioned? Parts of that trip were enjoyable, such as learning to play poker with someone else's money. But you have absolutely no idea how uncomfortable it is to hide an electronic stun gun and a vial of poison up your miniskirt all afternoon."

Steven half-laughed, half-snorted. "No, that I don't." His eyes angled up towards the ceiling for a second, and I could tell he was trying to picture me in a miniskirt as he ate the final piece of salmon.

"Poisoned a spy in Vegas, did you? I hadn't given it any thought before, but I guess you've had to use all the tools of the trade, huh? In West Virginia, I saw you use a gun and your bare hands. Add poison to the list and what else? A rifle? A knife? Ever managed to successfully drop that boulder on Road Runner's head—"

"No, never a knife," I said cutting him off mid-sentence. "Not for me anyway, even though Arnaud did exactly that on Saturday. It may look cool and macho in the movies, but it's rarely practical for me. I don't have the upper-body strength required to overpower most men, nor the height I'd need to reach their necks. It's also incredibly messy, especially if you go for the throat. Blood would get all over. The movies never show it, but the arterial spray spreads pretty far. There's no way I'd be able to get away cleanly—literally *cleanly*. It's messy enough when you make a headshot," I continued rapidly, enjoying being able to finally share something that I know with a man who is so much more of an intellectual than I could ever pretend to be. "It's not as though the person's heart stops beating all of a sudden. Blood still gushes out of the wound in spurts for a good long while. And with a gunshot, there's the blood, brain matter, and chunks of skull splattered all over the wall or car window—"

Steven's chair hit the floor with a *thunk* as he bolted from the table. At first, I didn't understand what was going on, but when he made a beeline for the bathroom, the realization hit me. I had spoken far too graphically when describing the gore involved in taking a person's life.

I detoured briefly on my way to the bathroom to get a washcloth and wet it in the sink to help comfort him. I felt terrible again, watching Steven retch, all because of my insensitivity.

"I know this is getting old, but I'll say it again. I am *so* sorry. That was terrible of me, going into too much detail way too quickly. And while eating, too. I know I've been saying this a lot tonight, honey, but I'm really, *really* sorry."

My apologies had little soothing effect on a shaken and shivering Steven as he knelt over the toilet bowl. Nothing else I could say would have been of much comfort to him, so I just wrapped my arms around him and held him gently.

As he recovered his composure and stepped to the sink to brush his teeth, I looked up at him from my seat on the edge of the bathtub. "I'll go clean up the dishes and meet you on the couch when you're feeling ready."

On my way back to the kitchen, I placed a tender kiss on his cheek.

***

I set a glass of ice water for Steven on one of his wood-and-cork Columbia University coasters on our coffee table and sat down on the sofa next to him. With my third glass of Chardonnay in hand, I sipped slowly, crossed my legs underneath me, and softly leaned my head against his shoulder. I tried to think of something to say but came up empty. My repeated apologies, while heart-felt, sounded stale, even to me.

Steven beat me to the punch. He asked simply, "What about Claude and Arnie?"

I just nodded my affirmation that we were all in the same line of work.

"I'm sure it's physically strenuous. Is it difficult mentally?"

"I cried a lot after my first mission," I admitted out loud for the first time in my life. "A lot. I was so confused. I guess that's understandable. Everything was so new to me. I knew what I had agreed to do, of course, but you never really, truly understand it until you've actually gone through with it. On the flight home, I got unbelievably paranoid. I was sure I'd get caught and the police would show up at my front door at any moment.

"For the next couple of days, I barely ate and practically barricaded myself in my apartment. For a little while, I was afraid of everything, every shadow, every bump in the night, as they say. I felt safer in my apartment than outside, but, still, I was sure that something bad was going to come my way. Eventually, I went out for a run. When I got home and no one was there waiting to slap the cuffs on me, I started to relax a bit. But it took time.

"Nowadays, I'll just go down to the Farm for a few days to escape the world and completely unwind. That's the one place in the world where I don't have to pretend I'm not CIA.

"Which is weird, if you think about it. I mean, that's where Case Officers learn in the first place to lie so convincingly about *not* being CIA officers, right? But for me, it's just about the only place to go where I can be openly Agency, talk to others who are there for in-service training classes, and we can have a beer or three and shoot the shit about some hell-hole of a country or the fouled-up traffic in such-and-such a city. We all know we're skipping over the operational details, but that's completely expected, so I don't have to pretend otherwise. We're all down there knowing full-well that we're holding out on each other and it's normal. We all expect it. For me, it's relaxing. Some guys call the Cantina the Liar's Club. I suppose it is. Maybe that's why I enjoy it so much.

"After that first mission, though, I was horribly conflicted about my feelings. So many emotions fought each other to get to the front of my mind. They were all over the place and at odds with each other. It seemed so unfair, because, if I were, say, an Air Force fighter pilot or a soldier back from a war, they'd give me a medal and a ticker tape parade. Instead, I had to live under an alias, hide the real me from my friends, and couldn't even tell people inside the Agency about my work. I wasn't sure if I was angry, scared, ashamed, or what."

Steven squeezed my hand.

Our intertwined fingers lazily explored the backs of each other's hands. "After a few days, things changed, but not so much for the better. Suddenly, I had all kinds of nervous energy and couldn't sit still. A very long run around the Reston golf course helped me burn it off. I just ran and ran and ran and have no idea how long it ended up being—hours at least. That exhausted me and made me incredibly hungry. My memories of the salty and sweet taste of the marinade the huge steak dinner I splurged on that night in Reston Town Center still excites me. The running definitely helped me get my head screwed back on straight, but I still have some... um... deep seated feelings maybe you'd call it, about that first mission. A hesitancy about it. The first one's always the hardest to come to terms with."

"I suppose it would be."

"And, in some ways, you never completely get over it. At least I haven't—not entirely. That's also when I started going to yoga classes a couple of times a week. Oh, man, what a great workout that is. How can anyone not love it? Back then, I just wanted the peace of mind everyone says you get from yoga. By the way, it doesn't happen right away—not at all. But over time, it has helped me stay focused mentally, and in good shape, too."

"You're certainly in fantastic shape. That's for sure. Do you find that you have any of the problems that are so common among soldiers who come back from combat? I mean PTSD or nightmares or anything?"

"I used to have some bad dreams and occasionally wake up in the middle of the night, but that hasn't happened in a while. The short answer is no, not much. I talk to the military guys I train with as much as I can, and I ask a few of them about it when I get the chance. They're mostly Army Green Berets and a few Delta operators, sometimes Navy SEALs. Almost all of them have been in combat. Most of them are not about to open up to a strange woman, especially a civilian who randomly shows up in one of their classes. A few have been willing to talk, though. I think there are two huge differences between what they do and what I do, which lets me keep my wits about me.

"First, when they're in a war zone, they're living every minute of every day in a hostile environment. They eventually get into the mindset that, at any time, someone may start shooting at them, mortars might drop into their compound, or a roadside bomb might explode while they're driving down some random street. There's so little safety for them in-theater. They're overstressed for so many months at a time that they can't come down from constantly living in a heightened state of alert. That's why some of them react so violently when they come home, and someone drops a book or something that would otherwise be trivial happens around them. Those guys are expected to magically turn off all their hard-earned survival instincts just because they're stateside again, but the human brain doesn't work like that. It's asking too much of them. For me, though, I don't spend enough time in-country for it to have become a problem."

"I'm glad for that," Steven said.

I nodded. "Me too. Second, and I see this all the time in training, the military guys have it drilled into them that they can only shoot *these* people and not *those* people. It's a constant struggle for them to always do target evaluation and selection on every person they see. Whether they're making entry into a hostile's house or just walking down the street, they're always having to calculate the shoot/don't-shoot equation. It's a constant state of stress heaped upon them by their commanders that they'll get disciplined or court martialed if they shoot the wrong person. The pressures on those soldiers never let up.

"I don't operate under the microscope the way they have to. I never worry that anyone is going to reprimand me for doing whatever I have to do to get to my primary target. When the decision is made to send our team in, then the decision has already been made that all other options have been ruled out. The Director knows at that point there are no easy ways to handle the situation. Michael accepts that we do whatever we need to do in the field to get the job done. There's no leash on us. No second-guessing from headquarters. No court-martials waiting when more than just the primary target—"

I stopped, unable to complete the thought in front of Steven, not wanting to seem cavalier about work I so dearly take to heart.

"Gets killed?" Steven asked.

I nodded. "It's serious business, and I never just go around shooting random people. It may sound weird, but I don't enjoy hurting people. I don't walk around thinking about shooting *him* or stabbing *her* when I pass people on the street. That'd be horrible. I really am a nice person!"

"You certainly are. I'm having a little trouble squaring the thought of the Michelle I know and love doing the kind of work you're describing."

"Thank you. I love you too."

"I'm sure this will sound sexist," Steven warned, "but I don't know how else to ask it. Is it harder for you, being a woman?"

I knew he'd ask that question at some point and smiled a little bit while answering. "At least you're willing to ask me directly, so thank you for that. Everyone else just looks at me with the same question on their minds, but no one has the guts to put it out there. The answer is simply that I don't really know. I have no way of comparing it to anything. The guys don't talk about it, at least not to me. Maybe they talk to each other. They are twin brothers, after all."

I couldn't imagine either Claude or Arnaud ever talking about his feelings, but if they did open up to anyone, it certainly would not be to me.

"Being an operator is not exactly the kind of job my mother would have chosen for me, that's for sure. I don't enjoy causing people pain and don't see this as hurting them. What I mean is that I'm not doing it specifically to punish them, but instead to prevent them from killing innocent people in the future. Let's not get into the gory stuff again," I said stroking Steven's forearm. "I just do what needs doing and get it over with. Most of them are bad people doing terrible things and we're all much, much better off—a lot safer—with them gone."

"'Most of them?'" Steven asked, echoing my own words.

"Well... sometimes people are just in the wrong place at the wrong time. As I said, I still have a—I don't know what to call it—a *hesitancy* about it."

"I'm pretty sure I don't want to know about *that*," he said softly.

"Maybe the only bad part of specifically being a woman in this job is that I don't have a girlfriend I can talk to. Women share everything. You probably think we talk too much, huh?" I smirked at Steven. "I wasn't able to talk to my mother about it when she was alive. When I talk with Allison, I'm always on guard to maintain my cover, so I never get to share specifically *why* I feel the way I do. Sometimes, when I can share my feelings with her, I have to make up an entire story about why I'm feeling that way. It gets complicated and can be more trouble than its worth.

"Now, maybe, I can at least talk to you and you'll understand why I'm feeling what I am, even if I still can't tell you all the details. You'll at least know enough," I said hopefully.

"Yes, of course. I'll always be here for you. Things have been somewhat bumpy for us lately, and I was convinced that you were holding out on me—holding something back. That's why I had to ask you today in my office. But, wow, *this*? I'm not sure whether my knowing is going to make things easier for me or not. Your analogy of the Air Force fighter pilot is a really good one. That makes sense to me. This is a lot for me to process, and I'm going to do it. You deserve it, and our relationship deserves it. You just have to give me some time, okay?"

I nodded and gave his arm a squeeze to let him know I appreciated his saying so. We both had work to do on our relationship.

I drained the little bit of dry red wine remaining and placed my empty glass on the coffee table. "So, how do you feel about all of this now that you know?"

"Well... I'm amazed, really. Even though I thought I was right about it, hearing that it's really true is something that'll take some getting used to. Here I have this kick-ass girlfriend, and I can't even tell anybody about her. Admittedly, I'm going to worry about you even more now when you travel."

Steven leaned over, gave me a kiss, and squeezed my knee for emphasis. He slid his arm around me and pulled me in firmly. We leaned against each other for mutual support, enjoying both the comfort of a lover and the closeness of an understanding and supportive friend.

After a time, he asked, "Are you going to tell Michael?"

I nodded again. "Yes, but he'll be okay with it. I think he expected you to figure it out sooner, actually. He knows that you'll keep it to yourself. And you *do* know that you can't tell anyone, right? Not Jon... no one at all."

It was his turn to nod.

"I'm not being dramatic, Steven. This really is serious stuff. Completely deniable. I'm always under non-official cover and my life is on the line every time I travel. You and I shouldn't even be talking about it here, and we can't talk in your office, at least not when anyone else could overhear."

I gently pulled his chin towards me for emphasis and looked him in the eye. "Tell me you understand."

"Yes, Michelle, I understand completely. You have my word."

Steven reached out to me and framed my cheek with his hand. He slid his other hand up the base of my neck to the back of my head and interlaced his fingers through my hair. I could feel his sincerity in the motion of his lips as we kissed. He told me verbally that I had his word, and with his mouth he was telling me that I also had his heart.

Steven had had a very difficult couple of days, and most of it was my fault. I let him know just how much I loved him by making it up to him, first on the couch and then again in bed that night.

PART EIGHT

CAYMAN PAIN

Chapter 28

Bang!

The blaze of pain consumed my left thigh even before the gunshot's echoes ceased reverberating through the lawyer's office on Cayman Brac. The searing heat of the bullet filled my thigh and buckled my knee. I collapsed to the floor with the ungainly clatter of a marionette cut from her strings. The all-encompassing wave of misery rushed up through my torso as if it wanted to escape through my ears.

My graceless impact with the floor jarred my right hand, sending an errant bullet flying off to who-the-hell-knows-where with a suppressed *thwwopp.*

Damn it! I got three of the bastards, I realized, *but must have just winged Sokolov.*

I braced for the pain my next movement was going cause. I twisted my hips, threw my legs back, flopped my arms over Chen's lifeless chest, and let the pain out through my clenched lips with a muffled, but forceful growl.

I brought my .45 caliber Sig Sauer down and pointed it in the general direction of Sokolov's mid-section. In rapid succession, I pulled the trigger twice. I know at least one bullet hit him because he fell back and moaned. The short Russian tried to raise the small pistol in his left hand but couldn't muster the strength to lift it. Blood erupted from the fat man's mouth and flowed along his cheeks like lava forced from a bubbling caldera.

A noisy chorus emerged from Sokolov as he tried to breathe through the same mouth, which also served as the only outlet for the blood filling his throat and lungs. He gurgled, choked, and convulsed as he tried in vain to simultaneously inhale air and expel blood.

To raise myself to a standing position, I pushed against Chen's torso and the wooden chair from which he had fallen just ten or fifteen seconds earlier. I hobbled across the room favoring my right leg, slaloming around the bodies littering the floor. I limped methodically between padded leather chairs in front of the hand-carved wooden desk and lowered myself roughly into the chair previously occupied by Sokolov.

I looked down at the large man at my feet and snarled to get his attention while he choked to death. Out of spite, I kicked him in his mid-section. My intention was good, but it failed in execution.

"Oww! Shit." The kick sent another wave of pain up my leg. I'm an idiot. That one I did to myself and I knew it.

A bubble of blood leaped from Sokolov's mouth. His laugh expelled the last of the air residing deep within his lungs. His convulsions diminished as he lost his battle for breath.

I stared directly into his still-alert eyes and forced the words out through the pain ravaging my thigh. "Listen up, dickhead. My name is Eden. This wasn't personal before, but it is now. I hope this hurts."

I fired another bullet into his lower abdomen as I did not want him to die too soon. I watched convulsions torture his face as he reacted to the explosion of pain.

"I don't want you to die right away, you son of a bitch. I want you to know that you shot me with your little toy gun, there. What is that, a Beretta .25? No. What is it? A Walther PP. Seriously? No one uses a .380 auto anymore. You watch too many old movies."

The next bullet I fired into the left side of Sokolov's belly barely registered on his face. Unable to breath for a minute now, he was fading swiftly.

I leaned forward, reached into the inside pocket of his sports coat, and removed the black leather-bound notebook—the real reason for my mission. I dropped the notebook into a zip-lock bag and returned the baggie safely to the pocket inside my windbreaker.

I reached down and drew out the blue-and-white silk pocket square from Sokolov's blazer. I removed the belt from my jeans and fashioned a makeshift bandage just above my left knee where the hole in the center of the growing red stain was graphically telling the story of my wound. The belt held the pocket square firmly in place, but I left it loose enough to not act as a tourniquet cutting off all blood flow. The improvised field dressing stayed in place well enough as I stood.

In Sokolov's mouth, blood pooled without a ripple. His eyes rolled aimlessly, unable to focus. He had drifted beyond the point of no return and was not worth the effort to taunt further. I administered the *coup de grâce* without further insult and turned to leave.

The two bodies in the outer office laid where they had fallen minutes before when I shot the pair of bodyguards from my perch on the fire escape. I exited the same window through which I had entered all of... what? Three minutes earlier?

I limped down the fire escape to my car for the fifteen-minute drive to what was then the Gerrard-Smith International Airport. The throbs coursing the length of my left thigh were more present than the pain, except for the few times I brought the Ford Escape to a stop. Fresh waves of agony cascaded up my leg as the car jerked during the unavoidable starts and stops.

I retraced the drive from my arrival only hours earlier to the sole airport on Cayman Brac. The airport's single terminal building accommodates commercial passengers who fly to the other two Cayman Islands or on the less-frequent flights to Miami. Passengers who play by the rules pass through security, customs, and immigration in the centrally located terminal.

Since I was limping, bleeding, and still had a bullet lodged somewhere inside my left thigh, I found it far more expedient to bypass that building completely. Understandably, security was not something I wanted anything to do with that afternoon. I slipped past the terminal building and made it to my plane by skirting the edge of the small maintenance facility just west of the terminal.

I pushed myself up the ten steps to board the Gulfstream III jet one painful stair after the next. I grimaced hard with each push of my arms on the handrails and bit my bottom lip to keep from grunting, which might have drawn the attention of the maintenance crew working on a nearby aircraft.

Upon reaching the top step, I was rewarded with a clear view of the name painted on the side of the plane, Caribbean Air Charter—a CIA front company. Like an aerial No-Tell Motel, they get our people and cargo to and from anywhere in the world, no questions asked. A *proprietary* in the vernacular of the spy business, it's the modern incarnation of the Civil Air Transport and Air America companies from the 1950s and '60s. Those companies became too well known and lost their effectiveness, so the CIA disbanded them.

"Wheels up," I tried yelling at the pilots lounging in two of the large brown leather seats in the small jet's passenger compartment. The raspy mixture of air and pain forced from my lungs sounded more like a loud wheeze than an urgent command. "Get us out of here now."

I collapsed into the front-row seat and reclined it to elevate my wounded leg as high as possible.

"I'll pull the chocks and do a walk-around," the co-pilot said, rushing forward to the cabin door.

"Make it a *run*-around, Doug," the pilot commanded on his way to the cockpit. "I'll get departure clearance."

"On it," the co-pilot replied from half-way down the stairs.

The G-III used most of the airport's six-thousand-foot runway to takeoff, launching us on our twelve-hundred-mile return flight to Virginia.

"What happened to you? How can I help?" co-pilot Doug asked as the pilot leveled the plane at an intermediate altitude on our departure leg, northbound over Cuba.

My grimace sufficed for the smile I couldn't quite bring myself to make. "I zigged when I should have zagged."

"How'd you get past security like that?"

"Security," I repeated. "Yeah, I kinda skipped that part." I unzipped my jacket and showed Doug my holstered Sig.

A look of concern crossed his face. "Is it cleared?"

"No, it's loaded. Best to leave it in the holster for now."

"Yeah. Let me take a look at your leg."

"If you have a first-aid kit, help me change the bandage," I said, more a directive than suggestion.

"Got one in the cabinet. Be right back."

I removed my blood-stained belt and the co-pilot cut away the left leg of my jeans. The conveniently located bullet hole served as a natural starting place for the medical shears.

I smiled weakly at Doug. "Normally, I get rather excited when a good-looking guy takes off my pants, but you'll understand if I say I'm not exactly in the mood, won't you?"

Doug returned my smile while he swapped out a sterile bandage for Sokolov's pocket square. "This would indeed be much easier if you were wearing a short skirt. Press down hard on this."

"Looks like my sense of fashion is as bad as my sense of direction today, huh? I did not plan well-enough ahead."

"It's still bleeding," Doug reported. "Let's get you on the floor and rest your leg up on the seat to elevate the wound above your heart.

"Tim," Doug yelled forward to the cockpit, "what's our ETA?"

"About three hours. Two-and-a-half if I push it to mil throttle. How is she?"

Doug responded hesitantly. "I don't know. I'm not really trained for this kind of thing."

"You're doing great, Doug," I said encouragingly. "What are our options?"

"Tim," Doug asked, squinting his eyes in thought, "what about diverting to Gitmo or Miami?"

"Let me look.... Guantanamo Bay Naval Base is forty-five or fifty minutes to our east. Miami is... over an hour northeast.... Is that too far? Key West has a Navy base and is under an hour due north. I can make that in the same fifty minutes. Yeah, that'll work. Twenty minutes out I'll declare an in-flight, ask for radar vectors to an extended straight-in with a hot stop straight ahead. They'll have the crash trucks and bus already waiting for us. That'll save time, too. Spooling up to mil power. The bean counters are going to hate me for all the extra fuel this burns, but screw 'em."

"I understood everything up to 'Key West,'" I said, taking my place on the floor of the aircraft. Doug gently lifted my left leg onto the seat I had just vacated. "You want to translate the rest for me?"

"Sure. Let me get you a pillow for your head, first. That hum you're hearing and the vibration in the airframe are because Tim's speeding up to the aircraft's maximum safe velocity. It's perfectly safe, just not efficient. It's ten- to fifteen-percent faster than our usual airspeed but uses thirty percent more fuel. He's just kidding about the bean counters—that's not a concern at all. That's just his sense of humor.

"Twenty minutes out from the Naval Air Station, he's going to declare an in-flight medical emergency, which will get us priority over all other traffic. We'll come straight-in and as well-aligned with the runway as possible to minimize the number of turns we need to make. Turning would require us to slow—"

Doug grabbed my chin and gently turned my head to face his. "Don't fade away on me. How you doing there?"

"Good. I'm good," I said softly, perhaps more to make it true than because it actually was. "How much longer?"

"A while. Hang in there."

"I'll be okay. Thanks."

"So, I was saying, we'll make as straight an approach to the runway as we can, coming in faster than we normally would. Military bases all have long runways, so we'll make an extended roll-out and stop at the end of the runway. We're not going to taxi to the terminal. When Tim announces the in-flight emergency, they'll send firetrucks and an ambulance out to meet us. You'll get door-to-door service. Valet all the way," he said, smiling and picking up my hand for comfort. "Nothing's too good for our passengers."

"Do you have a secure satellite phone on board?"

"Yes, both a STE and a Green phone. Which do you want?"

"Green," I replied.

"They're both up front. The cord won't reach this far back, and you're in no shape to walk up there."

"That's fine. Write down the number and the message. Just read it to whoever answers."

Doug pulled a ballpoint pen and small pad from the breast pocket of his white uniform shirt which was now blood-stained at the cuffs. He clicked his silver pen open, ready to write, and said, "Okay, shoot."

"Not the best choice of words," I replied with a pained smirk.

"Sorry. But I'm glad to see your sense of humor is still intact. That's a good sign."

"Dial 911-0911 and give them the following message: Echo Juliet Romeo Alpha Eight Niner Mike Sierra Whiskey. Also tell them where we're going. You can just say that part straight out."

Doug nodded and read the alphanumeric message back, confirming he had copied it correctly.

Doug stood up to make the call and said with a put-on Southern accent, "I'll see if Tim has a quarter for the payphone, ma'am. Y'all don't mosey off while I'm gone, now, y'hear?"

The laugh his joke got did not make up for the wave of pain that rolled up my left thigh, but I did appreciate his taking such good care of me. Especially since I was bleeding all over his beautiful airplane.

When Doug returned a few minutes later he sat down next to me, picked up my right hand again, and held it in both of his. "All she said was 'Palace Sentinel confirms receipt.' I hope that means something good to you."

"Yes. That's good. They'll know where to look for me now. For me and for this," I said while taking the bagged notebook out of my jacket. "I need you to hold on to this. Secure it in your crypto safe and keep it locked up until a white-haired man named Michael comes to get it. He'll be here... well, at Key West... in a few hours. I'll be in surgery and not able to protect it. I need to impose on you one more time. Do not leave the aircraft until he takes the book from you. Okay?"

"Okay. No problem."

"I'm serious. Promise me, Doug. Otherwise none of this was worth it."

"Yes, I promise," he said earnestly. "Should I also give him the bill for cleaning the blood off the leather seat?"

I just laughed, which didn't hurt as much this time. I was glad for that, but also concerned about what it might mean.

"In all seriousness, though, we're getting close. Do you want me to give the paramedics any information for you? Like, do you know what blood-type you are?"

I glanced down at my blood-stained thigh. "Yes, red."

Doug snickered. I didn't have the energy to join in.

"A-positive," I said softly. "I'm A-positive."

"Key West Approach, this is Charlie Alpha Charlie Niner Six Four on UHF," Tim said loudly from the cockpit over the air-to-ground radio, enunciating each word clearly. "DOD access code Three One Two Eight Zulu. I'm declaring a medical emergency and requesting radar vectors to a priority straight-in approach."

"Twenty minutes to touchdown," Doug said looking towards the cockpit. "How are you doing?"

"I'm good, actually. How about you?"

"Great. I never get to fly back here. I could get used to it. Although next time I'd prefer to sit in the seat, not just lean up against it. I hear they're quite comfortable."

"Only the executives get to sit *in* the seats. Us riff-raff only get to look at 'em," I countered.

We both smiled and silently enjoyed the last few minutes of calm before, we both knew, things were going to get rough.

"Doug. How's our girl doing? Need you back up here."

"Coming, Tim," Doug said towards the cockpit. Standing, he turned towards me. "Let's get you back in the seat and buckled up for landing. I'll apologize now that it'll be bumpy, but there won't be any lateral turns, so you won't be thrown left and right."

I appreciated his concern.

Even belted into the well-padded leather seat, the pounding of the landing gear on the runway bounced me roughly. On touchdown, my thigh muscles screamed their objections to being torn from the bone. My abdominal muscles seized up from one end of my belly to the other as if contracting in childbirth. Unable to exhale my pain away, my face contorted into a silent scream of repressed agony as I dug my fingers into the armrests in the hopes of finding some purchase for stability.

As the jet rolled along the runway, the reverse thrust of the engines slowing the plane made things worse—something I had not imagined possible. The physics of forward momentum fought the opposing force of the engines for dominance and something had to lose—me.

With the seat's footrest extended, I was lying almost flat. I slid forward until the seatbelt snagged painfully under my rib cage. The sudden stop bounced my lower body against the seat bottom and footrest. Pain like nothing I had ever felt before flashed through my thigh and up into my hips. The pain was no longer just a physical sensation. It became something I could see.

The pain had colors. White rays streaked from the windows and overhead lights like darts into my eyeballs. I held my breath and shut my eyes tightly, scrunching my cheeks up to reinforce the weak armor of my eyelids against the pinpoints of penetrating pain. Vicious, scalding waves of red agony flowed through my eyelids and up my optic nerves to sear the back of my brain. The aircraft bucked, and I could take no more.

Mercifully, the world faded to a cold, silent black.

Chapter 29

"...you hear me, ma'am?"
"...lost a lot of blood."
"...gun under her jack..."
"...hold on... going to be fi..."

Chapter 30

Michael sat in a blue visitor's chair across the room as the Navy surgeon in forest-green scrubs standing over my hospital bed finished explaining what my recovery would entail.

"...and in a week or two you can start physical therapy. It'll be moderately intensive at first. I'm sure you'll get through it just fine, Wendy. It's all about having the will to succeed. The PT med-techs will go over that with you at Norfolk."

"Thanks, doc. I can't tell you how relieved I am to hear that the bullet missed everything important in my leg," I said, gesturing vaguely to my tightly bandaged left thigh.

"By regulation, we had to turn the extracted bullet and your weapon over to NCIS. I'm sure they'll want to talk to you about that, but I just stick to medical matters. The rest is up to you, and I doubt I want to know anything about how you got shot." The surgeon glanced at Michael and continued, "I'll leave you two to get caught up and ask the nurse to bring dinner in."

"Thank you, doctor," Michael said as the lieutenant commander closed the door behind him on his way out.

"They checked me in as Wendy Mintner, I'm guessing?"

"Um hmm," Michael said, nodding. "You can stay as Wendy for another day or two. I'm glad to see you're in good spirits. Or is that just the painkillers you're on?"

"Yeah, that must be it."

"Now that you're awake and I know you're alright, I need to go make a few calls. I'll arrange for your transport to the Navy Medical Center at Portsmouth and ensure your hosts get paid for giving you these five-star accommodations," Michael said with a grin. "I'll bring you a few magazines when I come back later. On a more serious note, though, what do you want me to tell Steve?"

"Good question," I said, pausing to think of an equally good answer. "While I'm going to hate leaving him in the dark, it won't do any good for him to worry about me unnecessarily. He'd just try to fly down here. He may get angry at me for it, but don't tell him anything until I'm back in Virginia. I'll call him then. When I'm ready, he can drive me home from the hospital. His disappointment will be best for me to deal with in person. There's nothing I can tell him from here over the phone anyway.

"But you *can* tell Claude that I called him a few choice names. Use your favorite ones or make up something new, I don't care. This really was a two-man mission. I hope the flu is making him feel horrible. Misery loves company."

Michael walked up to the head of my bed, reached into his jacket pocket, and slowly withdrew Sokolov's black notebook. He waved it gently between his fingertips, looked at me and said softly, "You're truly something special, Eden. You know that? Wonderful work."

Michael paused and looked at me with what I can only describe as "serious eyes."

"When I first saw you in training at the Farm," he said, "I knew right away you were someone special. You had a fire in your eyes that none of your classmates had. Sure, they were all doing their best to get through a difficult training program, but you were giving it that something extra every day."

That surprised me. "You were watching me at the Farm? In person?" I didn't know how he had first spotted me and found myself itching to know the rest of the story.

"Yes. I'd been on the lookout for another team member for a while, and a contact of mine is one of the firearms instructors. Not surprisingly, your skills caught his eye. He tipped me off, so I drove down to watch you, both there and on a few of your off-campus practical exercises, as well. Do you remember the surveillance scenario at Baltimore's Inner Harbor?"

I nodded and chuckled. Our instructor assigned us to follow some random employee from one of the local financial firms on his lunchbreak. "Yeah, we had to scramble on that one."

"You didn't notice me, but I was in the office lobby that afternoon mopping the floor."

"You were? Seriously?"

"I wore a brown wig and brought a mop and bucket out of the instructor's surveillance van right into the office building lobby. Nobody ever notices janitors. When the rabbit returned from lunch and badged through the turnstiles, it stymied the rest of the team and they couldn't get through security to continue the pursuit. One boneheaded student took the initiative by jumping a turnstile, and practically got tackled by the guard."

I laughed softly and nodded. "Yeah, we all gave him crap for that stunt."

"I watched you take advantage of the distraction he had unintentionally created. You didn't hesitate. You jumped right in and did exactly what was needed. While the employees in the lobby were preoccupied watching the spectacle, you lifted one woman's building access badge right off her belt. She never felt a thing. You marched right through the turnstile as though you owned the place and kept your eye on the rabbit the whole time. That told me most of what I needed to know about you. You have the innate creativity required and are willing to do whatever it takes to complete the mission. That's why you're perfect for this team. You must have picked up quite a bit of your parents' can-do attitude from their time in the Army. It was that day in Baltimore that led me to have the firearms training staff run you through one additional simulation."

"I always wondered about that one. No one else in my class had to go through that video scenario."

"It's a customized setup my pal and I cooked up about a dozen years ago. We crafted the scenario of a small team breaking into an adversary's office to replicate our real-world work. In the simulation, you cleared the office and made certain no one was there before your virtual teammate got to work on the filing cabinets. The kicker is that no matter what the student does, the computer adds a guard who surprises you. You can't prevent that."

"I *knew* it was rigged!"

Michael smiled. "Yes, it was. The guard appeared around the corner in the perfect position to be able to attack your teammate from behind. Even though you couldn't see whether or not the guard had a weapon, you shot him to protect your teammate and complete the mission. That's what I needed to see. Your marksmanship skills told me you *could* pull the trigger, but it wasn't until that moment I could see whether or not you *would* pull it. That's what makes you so special."

Michael tapped his finger on Sokolov's black notebook. "Your willingness to do whatever it takes on these missions is what makes you unique. It's what makes you, *you*. Picking you for this team may very well have been the best decision I ever made."

I almost cried. Of course, that may have been because of the throbbing pain in my thigh and all the drugs the Navy had given me. I did, however, get choked up that Michael finally opened up to me about why he chose me. He could not possibly have said anything more important or special to me at that moment.

"Thank you, Michael, I never knew. Why didn't you tell me all this when I asked you about it a few years ago?"

He gave my shoulder a light squeeze. "You weren't ready to hear it back then. You are now. So, rest up, and I'll be back in an hour or so. Your job for the next two months is just to heal yourself. Body and...," pointing to my head, he finished the thought, "...mind."

"*People*," I said. "The magazine, I mean. And strawberry Twizzlers, if you can sneak them past the nurses. I hear their recuperative properties are practically magical."

Michael smiled and left me to watch the square ceiling tiles shimmer above me in the haze of some amazingly effective painkillers.

***

Allison ran her hand gently up my left thigh as I stretched out on the bed, resting my face comfortably on a pillow.

"That seems like an unusual place for them to go in for ligament-reattachment surgery," she said, looking over my two scars with the practiced eye of a nurse.

"It became partially detached when I was down in Charleston a few weeks ago and hurt like hell," I said, repeating the cover story I was given to use for my recovery. I never liked lying to Allison, but, in this instance, the last thing I wanted to tell her was the truth about what happened to me.

Allison's fingers traced a path up my thigh and explored the scar the Navy surgeon in Key West left when he extracted the bullet. "This one was exploratory?"

"Yeah. They said they couldn't see enough on the X-rays or sonogram, so they did that while I was under. They didn't find anything, which I guess is good, right? I get to keep the scar as a souvenir, though. No extra charge. You can't see that one too well unless I'm wearing a bathing suit. The other is more noticeable and is still pretty tender."

I rolled over so Allison could finish changing the bandages. Her hand traced gently across my left knee and pressed down firmly to secure the bandage onto my lower thigh.

"Arthroscopic surgery usually leaves three round scars. That's weird. This one," she said pressing down on the bandage harder, drawing a grimace from me, "is larger and with the raised ridge looks more like a..."

She left the thought hanging, and I was not going to help her finish the sentence or press the issue. I didn't want her sentence to come to its logical conclusion. Sometimes, there's no fooling a skilled eye. After being gone for most of three weeks, though, I had no choice but to let Allison be the nurse she is and change my bandages.

"Okay, you're fine, young lady. No infections, so put your pants back on and let's get some lunch," she said as she slapped her hand across my butt playfully. "Chinese food or that new SaladWorx place? What would you like?"

"A salad, definitely. All Steven knows how to bring home is Chinese carry-out from the Hunan place across the street. I have a fridge full of half-eaten leftovers."

"I thought he'd have you slaving away in the kitchen by now serving him seven-course meals each night."

"Somehow, I've gotten a bad rap in that department. I'm lucky if I'm even home from work in time to cook one or at most two dinners a week. And, as you well know, I like to eat, so I'm happy being the one to pick out the healthy meal of my choice. If he happens to enjoy it, too, then so much the better."

"I'm just kidding, girlfriend. *Sheesh.* No need to get so defensive about it," Allison said putting her hands up in surrender as we walked out the front door.

Maybe she's right and I sounded defensive. Who knows? With all the eating out I do when traveling, why can't I enjoy cooking healthy meals at home every now and then?

Over a couple of grilled-chicken salads our conversation stayed light. To my relief, Allison didn't ask any more probing questions about my "ligament surgery." She clearly had her misgivings about my story but is a close friend and clearly sensed I didn't want to provide any more detail than I had already volunteered. For that, I was grateful.

"So, your boyfriend is about to become an old man, huh?" she asked.

"Well, forty is not really all that old," I said, not quite sure if I was defending Steven or myself.

"Yeah, but you're still in your twenties. He's practically robbing the cradle."

"I have six months until his birthday, and I have no idea what to do. Of course, I'll get him something nice, but I also want to *do* something special. I have no idea what, though. Any suggestions?"

"Like spending a long weekend away at a B&B?" Allison suggested, forking a leaf of lettuce into her mouth.

"Yeah, maybe. We do that once or twice a year and both enjoy it. I'm also thinking about a week at one of those all-inclusive resorts in the Bahamas or Jamaica, or something like that."

Allison looked at me sideways with a devilish smile. "Sounds more like a honeymoon than a birthday. You making any plans I should be aware of? Hint, hint...."

"Nope," I replied. "We're fine just as we are, thank you very much. What about you? Is Rick *the one*?"

"No," she said as her smile turned into a frown. "I'm going to break up with him this weekend. I just don't want to do it over the phone."

"I'm so sorry," I said to comfort her. A pretty woman, she has never been very successful on the dating front. "That sucks."

"Nah. When it's not right, it's not right. Where did you meet Steven, again? Maybe they have more of those where he came from."

I responded with the cover story Steven and I agreed to use. "Union Street Public House in Old Town Alexandria. I've told you that. Great place, by the way."

Since we can't tell people that we really met at one of the CIA's covert training facilities, he talked Jon Brady and his wife, Linda, into backing us up on that particular lie, should we ever need the assist.

"Well," Allison replied wistfully, "I'll try to help you think of something special for your doctor, and maybe I can use the same idea later when I eventually land one of my own."

I smiled at the thought of Allison's on-going search for a physician to marry coming to fruition and their settling down. They'd have such smart kids.

Chapter 31

"Michelle. Michelle! Wake up. Are you alright?"

I bolted upright in bed as Steven gently shook me. "Wha...? Where?"

"You were dreaming," he said, looking up at me. "Are you alright? You were talking in your sleep again, and then you screamed."

"*Ugh,*" I groaned while rubbing my eyes. I flopped back down and pulled the covers up under my chin. "What was I saying?"

"I couldn't understand it at first. It was as if you were trying to talk but couldn't get the words out. It all came out as a stream of grunts, then it got clearer. You said, 'Oh no,' and then really clearly you said, 'I hope this hurts.' Then, you screamed, and that's when I woke you up."

I rubbed my eyes and tried to focus on the few rays of moonlight dancing on the ceiling. "Wait, what did you mean 'again?'"

"Well, this isn't the first time you've mumbled or talked in your sleep, but never so clearly. And you've never screamed like that before. This was different. Worse. That's why I woke you up. What did you mean about hoping it hurts? Who were you talking to in your dream?"

"No one. I don't remember. Never mind, it was just a dream," I lied, hoping that would end the conversation.

"Honey, I know you've been through a trauma and your leg will take time to heal. Maybe it wasn't just your thigh that got hurt. The Agency has people you can talk to. Just having someone to open up to can help."

"What, a shrink?" I spat out.

"They're fully cleared, and I'm sure they don't dig into the operational details. They're there to help."

"I'm pretty sure we both know that would not be a good idea."

Steven caressed my shoulder gently. "I won't try to make you. I just wanted to point out that it's an option."

"Thanks. Okay, it's good to know it's an option."

"At least consider it, Michelle."

"I will."

I didn't.

PART NINE

BEDROOM MANEUVERS

Chapter 32

"I've got the dad in his bedroom," Claude's disembodied voice reported through my earpiece.

"Good. We've got Junior here in the master bedroom," I responded while Arnaud used a pair of white plastic flex cuffs to bind the wrists of the fair-haired man on the floor. "I know it's a mansion, but Wilson was right. This place is huge."

I aimed my favorite Sig .45 at the younger of our two targets and keyed the throat mic again. "If we've got both men accounted for, then who the hell's in the bathroom?"

"I've got Junior wrapped up," Arnaud said as he pushed his charge to the ground in front of the king-sized bed. He nodded towards the closed door off to our right. "Go find out."

I threw the bathroom door open and confronted two nude blonde women cowering against the vanity. The pair knelt on the tile floor, whimpering and shaking in each other's arms.

With my menacing pistol and suppressor aimed their way, I barked my orders at them and gestured vigorously. I had no idea if they spoke English, nor did I care. "Out! Both of you, now!" Even if they only spoke German, my waving and pointing left no doubt about what I was insisting they do.

"*Schnell,*" I added for good measure, using one of the few words Claude taught me on the hour-and-a-half drive from Ramstein Air Base to the Fuchs' mansion outside Frankfurt.

The women raced forward as fast as their terrified bare feet could shuffle. I herded them towards the younger Fuchs' who squirmed on the floor. Arnaud covered the women with his pistol as they moved. I wasn't sure if he was paying much attention to anything except their shapely behinds, but either way, the two girls in their late teens or early twenties offered no resistance. I pushed the women onto the thick carpet, and zip cuffed their hands behind their backs.

"I need to work on Junior to get the safe open," Arnaud said to me quietly. "Why don't you get those two up on the bed where they won't be in the way or see too much?"

I nodded and moved the women, one by one, to the bed and laid them face down. I covered each girl's head with a maroon silk pillowcase to keep them from seeing any more of us than they already had. I knelt between them to keep a close watch over the pair.

At the foot of the bed, Arnaud began to provide the type of motivation he deemed necessary for Fuchs, Jr. to give up the combination to the safe built into the ornate mahogany night stand next to his bed.

If Junior had chosen not to cooperate, we could have readily cracked the safe ourselves. In hindsight, I think Arnaud had been looking forward to that particular part of the mission all week.

His version of *motivation* started with one kick to Junior's ribs and a pair of glancing blows from the butt of a Glock to the German's skull. Anyone could have predicted the back and forth yelling match between my teammate and the broker of chemical weapons fabrication equipment. First, Arnaud accused the two Fuchs men—father and son—of selling banned equipment to the Syrian government and other embargoed nations in the Middle East. Then, predictably, the younger Fuchs vehemently denied everything.

Personally, I didn't care to watch the brutal series of blows Arnaud inflicted upon the arms dealer. Instead, I focused my care on keeping the two women calm as they flinched in response to Fuchs' screams and pained grunts. To comfort the girls, I gently ran my hands along their shackled arms. Goosebumps pockmarked the girls' skin. Firmly and unhurriedly, I repeated the motion rhythmically as much for my own peace of mind as theirs.

The two women alternated between shuddering at the muffled crunches of blows landing on Junior's body and softly sobbing from their own fear. They writhed slowly in the impossible task of trying to get more comfortable while bound tightly by stiff plastic restraints biting into their thin wrists.

"The dad gave up pretty quickly," Claude advised over the radio. "He's a lightweight. I've got his bedroom safe open in here."

"*Ah bon, mon frère,*" Arnaud said. "*Bien joué*. Junior's giving me a bit too much Kraut attitude for his own good."

"Let the girls go," the younger Fuchs implored Arnaud in English, taking advantage of the pause in his beating. "They're not involved. They're prostitutes. They're nice girls. Let them leave, yes?"

That just angered Arnaud further, resulting in his delivering a pair of swift blows from his heavy boots to Junior's left shoulder.

I looked down to the girls at my knees and flipped through my mental catalogue of options for what to do with them. First, we could... well, I didn't like that idea at all. Second, we could...

We could what? Lock them in the bathroom after we killed the two men? After what they'd already seen and heard? Even if they didn't speak much English, they both saw our faces.

So, we could... what? Take them with us? Yeah, right. Get real, Michelle.

Arnaud was making progress with his human punching bag, and the girls had stopped flinching at each ensuing grunt or groan. Their emotional exertions had diminished their ability to struggle, but their sobs continued softly. They suffered their inner torments quietly, shaking from the ordeal or maybe just shivering from the winter's chill as they waited for the violence to end and the interlopers to leave.

So, what do *you do about them, Michelle?* I implored myself to answer. *You're a smart woman. How does this end?*

I knew just how this looked like it would end, but my gut twisted, telling me that somewhere, somehow an acceptable alternative had to exist. If not a happy medium, exactly, then at least a suitable compromise. But how? Ask them nicely not to talk to the cops? Drop them on the side of the road with some cash from the safes and trust them to keep their mouths shut?

With a spark of hope, I wondered if that could possibly work.

Claude joined us and watched his brother's aggressive questioning of the man sprawled on the carpet and bleeding profusely from his nose.

Finally, Junior decided he'd had enough and gave Arnaud the information he wanted.

Arnaud opened the night table and dialed the combination into the safe's lock.

Okay, Michelle, what do you do now? Think! Bribe the girls? Keep them here? Take them somewhere else? What's going to work? And how would it work? Knock them out and toss them in the trunk of the car? Possible, but not very practical. And if you did, then what? Drive them to... where?

My frustration grew as the time I had remaining to find an answer dwindled. There must be a way. I was certain of it. I just had to think of it and think fast.

You've gotten so good at taking lives, I castigated myself, now come up with a way to not have to.

Think, dammit!

First, how to keep them from identifying us? Money? They are prostitutes, after all, so maybe that could be the right motivator.

That and threats to come back and... do to them what Arnaud just did to Junior?

Would threats really work on them? You don't even know who they are. Are you kidding yourself? Are you willing to bet your life on trusting these two? More importantly, is Arnaud?

I looked up as Arnaud pulled the drawstring of his backpack closed with the contents of the safe secured inside.

As I watched the events unfold in front of me, the lack of alternatives left me stranded on an island surrounded by my own ineptitude, unable to find any possible escape.

It's your *fault, Michelle. You're not good enough!*

Thwwopp. Thwwopp.

The echo of ejected brass ricocheting off of the wardrobe in the corner of the bedroom wrenched my attention abruptly back to my teammates, standing over the now-dead body of the younger black marketer. My brain pulsated into the top of my skull. My time was up.

Arnaud holstered his pistol and nodded at me.

I remained still and stretched the seconds to try to think of something. Anything. Anything at all. Anything! Please, something!

"Come on," Arnaud said matter-of-factly. "Time to clean house."

As the word *house* cleared his lips, tears burst forth from the inner corners of my eyes and silently streamed down my face. I was awash in self-disgust lamenting my inability to think of a way out of this and not endowed with enough common sense to resolve the situation.

I had not created the situation, yet desperately wanted to bring it to a successful conclusion. If not for the sake of these two women, then for my own and how I wanted to think of myself.

I was once the kind woman who spared a housekeeper in Zurich all those years ago and even gave her money on the evening I killed her boss.

That was Michelle. That's no longer me, I realized with a start.

That was Michelle, but that's not Eden.

I looked down at the two young women alongside me and silently apologized to them that Zurich was then, but Frankfurt is now.

Kneeling between the pair, I ran my hands from their hair to the base of their spines. I stroked them one last time, calming each as best I could. Their labored breathing steadied. I traced my hands across their shoulders, down their sides, and back again. I pressed firmly. Gently. Calmingly. Reassuringly.

The muscles of their backs reacted, reassured by my touch as each gloved hand drew across their bare shoulder blades and along the sides of their naked bodies.

As I rose up on my knees, tears of disappointment streamed from my eyes and dropped onto my shirt. I brought my gun to bear and shot each woman in the head.

Chapter 33

Arnaud knocked on my bedroom door in the Ramstein Air Base safe house. Softly he asked, "Eden, may I come in?"

"What do you want?" I barked.

"Just to talk. Are you alright?"

"Leave me alone," I said indignantly.

He entered anyway, sat on the floor, and leaned back against the bed. I shifted away from him and curled my arm around the damp pillow into which I had cried earlier.

I didn't have the emotional strength for a confrontation after that evening's events and the long, silent drive back from Frankfort. I asked my simple question in a subdued tone, barely audible. "What?"

"I just didn't want you to think we don't care that you're upset. The drive back didn't seem like the time to talk. I wanted to come in to say I'm sorry this was so hard for you and to ask if there's anything you need."

For all my anger at myself—anger I associated with Arnaud's voice telling me it was time to "clean house"—part of me knew that it really was only Arnaud and Claude I can talk to about what we do. As much as I wanted to blame him for everything that had happened in my career up to that point and summarily throw him out of the room on his ass, I did want to have someone to talk to about my self-realization that night.

Call it an epiphany if you want. It was both eye-opening and, at the same time, a waking nightmare from which there was no escape in sight.

"Claude and I are going to get an early breakfast at the enlisted dining hall. It's open twenty-four seven. Want to come with?"

"No, thanks. It's three in the morning...." I said looking at my watch as my voice trailed off.

Part of me desperately wanted to talk to Arnaud, but I simply could not think of anything coherent to say. "That's all... It's 3 a.m. I don't know why I said that. I've got nothing else.... I'm just numb."

My eyes brightened momentarily, and I asked hopefully, "Actually, do they serve beer?"

"No, never in the dining hall. The officer's club does, but not until the afternoon. And if I might gently suggest, don't fight your feelings by jumping into a bottle. That'd be a rather self-destructive habit to take up. When I feel like that, I go for a long run. That's how I got into triathlons."

All that stress led to all that running, which keeps Arnaud in top shape.

"No, that's not it. I'm not trying to drown my sorrows or anything."

"Good. Maybe you can feel a little bit better if you think about how hard we worked to minimize who we thought would be in the house. We waited until Junior's wife bundled the kids off to see her family in Austria before we swooped in. That's a good thing, right? We're not intentionally cruel. None of us wants that, but no one could have planned for the guys calling in a couple of hookers this evening. I mean, prostitution is legal over here, but, even so, I can't imagine that the wife would have approved. We did what we could in advance to contain the situation. Just like we always do."

I thought about that for a moment before responding. "At the house tonight, I was really upset with myself that I couldn't figure out a way to avoid having to kill those girls. I don't care that they were prostitutes. That's their business. And leave it to *you* to even know that it's legal in Germany." I flashed a wry smile at Arnaud, half thinking he'd probably availed himself of such local entertainment in the past.

"I was trying to think of a way to let them live because that seemed like the right thing to do. In the house, I was pissed at myself for not being able to come up with a realistic plan. Maybe we could have bribed them or threatened them? But in the end, I knew there was no viable option. In Zurich, it worked with the housekeeper because we planned the mission to account for her right from the start. We got surprised tonight, and, well, it turned out the way it turned out."

I peered intently at Arnaud. "Back in Zurich, if I hadn't been there at all or let you leave after me, would you have left her alive?"

Arnaud thought for a moment and shook his head. He turned to me and said, "I could just say *yes*, but I think you know differently. Even if it isn't pleasant to hear, I hope you can appreciate the honesty, even if it may be brutal honesty."

"I know. And, yes, I'd rather hear it from you straight up than have to figure out whether or not you're BSing me. We need to be able to trust each other—and we do. Truthfully, I've always known exactly how it would have gone down that night if I hadn't insisted."

"In Zurich, you were the only one the housekeeper saw, and you incapacitated her right away. In this case, the girls saw and heard everything. Clearly, they spoke at least some English, so the two were very different situations. You know that, right?"

"Yeah, I know."

"I hope you also know that Claude and I think the world of you. After seeing you pull victory from the jaws of defeat when we went camping a few years ago, it was clear just how formidable a woman you are. You've got more balls than a hundred men. But we're all still human.

"When Michael first brought you onto the team, Claude and I were rather surprised, to say the least. Mike had said he was evaluating an Army officer, but then he showed up with you. Obviously, he changed his mind along the way. When we first met you, you were so young and inexperienced, like he brought you home from the hospital still wrapped in a baby blanket. We weren't sure what to make of you."

I laughed. "If this is your idea of how to sweet-talk a woman, you really suck at it. No wonder you can't keep a girlfriend for more than a few months at a time."

"What I mean is, that with a lot of training and experience, you've become exactly what Mike said you would. You've showed us all that you're smart, motivated, and dedicated to the team. You've proven time and again that you have our backs, and I just want you to know we have yours, too. Whatever you need, just ask, okay?"

Arnaud stood up. "I understand you feel bad for doing some of the things we have to do, like killing those prostitutes tonight. I just want to make sure you know that I'm always here to talk, if you need."

"Thanks, but I wasn't crying tonight because I'm upset about killing those girls," I said looking up at Arnaud's blue eyes and making a real connection between us, possibly for the first time in the decade I'd known him. "Sure, at the mansion I was sorely disappointed in myself for not being able to figure out a way to avoid it. I know we had no other option. I knew it then, and I know it now.

"This is different. I wasn't crying for them. I was crying for myself. I wasn't crying just now because killing people like those girls hurt, but because I realized tonight that it *doesn't* hurt anymore."

Chapter 34

"Allison, how do you know if you're a good nurse or not? Or if you're the best?" I asked over another of our post-yoga smoothie lunches.

"That's an interesting question. Is all of Jenni's talk of introspection during class starting to rub off on you?"

"Maybe. In sales, for example, you know with certainty if you've closed a new account or are making repeat sales. How does it work for you?"

"Well, one way is that you don't make mistakes. At least not ones that matter. But for me, it's really that when the excrement hits the rotary oscillator, the doctors are calling specifically for *me* to assist. When an ambulance radios ahead that they're bringing a critical case in, the more frequently the ER attending physician says 'Alli, you're with me,' the more I know I'm the one they trust with the most difficult cases. Makes me feel good, too, that I'm the one they can rely on when it counts the most."

"That makes sense. I suppose you know you're good when you get the hard jobs."

"Yeah, pretty much. And, girl, it sounds to me as if Jenni may be having a deeper effect on you than you want to admit."

"I do enjoy the serenity, but, man, it takes a lot of work to sit there looking like you're doing nothing."

"No one ever said that inner peace was quick or easy. Kinda like good sex."

I chuckled. Allison always had a way of turning serious conversations towards the tawdry. That's why I like her so much. She has the guts to come out and say what the rest of us only think.

PART TEN

GAZA TERROR

Chapter 35

My black burqa fluttered violently in the rotor wash as I sprinted away from the HH-60H Seahawk helicopter. Behind me, two Navy Red Wolves pilots from helicopter squadron HSC-84 lifted off and headed west, back to safety over the Mediterranean Sea.

I, on the other hand, rushed east, away from the coast and further into the Gaza Strip. East was definitely not the safe direction to go. *Safe* has never been in my job description.

I sprinted along unevenly spaced rows of crops, maneuvering through the dead of night by the green glow of night vision goggles. I carefully navigated my way from one memorized landmark to another, paying careful attention to the stony soil. A sprained ankle would almost certainly result in a failed mission.

The strawberry fields around the northern Gaza neighborhood of Al-Atatra had provided the necessary open space for the helo drop me off. Now, I needed to get away from the landing zone as fast as my legs would take me.

The complex dance of US military aircraft that got me into the Hamas-controlled stronghold of Gaza City was, for me, the easy part of the ingress. I just had to sit still and let two Navy Special Forces pilots do their thing and fly a nape-of-the-earth flight plan from a Navy helicopter landing ship at 3 a.m. in total blackness.

Now, I ran head-first into the chaos of a denied area in which US intelligence hasn't operated in decades. While the ingress was easy, the hard part—getting the hell out in one piece—was yet to come.

My untested plan for exfiltration distressed me but having no realistic way to abort the mission made me even more nervous. Quite frankly, if I thought about it for too long, it terrified me. The plan had sounded a whole lot more certain back in Virginia while sitting in the safety of our team's conference room.

I had to concentrate on the mission in phases or I'd never have gotten the fear of being caught crossing the Gaza Strip's heavily fortified border out of my mind. Thoughts of how damned few escape options existed would have completely consumed me if I didn't focus and take things one step at a time.

First, I had to find and kill Rashid. Second, and only then, I had to figure out how to make it to the border crossing at the southern end of the Gaza Strip. Until completing the first part, I had nothing to gain from worrying about the second. I had a Plan A, but always prefer to have options. Unfortunately, on this mission, options for a good Plan B didn't exist.

The mission profile said for me to run east and then south under the cover of darkness. I'd sprinted almost a mile before stopping to catch my breath and gauging whether or not anyone had seen me. I looked back to the west and imagined the Seahawk accelerating as rapidly as the pilots could coax the big black bird to go. Somewhere high above, a Navy EA-6B Prowler covered their retreat, jamming Israeli search and acquisition radars that might vector fighters to intercept our unannounced intrusion into their backyard.

An onshore breeze carried the usual mixture of ocean smells aloft—saltwater, seaweed, and rotting fish—but another scent also hung in the air. The nose-wrinkling, offensive stench of raw sewage was faint, but persistent. The wastewater treatment outflow pipes and open sewer pits common to both the northern and southern boundaries of the Gaza Strip were right where Wilson Henry said they'd be, and were frightfully obnoxious. Couldn't he have been a little bit wrong, just this once?

I continued south towards Gaza City, walking with purpose from landmark to checkpoint to intersection, all of which I had memorized from the satellite images in the mission briefing package. I trekked five miles south from my insertion point through farms and neighborhoods into more densely populated areas. As I approached more urbanized city streets, I tucked my night vision goggles safely into the pouch on my hip. I would need them again the next night.

Passing the Gaza Mall shopping center confirmed I was in the right place. A left turn on Khaled Al-Hasan Street and a right on Palestine Street, a major thoroughfare in the upscale Rimal neighborhood, put me within a half-mile of my target's house. I walked at a more leisurely pace along the next half-dozen blocks to fit in better with the early morning foot traffic as women walked slowly to the markets and men ambled to work. At least, that is, those men who had jobs.

The unemployment rate in the Gaza Strip sits somewhere over forty percent. While that's certainly bad for them, it was quite a benefit for me since I planned to blend in with the masses who had nowhere to go all day and little to do. Not that a woman covered head to toe by a burqa would ever stand out anyway—it's practically a cloak of invisibility in most of the Middle East. With only my eyes showing through the veil, I could see everyone and, in return, was ignored by them all.

Along Wassif Street in the village of Rimal, two blocks off the main drag of Omar Mukhtar Street, I found the house that Wilson showed me in a half-dozen grainy black-and-white satellite photos. In person, it ended up being quite easy to pick out. It was the only house in the area with two armed guards standing in front.

I marveled that the architecture of this area had one essential characteristic common to just about every aspect—it was all rectangular. The houses and commercial buildings would not win any design awards for creativity. If it was built in the Gaza Strip and was still standing, it was all right-angles. That, I saw, was going to both limit my options in approaching the target house, as well as help shield me from prying eyes.

The houses lining Wassif Street, while narrow, extended deeply into the block. Each backyard abutted the yard of the house to its rear. I surveyed the homes while walking around the neighborhood.

A privacy-enforcing trellis with nest of potted plants and vines hung between my target's house and the property immediately behind it. While the vines and colorful plants looked pretty, they would make getting over the dividing wall more complicated than I would have liked. It would be quite difficult to get through quietly on my way in, and I most definitely did not want to get stuck in the vines on my way out. I smiled inwardly at the thought that it'd be bad enough getting caught by a human on this mission but being caught by a plant was simply not something I would ever live down. If I lived through the mission at all, that is.

On my several reconnaissance orbits around the block over the course of the morning, I closely studied the houses on both sides of Rashid's. Each had a private walkway between the street and its front door. Painted cinderblock walls lined with a few colorful hanging plants separated one property from the next. Sans driveways, both houses had single-car garages that opened onto the street.

As I walked around the block, it felt more akin to "casing the joint" in a black-and-white 1940s detective flic than performing a professional recon of the area. Maybe having a pair of concealed forty-five automatics holstered under my burqa contributed to the sense of my firearm preference being a throwback to a bygone era.

I plopped myself down against a stone wall in a small park one block from Rashid's house. From that vantage point, I had a good angle to keep a watch on the front door, the guards, and approaching vehicles.

Just after 8:30 a.m., a small caravan consisting of a black Mercedes-Benz sedan and a white Land Rover SUV arrived. I didn't know in advance what kind of wheels Hamas would send to collect their guest, but a big Mercedes with a lead vehicle full of armed guards certainly fit the bill. A single guard from the SUV relieved the two who had stood guard overnight. Rashid climbed into the rear seat of the sedan, and the two-car convoy spun its wheels as they sped away for parts unknown.

A teenage boy being pulled by a large brown dog emerged from the house to the left of Rashid's. I couldn't tell for sure who was walking whom, but the formidable canine certainly posed a potential problem for me.

My immediate task was to figure out how to get into Rashid's house. Michael and Director Duncan had decided that getting at Rashid here in the hellhole that is the Gaza Strip would be easier than getting at him while he's back home in Tehran. After the fall of the Shah in 1979, Western intelligence lost most of its access to Iran and, as crazy as the idea of sneaking into a territory cordoned off by the paranoid Israelis is, it was still easier than trying to operate in Tehran. Easier for Michael and the Director anyway—not so easy for me. I imagined them sitting comfortably in their air-conditioned offices as I sat sweating under a palm tree in a park trying to figure out which approach would give me the highest probability of successfully breaking into my target's house.

I found I had four choices for getting into the house, assuming I didn't want to start a no-win firefight with the convoy's squad of heavily armed guards.

First, the house on the left seemed to have the fewest people living in it, but the dog concerned me. The little I could see of the backyard did not encourage me, either. I wondered whether if by buying a piece of meat and concealing a cyanide pill inside, the dog might just take care of himself. On one of my walks around the block, I snuck a peek into the backyard looking for anything that smacked of dog—a doghouse, a run with a leash, or anything that said pet. *Nada.* That didn't mean the family didn't keep the dog in the backyard at night and just close the gate, but planning on could or might does not work for me. I have to know and don't risk my life on guesses. Control is critical, and dogs are rarely controllable.

Second, the house behind Rashid's offered access, but the privacy trellis in the backyard made that avenue look more like quicksand than a quick exit. Third, I could make a quarterback sneak and go right up the middle—kill the two guards and walk in right through the front door. Hell, with guards out front, they probably didn't even lock the door. Of course, if either of the sentries managed to get off so much as a single shot, Rashid or a neighbor would be alerted and call for help. No go.

Fourth, and what seemed like my least-bad option, I could go through the house on the right and over the wall separating it from Rashid's. That house had at least a half-dozen people living in it. Over the course of the morning, I watched as a few men came and went in the pickup truck they kept in the garage. Two women headed to the market with an empty basket and returned an hour later with purchases they'd made up the road.

The guard in front of Rashid's was rotated with a fresh man every few hours. I tried to gauge the pattern of their shifts but wasn't seeing enough changes to figure out if they rotated every three- to five-hours or more randomly.

I had little to do while sitting in the heat under the palm tree watching people meander along the block. My mind occasionally wandered, and I thought back to my conversation with Steven just before I left DC.

***

"I really wanted you to come with me to New Jersey this weekend," Steven said. "My friend and his wife are expecting both of us. What am I supposed to say about why you're not there? Having to work again is not going to be that convincing. I tell everyone the same thing all the time, and it's wearing pretty thin."

"I know, I know. I'm thinking that this time my Aunt Francine in Los Angeles had a mild heart attack."

"That's terrible."

"It's just a fake mild heart attack. It's not like I'm killing her off." I regretted my blunder as soon as the words passed through my lips.

I threw up my hands energetically and acknowledged my poor choice of words. "That's not what I mean. What I mean is, it's not like you have to say that she died. I love my aunt and don't want anything bad to *actually* happen to her. But your college roommate, Ben, is unlikely to ever meet her, so—"

"No, no, I know. Don't worry," he said, trying to reassure me that my gaffe was not taken the wrong way. "I'll make excuses for you again." His pout and long face told me everything I needed to know about how he was feeling.

"Look, I have to run over to Tech Service's disguise and documents office in Arlington, then down to the Farm to get my gear, and be on a plane before noon tomorrow. You can tell them with a straight face that I'll be cooped up on an airplane while you're out having fun and you still want to enjoy the weekend, even without me."

"Alright," Steven said hesitantly. "This is getting a bit crazy, though."

"What's crazy is this mission profile," I muttered under my breath as I placed the last of my clothing into the suitcase.

Steven's voice rose an octave. "Wait, what do you mean by *that*?"

I waved my hand in dismissal. "No, no, nothing. It's fine, really. I'll be fine. I shouldn't have said anything." I looked him right in his beautiful hazel eyes to convey the full measure of my feigned sincerity. "I'll be *fiiine*," I reiterated with as much honest emotion as I could fake and squeeze into that single word.

With a tight hug and extended kiss, I left him as reassured as possible that I was going to come home without incident this time. I swore that he wouldn't need to pick me up from another Navy hospital the following week.

I knew that in this case if things went sideways, he would never even be told what happened to me nor even get my remains back to bury.

Chapter 36

A palm tree shaded my eyes from the worst of the afternoon sun. When the temperature under my black, full-length burqa got uncomfortably warm, I strolled around the block.

Back under the tree, I popped one of the green amphetamine pills from my pocket into my mouth and washed it down with warm Gatorade from the Camelback strapped between my shoulder blades.

I had quadruple-checked the color of the packet, the word *Green* on the outside, and the pill's round shape for absolute certainty that it was the right one. With my fingertips, I felt once more to confirm the triangular pill in its red packet remained securely sewn into the left collar of my burqa. I assured myself that the lethal "L-pill"—a fast-acting cyanide formulation—remained safely tucked away for later use if the situation ever deteriorated from "holy shit this is bad" to "now it's completely unsalvageable."

Sometimes the poison provided to CIA officers is concealed inside other items such as a pen or a watch, but in those cases, it's not color coded since there's nothing else to confuse it with. Back in the early 1960s when the Soviets shot down his U-2 reconnaissance jet, Francis Gary Powers carried a saxitoxin-laced needle concealed inside a hollowed-out coin. He chose not to use it and, fortunately, returned home after only three years in prison. Not all officers are so lucky.

When provided in packets alongside an amphetamine upper, each pill has always been color coded for the officer's safety. The CIA added printed words about thirty years ago after some unlucky Operations officer who didn't know he was red-green colorblind swallowed the wrong pill. I feel really sorry for the poor SOB. For whatever small consolation it may be, though, at least it was quick.

The white SUV and black Mercedes returned Rashid and a young brunette around 9:30 p.m. I assumed they had eaten dinner out. She hadn't left with him in the morning, so where had she come from? A gift from Hamas for their honored guest, perhaps?

A guard jumped out of the SUV and entered Rashid's house to inspect it before he would let his principal leave the vehicle. He didn't find anyone lying in wait, so he signaled to the other guards. The doors to the luxury sedan opened, and I half-thought about taking my shot right then. It was a fleeting idea. I knew that even if I got Rashid, there was no way that kind of firefight could possibly end well for me. I had to find a better way. Or if I couldn't find it, I had to make it.

Two guards replaced the solitary Centurion who had stood sentry duty since late afternoon. After that, the vehicles departed in a hurry.

I left the park a little after 10 p.m. To avoid passing right in front of the two guards, I walked the long way around the block and calmly up to the green-trimmed house to the right of Rashid's. The hour was late enough that all the residents were already home, yet early enough that they'd still be awake. Once off the street, a six-foot-tall cinder-block wall concealed me from the guards next door as I paraded up the walkway to the front door.

I picked up a small straw basket from a bench outside the house, placed one of my two suppressed .45 Sig Sauers inside, and covered it with the hood of my burqa. I didn't want my peripheral vision blocked by the veil as I entered the house.

I knocked lightly on the door and a man's face appeared in the adjacent window. Seeing a woman at the door, he gestured to someone else inside—a female, I was confident.

Two women appeared at the window and opened the front door.

"*As-salāmu alaykunna,*" I said, greeting them.

"*Wa alaykum as-salaam,*" the younger of the two women replied.

Without further pleasantries, I got right down to the very unpleasant reason for my late evening intrusion into the family's home. I aimed my Sig from under the black cloth and fired two suppressed rounds through the bottom of the basket.

My bullets found their mark in the upper chest of the twentyish woman standing in front of me. My next two hit the older woman straight-on—one penetrated her upper row of teeth and the other entered her skull at her hairline above a high forehead. I wasn't sure if the second woman was the mother or grandmother, nor did I stop and ask. In the span of a second and a half, the two dropped to the floor, dead.

The man who had come to the door stood about ten feet back and tried to escape into the kitchen. My first shot to the abdomen of the bearded man in his early thirties didn't kill him, but my second shot, which went through his head from ear to ear, did.

I did some quick mental math. Three people down and three to go. Six bullets fired and three remaining—two in the magazine and one in the chamber.

I rushed toward the kitchen where I confronted another of the house's residents. This man, a little bit older than the one in the living room, stood at the kitchen counter putting something on a plate.

In less than two seconds, I fired two rounds into the stationary target's head. In a single fluid motion, I reloaded my pistol with an extended magazine held to the inside of my right wrist by a tactical elastic strap.

Back up to eleven rounds. Check.

One elderly man and one teenager yet to find. Check.

Only eight seconds spent, and four of six targets already down. Check.

I moved purposefully from room to room, searching the rest of the small house's ground floor for occupants, but found no one. At the foot of the stairwell, I stopped and listened for any sound from upstairs. Nothing. With a time-on-target of less than fifteen seconds so far, the noise level remained minimal. A few *thwwopps* and *thuds*, but no loud noises. The family members upstairs would certainly have heard some kind of fuss going on downstairs, but the guards next door would still be in the dark.

So far, so good, I thought, and absolutely needed to keep it that way. With the downstairs clear, I prepared to move upstairs.

Stairways are hell, tactically. Once you're in one, you have no way to escape. If someone appears at the top with a gun, there are no corners to duck around and retreating down the stairs is always a risky proposition. If you're with a team, you have others behind you blocking your retreat. Either way, tripping and falling down the stairs while trying to run down them backwards is an excellent way to break your neck. There simply is no good course of action. You just have to pick the least-bad option, which is usually to shoot the person in front of you and advance as nimbly as you can.

I sprinted up the stairs taking two at a time. I stopped on the last one, swung my pistol around to my left, and aimed it down the hallway. An older man in a white thobe—the long traditional Arab garment that some derisively call a man's dress—walked down the hallway towards me.

I fired two quick shots into his upper chest and he crumpled to the floor in slow motion.

As he fell away, the teenage boy I had seen earlier came out of a room half-way down the hall. In his small hands, he held an AKM-47 with a collapsible stock. He ducked back into his bedroom before I could get a clean shot off at him.

The single word "Crap!" thundered through my mind. Everything had gone so well up to that point, but now I had a problem. Without a thermal scope to see what was happening on the other side of the wall, I had to take a chance, and pronto.

I aimed at the wall behind which the boy had just disappeared and fired four rounds spaced about a foot apart. A yelp from the bedroom told me that at least one of my shots hit its intended target, but still left me in the dark about just how badly. I had no time to debate the issue or doubts that as soon as he could lift the rifle, I would be on the receiving end of far too many rounds of 7.62mm ammunition. When faced with that situation, my favorite number is always zero.

I sprinted down the short hallway and took a leap of faith that with my training and experience—as well as not being injured— I'd be faster than the kid. The boy was likely panicking and, if I were lucky, he would not be entirely sure how to use the rifle.

On the other hand, I realized with a start, this is the Middle frickin' East and everyone has an AK-47 or two. Of course, he would know which way to point the noisy end.

I thrust myself into the bedroom, button-hooked to my left, and came face to face with the teenager. He was favoring his left leg and half stumbling towards the bed as he labored to raise the rifle. A red stain expanded across the thigh of his right pant leg. His face contorted, making plain the misery my .45 caliber bullet in his leg was causing. The squawks of agony he manfully tried to muffle grew steadily louder.

His sight of me rounding the corner and pointing my pistol at him only served to motivate the teenager more. No doubt he had seen me shoot what must have been his grandfather and this boy of no more than fourteen wanted to defend his family's home. For the two seconds I stood in front of him taking aim at his chest and squeezing the trigger, I respected his determination to not give up without a struggle.

I have seen so many people in his situation just give up at the end and simply accept their fate. As I pulled the trigger, part of my mind registered an amount of admiration for the young man who fought to the very end.

The low, guttural sounds of pain stopped, and his body crumbled to the floor with a thud. After the clatter of the wood-and-metal rifle hitting the wooden floor died away, a hush fell over the house. I stood still, appreciated the silence, and inhaled deeply to calm my adrenaline-fueled heart as it tried to pound its way out of my chest.

A high-pitched cry rose from one of the other bedrooms, shattering the silence and cutting short my brief bout of self-congratulatory back-patting. The wails of the shrill voice drove my already racing heart rate through the roof.

I sped across the small upstairs to the master bedroom and immediately found the source of the howling. I stood stock-still and looked down as sharp cries pierced the otherwise quiet evening. In a small wicker crib an infant squirmed, face half-twisted in that peculiar way only babies can achieve.

I stood over the crib and stared at the crying child. I didn't know if it was a boy or a girl, but either way, the kid's cries were growing louder. I could absolutely not risk any of the neighbors—much less the guards in front of the house next door—coming to investigate.

I never actually determined whether the baby was a boy or girl, but settled on calling her a *her* just... well, just because.

I angled the white plastic pacifier lying next to the tot into her open mouth and let go. She turned her head and spit it right out.

I hovered over the crib and peered down at the child dressed in her white one-piece wrap. My right index finger nervously tapped along the frame of my Sig Sauer as I weighed my options for silencing the crying girl. I holstered the firearm and ran my index finger across her nose and mouth, tracing the small outline of her lips with a fingertip of my black glove. One way or another, I had to silence her, but had a rather limited number of options available. The pacifier hadn't worked, so clearly, I needed to try something else. Something quiet, something quick, and most importantly, something effective.

The hair on the back of my neck rose uncomfortably as the baby's cries grew louder. Her piercing wails continued to increase the likelihood of her drawing unwanted attention to my intrusion into the house.

I fingered the small red pill as it sat at the ready, still secure inside my left collar. I shook my head in resignation at the writhing infant whose cries were getting louder. Knowing what I had to do next did not make the task any more pleasant.

Downstairs, I stepped over the bodies strewn across the floor on my way into the kitchen. These were the family members, I reminded myself, of the child whom I orphaned no more than three minutes earlier.

I found a glass baby bottle and plastic nipple in the dish rack next to the sink. The canister of baby formula in one of the cabinets had a plastic scoop inside. I mixed an admittedly inexact concoction which I could only hope would do the necessary job. I heated the bottle in the microwave for thirty seconds and brought it back upstairs. I wasn't going to win any "Babysitter of the Year" awards for this act—to put it mildly—but, deep down, I felt certain I had to do it.

I'm not in any way an expert on feeding babies, but then again, I've had to do a lot of things in this job for which the CIA doesn't offer training courses. This was definitely one of them. I lifted the infant into my arms, cradled her head in the crux of my left elbow, and fed her from the bottle.

Once she had emptied the bottle, I placed the silenced child into the crib. I left the room, turned out all the lights on the upper floor, and slowly walked downstairs past the bodies strewn almost casually about the house, my head held low.

I returned to the kitchen and looked along the counter for something I'd glimpsed there earlier. Car keys on a Toyota keychain rested at the end of the countertop, against the wall.

I grabbed the key ring and checked out the family's large Toyota pickup truck sitting silently in the garage. I made sure the key fit the ignition and left it there for later use. My getaway plan was starting to take shape. The King Cab pickup the men drove to and from work would be my getaway vehicle—the first phase of my escape. Already, I couldn't wait to back the pickup out of the garage and drive the hell out of there.

I turned off most of the lights on the first level and sat on the sofa in the living room to wait. The bodies scattered across the floor lay in silent testimony to my rushed entrance into the house a half-hour earlier. The grandfather and teenager upstairs lay as soundless witnesses to my... what? Professionalism? Expertise? Ruthlessness?

The sight of the blood pooling on the now-stained living room carpet contrasted in my mind with the cleanliness of the master bedroom. The girl in the crib upstairs also lay silently.

I sprinted for the bathroom and barely made it to the toilet before vomiting. My entire midsection convulsed painfully as I heaved up what little I'd eaten earlier. The gut-wrenching heaves continued for minutes that seemed to stretch long beyond the sixty seconds the clock says each one contains.

When the torment stopped, I sat on the tiled floor feeling only barely relieved. Beads of sweat stood out across my forehead and waves of heat rose from my face. Slowly, I composed myself to the extent I could and cleaned up at the sink.

Unable to face the scene in the living room again so soon, I walked upstairs. I lowered myself into a wooden chair in the one unoccupied bedroom and sat in the darkness, grateful for a few moments of calm—the calm before the storm I knew was coming.

I set the alarm on my watch for 3:30 a.m. just in case I fell asleep. It certainly would not do for me to sleep through the night. I would not get a second chance at this target. As difficult as operating in Gaza was, I couldn't imagine trying to get into, much less out of, Iran. That was simply not something I could even conceive of. Best to get Rashid that night, I reassured myself, while he's sleeping less than a hundred feet away.

With my feet flat on the floor, I placed my hands on my knees and started my yoga meditation routine. For the first few minutes, I inhaled deeply and exhaled smoothly. In and out. Again, and again. Slow and steady. In and out.

I focused my attention on my breathing. Visions of the living room intruded, and I redirected my attention to feeling each breath as it left my body. I replaced encroaching thoughts of the baby down the hall by visualizing the air filling my lungs upon each inhale.

Years of practice in Jenni's classes with Allison at my side had taught me how to focus my attention on breathing. I've always felt the benefits I receive from yoga are mostly physical, largely in flexibility and strength. I enjoy the strenuous workouts and, of course, the close friendship.

That night in Gaza, though, I relished the more mindful benefits of yoga and promised myself that if I made it out of there in one piece, I would pay more attention to Jenni during those parts of her classes. In the short span of my meditation that night, I realized that by focusing mostly on the physical aspects of yoga, I shortchanged both of us.

At that moment, I finally understood that I owed her more than just being in class physically. She deserved my being present in both mind and body.

Chapter 37

I turned the alarm on my watch off at 3:27, before it had a chance to bark out its order for me to get to work. I nodded to the black digits in a mute acceptance that it was now time to do what I'd come halfway around the world to do.

I left the front door unlocked and stepped outside towards the street. With a sneak-peek around the corner, I confirmed the two guards were still standing sentry duty in front of the house.

I quietly retreated and climbed over the cinder block wall. Deftly, I dropped to the ground, froze in place, and listened to see if I'd alerted the guards. With no indication that they'd heard anything, I picked the lock on the side door to the garage and slipped inside.

The garage was empty. I wondered if the lack of a car was meant to ensure that if the guest staying in Hamas' safe house wanted to leave, he'd have to take his guards with him. Or perhaps it was to dissuade visitors from venturing out at all.

I tested the knob to the inner door and found it also locked, but even easier to pick than the exterior door. I'd been training on European-style locks for years and smiled at seeing the extra practice was paying dividends. I was through it in six seconds.

Inside, the two-story house looked comfortably appointed. Through the green tint of my night-vision goggles, I scanned over the leather chairs and plush L-shaped sofa that faced a large Samsung flat-panel television in the living room.

I walked up the stairs, one slow and quiet step after the next. The door to the master bedroom stood open, and I peeked in, pistol at the ready.

Two forms laid quietly in the bed against the front wall of the house. I approached from the left and stood a few feet away from the sleeping Rashid. His chest gently expanded with each breath. My NVGs tinted his face a fuzzy shade of green.

I tilted my goggles up and looked at the sleeping pair and reminded myself that I didn't have much time. Standing near the front wall of the house, I was practically above the duo of armed sentries downstairs. If either of the two naked people in the bed woke up and called for help, I would have my hands full in a hurry.

I lifted my Sig and aimed it at Rashid's temple. I angled the weapon somewhat awkwardly to ensure the bullet, which was certain to travel through his skull completely, would not penetrate the front wall of the house and alert the guards.

I squeezed the trigger smoothly. The *thwwopp* of the sub-sonic round killing Rashid sounded quite loud in the silence of the evening. The ejected cartridge ricocheted off the far wall with a dull *thunk*.

Some sleeping people seem to *feel* the presence of someone approaching. Perhaps it's a sixth sense—I don't know, but probably not. Some people are just light sleepers. Maybe that's what the brunette was.

Of course, it could also have been some combination of the metallic sound of the Sig's slide racing across the frame, the ejected brass *thunk*ing against the bedroom wall, the pungent scent of burnt gunpowder, or the rush of hot air from the barrel of the suppressor. Whatever the case, she woke up.

She rose up on one elbow, squinted, and looked at me. Still not fully awake, she scrunched her face as she tried to focus her eyes in the dark.

"Shhhhh," I whispered. Then, quietly in Arabic, said, "Go back to sleep."

Calmly, I hefted the weight of my Sig Sauer into my sightline and smoothly pulled the trigger, firing one round into her upper chest. The impact of the bullet just above her bare right breast knocked her back onto the bed.

She convulsed in shock and gasped desperately to inhale in spite of the savaging rupturing her chest muscles and right lung suffered from my bullet. The surprise on her face gave way to exquisite anguish and then faded as she started to lose consciousness. With another deliberately aimed shot into her head just above her left eye, I ended her suffering—and her life.

I stared at her briefly and my thoughts drifted back to Gutierrez's girlfriend in Aruba. I'm not sure what connected the two in my mind. Maybe it was that they were both women with long brown hair. Or maybe it was just that one was the first person I killed, and one was the most recent. I don't know. But I did know I had to get out of there.

Get your ass moving, Michelle, I castigated myself silently in a voice reminiscent of Michael's slight Texas drawl.

Quietly, I walked back downstairs and out the side door though which I had entered less than four minutes earlier. I pulled hard several times and heaved with great difficulty to hoist myself back over the wall. My arms buckled and complained that I must have weighed a thousand pounds. I made it over with a solemn promised to myself that if I got out of Gaza alive, I'd start doing more pull ups during my workouts while wearing a vest full of gear. I was in good shape, but... damn. The combination of tactical equipment, an empty stomach, and not having slept for almost two days added up to my arms shaking feebly while straining to haul my sorry ass over the cinderblock wall.

Back inside the green-trimmed house, I camped out on the hallway floor near the garage door, itching to make my escape. I sat facing away from the bodies littering the main level of the house and did my best to ignore the result of my earlier intrusion into what had, until my arrival, been a perfectly peaceful abode.

My watch gave me the bad news that I still had two hours to spend sitting still until I could get into the pickup truck and head south. Driving out of the garage in the middle of the night might unnecessarily alert the guards next door, so I wanted to wait until a little after 6 a.m. Well, I certainly did not *want* to wait but felt strongly that I *had* to.

As long as the guards thought Rashid and his lady friend were still asleep, there'd be no reason for them to check. I detested the thought of spending any more time than absolutely necessary so close to my recently deceased target, but wandering around the Gaza Strip in the middle of the night sounded even worse.

Besides, I knew the border crossing wouldn't open for another five hours and had nowhere safe to wait between that house and the border anyway. So, waiting right there on the floor was just as good—and just as bad—a choice as any.

Time passed slowly in that hallway. Waiting always takes its toll on my nerves. I despised having to sit in a house full of dead bodies feeling so exposed. Every inside *creak* of wood and outdoor *whoosh* of wind had especially eerie edges to them.

The narrow, dark hallway grew smaller over time, constricting in on me.

I had nothing to do but mentally replay my killing of the people lying on the floor behind me. The ruthless efficiency visible on my cerebral silver screen ate away at my insides. Every remembered *thwwoop* reverberating through my mind became another itch on my brain I could not reach inside to scratch.

The emotional pendulum in my head had swung back and forth many times over the years. So very many times. On countless missions, I felt perfectly at peace doing what my team and I do—killing the WPWTs didn't bother me at all. Other times, though, parts of me were disgusted at the randomness. The silenced infant in her crib upstairs and what I had done to her parents forced me to deal with a multitude of feelings—some long suppressed and others newly created.

Like a sea slowly rising, its tide unstoppable, my inner debate over whether killing Rashid was worth such a high price grew too loud for me to ignore. The rising gloom of dour self-doubt and unanswerable second-guessing gusted turbulently through my mind. The thoughts pulled my conflicted emotions in too many directions at once.

On one hand, I should be happy to have rid the world of another creator of terrible weapons, shouldn't I? Even if he himself never pulled the proverbial trigger, he was still giving dangerous people the technologies needed to manufacture and deliver poison-gas weapons. We have absolutely got to keep such things out of the hands of terrorist groups. If Hamas or Hezbollah obtain the means to make them, they are certain to use them as terrorist weapons of mass destruction around the world and not just in the Middle East. The world is much better off without men like Rashid in it, right?

But the high cost of this mission tugged me in the other direction, too. I have to live with what I've done while the family whose bodies were at that moment strewn about both floors of the house in which I sat and brooded did not get to live anymore. Would anyone ever know if the lives I saved were worth the cost of the lives I took? The family in that house paid a high price. Was *that* worth it?

Was *that* fair? Even if life isn't always fair, did I choose the right approach to the mission? Could I have saved three or five or who-knows-how-many lives by going into the house with the dog, instead? Should I have put the mission and my life at risk to spare the lives of a new mother and those around her? What about the baby? What about her?

The pulsing inside my head grew steadily.

Wasn't getting rid of a merchant of death like Rashid worth the price? He certainly was a merchant of death. Of that, I had no doubt. And so, it's best for all of us now that we were rid of him. Right?

Yes, that's right, right? But of that, I could only be *mostly* certain.

If Rashid was a merchant of death, what did that make me? An instrument of death? What makes me right and good, but him wrong and bad?

Rashid got paid for what he did. I get paid for what I do.

Rashid traveled the world to ply his trade. I flew halfway around the world to find him and do my job.

The ache inside my head grew as rapidly as my level of self-respect dropped. I questioned who I was and what I did. More than that, I couldn't decide whether I was losing my grip on myself—on the real me—or if that ship had already sailed. Who am I? Who is Michelle? Who is Eden?

Who are we? I mean, who am *I*?

Which one is the real *me*? Or at least, which woman *should* I be? Who's in charge?

Rashid was not in charge of Iran's chemical weapons program. He was just an engineer with specialized knowledge.

I was not in charge of my missions and did not choose my targets. That was left up to Michael.

Rashid just followed orders. I just....

What did that make me? A mindless automaton? An honorable soldier? An expendable pawn? The Grim Reaper?

The pressure in my head became a painful distention of emotion saturating my mind with visions of those lying dead not twenty feet behind me. The silent corpses were a testament not only to what I did, but how I viewed myself. Darkness clouded my mind, fogging my thinking.

I held my face in my hands, shook my head, and struggled to regain control. I badly wanted to cry, but no drops would form. I begged tears to flow so they would wash away the thoughts I could not get out of my head by force of willpower alone.

My temples throbbed with the unshakable burden of my thoughts.

My actions.

My feelings.

My uncertainty.

My reasoning.

My rationalizations.

My justifications.

My life.

I drew from its holster under my left arm the same Sig Sauer I had used an hour earlier to kill the family in whose house I sat. I raised the barrel to my head and pressed the blunt end of the suppressor into my right temple until it hurt.

The cold metal felt like an ice cube on the frying pan of my scalp. My mind recoiled from the juxtaposition of icy steel outside and boiling thoughts inside. An electric arc of emotions leapt across the thin barrier of my skull connecting the two—the cause and the effect. The one, my gun that takes lives, and the other, my life, which it leaves behind each time to bear the burden.

What if it didn't? What if I pulled the trigger? Who would even know or care?

Steven would, of that I was certain.

Allison would, I hoped.

I thought they might make a good couple. If I didn't make it home, they could end up with each other, couldn't they? Allison has that cherry-lipped traditional look Steven likes so much. Could it happen? She's still young enough; they could have kids.

Kids. Children. Infant—

The dam broke, and my eyes filled with the tears that had refused to form earlier. I buried my mouth into my elbow and muffled my howling cries of pain so only the dead could hear my torment. Tears flowed in torrents down my face. The mass—indeed, the mess—of accumulated emotions forced themselves forward, my ability to resist them having faded completely. The natural process followed its own course. My body knew what it needed to do and wrested control from my brain. Maybe it was a rebellion, or perhaps a mutiny.

I don't know how long I spent crying. Time had no meaning at that point. Eventually, the streams from my eyes slowed to trickles. The sleeve I soaked through with tears was also drenched with the emotions that had built up inside me over the previous few days. Or maybe the past few years.

A gentle ripple of electricity flowed slowly across my forearms, down each finger, and across each unpainted nail to the tip where the current jumped off into the air. I wiggled my fingers and smiled at the tingling sensation.

I had more than simply a sense of being lighter or having sloughed off an unbearable burden. My head had cleared—drained of the suffocating darkness, at least for the time being.

Even if it was only temporary, my liberation from emotional paralysis brought me back to the moment and the pressing need to make my escape. To coin a phrase, I needed to live today to cry again another day.

I washed up in the bathroom and returned to the hallway. There I resumed my silent vigil until daylight would signal the time for my departure had arrived.

I passed the time by gathering my tactical equipment together. I couldn't bring weapons or anything incriminating with me across a border where I risked being searched. I also did not want to leave functioning weapons or night-vision goggles behind for terrorists to use for their own purposes.

I unloaded my weapons and laid them out on the floor in front of me. I leaned the Sigs up against the wall and stood on each, jumping up and down a bit. I double checked to ensure I bent the threaded tips of the suppressors where each sat at the end of the pistol's barrel just enough that neither could be used by whomever found them. Firing one in that condition would be more dangerous to the shooter than the target.

I dropped the weapons, ammunition, freshly broken lock picks, and NVGs with their lenses shattered into a trash bag from the kitchen and placed it next to the garage door to take with me later.

With that accomplished, I returned to the intensely time-consuming process of doing absolutely nothing and doing it quietly. I flipped lazily through the Mexican passport the OTS documents team gave me to use at the border later in the day. The cover's heavyweight paper stock felt rough on my fingertips. The dim light of the hallway made it impossible to read it or the two other sheets of paper OTS forged to support my trip across the border, so I settled for just holding them all in my hands for reassurance. In a very real sense, I held my life in my hands.

I tried meditating again to pass more time, but my nervousness prevented me from centering myself.

Fortunately, the butterflies that typically inhabit my stomach were taking the night off. I didn't suffer the usual fluttering, but my gut remained unsettled. I hoped I wasn't going to vomit again. Once was more than enough.

By 6 a.m., I had had it. The sky was starting to lighten in the east and the ants in my pants were having a field day. I decided to get on the road, but first I made one last trip to the master bedroom upstairs.

I looked down at the form in the crib and watched her for a few seconds. I didn't even realize I was holding my breath until I saw her take one of her own. Her chest rose and fell rhythmically as the little girl slept peacefully. I smiled, ecstatic that the bottle I fed her sufficed to hold her through the night. I smiled, thankful that she had cooperated enough to stay quiet when I needed her to. I put the thoughts out of my mind of what I might have been forced to do if that had not been the case.

In two or three hours, Hamas' security team would find Rashid's body next door. At that point, they would kick in the doors to every house in the neighborhood looking for me. They would find the little girl in her crib hungry and wet, but alive. What happened to her then was out of my hands, but at least she would be found.

Finally, it was time for me to leave.

I threw my bag of now-broken equipment onto the floor of the pickup truck and backed out of the garage. I drove down the street and away from Rashid's house so the guards would see nothing more of me than my black-cloaked head in the pickup's red tail lights.

I labored for two hours through mostly urban side-streets on the twenty-mile drive to Rafa. Along the way, I made one pit stop at a garbage can to dump the bag of ruined equipment.

I stopped a half-mile before the border crossing and abandoned the truck outside a local market, leaving the keys in the ignition. It wouldn't stay parked there for long—someone would enjoy stealing a nice new Toyota pickup truck later that day.

As Wilson Henry had briefed me to expect, a line formed at the border well in advance of its 9 a.m. opening. Once the checkpoint opened, the line inched forward.

I nervously fingered the passport in my pocket. Once again, I found myself having to trust the technical services professionals who specialize in providing the myriad travel documents—forged or otherwise—we undercover officers need. Of course, at that point, I didn't have much of a choice.

Gusts of wind tossed sand around the Rafa checkpoint, the only legal portal between the Gaza Strip and Egypt. The portal was a desolate dam designed to stem the flow of would-be travelers between the crowded and battered Gazan side of the wall and the empty expanse of Egypt's Sinai Peninsula.

The tall, angular metallic structure of the checkpoint loomed ahead of me. Palestinian guards armed with AK-47s patrolled the area and closely scrutinized those of us who dared to queue up and wait hours to leave Hamas' seaside stronghold.

The heat of the day remained hours away, but the rising sun combined with the mass of bodies slowly moving forward had already raised the temperature under my burqa to an uncomfortable level. I pulled at my clothing repeatedly, billowing it for even a modicum of relief.

With little else to do, I tried to recall the last time I had showered. Aboard the Navy ship, certainly, but when was that? Two days ago?

Four days? I had lost track. I hoped feverishly that no one else noticed how bad I smelled. Then again, stuck in that mass of humanity standing in the open under an unyielding desert sun, I doubt I stood out any more than those around me did.

The would-be parade of hopeful travelers wheeled their luggage forward at a snail's pace as the clock ticked ahead ever slowly.

An inspector in a wrinkled khaki uniform checked everyone's travel papers. Upon reaching the front of the line, I handed over my passport and forged Gaza transit letter to him. At that point, I could only hope for the best. He looked at the picture and politely asked me to remove my veil. I complied. Alternatingly looking at me and the photo on my travel documents, my heart leapt into my throat when he signaled for another officer to come over.

My pulse raced as an older officer dressed in a blue camouflage military outfit approached. Fear of having been discovered surged forward in my mind. Slowly, I inhaled deeply to settle my racing heart. With no weapons and no way to make a run for it, my lying skills were about to tested. I desperately hoped it would not be my final exam.

"What is your name?" the mid-level officer asked in Arabic.

"Maria Nunez-Nunez," I replied in the same language.

"How long have you been here?"

"Three weeks."

"Where are you going? Back to Mexico?"

"No, I'm going to Geneva, Switzerland, to purchase medical supplies and bring them back to the Al Ahli Hospital in Gaza City." From my pocket, I withdrew the other piece of paper prepared by the DS&T documents team. In Arabic, they had written a long list of medical supplies. I showed it to the inspector.

My entire escape plan hinged upon my being able to convince the border guards I was a foreign national visiting Gaza to provide humanitarian support. Only half of that story was true.

"Are you a nurse?" he asked.

"No," I replied calmly. It was one of the few truthful answers that I gave him, so it wasn't hard to get the point across convincingly. "I have had only a little first-aid training, so I just assist the nurses when they ask. I mostly clean up the medical waste and disinfect equipment between treatments."

As the questioning continued, my hopes for an easy transit across the border slowly sank. In the recesses of my mind, I knew full-well that there was no such thing as an easy way to get across the borders between Egypt, Israel, and Gaza. I hoped beyond hope that my documents would be accepted at face value, and things would go smoothly.

"Wait here," the officer ordered. Much to my dismay, he walked away with my passport.

Crap, I thought while concentrating on keeping my feelings from showing across my face.

The officer returned with an older man, who also sported blue mottled camouflage fatigues.

"I speak Spanish," the obviously more senior officer said in that language. "Where are you from?"

"Mexico, *señor*."

"Which part?"

Home addresses are not printed in passports, so I guessed that the ranking officer was just testing my ability to speak Spanish. If that's what he wanted, I thought happily, I'd give him a show.

"*Señor*, I'm from a town called Chunhuhub in the Mexican state of Quintana Roo. It's on the Yucatan Peninsula. It's an area popular with tourists who come to see the ruins of Aztec pyramids like those up in Tulum. They're not anywhere near as grand as the pyramids in Egypt, of course, nor as old. I'd love to see the pyramids in Giza someday, but I don't really have the time or money for that, unfortunately."

Having rattled off my prepared speech about some of the Mexican geography I'd picked up in my travels, I figured I'd more than demonstrated my fluency in Spanish and felt it was time to turn the conversation back around to him. "Have you been to Mexico? Is that where you learned to speak Spanish so well?"

I hoped my false compliment would play to his self-esteem and work in my favor, at least a little bit.

"No, but I have been to Madrid," he said in halting Spanish. I got the distinct impression that he had not followed most of what I had said, which was fine with me. He clearly caught the last part, though, and if he wasn't convinced I was Mexican, I didn't know what else I could do.

"I've never been to Madrid, *señor*, but I have been to Barcelona on the Mediterranean coast. Once." The best way to lie, I've found, is to do it by telling the truth, and the truth was that I had only been to Barcelona once. And Madrid, and Toledo, and the Navy base in Rota... but this officer certainly didn't need to know any of that.

Switching back to Arabic, he asked, "Where is your luggage?"

"I'm leaving most of my belongings here since I'm coming back so soon. I have just what I need to travel in my backpack," I said, with as much falsified emotion as I could muster. I held up for him to see the small black satchel I'd filled with a few toiletries from the house I'd commandeered the previous night.

The senior officer looked over the list of medical supplies that the junior inspector held up for him to read. The older man snatched the paper and held it up to the light.

The moment of truth had arrived. He scrutinized the fabricated list of medical supplies and debated my fate. I stood poised on the verge of escape from one of, if not *the*, most difficult places on earth for the Agency to operate and would soon find out how realistic CIA's forgeries appeared to an expert.

I focused on breathing normally—holding one's breath unintentionally is a good indicator that the person is under stress and probably lying.

Nervous sweat oozed from more places on my body than I could count. My armpits were flooded in a mixture of perspiration from the heat of the day and the angst of the exit interview I was working so energetically to pass.

"Hurry back from Geneva," the senior officer said as he returned the folded list to the junior inspector. "We always need more medical supplies."

"*Insha'Allah*, I'll be back in three or four days."

The younger inspector stamped my passport and handed my documents back to me. I walked to the checkpoint on the Egyptian side of the border more relieved than I could ever remember feeling. The late morning sun rising to my left had baked me for a day and a half on the other side of the border. Now, I relished it as a bright and shining beacon welcoming me to freedom.

A dry gust of wind blew across my face, and I relished the modicum of relief it provided. I lifted my arms to air out my body. As the wind carried the sweat away, my nervousness evaporated with it. With every step away from Gaza, I walked lighter and felt freer than I had after any other mission.

At that moment, I savored the thought of just how much I was going to enjoy a long hot shower that afternoon in the Cairo safe house.

As trying as the mission in Gaza had been, the difficult task of facing Steven when I got home loomed ahead of me. I had survived the one but remained unsure if the coming encounter with the man I loved would leave our relationship intact or DOA.

Chapter 38

"We're in here," I called to Steven as the condo door closed and locked. "In the living room."

He sounded puzzled. "Who's 'we?'"

I held up my pint of chocolate chip cookie dough ice cream for him to see and clarified, "Ben, Jerry, and me."

I plopped my comfort-food substitute for a real dinner onto the coffee table with a dull thud, rose, and hugged him.

I gripped him tightly and rested my head against his chest. He pulled me into that wonderful hug of his that tells me just how much he missed me. I snuggled the top of my head against the side of his chin, my ear against his upper chest.

His heart beat energetically.

"I'm glad you're home," he said. "You were gone for two-and-a-half weeks. I wasn't starting to worry, but that's longer than usual." He held me firmly, crossing his arms all the way across my back. "I'm glad you're safe."

"You kept me safe," I said softly.

"How did I do that?"

I paused to think of the right words. Not the truth, or at least not the whole truth, but not a lie, either.

"By being here for me. By being the one I want to come home to every time. You anchor me to the real world, so I don't get lost in the web of fictions that I live in the field. You're my reality. When you're holding me, I know everything's okay."

"I'm happy to help in whatever small way I can."

Steven's words were reassuring, although I could tell he didn't understand what I really meant. That's okay. It was good enough for me.

"We both agree that I travel far more than you'd prefer, and my job is not exactly *Good Housekeeping*-approved. My unpredictable schedule been a strain on us for a while, and now more than ever we both deserve to know where each other stands in this relationship. *Our* relationship. You need to know that I don't *ever* take you for granted. It's at times like this past week that I realize just how much I cherish you and miss you. You keep me centered and sane in this crazy world of ours. I need to do a much better job telling you how important you are to me and how much I love you. And I will. I promise."

Steven rubbed my back gently. "I've been thinking, too. With you away, I've been alone with my thoughts a lot."

A sinking feeling descended over me about where the conversation might be going. I had just gotten back and was suddenly afraid that the home we'd shared for so many years might not be *ours* for much longer. Our condo—and *my* Steven—had drawn me back from the brink in Gaza and suddenly the fear that I might be on the verge of losing them both flooded my mind. I needed him to say what he had to say, but tightened my grip around him, not wanting to hear it. I braced for the worst.

"I drove up to New Jersey the weekend you left."

"Did you have fun?" I asked hopefully.

"A little, but it just wasn't the same without you. It's always great to see Ben and Marci, but all I could think about was you. I wanted you there with me. Part of me thought you wanted to be there, too, but...."

My eyes flew open involuntarily at the sound of that fateful word: *but*. But what? But it's over? But I can't take this anymore? But you're a psychopath, and I want you out of my house right this instant?

"But what?" I asked softly, not sure I wanted to hear what he would say next.

"But I don't know if you have it in you to give me what I need. I need more from you. I do love you, but things feel as if they've been on autopilot for quite a while. I don't need a bigger commitment from you. I'm not going to ask *The Question*." Steven laughed. "The *other* question, I mean."

I smiled, knowing full-well what he meant. "What, then?"

"If we're truly in this relationship together, then let's be in it *together*. I need to know you're fully *in*. It seems to me sometimes—not always, but sometimes—that when you *are* here, it's just a way station or pit stop for you between missions. I want more than that from you. I *need* more than that from you."

"Like what?"

"Like going out together as a couple, for starters. I mean with other people. You rarely go with me when my friends from work go out socially. All the other guys' wives are there. Even Maria Park's husband comes most of the time. But I'm alone. Sure, I want to be part of *your* life, but I also want you in *mine*. I even went camping with you and your co-workers, and we know how that turned out." Steven gave a half-laugh, half-snort at the memory.

"Dinners with my friends are far less, umm, memorable than that. But just the same, I want you to be a part of the group. I hate always having to fly solo. Another example is the annual DI holiday and awards dinner. I want you to attend those with me, okay? There aren't that many people there who know you're a UC employee. You can live your cover and wear a red visitor's badge if you want, but I would very much like you to attend with me. I want us to show the world that we're a couple in love and not just two people who get their mail at the same address. If you can't always make the big weekends away, then at least show me you're trying with the little things here closer to home."

I felt terrible for not being able to get across just how much he means to me. "I'm sorry I've made you feel that way. That's certainly not how I feel—not at all. I can't even put into words how important you are to me. On missions such as this last one... you have no idea. I don't want this to come across the wrong way, but it really is you who gets me back in one piece every time. I always think of you and... you're my motivation. More than self-preservation, I just think of getting back to you, and then I know everything will be alright."

"Am I asking too much, Michelle? Because I don't think so. Is this something you can do?"

"Yes, I *will*. I promise." I meant it.

"Can we sit down, now?"

"Not yet. I have two weeks of hugging to catch up on."

His heartbeat drummed slowly and reassuringly in my ear.

Some people say that men are taller than women because they're the right size to be hunters and we're the right size to be gatherers. I never quite bought into that theory.

At least in our case, Steven is the perfect size to completely envelop me in the warmth of a hug that is all-encompassing. A strong, full-body embrace, his is the hug I think of on cold nights when I'm sitting alone on the floor of some dusty, distant part of the world. Even when I'm alone, I can still feel his arms around me, his hands on my back pulling me against his body.

His heartbeat thumped throughout his chest. My heart—separated from his by only a few inches of skin and clothing—beat in time to his.

My love and need for Steven saved my sanity on more occasions than I can count. Our mutual commitment—truly a *re*commitment—to each other is what enabled us to mend our relationship. Competing stresses had strained our bond, but it never broke. Our connection thinned at times, but survived intact, although admittedly I sometimes took it—and him—too much for granted. Never again, I committed to myself silently and to Steven aloud.

I lifted my head from his chest and looked up at him. "You really are the reason I make it home every time, Steven Krauss. Because... I choose you."

PART ELEVEN

DREAM BOAT

Chapter 39

I sat in my plush red velvet theater seat watching the soloist belt out the final song being performed by the cruise ship's singers and dancers. As I had found myself doing so often during the cruise, I thumbed the engagement ring and wedding band newly adorning my left hand. I was still getting used to the feel of the three-stone princess-cut diamond setting that had not left my finger for a moment over the five sun-filled days since Claude and I boarded the *Jade Queen* as newlyweds at the port of Yokohama, outside of Tokyo.

As the shimmering green curtain descended to signal the end of the performance, enthusiastic applause rose from the audience in appreciation of the exquisite show given by eight very talented Japanese performers.

Throngs of our fellow passengers trickled into the aisles and slowly filtered up the stairs. The crowd navigated the narrow walkways as they headed for the two primary exits in the rear of the theater.

I smoothed the black dress across my tummy and balanced myself on a pair of three-inch heels. Not my usual attire on a mission, my "barely there" dress had a single spaghetti strap across the back, an oblique skirt half-way up my left thigh angled down to my right ankle, and a plunging neckline—all of which combined to leave little to the imagination. I felt as beautiful as I looked.

Although I was certainly dressed to kill, on this mission I was just the distraction and not the shooter. In fact, there was no shooter.

The horde of theatergoers drifted past our back-row seats two at a time. Anxious to get out of the theater and on to other shipboard activities, some headed for the casino and others back to their staterooms—no doubt to make their own entertainment.

I stood facing the aisle. After watching the crowd with disinterest for a minute, I felt Claude step in close behind me and rest his hands on my waist. He looked dashing dressed in his well-tailored tuxedo. His black shirt under a white vest brought a modern twist to a classic look.

Before long, Claude ran his hands up my arms and gently caressed my bare shoulders with a caring, if slightly exaggerated, motion.

Michael saw Claude's hands on my shoulders—the signal—and pushed his wife's wheelchair into the aisle across from me. On cue, I stepped briskly into the aisle from my side, bumping into Mona's wheelchair and clogging the pedestrian artery completely.

I let loose a tirade upon Michael in Spanish in a way that I had never done before. I berated him for his clumsiness in steering the wheelchair into me in the aisle and any number of other reckless acts which I'd queued up in my mind over the last week just for this purpose. My verbal assault on my beloved boss used vocabulary I would never have said to him in English. I must say, I did so enjoy the play acting!

I channeled as much of my high-school friend Carmen's mother, Cecilia, as I could muster. A fiery Latina with jet-black hair, Cecilia was a wonderful mother of six children. Sometimes we joked that I was her seventh child since I spent so much time at their house, especially after my father walked out on us. With a household of two Type-A parents and six active children all vying for their attention, the only way anyone in that family could be heard was to amp up the volume. No one excelled at being heard over her brood quite the way Cecilia did. I hoped I did her proud that night.

The line of theatergoers backed up along the aisle and, like an accordion, compressed well-dressed people against each other.

I waved my arms and gestured first at Michael and then at the growing line of couples wanting to leave the theater. I put on my best *Cecilia* act, paying homage to my surrogate mother. My voice rose in volume and pitch as my diatribe grew more animated. I accused Michael of just about every wickedness under the sun. How inconsiderate could one man be? Was he blind? Did he not see there were a thousand people waiting because he couldn't steer a wheelchair? What made him think he was so special?

Mona apologized frantically, embarrassed and feeling as if she had caused the commotion.

I felt terribly for her—that she was unknowingly being used as a prop in our charade—but this mission sprung up abruptly, so Michael didn't have time to find a CIA officer to play the part. Instead, he made an otherwise fun two-week trip of it for himself and his wife who, in reality, did rely on her wheelchair for mobility.

I prolonged my rant until I felt Claude reach his hands around my waist and pull gently. That was my signal to stop.

It was done.

Claude drew me back out of the aisle and away from Mona. Michael angled the wheelchair toward the exit and the anxious crowd breathed a collective sigh of relief that the *gaijin* obstructions in front of them had gotten the hell out their way.

As they receded into the distance, I heard Mona complain to Michael. "That young woman was very rude. And, oh my, that *dress*! I have slips that cover more than her dress does. She should be ashamed of herself." I choked down a laugh as I turned to face Claude.

Claude draped his arms around my neck and drew me in close. His imitation of a loving embrace helped us both avoid looking at the target of this mission—someone we had not met aboard ship and would have no reason to know, much less stare at awkwardly. After my public outburst in the aisle, I didn't want to give anyone else any more reason to remember us.

From the corner of my eye, I watched Arnaud walk along a row of seats toward a side exit. In his pocket, I knew, he held the auto-injector pen he'd just used to poison the Yakuza don who had been causing a tremendous amount of trouble for the US military on Okinawa over the past few years.

A sophisticated coating around a pellet of concentrated sedative now slowly dissolved in the buttock of the elderly Mafioso. According to Wilson's mission briefing, it would gradually and irreversibly weaken the man over the next three days. One night soon, the old man would stop breathing and die peacefully in his sleep of "natural causes."

I watched Arnaud pass through the arched exit and disappear. Within a minute or two, he would toss the spent injector overboard, disposing of any evidence that anything untoward had happened aboard the *Jade Queen* that evening.

I reached up and wrapped my arms around Claude's neck. I pulled myself close to him and laid my head on his shoulder, holding him firmly.

I stood against Claude, biding my time while waiting for the crowd behind me to empty out of the theater. I thumbed my CIA-issued wedding ring behind the neck of my fake husband and thought about the kind of ring I might someday wear for real while holding my true love—Steven—close.

Not anytime soon, I reaffirmed to myself, but someday.

Someday, eventually.

Someday, after all of this is behind me.

Only then would Steven and I get to wear matching wedding rings and live out our very own version of "happily ever after."

In the meantime, I leaned against Claude and beamed silently. Arnaud's departure from the theater signaled yet another successful mission we pulled off as a team. Years of busting my ass to fit in and prove myself a first-rate operator had paid off better than I could have ever imagined or hoped for. From my early solo missions to this nautical full-court press, we had come together as a smoothly operating machine—a machine which Michael had tuned perfectly. After more than a decade of training, run-throughs, missions, and debriefings, we could practically read each other's minds. We had each other's backs all day, every day. The three of us practically operated as one.

After my early years of being on the outside as the new kid, I had become a driving force and mainstay of our traveling troupe. With my brothers-in-arms both *at* my side and *on* my side, I was happier than I'd ever been.

With my arms gently encircling Claude's neck, I smiled a bit wider and nudged my head into his shoulder just *that* much deeper.

As ecstatic as I felt during those two weeks at sea, if I'd known in advance what our next mission held in store, I would have quit the team right then and there.

PART TWELVE

DRAGON'S BREATH

Chapter 40

The conference room in Mossad's Tel Aviv office was spartan by American standards. The bare-bones table and chairs were functional, but not luxurious. Colorful posters of cultural and religious sites around Israel hung on the walls. At least the bottled water was cold.

"An amusement park?" I asked, astonished. "They have those in Syria?"

"Of course, why wouldn't they?" Dov asked, amazed at my surprise. "Do you think they only build amusement parks in America and Europe? We have them here, too."

"No, I mean.... I don't know. I'm sorry. It just surprised me, that's all. It never crossed my mind that this kind of thing would be going on at an amusement park. I just can't imagine an operational trip to someplace like Disneyland, that's all."

"I've had three surveillance missions to Disney World, as it happens."

"Really?" I blurted out, even more astounded than I was earlier. The Magic Kingdom is not what immediately comes to mind when one thinks of the most likely places for Mossad to conduct intelligence operations in America. Washington, New York, or Los Angeles, sure. But Orlando?

Reuven interrupted. "Let's keep the conversation focused on this particular mission, shall we?"

"Sorry," I apologized to Michael's Mossad counterpart. For our team's week in Israel, Reuven was serving as our gracious host and the coordinator of the joint operation.

Reuven continued the briefing. "The warehouse we've been watching is not actually inside the Pride of Damascus Park, itself. It's a support building at the edge of the park's maintenance area, adjacent to a rail line. Our human intelligence sources indicate that weapons are being transshipped through the warehouse. Some of the weapons Syria receives from Iran are siphoned off, sent through this warehouse, and end up in Lebanon, Africa, and other areas for use by Hezbollah, various terrorist groups, and their proxies. Our reconnaissance drones and your satellites haven't seen anything more than the movement of crates. None of that is concrete enough confirmation of the presence of weapons for the leaders of either of our countries to use to justify direct action."

Michael added his emphasis to the importance of the mission. "Both of our nations have a strong interest in containing Iran's expanding influence and preventing the distribution of missiles and weapons to Hezbollah, Al Qaeda, Boko Haram, and others. Any arms we can keep from reaching the battlefield is a win for all of us."

"Unfortunately," Reuven said with a frown, "remote sensors can only do so much. For real confirmation, we need to get eyeballs on the target. Neither of our governments is willing to be seen as having bombed an amusement park just on the strength of the information received to date. That's why the six of you are here. This mission will confirm or refute overhead and HUMINT reports and provide hard evidence such that world opinion can be successfully managed if or when either of our nations decides to act overtly. To get in, take pictures, and bring back conclusive evidence, a joint six-man mission is the only way. Excuse me, four men and two women. My apologies, ladies."

"No offense taken," I said with a glance across the conference table at Rachel.

Along with Claude, Arnaud, and Rachel, Mossad assigned two other officers, Dov and Noah, to round out our six-person recon team.

Reuven summarized the plan. "You'll travel in three teams of two. Dov and Noah will fly in one day before the others to secure the two vehicles and assortment of tactical equipment you can't take with you on commercial aircraft. Mossad's logistics arm has been working on this for a month and confirmed yesterday that your weapons, radios, and tools are already in place. The other teams will fly to Damascus through Cairo, Egypt, and Amman, Jordan. The park is southeast of the capital."

Michael ran his fingers through his shock-white hair, pushing it straight back over the top of his head. "Normally, recon missions are the ones you want to get done without being seen. Stealth in, stealth out, and zero residual presence. In this case, that may not be possible. The warehouse is rarely left unguarded. That alone is strong evidence that something important is kept there. But either way, you'll need to get inside, open a few crates, and take photos. If that means going through a half-dozen guards to do so, then that's what you'll have to do."

The heads nodding around the table told me that the Mossad team was also experienced in such missions. No doubt, I was sure, that's why the six of us were specifically chosen for a recon mission that would otherwise have been assigned to a team whose real job was defeating locks and alarms, not armed guards.

Reuven continued. "Concealed within each car is one silenced sniper rifle, handguns, digital cameras, night-vision goggles, and the other equipment you either requested or provided yourselves. Dov and Rachel are our primary sharpshooters, and that's the way our training scenarios will be organized over the next few days. We'll have two training days this week for team familiarization and practice scenarios. After that, it's game time, as you Americans say. Any questions?"

There were none.

Chapter 41

The Dragon's Neck roller coaster loomed in the distance across the empty parking lot. The green-tinted glow of its steel tracks bloomed in my night vision goggles as the dragon lay sleeping in the early morning hours. Our team of six intrepid adventurers had no intention of stealing the beast's treasure—we just needed to get a few good pictures of it.

Dov peered through the night-vision scope of his rifle and confirmed what Rachel had just reported over the radio. "I see two armed guards, as well. One next to the train tracks and the other upstairs on the balcony outside what must be the office. I have a clear shot at both. Pick your target."

Rachel responded. "I can only get the target upstairs. The other keeps going between the rail cars. On three...."

I knelt next to a wooden shack about a hundred yards from the warehouse and waited. Dov counted to what I can only assume was three in Hebrew. A moment later, I saw the guard on the balcony plummet to the ground. The clatter of his AK-47 hitting the pavement broke the silence briefly.

Radio calls of "target down" and "moving now" flooded my earpiece. Dov reported that he would stay on overwatch from his sniper's perch and cover our collective backsides.

I sprinted for the warehouse's southern door, just underneath the balcony. Arnaud arrived before me and held the door open. I mused briefly as I rushed through the doorway, pistol out in front of me, that this is one of those few times in life that a policy of "Ladies First" is not necessarily to our advantage.

Inside the warehouse, we began clearing the areas between stacks of crates, looking for other guards.

With none in sight in our part of the warehouse, Arnaud and I maneuvered back to the door and regrouped with Noah.

"One or two guards here on the north side," Claude reported over the radio. "Moving."

Noah charged off to help Claude and Rachel deal with the guard on the main level. Arnaud followed me upstairs to clear the office.

Cluttered with a half-dozen desks and twice as many filing cabinets, the main part of the office had an open floorplan. We could easily see it was empty. We rushed through the sparsely furnished office and ensured the kitchen, bathroom, and two storage rooms were equally unoccupied.

Cracks of rifle fire from below were followed by Noah's screaming into the radio. "Eden, Arnie, one's coming your way. There were three down here, and one got by me. He's heading towards the south door."

Arnaud sprinted for the stairs. I stepped outside onto the balcony into position to engage the guard from above if Arnaud didn't get him before he made it through the door. Dov might also be able to get a shot off from across the parking lot, but it's hard for a sniper to hit a running target.

I steadied myself on the balcony and held my pistol at the ready to get a clean shot at the guard about to appear below me.

The reports from an AK-47 on the north end of the warehouse continued sporadically. I couldn't hear our team's suppressed pistol shots, but the *ping*s and *clink*s of ricochets told me there were bullets flying in both directions.

"Got him, Noah," Arnaud called out over the radio. "Target down at the south door. I'm coming to help."

The ear-splitting *bang* of an explosion from the north end of the warehouse rang out into the still night air.

My teammates screamed through my radio earpiece.

"Grenade!" Noah warned.

"I'm hit. My leg—" Rachel cried, her voice straining through the pain.

I spun to go help the team with the grenade-throwing guard downstairs. With the dragon-shaped roller coaster rising in the distance beyond the warehouse, I moved toward the balcony door.

Then, the dragon breathed.

An angry roar rebuking us for our trespass rose from downstairs.

A maelstrom of flame shot through the windows and door of the office. The force of the blast threw me off the balcony and sent me tumbling.

The world turned orange.

Then everything went black.

Chapter 42

White. Everything was white.

White haze flowed through my head like clouds on a windy day.

White acoustic ceiling tiles above me were punctuated with thousands of black pinholes.

White ceramic wall tiles surrounded a wide, pinewood door with a stainless-steel kick plate at the bottom.

White drapes. White with squiggly green lines. Or waves? Were they supposed to be waves? They surged endlessly like swells never reaching the shore.

White vinyl floor tiles. White with gray speckles. Ugly. Industrial.

White bed sheets under my arms.

Even the cast on my right leg was white.

Wait, what? A cast? I screamed—or at least I tried to. Through the haze, even to me it sounded more like a muddled, "Whaaaa thuuuhhh?"

White haze, I thought. Not as good as Purple Haze, I smirked. Or Deep Purple—even better. White hazy smoke in my head. No, smoke on the water. Yes, that was it. It was Frank Zappa and the Mothers!

I laughed aloud at my song-lyrics joke and stopped abruptly.

I am soooo high, I realized. *Completely stoned! Holy shit,* I thought smiling and chuckling again. *So that's what really good drugs feel like. They're so much better than the pot Jimmy Hernandez used to get for us from his older brother back in high school.*

High school. Get it? I really amused myself.

I strained to look at the cast. A greenish-grayish sling suspended my leg above the bed—a hospital bed with arm rails. The question of what hospital I was in flashed briefly through my mind, but didn't stick there for long. I fixated on the cast encasing my leg. I had a burning need to touch it—to see if it was real or just a figment of my imagination. I half expected it to jump off my leg, fold itself into a snow-white dove, and fly away.

If it had done so, I would have surely enjoyed the show.

I reached down to feel the cast but couldn't stretch my arm far enough. The cast ended below my knee, and I had to sit up to try to reach it.

As I leaned forward, a wave of agony rolled through my stomach. The stabbing pain in my gut dropped me back onto the bed, my face contorted by the torment. I laid motionless for a minute to catch my breath and figure out what was going on.

I patted my stomach through the bedsheets and felt something bulky lurking underneath. I pulled up the white gown covering me and stared at the bandages taped to my abdomen. Lots of white bandages.

More white. Everything was white. Well, the gown had some red pinstripes in it. Those were pretty, I thought, as my mind wandered away.

I shook my head to clear it and a wave of dizziness washed over me. I gripped the bed's handrails in a vain attempt to arrest the world's sudden spiraling. I leaned back and laid still for a little while in the desperate hope that the room would soon choose to stop swirling around my head. I held my pulsating head in my hands for a painful minute and wished for the world to stop—I wanted to get off.

While resting, I got back to thinking about my situation. *Obviously, I'd been captured, but by who? Or is it by whom,* I wondered. *I've never understood the diff—*

Get a grip of yourself, girl, I thought, interrupting my floating off on yet another tangent. *Man, the painkillers are killer,* I realized.

My captors had not restrained my hands, but I was not truly free. With my leg in a cast, whatever the hell was going on under the bandages on the right side of my abdomen, and the drugs (the wonderful drugs!) they had me on, even in my condition I could readily see that my mobility was limited. Just standing up was going to severely challenge me. Running away was more a hope than a plan.

But run to where? Where was I? What were my options for escape and exfiltration? And where were the other five members of my team? Were they here in the same facility? Down the hall or maybe on another floor? I had far more questions than answers.

Before anyone discovered I was even awake, I needed to figure out quite a lot.

To my left, the half-drawn drapes partially concealed a metal security screen over the window. I could make out a white plastic panel or some such obstruction between the screen and the glass, blocking my view.

Okay, so they didn't want me to know where I was. Got it. That's rule number one for interrogation—disorient the subject.

Knowing that much gave me a basis for assessing my situation. It was a start.

Now what? What's my next step?

Step being more a figure of speech than a literal possibility at that point. If I couldn't so much as bend at the waist, I wasn't sure how I'd be able to stand up, much less walk. Forget running. I was going to have to sneak out of here—wherever *here* is.

Sometime later—in my condition, I had trouble gauging the passage of time—a woman in pale blue scrubs entered the room. I guessed she was a nurse, if only because she checked my IV.

Until that point, it hadn't even occurred to me that I had an IV in my arm. Damn, I was really out of it.

The thought that an IV needle could be the beginning of a makeshift sharp weapon provided a faint glimmer of hope.

The nurse asked me a question in a language I didn't recognize. Probably asking how I felt, but I couldn't make heads or tails of the guttural sounds and hard *chhh* intonations. It wasn't Arabic, of that I was sure. It also wasn't Russian. I don't speak Russian, but after spending enough time around Claude and Arnaud, I could recognize it most of the time.

I thought through various scenarios, trying to answer the question of what the Syrians would do with a captured enemy spy or saboteur. We weren't carrying any identification, so I thought it highly unlikely they'd immediately think I was American. Maybe they'd suspect me of being part of a local resistance group? A Kurd, perhaps? Not that that'd be any better—they'd treat me as if I were a terrorist. Which would be worse, being treated like a terrorist or an American spy? I wasn't sure, nor did I want to find out.

Or, they could think I were Israeli. Oh, crap. *That* would certainly be worse for me.

So, if she weren't speaking Arabic, I pondered, *she's probably not Syrian. Then, who are my captors? If I weren't in Syria, where had they taken me?*

Who are Assad's allies? The Russians, for sure. But she wasn't speaking Russian. Not the Turks, Iraqis, or Jordanians. They all pretty much hate the Syrians, or at least the Assad regime. So, who, then? The Iranians?

Shit! Was she speaking Farsi? I wouldn't recognize Farsi if they handed me a textbook, much less spoke it in front of me.

I had no idea how long I'd been unconscious. Hours? For sure. Days? Possibly. Certainly long enough for them to fly me to Tehran. To me, that was the very definition of an unmitigated disaster.

I looked at my left wrist for my watch, but it wasn't there. If I had my watch, the poisoned needle concealed in the stem would be my last-ditch option. An option I didn't relish, but one I would certainly prefer to enduring weeks or months of torture before being dragged before a kangaroo court for a sham trial. All of which would have been carefully orchestrated for the world's viewing pleasure. After that, I knew, I would be led to a highly public execution staged for maximum propaganda value. In either case—needle or noose—I would end up dead. Personally, I would rather be the one to determine my own fate and decide how I exit the world's stage.

Maybe my clothing was in the cabinet against the far wall, I speculated, half wondering and half hoping. I needed to find out. There was no chance my weapons were in there, though. That'd make it too easy.

The nurse finished checking the monitors alongside my bed. She again asked me something I couldn't understand, and I chose to remain silent. It seemed they didn't know I spoke English, so there was no reason to expose that fact just yet. I suspected they'd try Arabic, next.

She held up one finger in what I interpreted as the universal hand sign for "wait one minute," and left the room.

As the door swung shut, I caught a glimpse of an armed guard in fatigues standing just outside. That confirmed what I had already suspected: I was a prisoner.

For the moment, I couldn't even get out of the bed. At some point, though, I'd regain my strength and be able to stand. I resolved to conceal my strength as it returned. At best, I'd get only one opportunity for a surprise rush out the door. After that, if I weren't successful, they'd surely strap my hands to the bed. My one chance had to count.

The door opened and a man wearing a white coat and stethoscope entered behind the nurse. Even in my condition, it wasn't much of a leap for me to mentally label him the doctor.

His questions were equally unintelligible. I didn't try to respond.

He pressed ever so gently on my bandages and I winced at the sting. I let him continue his examination, choosing not to start resisting just yet. I wanted to see what my captors' next step would be.

It turned out their next step was to simply leave the room. Frankly, that surprised me.

The nurse returned before long with what was either lunch or dinner. The sight of food reminded me that I had no idea what time it was. Still disoriented, I ate with my fingers. Not surprisingly, she didn't bring me utensils. No sense giving your prisoner a knife, I mused.

I awoke sometime later as the nurse entered my room. A scream from somewhere down the hall flooded through the open doorway. Instinctively, I bolted upright—or at least tried to. A wave of pain washed over me, and I cried out in my own wail of agony.

The nurse pushed my shoulder down onto the bed—well, more guided than pushed. Gently, she patted my shoulder as I grimaced. My eyes watered as I labored to breathe through the pain. I could have sworn that the way she squinted her eyes and drew her lips back was a genuine display of sympathy. It seemed to me she would not likely be part of the inevitable interrogation team. I briefly wondered how I might turn her into a sympathetic ally to help me escape. That would, no doubt, be a high hurdle as we didn't even speak the same language.

The nurse withdrew a syringe from her pocket and injected it into the IV stream. With the pain in my side subsiding only slightly on its own, I was grateful for whatever relief she was giving me from the flame burning across my belly. There was no doubt in my mind that I'd be wishing for more of whatever was in that needle once the coming inquisition began.

Chapter 43

A loud noise from somewhere down the hall woke me with a start. Was that a scream? One of my teammates? Is that what's in store for me, too?

I looked around the room and found I was alone. The effect of the medications had abated while I slept. My head throbbed directly behind my left eye while my abdomen felt like the Los Angeles Dodgers had taken batting practice on it while I slept. Damn them, I would have to start rooting for the Yankees from now on.

I peered intently at the narrow wooden cabinet against the wall opposite my bed. Only fifteen feet away, it might as well have been across an ocean. I made it my goal to walk to it before the nurse returned. I needed to know if my watch or clothes were inside.

If so, even a belt could be turned into an improvised weapon. If not, I needed to figure out what else to use. Shoelaces would be a good start. I thought about making a blackjack out of the pillowcase with something heavy inside, or maybe jabbing the IV needle into the guard's eyeball to steal his sidearm. Or perhaps those thoughts were more wishful thinking than realistic planning. Who knows? It had the makings of a plan, although it hinged on my getting my sorry ass up and out of bed.

The nurse's return interrupted my planning. She pushed a stainless-steel cart of medical supplies into the room. A doctor I had not seen before followed closely behind.

While the nurse laid out new bandages on top of the cart, the doctor pulled on a pair of white latex gloves. As he carefully peeled back the red-stained surgical dressings from my skin, I got my first look at my injuries.

Sutures in the shape of a jagged number four adorned my abdomen and stretched around to my right side. Fading yellow streaks of surgical antiseptic stained my sallow skin.

After a few minutes, the door cracked open and the doctor who examined me earlier poked his head in. He said only a few quick words to the man at my bedside, but it was enough to spook both him and the nurse. The look on all three faces was identical—grave concern. More for themselves, I decided, than for me.

After a few words to the nurse, the doctor changing my bandages followed his colleague out the door. The nurse finished applying new dressings and pulled her cart behind her as she departed.

Ready or not, I had to make my move. Whatever had so concerned the doctors could not possibly be good news for me. It was now or never.

I mustered what little physical strength remained in my battered muscles and gritted my teeth to brace for the pain waiting in front of me. With a grunt and a twist, I swung my body to the left. My left leg eagerly led the way, flopping over the side of the bed on its way to freedom. My torso cajoled the rest of my body to follow, but my right leg rejected the order to move. Instead, it swung like a pendulum in the harness suspending my cast above the bed.

My right side exploded in scorching pain collapsing me back onto the bed in agony. Streaks of white-hot sparks shot throughout my mid-section. My eyes watered, blurring the room for a moment. I clenched my teeth and hissed the pain out slowly, determined to not call attention to myself by screaming and squandering my one chance to escape.

Splayed across the bed in a half-split, my left leg dangled off the edge while my right still hung securely above me. How the hell could I have possibly missed my leg being up in the air while trying to get out of bed? I cursed myself for being an idiot. The painkillers were seriously messing with my mind.

The sling hung too far away to reach, especially since I couldn't bend forward to even touch my knee. Maybe I could just pull it straight towards me and out of the sling?

With a *clang*, the door burst open and the nurse entered with her lips drawn thin and brow furrowed—a degree of concern I had not seen her show before. I was caught in the act of escape and now found myself boxed in by the nurse.

Behind her, a procession of four men hurried into my room. I watched as one after the other entered, practically tripping over each other to get to my bedside. I stared in complete disbelief as the first man through the door spoke.

"Glad to see you're awake," Reuven said, smiling. "How do you feel?"

"What the...?" I blurt out, mouth agape at the sight of my new visitors. How could Reuven be here? Was this a trick? Is he part of the interrogation?

The room spun, and my head careened into the pillow behind me. I grabbed a fistful of bed and squeezed until my hand was the same bloodless color as the sheets.

The faces of the four men steadied and slowly came into focus. My eyes watered, and a tear slide down my cheek.

"Michael. Steven!" I cried, joyously. "Why is—? How did—? What are you doing here?" My mind swung abruptly, swirling from pain to joy, my thoughts ricocheting from imprisonment to bewilderment. "And where the hell is *here* anyway?"

On one side of me, the nurse lifted my left leg back onto the bed. On the other, Steven snatched up my hand and held it tightly, intertwining his fingers with mine. Although he smiled with his lips, his eyes told a different story.

"Are you alright?" he asked softly. "They said it was touch-and-go for a while. I was so worried when Mike told me what happened and knew it had to be really bad for him to invite me to come with him to see you."

Steven's eyes fought a losing battle to stay locked with mine. Those beautiful hazel orbs snuck a few glances at my head. "What happened to your hair?"

"My *what*?" Confused, I ran my free hand through my hair, or what was left of it. My fingertips ran unimpeded along the scalp above my right ear. Along the rest of my skull, a good third of my hair was simply gone.

I looked at Reuven. "What happened? Where are the others?"

Michael answered my question by shaking his head silently.

"I'm sorry," Reuven said softly.

"What do you mean?" I hissed hoarsely. "What the hell happened?"

I looked closely at Michael. He stood silently beside Steven. The whites of Michael's eyes ran thick with red streaks. He appeared older than I had ever seen him look. What might have seemed to an outsider as the world's worst case of jetlag, I knew, was not the case—I could just tell. I knew Michael well and had never seen him so sullen. The bright trails of red that crisscrossed his eyes stood in stark contrast to the pallor of his cheeks.

My head snapped back as I grasped what had happened: Michael had been crying.

The pain in my abdomen flared from the physical aches of my wound to an emotional kick in the gut.

Reuven's eyes sagged. That he found the news so terrible that he struggled to even deliver it paralyzed me. I couldn't breathe.

"Dov brought you back safely," Reuven said softly. "When the warehouse exploded.... I'm sorry. None of the others survived."

I could barely muster a whisper. "None?"

A weight descended upon my chest. I could draw only shallow breaths. I hardly knew Rachel or Noah but had spent the past decade working with Claude and Arnaud. After so many years of struggling, we had finally become close. We trained together. We traveled the world together. We relied upon each other operationally and, as had eventually become the case, emotionally.

I turned away and stared at the metal grate over the window. I let my vision go blurry and melt into the white panel diffusing the light trying to stream through. I fought to catch my breath. The suddenness of the news was too much to process. I gasped for air.

"During his debrief," Reuven continued slowly, "Dov said he heard over the radio that one of the guards was throwing grenades. Not a very smart thing to do in a warehouse full of arms and explosives. Did you see anything else?"

"No," I said, shaking my head slowly. A tear slid slowly down my right cheek. "I didn't engage the guards. The others had that covered. I was upstairs on the balcony. I set up to take out the guard heading out the south door if he made it that far, but Arnaud got him first while they were both still inside."

I looked at Steven as he ran his hands across my chin. He wiped away a tear and caressed my jaw. This was the first time he was hearing the tactical specifics of any of my missions. He was an analyst through and through, and I worried how he'd react to hearing the unfiltered details. Years before, my overly gruesome descriptions of my work disgusted him when he first learned the truth. I hoped he'd hold up better this time.

"You were successful in learning what we needed to know," Reuven went on, "but at such a high cost. I'm sorry for your loss."

"Thank you," I said softly, looking up at the Mossad unit chief. "You have my condolences for your team, as well. I didn't know them that well, but I liked them all. They were good officers. Good people."

I looked at the fourth man in the room and realized he'd been standing by silently so far. "Who's he?"

"Howie Miller," Michael answered. "Deputy Chief of Station, Tel Aviv. He's going to arrange for your medical evacuation to Ramstein Air Base in Germany."

"Where am I, anyway?" I asked Reuven, realizing I didn't even know that much. My failed attempts to escape suddenly struck me as ludicrous, if not pathetic. I had schemed every which way I could think of to plot an escape from that hospital—the one place I should have been fighting to stay *in*. My cheeks flushed with embarrassment.

"You were badly injured," Reuven explained. "Dov drove you to a pre-surveyed extraction point further south and called for an Israeli Special Forces helicopter to pick the both of you up."

"You flew into Syria to rescue me? Rescue us?" I asked, almost stupefied. Being so used to operating completely on my own in the field, I'd forgotten how it felt to have a way to dial 9-1-1 for reinforcements or extraction.

Reuven nodded. "I don't want to say we do it all the time, but, yes, we know how to get in and out of Syria and Lebanon when we need to," he said with a sly grin.

"As I said, you were badly injured and lost a lot of blood, so you were brought to the closest hospital in Israel. You're in the Golan Heights. They don't have a military or police wing here—it's a very small hospital by Tel Aviv or Jerusalem standards. The most secure part of the facility is the psychiatric ward. We checked you in here under an Israeli pseudonym and had the local police post a guard outside for your protection."

I laughed, which hurt my side. "Being in the psych ward seems somehow appropriate, doesn't it? That explains the grate over the window. What happened here?" I pointed to my side.

"Shrapnel. The surgeons said they patched you up as best they could, however you may need a follow-up procedure."

"Thank you, Reuven. I really don't know what else to say. Just, thank you."

"No, it is *I* who should be thanking you. You are everything Mike said you were and then some. So, thank *you*, Eden."

Steven glanced at Reuven with a puzzled look on his face.

"*Eden*?" he asked me.

I squeezed Steven's hand and smiled. "I guess we have a lot of talking to do when we get home."

Chapter 44

"It looks like the Air Force took good care of you in Germany, Wendy," Doctor Patel said to me as he closed the medical chart and returned it to the folder at the foot of my hospital bed. "Your second surgery was a complete success. Where did you say the first procedure was performed?"

"I didn't, but nice try, Doc. That's classified," I said with a bit of a devilish grin. I couldn't blame the guy for trying.

"Well, we'll be taking good care of you here at Portsmouth, as well. The Navy's physical therapists downstairs will challenge you, but if you work *with* them instead of *against* them, they'll have you back on your feet in no time. And there's a beauty salon on the first floor if you want to have them even out your hair."

"I'm going to leave my hair as is for now," I said as he turned to leave the room, "but thank you."

Michael rose from his chair at the side of my bed. "Seems like a nice guy."

"Sure, I suppose. Although, he's not the one who has to endure dealing with the physical torturers in the PT department. And by the way, if I never hear the name Wendy Mintner again as long as I live, it'll be fine with me."

"Same hospital, same medical records, same name—that's the way it works. But, if not having to hear that name again is the motivation you need to not get wounded again, then good. Now I know how to incentivize you to stay healthy. On a more serious note, for the next two weeks of inpatient PT, you'll stay here. After that, you can rehab at the Farm. I'll make the transportation arrangements."

"No need. I'll ask Steven to drive down from DC to get me, but thanks just the same."

"Okay, Michelle. You relax and get better. That's your only job for the next six months, and it's an important one."

"I will. And Michael," I said hesitantly, "please tell Monica I'm sorry I missed the memorial service for Claude and Arnaud. I really wanted to attend."

"I know," he said, "and she knows it, too. She sends her best wishes for a quick recovery. She said she's going to move back to Minnesota so she's closer to her family."

Michael picked up the briefcase from beside his chair and laid it on the table next to my bed.

"This is for you. You've been through a serious trauma and have had a difficult time lately. And I don't just mean after this particular mission. I know you've been struggling after the last few. I've been there myself, and I can see it in your eyes. Believe me, I know. Sometimes, in this job it can be difficult to separate yourself from the mission. One minute you're Wendy and the next you're Eden, but underneath, you're always Michelle. You don't seem to want to talk about it to me, and I know you keep the worst of it hidden from Steve."

Michael pulled a laptop computer from his briefcase and set the computer on the table.

"This is an encrypted PC that you unlock with your thumbprint on the scanner down here," he said, pointing to a spot below the keyboard. "It's the same kind of secure computer that Agency executives use when traveling. I'm not saying that you have to, but if you wanted to, you can use this to put your thoughts and feelings down on paper. Call it an electronic diary, if you like. No one else has to ever read it—it's just for you. Think about it, and if you decide it might help, then it's here for you to use as you please."

"I don't think that's really my cup of tea, Michael. I wouldn't even know where to start. What would I write about?"

"That's up to you. Write about your thoughts and feelings, if you want to. As for where to start, well, I suppose you can always just start at the beginning."

He pointed at me as he headed for the door. With a parting smile Michael said, "Feel better. I'll stop by again early next week and bring you a couple of issues of *People*."

I laughed, which didn't hurt nearly as much anymore, and thanked him as he left.

I looked over at the computer, its screen blank as it sat silently on the table next to my bed.

Start at the beginning?

I laid back on the bed and stared at the ceiling. What in the world I would even *want* to write if no one else would ever read it? My emotions over the past year or so had swung wildly from one horrible extreme to the other. Would any of it make sense, even to me?

I looked at the computer again. It sat noiselessly on the table, waiting patiently for me to make a decision. That's what it's all about, after all, I reminded myself, making decisions. Making the right decisions.

Michael suggested I start at the beginning. From that hospital bed, the beginning seemed like a lifetime ago.

Chapter 45

She pushed my head down below the surface of the water, wrapped her hands around my throat, and squeezed with all her might. Her sharp fingernails pinched my neck as they dug into the skin around my trachea. Her slender fingers compressed my windpipe, sure to crush it at any moment.

She sat on my stomach, clutched her hands around my neck squeezing the life out of me, and pushed my head down to a watery grave. I held my breath—not that I had much choice in the matter—thrashed about wildly, struggling with all my might to get free.

As she leaned over me staring down into my face, I looked up through the ripples of the water at her flawless complexion and long brown hair. Rodrigo Beltran Gutierrez's girlfriend pushed down, crushing my throat, and looked at me with an expression of shock splayed across her face.

Why was she so surprised? Because she had gotten the better of me? She was the one killing *me*. I was the one who didn't see this coming.

I pushed up as hard as I could in one failed attempt after another to break her grip, but the woman in the short silver dress would not budge. I rocked backwards to get some forward momentum going and pushed against her again. And again, and again, and again, with no more success than I had had the first dozen times. Her strong arms held me fast.

Fragmented thoughts born of my own panic ricocheted across my brain. My own confusion conspired with my adversary to rob me of my life.

Her fingernails pinched deeply into the sides of my neck while her thumbs pressed harder and harder on the front of my throat. The last seconds of my life ticked away. I knew she was squeezing the life out of me and dug deeper to summon the strength I needed to fight back harder.

My instincts conflicted, adding confusion to the pain. My lungs burned for me to breathe deeply, but I knew I needed to hold my breath until I could raise my head above the surface. One instinct screamed that if I wanted to live, I had to breathe, but another countered just as forcefully that to even try to breathe was certain death. I fought against myself as much as I fought against her.

I desperately needed to inhale, but I couldn't let myself give in to the temptation to draw a breath. To do so would be to drown.

To die.

To lose.

Pushing was not working. I had to pull. Yes! That was it, I told myself, pull her!

I leaned back further as if to help her drown me while a part of my brain screamed in protest against my complicity. I lifted my left leg up across my body and around her head. I squeezed my knee closed, twisted sideways, and rolled to my left reversing positions with her. As my head cleared the water, I inhaled deeply and rolled myself on top of Gutierrez's girlfriend. I reached down and firmly pushed her face beneath the silvery surface of the still water.

Now with my hands around her throat, I choked *her*. I wrapped my hands around her neck and pressed with my thumbs across the smooth skin of her neck. With a grin running from ear to ear, I shouted into her face, "I am not going to lose!"

I lifted her head out of the water and repeatedly plunged it back underneath the smooth surface. I pushed her into the cold, clear water where her muddled cries bubbled up as nothing more than an unintelligible *Guuk*.

No.... I was pushing but I must not push. I knew I had to do this the right way. I had to pull. Yes, that's it, I ordered myself. Pull her.

I released her throat and reached around to the back of her head. I grabbed ahold of her long, wavy brown hair and pulled. Yes, pull, Michelle. That's it, pull with all your might!

I made a pony tail out of her loose, wet hair and yanked her head down underwater. She bobbed up and down trying to escape my grasp, gyrating wildly to lift her face above the surface and catch a breath of life—a breath of the air that was only an inch away from her ruby lips.

An inch was all I needed.

She struggled in vain. I was not going to let her up. She could see it in my eyes.

I held her head down just below the surface and stared directly into her eyes. Face to face, separated by only an inch of the water into which she had tried to drown me, I knew I was not going to lose. I was on top and would win this life-and-death struggle with... who?

Who was she anyway? Did it matter?

The Girlfriend. That's all she'd ever be to me. She was the only thing that ever stood between me and the career I was destined to have. There was no way I'd let her keep me from being the best possible *me*.

"You're nobody," I screamed into her face at the top of my lungs. "You don't even have a name, but I do! My name is Eden!"

She pushed hard, but I didn't budge. She twisted, but I sat on her stomach like a championship bull rider not giving an inch as she bucked.

"No. You can't drag me down. I win," I yelled, staring directly into her eyes, proving my dominance. "I win, do you hear me? I win. I *win*!"

My refrain grew from a victorious cry to a hair-raising shriek.

"I win! I win! I—"

***

"Michelle, Michelle! Wake up, dear, you're okay, wake up."

I bolted awake to find Nurse Sarah gently rubbing my back. I was kneeling on the bed in the Infirmary at the Farm, face down in my pillow, heart racing, and chest heaving for air.

Sarah's face furrowed. "Are you alright, Michelle? You were screaming that 'you win' or 'you won,' or something. Are you okay? You're safe now, honey. How do you feel?"

I looked at my worried nurse while gasping for air, mouth wide open and fighting for each breath. Bright light streamed through the doorway into the Infirmary's small bedroom. I squinted my eyes as they painfully adjusted to the glare of the hallway's fluorescents. My pounding heart did its best to push its way out of my chest.

Without a word I nodded, stood, and limped into the main treatment area. From a tray on the counter, I selected a pair of medical shears and silently led a hawk-eyed Sarah into the bathroom.

In front of the mirror, I looked at my reflection. For the first time since my return from the Middle East, I saw myself clearly. Dressed in a white Infirmary-issued t-shirt—the red, white, and blue CIA seal perched prominently over my left breast—I smiled and turned my head slowly from side to side, inspecting my half-a-head of hair.

My reflection smiled back as we—the two *mes*—reminisced about the years it took my hair to grow nearly down to my waist. Years of training. Years of missions. Years of accumulated pain and joy and stress and confusion and love and, now, mind-numbing loss. Over more than a decade, the incessant envelopment of conflicting emotions had swaddled me in stifling layers shrouding what remained of the Michelle I once knew. Deep inside, she cried to be heard and begged me to slough off the amassed burden so the two mes could finally come together.

The Infirmary at the Farm served quite possibly as the perfect place for me to have my nightmare, my revelation, and my emotional cleansing.

I looked closely at the woman in the mirror and recognized that particular *me* by the shape of her face. My face. We share the same heart, even if we will forever occupy disconnected worlds.

I know who that *me* is. Although this is a medical facility and she's not a doctor, she is a surgeon of sorts, I told myself. There is cancer in this world and someone needs to cut it out. That's her job—*my* job. I excise the tumors Michael says to, cutting the diseased parts from the body so they can do no further harm. Sometimes, adjacent healthy tissue must be sacrificed in the process if it's in the Wrong Place at the Wrong Time. That's unfortunate, but it's the price society has to pay to rid itself of the diseases infecting it.

I looked again at my reflection and beamed.

With shears in hand, I held up the remnants of my hair and sliced it off in bunches. Snip by snip, I dropped yard-long handfuls of brunette tresses into the trashcan. Up the back and over the top, I cut, cropped, snipped, and all but shaved the remaining shocks of hair from my skull and dropped a lifetime of accumulation into the garbage pail.

The resulting ugly, scraggly mess drew a self-shaming laugh. Shorter on the right where the Israeli nurses had trimmed away the scraggly burnt ends, the left side I had just shorn was an uneven, patchy hack job.

Still, it was freeing. Liberating. Unburdening. I relieved myself of years of amassed pain, dropped it into the trashcan, and walked away. Well, limped away.

"Yes, Sarah, I'm alright. Thank you," I said softly as I turned and handed the borrowed scissors to her. "I did win after all. I lost friends and still need to grieve for them. But I'm winning the battle with myself. More importantly, I'm winning the battle *for* myself."

The Infirmary's unflattering fluorescent lights illuminated my reflection in the mirror, but I told myself in a more becoming way what

I knew I needed to hear. "I know who I am and what I am. I know what I do and why. Most importantly, I like myself. I like the *who* that I am now," I told the woman in the mirror in no uncertain terms. "And I'm damned good at being who I am."

No, I realized, that's not right. "I'm *great* at who I am."

The explosion in Syria had burned away not just my beautiful hair but my ugly outer shell and showed me the wonderful woman underneath.

Wounded, but not dead.

Limping, but not lost.

Healing and hopeful.

Eden... and Michelle.

Chapter 46

A few days after returning home from the Farm, I met with the Agency Human Resources rep at headquarters about my government medical and disability benefits.

After leaving her office, I hobbled back through the main lobby of the Original Headquarters Building to catch the shuttle to the parking lot. I fumbled with my blue ID badge and crutches through the security turnstiles and shuffled over to where a small crowd had gathered in front of the Memorial Wall. The Agency's contract stonemason had arrayed his tools on a portable table in front of the marble edifice.

I looked across more than one-hundred black stars adorning the white wall. Below the ranks of stars sat the Book of Honor in which were recorded the names of all acknowledged officers killed in the line of duty. A blank line in the book sits awaiting the day—perhaps decades in the future—that an unacknowledged undercover officer's name may finally be listed and all due honors ultimately bestowed.

On the lowest row of stars, the stonemason had stenciled outlines where he would soon etch two more. My throat parched at the realization that the newest pair being forever added to the wall were for Claude and Arnaud Payeur. Those additions would be a permanent reminder of my loss—literally etched in stone. I didn't have to see the book's open page to know there would be two blank lines left empty for years to come until their sacrifices could be recognized publicly.

A tear welled up in my eye blurring the stark outlines of the rows of dark stars carved into the alabaster monolith.

My thoughts drifted back to the first time I met the twins who would become my teammates, confidantes, and constant companions. In my mind's eye, I could clearly see the bright blue sky of that brisk day on the Farm's firing range when Michael first introduced us. He had arranged for shooting drills, knowing I would make a good first impression. I spent years after that working damned hard to get them both to accept me, and now they were gone.

My eyes watered rapidly, and rivulets of tears slid down my cheeks. A few of the employees around me turned at the sound of the gentle sobs I could not muffle. Those standing closest stared as I peered up through fogged eyes at the stark reminder of the high price Claude and Arnaud paid in Syria.

My weeps grew louder, and my chest heaved as the sadness welled up from deep inside. The dull ache of my healing abdomen was replaced by the sharp pain left by twin holes in my heart—voids left by brothers I had entrusted with my life more times than I could count.

An emptiness I had not felt in over a decade climbed my spine and slowly wrapped its tentacles around the back of my head. It was the loneliness of being on my own.

Again.

My clenched jaw ached as I tried unsuccessfully to muffle my cries. My shoulders shook uncontrollably. My arms flailed and refused to prop me up on my crutches any longer. I struggled unsuccessfully to balance and crumbled to the cold tile floor in an ungainly cascade of limbs, crutches, and leg cast.

An instant is all it had taken for some Syrian guard I never saw to rip Claude and Arnaud away from me in a dark warehouse in that shitty little third-world country. My friends were torn from my world, wrenched away before I could even say goodbye. The star-encrusted wall on which I could no longer focus my eyes would be all I ever had to remember them by. Now, we were no longer a team—the team I had worked so hard to be accepted on. All that work... all those years....

There was no team anymore. There was only me. I was alone.

Again.

I heaved as the pain flowed up from deep within me. One by one, waves of heartbreak washed over me.

A woman sat down next to me and pulled me towards her. With one arm she offered comfort, and with the other she pressed a kerchief into my empty hand.

The spectacle of my collapse drew the attention of the guards. A SPO at the duty desk summoned the headquarters nurse.

I half-sat, half-laid on the speckled tile and cried. The crowd parted as the white-uniformed nurse arrived and knelt in front of me.

"Are you okay?" she asked.

I couldn't answer her. I was not okay. I didn't think I'd ever be truly okay again. After what had happened, how could I ever be a whole person again?

The nurse gave a pointed look to the crowd. Employees acceded to her unspoken order and began to filter away, heading back to their offices. As the crowd parted, the stonemason standing next to the Memorial Wall caught her attention. Behind him, she spied the pair of newly stenciled outlines where new stars would be cut that afternoon.

Softly she asked, "Did you know them? The two officers who were killed?"

I wiped my eyes and looked up at the enduring reminder of my loss. My vision slowly cleared, and I could see the concerned face of the stonemason standing beside his table. I sat up, looked again at the wall, and then over to the man who would permanently embed upon it the twin reminders of my loss. Forever ensconced on the Memorial Wall would be a totem with which I would be faced every time I walked through the lobby of CIA's Original Headquarters Building.

I could not bring myself to answer the nurse. As much as I wanted to verbalize it, the drama playing itself out on that tile floor was enough overt acknowledgment of my involvement in the events that cost my teammates their lives.

With the nurse's help, I stood and perched myself back upon my crutches.

With a motion I repeat to this day whenever I walk past the Memorial Wall, I blew a kiss to each of the two new stars—my silent salute to my closest friends.

Chapter 47

"You were gone for a month and a half," Allison DeMott said in exasperation, her voice rising several octaves. "I was worried to death about you! Steve told me over and over and over again that you were in a bad car accident in Los Angeles, but he wouldn't tell me which hospital you were in. I wanted to fly out to see you, but he adamantly refused to tell me where you were. I've been so mad at him."

"I know, and I *am* sorry. Please don't blame him. I ended up staying with family for a while, and it was already a real burden on them. They don't have a very big place. But you're such a dear, thank you."

"So, what happened?" she asked with a mixture of concern and frustration. "He told me that you fractured your leg, had a severe concussion, and suffered an abdominal puncture, too?"

"Yeah, it was really scary after I woke up in the hospital. Very disorienting. I didn't know where I was or what had happened. Once Steven showed up, though, I knew everything was going to be alright. Fortunately, my leg wasn't hurt too badly after all, and I got the cast off yesterday. I'm able to get around much more easily, now."

"And your abdomen? What was that about?"

"Pieces of metal from the car, they said. It took two surgeries for them to get it all out and patch me up properly."

"Were you wearing a seatbelt?"

"What are you now, my mother?" I asked, jokingly.

"Just answer the question."

"Yes, *mommy,*" I said with a sarcastic sneer. "I was wearing my seatbelt like a good little girl."

"Does it hurt here?" Allison asked, gently placing two finger tips in the center of my chest.

"Nooooo...." I responded slowly, eyebrows raised at my friend the nurse and her apparent interest in playing doctor.

"What about now?" she asked, pushing harder.

"No. Why?"

She laid the heel of her hand between my breasts and pushed uncomfortably hard. Allison tilted her head and asked again, "It never hurt here?"

"No, Allison, it didn't," I said resolutely.

She put both hands on her hips and looked at me intently. "So, let me get this straight. You were in a wreck bad enough to give you a severe concussion, fracture your leg, have pieces of metal lodge in your abdomen, and you say that you were wearing your seatbelt. But you didn't end up with either a sternal fracture or any subcutaneous bruising where the seatbelt crossed over your chest and prevented you from being impaled on the steering column as the car got turned into a mass of twisted steel? Is *that* what you're telling me?"

Allison thumped my chest firmly with her index finger and her tone turned accusatory. "I've been an ER nurse for a long time, and I've seen a lot of patients survive all sorts of nasty car crashes, but I've never seen *that*."

Allison looked directly into my brown eyes with hers and asked me the question I hoped with all my heart I would never have to answer. "Michelle, what *really* happened to you? What aren't you telling me? Tell me the truth, please. I know what Steve does for a living, but what are you? Some kind of super-secret—"

I lifted one finger to Allison's lips, and she stopped mid-sentence. Her eyes narrowed in confusion, then burst open and shone as bright as headlights. That gesture served as my silent way of telling her without telling her. It was as far as I could risk going down that path. She would never be ready to know the truth, the whole truth, and nothing but the truth. Few people are. I would always have to maintain some semblance of a cover with her, and that's fine with me, but now she was one step closer to knowing the real me.

Over the years, I've always found it hard to lie to her about my supposed "tendon surgery" when I'd been shot on Cayman Brac. She always knew something was odd with that story, but, thankfully, she let it go without a fight.

Now, I shuddered to think I might not be as lucky this time. Letting on to her a little bit was infinitely better than opening up as much as she would have liked.

My mouth dried, and I had to lick my lips so I could respond with a believable tone and not just a faint hiss. "The truth, Allison, is that I love you. I'm recovering from two serious surgeries and, more than anything else in the world right now, I need your friendship and support to get better. I really do, okay?"

I side-stepped her question and desperately hoped our friendship was strong enough that she would take the modicum of new-found knowledge and give me the benefit of the doubt. Or failing that, at least just let it go with what little acknowledgement my finger to her lips offered. I didn't want to lie to her again. I just didn't have the strength for that. I never liked keeping her out of my real professional life, but there was no doubt in my mind whatsoever that if she knew the truth, I would never see her again.

"I love you, too," she said softly and wrapped her arms around me gently. Her eyes returned to their usual, lovely size and Allison nodded. She understood. "I'm sorry, I just want to help get you better, that's all."

I hugged her back and slowly let out my breath in relief. Our friendship has endured a decade of ups and downs. We'd been through quite a lot together, from boyfriends and breakups to hangouts and hookups. At that moment, I needed the support of my best friend at least as much as I needed the air in the room. Maybe more.

I squeezed Allison firmly and knew she truly wanted nothing more than to help me recuperate. I very much needed that help to heal myself—both mind and body.

Chapter 48

Wilson Henry, our team's Directorate of Intelligence analyst, hugged me gently as we stood in the hallway outside Michael's office.

"I'm glad you're back safely, Eden. Welcome home."

"Thanks, Wilson. I've been taking it slowly and am making pretty good progress."

"Whatever I can do to help, just ask. Anything you need, anything at all, I'm here for you."

"I know and thank you. That means a lot to me."

I sat down gingerly on the sofa across from the desk in Michael's office. Michael closed the door and sat down at the other end of the brown leather couch while he pushed a wayward lock of his white hair back up over the top of his head.

"Danny Vickers, the director of the Special Activities Division, asked me to let you know that he wanted to visit you in the hospital in Germany," Michael said, "but he ended up shuttling between Pakistan and Afghanistan for operational meetings. By the time he made it to Europe, you were already stateside, and then he was off to Monaco. Apparently, SAD is in negotiations to buy another undercover yacht, and he wanted to see it first."

"Must be nice to hang out on a yacht in the south of France all the time," I said, more out of fascination with the thought than any real interest in the possibility. "Maybe I should transfer to the Maritime Branch?"

"I'd support your transfer anywhere you choose to go, if that's what you want to do," Michael responded.

I'm sure my eyes went wide just at hearing the words come out of his mouth. I was flabbergasted. It never crossed my mind to ever consider such a thing.

I spoke louder than intended and my voice dripped with a mix of surprise and accusation. "You seriously want me to leave the team?" I hadn't expected to have a conversation like this today. I'd only gone into the office to get out of the condo for a few hours and say hello to

Wilson, not to have a discussion anything along the lines of where our talk was suddenly headed.

"No, of course not, but we don't really have much of a team left, do we? I'm an old man, and you've got a clipped wing. You'll heal soon enough, but I'm not getting any younger. If you had any thoughts about doing something else for your career, Michelle, no one would blame you. Certainly not me. I'd support you no matter what you wanted to do."

"I'm still working to come to terms with the loss of Claude and Arnaud," I said. "That's been devastating, both professionally and personally. But I assumed you would be looking to recruit some new team members. Honestly, I hadn't thought much about it. Are you?"

"Yes, I am. There's a former Navy SEAL I'm considering. He's been working in SAD as a paramilitary officer. It'll take a while for me to determine if he's the right guy for the job or not, and that's fine. But if you do want to consider an assignment elsewhere in the Agency, just let me know."

"Michael, I would never abandon you. You know that, right? I may be sidelined for another few months, but I'm not going anywhere. I more than appreciate everything you've done for me and can't imagine doing anything else. I'll be back in the saddle in a few months. Maybe I can help you vet candidates in the meantime, if you want. But, you *do* know I'd never leave you, right?"

"You have the attitude of a true professional. I can't tell you how much I've relied on you for the past few years and I don't want to even imagine doing this job without you on the team. I'm glad to hear that you're not considering leaving. You've done a tremendous amount of good for both the Agency and the country."

"Thank you for saying that, Michael. I appreciate the kind words. Who knows... maybe the pep talk will even help my clipped wing heal that much faster? And by the way, you are *not* old."

Chapter 49

Steven ran the tips of his fingers affectionately through the remaining two inches of my hair.

"I've never seen it this short," he remarked, "or this particular color. It's always been a darker brown, hasn't it?"

During my convalescence at the Farm the month before, Nurse Sarah had taken pity on me and shuttled me out to her beauty salon one evening. Her rather surprised stylist did what she could with the ragged remnants that remained after my late-night outburst in the Infirmary.

The short strands of what little hair survived made me do a double-take whenever I passed a mirror. It was going to take me some time to get used to my new look.

"Yeah, well, there's not nearly enough left to color," I said somewhat sullenly. "A year from now it'll be back down to my shoulders, but for the time being, I think the style makes me look like a ten-year-old boy. Do you like it?"

"I'm not really partial to ten-year-old boys," Steven retorted.

I pursed my lips in scorn and clarified, "I meant the color, Bozo."

"Oh, that. Yes, it's very pretty," he said, grinning ear to ear.

As we sat on the couch holding hands, I felt it was time for me to find out where he really stood regarding my particular and certainly nontraditional line of work. I love Steven with all my heart, and I wanted to know what he was feeling at that moment. The events of the previous two months had caused him more stress than the rest of our decade together, combined. I had survived my ordeal. Now, I needed to know how he felt about that, about us, and about me.

"I talked to Michael last week," I said in a tone reflecting the seriousness of the coming conversation. "He said that if I wanted to request a transfer, he'd support it."

"Did you *ask* for a transfer?" Steven asked in bewilderment.

I ducked his question. "Do you think I should?"

"That's not a fair question to ask me, and you know it. You can do anything you put your mind to. If you're asking whether I think there are other jobs within the Agency at which you would excel, the answer is an unqualified yes. If you're asking me whether I would want you home more often, so I can keep my arms around you all day and all night, then it's *yes* again, albeit a selfish one. If you're asking whether I want you to always be safe, the answer is an unequivocal yes. That goes without saying."

Steven lifted my hand up and pressed it against his chest.

"But if you're asking me whether I think you *should*... well.... I can only say that if you did transfer, I think you'd be miserable. I'm sure there are other field jobs you could choose that aren't nearly as dangerous, but you're the adventurous type at heart. I think you'd be gloomy sitting at a desk all day or teaching others to do what you feel deep down that you should be out in the field doing yourself."

I smiled at his characterization of me as the 'adventurous type.' I would not have used those words, but it made me realize how well he knows me.

"Of course, I'd support you no matter what you choose, but the thought of you leaving Mike's team is...." Steven searched for the right words. "It's inconceivable. You two are inseparable. I think you'd leave me before you'd leave him."

I shuffled closer to him and put my head on his shoulder.

"I'm not leaving you. And I'm not going to leave the team either. I appreciate your supporting me, whatever I decide. The talk about transferring wasn't my idea. Michael brought it up. I think he said it just to give me an out in case I had been thinking about it while cooped up in one hospital or another. I still need another few months to heal and get back into shape. After that, I'll end up on a plane headed for some pissant little country somewhere to do what needs to be done."

"I know you will and, as much as you'll hate it, you'll love it. And if you can think of it next time, please don't forget to duck."

Hating it and loving it. Steven got that exactly right. I've been struggling with that schism since the beginning.

My convalescence at the Farm gave me the time needed to come to terms with the work I do and my feelings about both it and myself. The job needs doing, and I want to be the one to do it. The feeling of power it gives me is addictive. It's real, tangible power over people. I can practically taste it. It's not a façade for show or the kind of make-believe power that someone claims they're delegating via memo while safely sitting within the confines of a sterile office.

It has come to define me. I love it, and I love myself.

Perhaps Michael gave me this computer into which I've poured my fears and loves specifically so I would come to these specific self-realizations and get back to work on his team. If so, then all I can say about him is that he's fucking brilliant.

That night, when Steven and I climbed into bed, I pulled back our old blue bedspread and got under the covers. I snuggled up to him, laid my head on his shoulder, closed my eyes feeling peaceful and safe, and smiled.

About the Author

Scott Shinberg has served in leadership positions across the US Government and industry for over twenty-five years. He has worked in and with the US Air Force, the Department of Homeland Security, the Federal Bureau of Investigation, and most "Three-Letter Agencies." While in government service, he served as an Air Force Intelligence Operations Officer and a Special Agent with the FBI. He lives in Virginia with his wife and sons.

Website: www.ScottShinberg.com
Facebook: @ScottShinbergAuthor
Twitter: @Author_Scott

What's Next?

The unthinkable happens in the skies over Florida, when someone hijacks the CIA Director's flight as he returns from his daughter's wedding.

DIRECTIVE ONE
Michelle Reagan - Book 2
(Releases Fall 2019)

Michelle Reagan—**code name Eden**—and an elite team of US Navy SEALs are sent halfway around the world to rescue him. Their high-risk mission to rescue the director and his wife becomes a full-scale assault on a heavily fortified military base. If rescue becomes impossible, Eden will have to carry out the CIA's best-kept secret: Directive One.

EVOLVED PUBLISHING PRESENTS a non-stop thrill ride with action galore, insights into covert action tradecraft, and descriptions of exotic locales around the globe so detailed you can smell them. *Directive One* is perfect for fans of Tom Clancy, Robert Ludlum, Dean Koontz, Brad Meltzer, and Len Deighton.

More from Evolved Publishing

We offer great books across multiple genres, featuring hiqh-quality editing (which we believe is second-to-none) and fantastic covers.

As a hybrid small press, your support as loyal readers is so important to us, and we have strived, with tireless dedication and sheer determination, to deliver on the promise of our motto: **QUALITY IS PRIORITY #1!**

Please check out all of our great books, which you can find at this link: **www.EvolvedPub.com/Catalog/**

Thank you!

CPSIA information can be obtained
at www.ICGtesting.com
Printed in the USA
BVHW030650100519
547942BV00025B/100/P

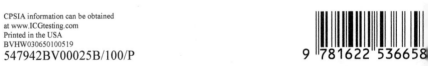

9 781622 536658